Chris Ryan Extreme: Night Strike

Chris Ryan

CORONET

First published in Great Britain in 2012 by Coronet
An imprint of Hodder & Stoughton
An Hachette UK company

First published in paperback in 2013

2

Copyright © Chris Ryan 2012

A CIP catalogue record for this title is available from the British Library

B format ISBN 978 1 444 72960 3
A format ISBN 978 1 444 75689 0

Printed and bound by Clays Ltd, St Ives plc

Hodder & Stoughton policy is to use papers that are natural, renewable
and recyclable products and made from wood grown in sustainable forests.
The logging and manufacturing processes are expected to conform
to the environmental regulations of the country of origin.

Hodder & Stoughton Ltd
338 Euston Road
London NW1 3BH

www.hodder.co.uk

acknowledgements

To my agent Barbara Levy, publisher Mark Booth,
Charlotte Hardman, Eleni Lawrence and the rest of
the team at Coronet.

one

His name was Hauser and he moved down the corridor as fast as his bad right leg allowed. The metal toolbox he carried was heavy and exaggerated his limp. He paused in front of the last door on the right. A yellow sign on the door read 'WARNING! AUTHORIZED PERSONNEL ONLY'. He fished a key chain from his paint-flecked trousers and skimmed through the keys until he found the right one. His hand was trembling. He looked across his right shoulder at the bank of lifts ten metres back down the corridor. Satisfied the coast was clear, he inserted the key in the lock and twisted it. There was a sequence of clicks as the pins inside jangled up and down, and then a satisfying *clack* as the lock was released.

Hauser stepped inside the room. It was a four-metre-square jungle of filing cabinets, cardboard boxes and industrial shelves with a tall, dark-panelled window overlooking the street below. Hauser hobbled over to the window. An electric pain shot up his leg with every step, like someone had taped broken glass to his shins. He stopped in front of the window and dumped a roll of black tarpaulin he'd been carrying under his left arm. Then he set the toolbox down next to the tarp and scanned the scene outside. He was on the fourth floor of an office block adjacent to the Lanesborough Hotel at Hyde Park Corner. The current tenants were some kind of marketing agency who, he knew, were badly behind with their rent. They'd have to relocate soon. Shame. From that height Hauser had quite a view. The pavements were packed with commuters and tourists flocking in and out of Hyde Park Corner Tube station. Further in the distance lay the bleached green ribbon of the park itself.

Yep. It was quite a view. Especially if you wanted to shoot somebody.

Hauser was wearing a tearaway paper suit that had been vacuum-packed. The overalls came with a hood. He also wore a pair of surgical gloves. The suit and gloves would both prevent his DNA from contaminating the scene, as well as protecting his body from residue such as gunpowder. Now Hauser knelt down. Slowly, because any sudden movement sent fierce voltages of pain up his right leg, he prised open the toolbox. It was rusty and stiff and he had to force the damn thing apart with both hands. Finally the cantilever trays separated. There were three trays on either side of the central compartment. Each one was filled with tools. Hauser ran his fingers over them. There was a rubber-headed hammer, tacks, putty, bolt-cutters, a pair of suction pads, a large ring of different-sized hexagon keys and a spirit level.

There were two more objects in the bottom of the main compartment of the toolbox. One was a diamond cutter. The other was a featureless black tube ten inches long and three and a half inches wide. Made of carbon-fibre, it weighed just 300 grams, no more than a tennis racquet. Hauser removed the tube. There was a latch on the underside. Hauser flipped this and a pistol grip flipped out, transforming the tube into a short-barrelled rifle.

Hauser cocked the bolt. The whole operation had taken four seconds. Four seconds to set up a selective-fire rifle effective up to 300 metres.

Hauser set the rifle down and took the diamond cutter from the toolbox. Moving with speed now, he ran the cutter around the edges of the window until he had cut out a rectangle of glass as big as a forty-inch TV. Then he took out the suction pads and, with one in either hand, pressed them to the sides of the cut-out sheet. The glass came loose easily. Hauser laid this down on the floor with the suction pads still attached. Then he took the black tarp, hammer and tacks and pinned one end of the material to the ceiling, allowing the rest to drape down over the opening. Seen from the street below, the tarp would give the appearance of reflective glass. If anyone looked up at the window, they wouldn't see shit.

Going down on one knee, Hauser tucked the stock tight into the Y-spot where his shoulder met his chest. His index finger rested on the trigger, then he applied a little pressure. He went through the drill he had practised thousands of times before.

Breathe in. Breathe out.

Keep the target in focus.

Firm shoulder. Left hand supporting the right.

The woman in his sights meant nothing to him. She'd simply been the first person he targeted. She was sitting on a bench and eating a sandwich. The optics were so precise that Hauser could identify the brand. Pret A Manger.

He pulled the trigger.

She was eating a sandwich one second and clutching her guts the next.

The subsonic .22 long rifle rimfire round tore a hole in her stomach big enough to accommodate your middle finger.

And he went for the stomach with the next seven targets too. Unlike head shots, gut shots didn't kill people, and Hauser had been specifically told not to kill. Only maim. He kicked out the rounds in quick succession. Two seconds between each. With each shot the muzzle *phtt-ed* and the barrel jerked.

The bodies dropped.

The crowd was confused by the first two shots. The built-in suppressor guaranteed that the shots didn't sound like the thunderous *ca-rack* of a bullet. But when the third target fell they all knew something terrifying was happening. Panic spread and everyone ran for cover.

Twenty-four seconds. That's how long it had taken Hauser to leave eight civilians sprawled on the pavement soaked in their own blood and pawing at their wounds. The victims were strangely silent. No one else dared approach them. Any sane person would wait for a clear sign that the shooting had stopped.

Hauser stepped back from the window. He was confident no one had seen him. The suppressor had phased out more than ninety per cent of the sound, making it difficult for anyone to clearly understand that they were gunshots, let alone pinpoint their origin. A breeze kicked up. The tarp fluttered. Hauser quickly folded up the weapon and stashed it in the toolbox. He removed the overalls and stuffed them into the toolbox. The overalls he would dispose of shortly, in a nearby public toilet, courtesy of a lit match and some wetted toilet paper to cover and disable the smoke detector. He left the room.

Police sirens in the distance. And now screams from the crowd, as if the sirens gave them permission.

two

He downed it in three long gulps that had the barmaid shaking her head and the three gnarled alcoholics at the other end of the bar nodding welcome to the newest member of their club. Joe Gardner polished off his London Pride and tipped the foamy glass at the barmaid.

'Another,' he said.

The barmaid snatched his empty glass and stood it under the pump. Golden beer flowed out of the nozzle and settled into a dark-bronze column. She cut him a thick head and dumped the glass in front of him.

'Cheers, Kate.' Gardner raised his glass in a toast but she had already turned her back. 'But you're forgetting one thing.'

Kate sighed. 'What's that?'

'Your phone number.'

'The only thing you'll get from me is a slap.' A disgusted expression was plastered over the right side of the girl's face. Gardner doubted her left side was any more pleasant. 'That's your last pint till you settle your tab.'

'Give us a break,' Gardner grunted, rooting around in his jeans pocket for imaginary change.

Then a voice to his left said, 'This one's on me.'

On the edge of his vision Gardner glimpsed a red-knuckled hand slipping the barmaid a pair of crisp twenty-quid notes. She eyed the queen's head suspiciously before accepting it.

'Thanks. This'll about cover it.'

'My pleasure,' the voice said. 'After all, we've got to look after our own.'

The voice was hoarse and the man's breath wafted across Gardner's face and violated his nostrils. It was the smoky, medicinal smell of cheap whisky.

'Didn't I see you on the telly once?'

Gardner didn't turn around.

'Yeah,' the voice went on. 'You're that bloke from the Regiment. The one who was at Parliament Square. You were the big hero of the day.'

The voice swigged his whisky. Ice clinked against the glass.

'You look like a bag of bollocks, mate,' said the voice. 'What the fuck happened?'

Gardner took a sip of his pint. Said nothing.

'No, wait. I can guess what happened. I mean, fucking look at you. You're a joke. You're a right fucking cunt.'

Gardner stood his beer on the bar. Kate was nowhere to be seen. Then he slowly turned to face his new best friend.

'That's right. A complete and utter cunt.'

He looked as ugly as he sounded. Red cheeks hung like sandbags beneath a pair of drill-hole eyes set in a head topped off with a buzzcut. He was a couple of hundred pounds or thereabouts, half of it muscle and the rest fat that had been muscle in a previous life. The glass in front of him was half-full of whisky and ice. The glazed expression in his eyes told Gardner the drink had not been the guy's first of the night, or even his tenth.

'I'm not looking for trouble,' Gardner said quietly.

'But you found it anyway. You know, there's nothing more tragic than a washed-up old Blade.' The man pulled a face at the prismatic bottom of the tumbler. 'Know what? Someone should just put you out of your fucking misery now.'

Gardner attempted to focus on the guy and saw two of him. Sixteen pints of Pride and a few shots off the top shelf will do that to a man. Rain lightly drum-tapped on the pub windows. The guy leaned in close to Gardner and whispered into his left ear.

'Me, I'm from 3 Para. Real fucking soldier. Real fucking man.' He winked at the barmaid. 'Ain't that right, Kate?' She smiled back flirtatiously. Then the guy turned back to Gardner. 'Now do me a favour and fuck off.'

A shit-eating grin was his parting gift.

Gardner swiftly drank up. Made for the door.

Outside in the deserted car park the rain was lashing down in slanted ice sheets. Gardner zipped up his nylon windcheater to insulate himself against the cold and wet. The Rose in June pub was set on the outskirts of Hereford and the low rent was probably the only reason it hadn't shut down. Gardner made his way down the back streets, snaking towards the Regiment's headquarters. He navigated around the housing estate that used to be the site of the old Regiment camp on Stirling Lane. Now it was all council-owned. The rain picked up, spattering the empty street that edged the estate. Gardner couldn't see more than two or three metres in front of him. A ruthless wind whipped through the street and pricked his skin. Gardner closed his eyes. He heard voices, subdued beneath the bass line of the rain.

When he opened his eyes a fist was colliding with his face.

three

The fist struck Gardner hard and sudden, like a jet engine backfiring. He fell backwards, banging his head against the kerb. A sharp pain speared the base of his skull and it took a moment to wrench himself together. You're lying on your back. Your cheek is on fire from a fucking punch. And Para is towering over you.

Para's hands were at his side and curled into kettlebells. He hocked up phlegm and spat at Gardner. The gob arced through the rain like a discus and landed with a plop on his neck.

'Get up, prick.' Para's voice was barely audible above the hammering rain.

Gardner wiped away the spittle with the back of his hand.

'I said, get the fuck up.'

Gardner noticed two guys with Para, one at either shoulder. The guy on the left was shaven-headed with black dull eyes and the kind of hulking frame that you only get from injecting dodgy Bulgarian 'roids. He wore a grey hoodie and dark combats. Gardner noticed he was clutching a battery-operated planer. The guy on Para's right stood six-five. A reflective yellow jacket hung like a tent from his scrawny frame. He smiled and revealed a line of coffee-brown teeth. He was holding a sledgehammer. Raindrops were cascading off the tip of its black head.

'Call yourself a Blade,' Para said. 'You're just a washed-up cunt.'

Hoodie and Black Teeth laughed like Para was Ricky Gervais back when he was funny.

Gardner began scraping himself off the pavement. The rain hissed. The guys were crowding around him now. He swayed uneasily on his feet.

Black Teeth was gripping the sledgehammer with both hands. He stood with his feet apart in a golf-swing posture and raised the hammer above his right shoulder. Gardner knew he should be ducking out of the way but the booze had made him woozy. Dumbly he watched as the hammer swung down at him.

Straight into his solar plexus. *Thud!*

A million different pains fired in the wall of his chest. He heard something snap in there. Heard it, then felt it. His ribcage screamed. He dropped to his knees and sucked in air. The valley of his chest exploded. He looked up and saw Black Teeth standing triumphantly over him.

'What a joke,' he said.

Black Teeth went to swipe again but Hoodie came between them, wanted a piece of the action for himself. He'd fired up the planer and was aiming it at Gardner's temple. Gardner managed to climb to his knees. He didn't have the energy to stand on two feet, but he wasn't going to lie down and leave himself defenceless. First rule of combat, he reminded himself: always try to stay on your toes. The planer buzzed angrily. Gardner was alert now, his body flooded with endorphins and adrenaline. In a blur he quickly sidestepped to the left and out of the path of the planer. Momentum carried Hoodie forwards, his forearm brushing Gardner's face, the planer chopping the air.

Then Gardner unclenched his left hand and thrust the open palm into Hoodie's chest. Winded the cunt. Hoodie yelped as he dropped to the ground. The planer flew out of his hands and Gardner reached for it, but Black Teeth was on top of him and bringing the sledgehammer in a downward arc again. Gardner feinted, dropping his shoulder and leaving Black Teeth swiping at nothing. Out of the corner of his eye Gardner spied Para fishing something out of his jacket. Gardner folded his fingers in tightly and jabbed his knuckles at Black Teeth's throat. He could feel the bone denting the soft cartilage rings of the guy's trachea. The sledgehammer rang as it hit the deck.

Para had a knife in his hands now. Gardner recognised the distinctive fine tip of a Gerber Compact.

'Fuck it, you cunt,' said Para. 'Come on then.'

Para lunged at Gardner, angling the Gerber at his neck. Gardner shunted his right hand across and jerked his head the same direction, pushing the blade away. Then he launched an uppercut at Para's face. His face was a stew of blood and bone.

Gardner moved in for the kill. He grabbed the planer and lamped it against the side of Para's face. Para groaned as he fumbled blindly for the Gerber.

Too late.

Gardner yanked Para's right arm. He pinned his right knee against the guy's elbow, trapping his forearm in place. Then he depressed the button to start the planer. The tool whirred above the incessant rain as he slid it along the surface of Para's forearm. The blade tore off strips of flesh. A pinkish-red slush spewed out of the side of the device. Gardner drove the planer further up Para's arm. His scream turned into something animal. The skin below was totally shredded, a gooey mess of veins coiled around whitish bone. It didn't look like an arm any longer. More like something a pack of Staffies had feasted on.

Pleased with his work, Gardner eased off the button and ditched the planer. It clattered to the ground, sputtered, whined and died.

The rain was now a murmur.

'My arm,' Para said. 'My fucking arm!'

'I see you again, next time it's your face.' Gardner's voice was as sharp as cut glass. 'Are we fucking clear?'

Gardner didn't wait for an answer. He gave his back to the three fucked-up pricks and walked down the road, past the construction site. He had reached a crossroads in his life. Lately he'd been getting into a lot of scraps. And deep down he was afraid of admitting to himself that fighting was all he was good for. The problem was, he was no longer an operator. His injury had reduced him to cleaning rifles and hauling HESCO blocks around Hereford, and the suit did not fit a fucking inch.

He was a couple of hundred metres from the site when his mobile sparked up. A shitty old Nokia. Gardner could afford an iPhone 4, but only in his dreams. The number on the screen wasn't one he recognized. An 0207 number. London. He tapped the answer key.

'Is that Mr Joseph Gardner?'

The voice was female and corporate. The kind of tone that belonged on airport announcements. Pressing the phone closer to his ear, Gardner said, 'Who's this?'

'Nancy Rayner here. I'm calling from Talisman International.'

Gardner rubbed his temples, trying to clear the fog of booze behind his eyeballs. The name sounded vaguely familiar.

'The security consultancy?' the woman went on. 'You submitted a job application . . . let me see . . .' – Gardner heard the shuffle of papers – '. . . two weeks ago.'

Her words jolted his mind. Fucking yes. He did recall applying for a job. He also recalled thinking he had next to no hope of getting it. Talisman were one of the new boys on the security circuit. He'd not heard anything, and figured it was the same better-luck-elsewhere story.

'We'd like to invite you for an interview.'

Gardner fell silent.

'Mr Gardner?'

'Yes?'

'How does tomorrow sound? One o'clock at our offices?'

It sounded better than good. It was fucking great.

He said simply, 'OK.'

'Excellent. So we'll see you tomorrow at one.'

Click.

Gardner was left listening to dead air. Suddenly the drunken mist behind his eyes was lifting. He tucked the mobile away, dug his hands into his jacket pockets and quickened his pace.

Maybe he wouldn't be hauling gravel around Hereford for the rest of his miserable life.

four

As the First Great Western train slithered into Paddington, the passenger announcement shook Gardner from his slumbers. 'All change.' The doors bleated and opened, and Gardner made his way to the Underground. The concourse was crawling with armed police patrolling around with their Heckler & Koch MP5K submachine guns strapped around their chests. Gardner afforded himself a wry smile. These coppers couldn't shoot their way out of a wet bog roll yet here they were prancing around like fucking Rambo. He parted with six quid for a one-day Travelcard and caught the Bakerloo Line towards Elephant and Castle. Twelve minutes later the Tube coughed him up at Charing Cross.

Life had not been kind to Gardner since he had stopped MI6 agent Leo Land from engineering a conflict between Israel and Iran. Land had been publicly humiliated and war narrowly averted, but the media didn't give Gardner any credit. Not that he wanted it. Aimée Milana, the journalist he had been protecting, had been killed by a sniper's bullet in London's Parliament Square in front of the world's media. The 7.62x51mm NATO round entered her left eye, bored through her brain and exited via her left shoulder. Aimée died immediately, and in death she became both martyr and the intrepid investigator who had uncovered the plot. Gardner hadn't loved her, but he cared enough to let her take the afterlife glory.

He emerged from the Tube into the chaotic embrace of Charing Cross. More coppers. The crowds were thinner than he recalled from his last visit. The shooting at Knightsbridge had put everyone on edge. Copies of *Metro* carpeted the ground, stamped with shoeprints and bird shit. He caught half of a headline, the word 'HORROR' in big bold letters next to a pixelated CCTV image of a woman covered in blood. He hooked a left onto the Strand and kept an eye on the clouds, bulging like overfilled flour sacks.

Gardner quickened his stride and tried to feel at ease in the cheap suit he was wearing. He carried on down Whitehall and the classical buildings imposing themselves between old boys' boozers and souvenir shops. At the back of the Household Cavalry's headquarters Gardner hung a left onto Horse Guards Avenue and tipped his head in quiet respect at the statue of the Gurkha outside the Ministry of Defence. Left again and he found himself on Whitehall Court. Twenty metres down the street he found the place he was looking for.

Compared with the ostentation around it, the building looked subdued. It was three storeys tall with a stucco front and an oak door, above which a dark glass fanlight framed the company name in finely etched gold letters: Talisman Security. The 'International' had been shortened to 'Int'l'. Gardner approached the intercom to the right of the door and pressed the buzzer.

'Yes?' a woman squawked.

'Joe Gardner. I'm here for the interview.'

Static crackled from the speaker. Gardner scratched his freshly clipped beard, straightened his tie.

'Please enter.'

There was the diplomatic click of a lock being released. Gardner gave the brass doorknob a twist and entered the reception. The woman who had spoken to him through the intercom greeted him with a stern face. She was disappointingly old and fat. He was signed in and given a visitor ID badge.

He rode the shuddering box lift up to the first floor. When he stepped out he got a surprise. This floor was nothing like the gentlemen's club décor of the reception. Gone were the dark-framed portraits and the musty smell of old money. Instead he was in a white-tiled corridor with frosted-glass office doors. A fragrance like freshly chopped pinewood hung in the air. He stopped outside the interview room for a moment and wiped his brow.

Gardner had faced down terrorists and been shot at by African warlords, but job interviews scared the shit out of him. Fuck it, he thought. Let's get it over with. He opened the door and entered a long and wide meeting room. A white walnut table faced him. A deck of Cisco phones were lined up on the table, along with a projector, and at one end of the room was a pulled-down white screen.

Three figures were seated at the far end of the table.

On the left was a woman. Slimline body, small breasts, early thirties. Her brunette hair was tied back in a businesslike manner and she was dressed in an understated skirt suit. On her wedding-ring finger she wore a discreet band that depressed Gardner.

The guy on the right was almost as thin as the bird. He was sitting stiffly in his chair and scribbling on a notepad. Conservative-blue suit, white shirt, grey tie. His face was smooth and clean-shaven, his fingernails immaculately cut. He didn't look like he had ever lifted a weight, let alone spent a night in the jungle.

Then Gardner set eyes on the figure sitting in the middle, and did a double-take. He blinked. His eyes were not deceiving him. The man was sitting with his hands splayed in front of him and broadcasting a smug, taunting look at Gardner.

'Hello, Joe,' he said.

There was a long pause while an invisible rope tightened around Gardner's chest.

'This is Nancy Rayner,' said the man, gesturing to his right. 'And this is Danny, my PA,' he added, nodding at the corporate twat to his left.

But Gardner couldn't take his eyes off the man in the middle.

'You two know each other?' Rayner asked, her eyes flicking between Gardner and the man sitting next to her.

'We do,' breathed Gardner. 'Hello, John.'

five

John Bald looked good for a dead man. He was decked out in an olive-green Ralph Lauren polo shirt, stone-washed jeans and brown Timberlands. The muscles on his forearms bulged like a pair of knotted garden hoses about to burst. A TAG Heuer Aquaracer watch glinted on his wrist.

'You're not here,' Gardner said. 'You're fucking dead.'

Bald leaned back and laughed at the ceiling. It was a full-bellied, confident laugh and it made Gardner feel like he was something Bald was scraping off the bottom of his shoe.

'And now I'm back,' said Bald. 'Hallelujah! It's a miracle, Joe – isn't it?'

Gardner edged closer. Deep, thick scars were pressed into Bald's cheeks like barbed wire. His forehead was marked with pink gashes. Scar tissue. It all came hurtling back at Gardner. The village of Brezovan. The Presevo Valley, Serbia. He had looked on helplessly as Russian mafia goons pumped Bald full of hot lead. The rounds had rent terrible damage, thundering through Bald's body and tearing off clumps of flesh. And Gardner hadn't been able to do a thing about it.

'But I saw you with my own eyes. You had more holes in you than a fucking choirboy.'

'I got lucky,' Bald said. 'I was out of it for hours. Lying there in that fucking foul ditch. Left for dead. Then I came to. It was dark but somehow I managed to drag myself to the nearest town. God knows how I made it that far. Some farmer found me. Drove me to the hospital. I remember bright lights and a doctor telling me I wouldn't make it.'

Bald's eyes shone like polished steel.

'It took me six months to recover,' he said, his gaze now dropped. 'I was so weak I could barely lift a spoon to my mouth.'

Gardner tried to take in what Bald was telling him. The pain flared up in his ribcage again. He put a hand to his chest and caught his breath.

'You OK?' Bald looked genuinely concerned.

'I'm fine,' Gardner said much too quickly.

'Why don't you have a seat?'

Gardner deposited himself on the chair facing Bald and accepted a tumbler of chilled water from the PA. Now Rayner was flicking through a neat stack of papers in front of her. Danny had his thin lips sealed. Something didn't seem right about him in Gardner's mind. He knew John Bald better than most. And Bald would never hire a bloke as a PA. He'd go for a smoking-hot blonde every time.

'Let's get down to business, shall we?' said Bald. 'That's what we're here for, after all.'

Gardner nodded and gave Bald a chummy smile.

''Course,' Gardner said. 'I'm glad you're alive, mate.'

'Likewise, Joe.' Bald was grinding his jaws like he was chewing tarmac. 'It's fucking good to see you. Not many of us old Blades left in the world, is there? You're practically family.'

Gardner smiled and felt the lead weights lift from his shoulders. No one knows me better than John, he was thinking. John was a lying, thieving bastard, but he was also an old mucker. I'm fucking in here, he told himself.

'Thanks for inviting me up here,' Gardner said, framing his premium-grade smile. 'I really appreciate you giving me this opportunity, John.'

'Don't mention it,' Bald said, generously waving aside the compliment. Rayner placed a sheet of paper in front of him. Bald took a breath mint from an expensive-looking little metal case and popped it into his mouth. Gardner caught a glimpse of the paper and recognized it as the CV he'd emailed to Rayner when applying for the job.

'Very impressive credentials,' Bald said, raising his bushy eyebrows. 'I mean, seriously fucking good. Says here you were awarded the MM in 2 Para by the age of twenty-one, applied as a candidate for Selection aged twenty-three and passed at the first attempt.'

'Yeah, that's right,' Gardner said. His smile began to crack at the edges as he wondered, what's John trying to get at? He knows all this shit already.

Bald said, 'You finished second overall in the long drag. Who was first?'

'You were.'

Bald slapped a hand dolefully against his forehead.

'Fuck me, that's right. I'm always forgetting that.' Rayner suppressed a laugh while Bald returned to the CV and read on. 'One tour of duty in Kosovo, undercover work with the SRR in Northern Ireland, two combat tours in

Iraq as part of Task Force Black, then combat operations in Afghanistan. And then – oh, what's this?'

He tapped at a note at the bottom of the page.

'Says here you sustained combat injuries in Afghanistan.'

Gardner was still trying to hold the smile. Bald stared down the barrel of his bulbous nose at him. His voice was growing louder, his Scottish accent more pronounced. 'I know that too, of course. I was there. I was the one who saved your fucking life.'

'And I'll always be grateful—'

'Lost your hand, though,' Bald cut Gardner short.

Gardner instinctively covered his artificial left hand with his right. Bald passed the CV back to Rayner and shook his head.

'No. I'm sorry, Joe. But your combat injury, your fucked-up hand, whatever you want to call it – I can't consider you for this job. We're looking for someone who can, well, really grasp this opportunity with both hands.'

Rayner laughed, this time out loud, unable to hold it in. Gardner could sense his temper breaking loose. He slammed the glass down on the table.

'The hand's not a problem,' said Gardner. 'Come on, mate.'

Bald shook his head. 'Sorry. *Mate.*'

'But no one else has the experience I've got. You know that. Come on, John. Give me a fucking chance and I'll not let you down.'

Bald shrugged with his lips.

'That's all well and good. But we need someone who can blend in.'

Gardner frowned. 'What do you mean?'

'I can't go into too much detail, Joe. But our client believes they have a terrorist sleeper cell operating at the very heart of their organization.' He glanced hesitantly at Danny. 'We're looking for someone inconspicuous. And that hand of yours? Well, it stands out like an Arab at Gay Pride.'

Gardner felt his jaw muscles twitch. It had taken him the best part of six months to get his foot in the door with the security companies. Most of them had more operators than jobs, especially now the work in Afghanistan and Iraq had dried up. Opportunities elsewhere were limited to guarding Saudi princesses and protecting African diamond mines. As for MI6, they had cast him out without so much as an iTunes gift certificate.

Bottom line: this interview was Gardner drinking in the last-chance saloon. And John Bald, the mate he thought had died in a hellhole village in the Balkans, was pissing all over his dreams.

'I can do this, John,' Gardner said.

'With that thing?' Bald angled his head at the prosthesis. 'I don't think so.'

Danny excused himself and left the room. Gardner watched him leave and turned back to Bald.

'Don't do this to me.' His voice echoed off the walls. 'We fought alongside each other, for fuck's sake. I'm not asking you for a favour, I'm just asking for an honest chance. I know—'

'I'm sorry, Joe.' Bald held Gardner's gaze. The look in his eyes was pure, unfiltered indifference. That was the worst of it for Gardner. His old mucker didn't hate him. He just thought he was a fucking joke. 'Now, if you'll excuse me, I have other business to attend to.'

Bald strode confidently towards the door. He rested a hand on Gardner's shoulder.

'Never mind, mate. There's always your local Jobcentre.'

With that Bald exited the conference room. Rayner trailed in his wake. Gardner was left alone with nothing but a glimpse of bling and a life rapidly disappearing down the shitter. The notepad Danny had been writing on was lying on the table. Gardner craned his neck at the open page. It was covered in doodles. The cunt hadn't even been paying attention.

They had invited him down for nothing.

Gardner was humiliated. He didn't own a watch, having pawned his Breitling SAS watch in order to pay off credit card debts. But the stylish antique clock on the far wall told him it was just past two.

He needed a beer.

He pissed off out of Talisman's offices and tramped back up towards the Strand. Finding a boozer that charged less than four fucking quid a pint was impossible, so Gardner bought twelve tinnies of cheap lager from a corner shop for a tenner and headed for Temple Tube. Beside the station, with its scattershot of grey-faced street sellers, was a tiny park. South of this ran the Victoria Embankment. On the other side Arundel Street climbed up to the Strand east of Somerset House and the Savoy. Gardner settled on a park bench and knuckled down to the important work of getting shitfaced. He lost track of time. At some point the peat-bog sky dulled into a cocktail of purple and orange clouds as night closed in over London. Earlier the area had been throbbing with important people. Now it was abandoned.

Gardner kept on drinking.

By the time he cracked open his eleventh 500ml can of imported Czech piss it was gone ten o'clock and he was the last fucker left in the park. He tipped more lager down his throat. Then he wondered again about Danny the PA. No, hiring a bloke as a secretary wasn't like the Jock bastard at all.

Gardner downed his twelfth beer and was surprised when he reached down to the black plastic bag only to discover it was empty. The bag fluttered along with the breeze. Urban tumbleweed. The world had stopped being a grid of straight lines and distinct edges. Now things were blurred and vague and dreamy. Gardner checked his pockets for loose change. Seventy-three pence. Not enough even for one fucking can. He stood up, rearranged his balls and headed for Temple station. Caught sight of the clock in the station and realised he was too late to make the last train back to Hereford. But then, in the glow of the street lights, he spotted Bald striding confidently down Arundel Street from the direction of the Strand.

Gardner put his plans on ice.

six

Bald wasn't alone.

There was a woman on his arm, all high cheekbones and thin lips fish-hooked at either corner into a sly smile. Gardner guessed Eastern European. Her eyes were wide, round as marbles and lime green. She was wearing a short black skirt that showed off her catwalk legs and a white blouse that gave Gardner a sneak preview of her tits as the couple drew nearer. Large and probably fake, but who cared? She was the kind of package Gardner would peel off his eyelids to spend the night with. She reminded him of the painful fact that it'd been a year since he'd last had his end away.

She had her arm entwined around Bald's. They were so absorbed in each other they were oblivious of Gardner. When they were just metres away, he retreated into the shadows of an anonymous office building at the bottom of Arundel Street. Bald and the woman carried on towards the Victoria Embankment.

A small voice in the back of Gardner's head told him to follow.

Gardner counted to ten then stepped out onto Arundel Street. Bald and the woman were now approaching the

Embankment, where traffic screamed by, red and white car lights zipping along like neon dragonflies. Gardner watched the couple stop on the corner. The woman stood on the tiptoes of her six-inch heels and whispered something into Bald's ear. For a second Gardner thought he'd been rumbled. But then Bald traced a hand from the woman's cheek all the way down to the subtle curve of her arse. With his other hand he hailed a black cab. Then Bald reached into his wallet and handed the woman a blue keycard of the kind you get in fancy hotels. The cab pulled over. Bald held open the rear door and Mrs Eastern Europe 2011 gave him a final kiss before climbing inside, and the cab catapulted off into the night traffic.

Alone now, Bald set off westwards along the Embankment, towards Waterloo Bridge. Gardner followed. He kept a safe distance of forty metres between himself and Bald. At his nine o'clock the Thames slithered like a lake of jellied eels.

The traffic thinned out the further along the Embankment Gardner went. After four hundred metres Bald passed Waterloo Bridge and Gardner wondered where his old mucker was going. Another three hundred metres and they were beyond Villiers Street. Now Bald scaled the steps leading up to the Embankment Bridge two at a time. He had a long stride and Gardner had to push himself to keep up. He couldn't afford to slip any further behind. By the time he reached the footbridge he was sweating hard. The London Eye hung on the southern canvas of the Thames, skeletal and still. The walkway was deserted. Support pylons straddled the bridge at fifty-metre intervals, drawing up lengths of steel cable high above the walkway. He could hear the sludgy lapping of the river fifteen metres below.

Just you and John, that voice in Gardner's head said.

Time to get revenge.

Gardner broke into a run. Twenty metres became ten and suddenly Gardner was drawing up behind Bald and fighting the urge to smack him in the back of his head.

'Hey,' Gardner said. 'I want a fucking word with you.'

Bald stopped dead in his tracks. He did not turn around. As if he had known all this time that Gardner had been tailing him. Instead he dropped his head and his shoulders and said wearily, 'What is it, Joe?'

'That interview was a load of bollocks. You were never gonna give me the gig, and fuck you for making me come all the way up here for nothing.'

Now Bald turned around. He kept his hands casually tucked into his jean pockets. A rage Gardner had never known before surged in his bowels. He could feel it at the back of his throat. There was six metres between them. Then Bald took a few strides closer to Gardner.

'You're drunk, Joe. Go home.'

But Gardner stood his ground. 'I'm as sober as I've ever been.' He was surprised at how badly he was slurring his words.

'Your mouth smells like a rat pissed in it.'

'We were mates,' Gardner said, shaking his head in the vain hope of clearing it. 'You don't treat a dog that way.'

Bald stepped up to Gardner's face. Gardner could make out each individual scar on Bald's face, the two men were so close.

'Mates?' Bald said disbelievingly. 'We stopped being mates the day you left me for dead. Now be a good boy and fuck off back to Hereford.'

Gardner responded with a fist, launching a right-hand uppercut at Bald. But Bald reacted quickly. He thrust his left hand up and deflected the punch. Then he reached out with his right hand, trying to grab Gardner's vulnerable prosthetic hand.

Gardner's blood was up. Bald had his back against the railings and his fists level with his chest, expecting another punch. But Gardner knew the key to winning any fight was surprise. He launched his head forward, poised to give Bald a Glasgow Kiss.

But Bald was surprisingly agile. He quickly stepped to one side and left Gardner nutting thin air. And now Gardner was thrown off balance, momentum pushing him forward. Bald's giant hands clamped around his neck and lifted him off his feet. Gardner was being dragged up and over the railings. Suddenly the ground below him disappeared. The world was spinning wildly out of control. He felt his heart pumping wildly, the wind rushing around him. Now his world was the Thames void. He tumbled into the slick blackness.

seven

Bald peered over the frosty railings at the waters below.
The night was surprisingly cold, after a mild day. The tip
of each wave glimmered cold and white as a knife point. A
pool of white foam marked the spot where Gardner's body
had broken the surface. For a brief moment Bald considered calling the emergency services. Then he reminded
himself how Gardner had once left him for dead. No,
he thought. Gardner drowning in the Thames just about
evened things out.

'Fuck you, you cunt,' Bald said to the evaporating foam.
He moved on.

With the chunky blocks of the Southbank Centre
silhouetted to his left, he descended from the bridge
into Belvedere Road. He walked quickly south towards
Waterloo Station, passing a gaggle of students jabbering away in some foreign language. By the time he scaled
the Portland stone steps of the station's Victory Arch, Joe
Gardner was ancient fucking history and Bald was looking
forward to nabbing a quick pint at the station boozer, then
heading across to the Waterloo Novotel, where a Russian
blonde called Lena would be waiting for him naked in
bed. Christ, he was looking forward to smashing that arse.

'Leaving so soon?'

The voice came from his four o'clock. Bald froze on the top step and slowly turned to face the guy. He was leaning against the high wall next to a bronze plaque that commemorated 'The 626 men of the Southern Railway who gave their lives in the 1939–1945 War'. The man was sucking on a cigarette.

'Cave,' Bald said. 'What the fuck do you want?'

The man tut-tutted, took another drag and flicked the butt down the steps. 'Bad habit,' he said. 'Cut myself down to five a day but that's as far as I can go. Too much stress. Nice to see you too, John. Though I'd prefer it if you just called me Danny. Cave sounds so fucking formal.'

How about I call you cunt instead? thought Bald.

Danny Cave inspected his manicured fingernails. In another life he would've been an estate agent peddling studios in Camden. 'That was a nice touch at the interview – calling me your secretary,' he said. 'I think our friend Joe even believed you.'

'Yeah, well.' Bald wiped sweat from his bristled scalp. 'I could hardly tell the lad some tosser from the Firm was sitting in on his interview. He would've clammed up faster than an arsehole in a prison riot.'

'Good job I can take a joke better than my predecessor.' Cave brushed imaginary lint from his jacket and went on. 'The thing is this, John. I didn't just come here to shoot the breeze with you.'

Bald didn't look surprised, because he wasn't. The Firm didn't do idle chit-chat. Everything they said, everything they did, it was calculated and was only ever a half- or quarter-truth.

'I wanted to talk to you about the job,' Cave said.

'I haven't found the right man yet.'

'Oh, but I have.'

Cave glided up the steps until he was alongside Bald. He put a bony hand on Bald's shoulder and nodded towards the street below as a Lexus GS rolled into view. Bald admired the chrome bodywork and heavily tinted windows. Clearly the MoD cutbacks hadn't extended to the company car scheme. Fucking typical, Bald thought. It was all right for squaddies to get lumbered with shit equipment but God forbid if anyone deprived the pen-pushers of their executive cars and expense accounts.

A driver stepped out and held open the rear passenger door.

'Need a ride?' Cave asked Bald.

'I'm fine.'

'Nonsense, man. Get in. We can have ourselves a little chat along the way.'

Bald sighed. Ever since he'd signed on the dotted line with Talisman International, Bald had kept Cave at arm's length. But now the Firm had come knocking and if Cave wanted to talk, well, he would just have to fucking listen.

Bald shrugged off Cave's hand. 'Let's get this over with.'

They walked down the steps and Bald folded himself into the back of the Lexus. It was a tight fit. Bald had packed on almost three stone in the last six months. Not so long ago he'd had a lithe thirty-inch waist, but the four inches he'd put on betrayed a life of lavish lunches. He felt slow and cumbersome.

They eased out of the station and headed south down Waterloo Road, then east towards the Elephant and Castle. Further and further away from his shag. Two tower blocks jutted out in the iron-grey skyline like a pair of giant fingers giving the rest of the world a big 'fuck you'.

'So tell me something,' Bald said. 'How did a common prick like you end up in the Firm?'

Cave rubbed his meticulous stubble and said, 'What a drunk Scottish tool like you doesn't understand is that people like me are the new flavour of the month in Whitehall. Those old farts with their posh accents and their fucking principles, the Leo Lands of this world – their time has gone. The world is changing, John. And so is the Firm.'

'Nah, I don't think you change. Bringing someone like you in is just window-dressing. Everything else stays the same.'

'Look, let's skip the bullshit,' Cave said. His voice was matey wideboy rather than public school. 'I want you in on this job.'

Bald laughed. 'I already am.'

'No, I mean I want you to do it *personally*.'

The words shot up Bald's spine. In the months since his rehab, during all the tortuous phys and stretching exercises as he painstakingly coached his legs back into action, never once had it crossed his mind to go back into operations. Bald's vision of his future included beer and golf in the Algarve and the occasional jet-ski ride.

'I'm retired.'

Cave raised a hand to protest. 'Think about it, John. You're the perfect man for the job. You've done your years in the Regiment. You've got experience operating as the grey man. Christ, it makes perfect sense.'

'Forget it,' Bald replied. 'Those days are behind me.'

Cave slipped into silence for a while. As they glided along the Old Kent Road, Bald saw garish supermarkets squeezed between black-eyed postwar terraces, gum-spattered pavements populated by Arab women in black and white burkhas, drunks shuffling along, holding up their piss-stained trousers. He remembered why he hated London and had resisted moving there despite the job with Talisman. He'd grown up in Dundee – Scumdee to the locals – but every weekend he'd escaped to the Cairngorms, where he learned to run and ski and row and fish. And there, in the unforgiving Scottish Highlands, John Bald had honed the skills he would one day need to become a Blade.

London could go fuck itself.

'Shall I let you in on a little secret? There's one or two things about this job that you don't know,' Cave said while staring out of the window. 'Stuff that's on a strictly need-to-know basis.'

That got Bald halfway curious. He'd been drip-fed intelligence on the operation, but as with everything else the Firm did, they told you only what you needed to know, or rather what they wanted you to know. Bald had been obliged to share that int with Gardner, because although he'd brought Joe down from Hereford to take the piss out of him, Cave hadn't known that. He assumed Gardner was another candidate for the job, not some sad prick Bald wanted to get revenge on.

'Such as?' said Bald.

Cave crossed his legs. 'What if I told you that the employer was a contractor that works at the cutting edge of the defence industry.'

'I'd say that's very fucking interesting. But so what?'

They had passed New Cross and started down the Lewisham Way, on the A20. Bald said, 'Where the fuck are you taking me?'

Cave stared rigidly ahead and pretended not to have heard. 'The company is Lance-Elsing. They work under the radar, developing the kind of new technologies that will blow that drunken little brain of yours.'

'I don't care if they make fucking Jaffa cakes,' Bald said. 'I'm not doing it.'

Cave stared grimly at him.

'You forget who you're talking to, John Boy. You'll do whatever I say. I say, clap your hands, you'll fucking clap. I tell you to jump, you'll go running off the nearest cliff.' He looked away again. 'And if you don't do the job, millions of people will suffer.'

'What do you mean?'

Cave faced him again.

'If the sleeper succeeds in their mission, in three days' time they'll reduce the West to rubble.'

eight

2359 hours.

Cave took out his BlackBerry Torch and started tapping out emails and bossing subordinates on the phone. Bald saw London's lights fading on the horizon as the driver pulled onto the M20. The land had become a basin of dense shadows, as if black snow had fallen from the sky and blanketed the fields and trees. Bald could feel his brain pounding inside his skull. They skated past Ashford International Airport, the Lexus clocking eighty, and Bald feared that things were about to get bad for him.

'We've been in close contact with the CIA for the past three months,' Cave said after ending a call. 'Usually the Agency wouldn't share their lunch with us let alone operational info. But in this case they've got no choice. They know the sleeper's bosses are planning to attack Britain.'

Bald said, 'Who's the sleeper working for?'

'Take a wild guess.'

'The Taliban? Al-Qaeda?'

Cave pulled a face, as if he'd just drunk a glass of piss. 'Get real, John. The Taliban are bogged down in Afghanistan. And as for Al-Qaeda, those jokers been irrelevant for longer than the White House would dare to admit. We're talking about a sleeper cell being groomed for several years. Possibly since they were at university. That level of planning and foresight is alien to such groups.'

'Then who?'

'They call themselves Lashkar-e-Taiba. They're the sadistic bastards who masterminded the Mumbai terrorist attacks.'

A couple of miles south of Ashford the driver pulled off the M20 onto Bad Munstereifel Road. Cave continued, 'Killing Bin Laden hasn't changed a thing. Al-Qaeda were already a spent force. You will appreciate that we all knew that. We just couldn't say it publicly. But the important thing about Bin Laden's death was that he was holed up in Pakistan, right on the doorstep of the biggest military base in the bloody country. Pakistan is where the next generation of terror groups will come from, and Lashkar-e-Taiba think big. They've got funding and they're not afraid to kill. And with Bin Laden out of the way, they sense this is their big moment.'

'Bully for them,' said Bald, and rubbed his temples.

Cave frowned. 'You don't sound very concerned about any of this?'

Bald closed his eyes. He could feel the pressure building. The invisible band around his head tightened. He looked down at the palms of his hands. Not this, not now, he thought. 'Those dickheads at the Agency are big boys,' he said. 'I'm sure they can take care of the sleeper themselves.'

'But that's my point.' Cave squirmed irritably in his seat. 'They can't. You know this, for fuck's sake. You've been in charge of recruiting for the job.'

Bald said nothing.

'I saw how you handled yourself in those interviews and of course you're the dirtiest fighter we have, John Boy.

So this is what's going to happen. You're going to go to America and kill the sleeper. We'll fly you in and give you all the supplies you need. But—'

Cave left the sentence hanging in the air while he again attended to the Torch. The screen was flashing with an incoming call. Cave smiled wanly at Bald.

'You know the drill. If it goes tits up, we'll deny all knowledge of the operation. So will the Agency.'

Nothing new there, thought Bald. The Firm's SOPs were basically a roll-call of the many devious and original ways by which they planned to fuck you in the arse. Bald rubbed his eyes but the shimmering refused to go away. His iPhone trilled in his jeans pocket. He dug it out. Lena was calling. He tapped the 'Decline' tab. I shouldn't be here right now, he thought. I should be in a hotel banging the finest piece of Russian arse the world has ever seen. His mind ran through all the good shit that had happened to him since Serbia. The women. The job. The fucking money. The big house in Guildford. Lena. Cave was out of his fucking mind if he thought he would want to risk going back into active service.

He thought, too, about the migraines. It wouldn't just be a risk doing the job. It'd be a fucking disaster. That was why he'd never considered himself for the contract to begin with. He thought about sharing his thoughts with Cave, but the MI6 man was waffling away on the Torch.

'Yes . . . No . . . Yes. Of course.'

They were fast approaching the Kent coast. The land had flattened out. Cave killed the call.

Bald wasn't prepared to deal with this crap any longer. He wanted out. He tapped the driver's headrest and said, 'Stop the car.'

Cave snorted, half amused, half annoyed. 'Don't you want to hear my proposal?'

'Shove it up your crack. I've got a good job. A good fucking life. I don't need this shit. Get some other cunt to do it.'

With that Bald sunk into his seat and rooted around in his jeans pocket. He pulled out a small plastic container, unscrewed the lid and popped three white tablets into his mouth.

'On the happy pills now, are we, John Boy?'

'These fucking headaches—'

Cave snatched the container from Bald and read out the word 'Sarotex'. He tossed it back into Bald's lap. 'For God's sake. You're on anti-depressants now?'

'It's for my head,' said Bald.

'That's the stuff they prescribe for the boys coming back from Afghanistan with PTSD.' Cave was quiet for a moment. Bald faced forward but he could feel the wanker's eyes burning holes in him. 'Lance-Elsing are willing to cough up $5 million for this job.'

Bald said, 'It's worth a lot more to the Firm.'

'You want to concentrate on getting your act together. You can't cock this one up.'

'I told you: get someone else to do it.'

'There is no one else.'

Bald soothed his forehead. He prayed for the amitriptyline to kick in super-fast. Bald was a tough guy, he had grit, had balls, but when the migraines came on he wanted nothing more than to put a bullet between his eyes.

'Five million,' repeated Cave. 'That'll set you up for life. You can go and live in a chalet in the Alps, drink whiskey and eat deep-fried kebabs, or whatever it is you people do.'

Bald said nothing.

Cave dropped his voice. His eyes were smiling. 'But know this. You walk away and I make one phone call. That's all it takes. One phone call and your life becomes a living nightmare.'

Bald's mouth was suddenly very dry.

'You remember Rio, don't you, John?' Cave went on. 'I'm sure the Brazilian authorities would love to talk to you about the cops you killed and the drugs you smuggled out.'

Cave now turned to face Bald. His demeanour had changed. His voice was threatening.

'If you won't cooperate with us, I'll put you on the next flight to Brazil. The police will have you wearing steel bracelets before you put a foot on the tarmac. They'll try you for murder, John Boy. They'll send you to a prison where the local gangs will ride a train up your arse so hard their dicks will be tickling the back of your throat.'

Bile rose up to Bald's mouth. He could taste it. It was bitter and lumpy. He swallowed it back down, breathed in air-conned air and glared at Cave. 'I do this one job, we're quits?'

Cave smiled broadly at Bald. 'Good man.'

A road sign indicated they were five miles north of New Romney. The sky had been stripped bare of clouds. In its place was a low mist that rippled and swirled as it blew in from the sea, dousing the fields and the trees.

'Almost there.'

'Almost where?' asked Bald.

'Lydd Airport.'

The mist thickened. Irrigation dykes tapered away either side of the road, hemmed in by slanting fence posts.

Bald caught sight of the GPS navigator on the dash. They were racing south down Swamp Road. The navigator reckoned 1.2 miles to their destination. Swamp Road fed into Dennes Lane and the road shrunk to country lane. It was bumpy as fuck and at the speed they were travelling the car jerked and rattled, Bald's guts doing somersaults. The words of his old mucker Dave Hands came back to him. Hands had always been a cunt but he was on the money when it came to dealing with Whitehall. However smart you are or think you are, he'd said to John, the Firm will fuck you.

But they'll fuck you so gently you won't even notice it.

Cave checked his Torch again. Without looking at Bald he said, 'There's a private Gulfstream jet waiting for you. It'll fly you to Mexico City. From there you'll have to make your own way across the border.'

Bald asked, 'Why Mexico?'

'We can't send you on a flight directly to the US. Even with the Agency's help, there's no way of sneaking you in without your name and fingerprints being recorded.'

Bald shook his head vigorously. 'No fucking way. I can't just get on a flight and bug out of here. I've got business to take care of.' Lena's arse flashed into his mind.

Cave shrugged. 'Tough luck, John Boy. The sleeper is planning to act in three days. That gives us a window of seventy-two hours to stop him.'

Cave paused to consult his watch. He was wearing a Cartier – eighteen carats of gold that had Bald wondering how much a prick like him banked each month.

'I have meetings—'

'I'm afraid you don't,' Cave said. 'As of midnight you're officially on the Missing Persons list. Suspected of falling off the Embankment Bridge along with another ex-Regiment bad-luck story, Joseph James Gardner. Media reports will suggest you were both drunk. They'll write it up as the tragic end to two glorious military careers.'

Bald felt his face blaze up.

'Don't bother playing innocent,' Cave said. 'I saw what happened on the bridge. I was watching you the whole time.'

The heat spread down Bald's neck. Tiny sparks singed each hair on his forearms. 'But if you saw me, why didn't you do anything to stop me?'

'One less problem to take care of. Gardner was a bundle of trouble. You did us a favour there.'

Sweat trickled down the nape of Bald's neck. The Lexus was churning out frosted air that made the sweat unpleasantly cold. They were east of Lydd now. The medication was taking effect. A fog was settling behind Bald's eyes and making him feel drowsy. The palpitation in his hands and chest was petering out. He gazed out of his window. Nearly one o'clock in the morning and the moon was on full blast, coating a single aircraft hangar and a half-dozen surrounding structures in a sticky luminescence. Lydd Airport.

The runway was lit up. Everything else was encased in darkness. It wasn't hard to spot the Gulfstream poised at the near end of the runway. Sea mist ghosted around the perimeter of the airport. Take a good look, said the voice in the back of Bald's head. This might be the last time you see Britain for a while.

The driver slowed the Lexus to a fast walk. Its headlights danced across the body of the Gulfstream.

'Everything's ready, Johnny. Are you?'

'What do you fucking think?'

A smile crawled up Cave's right cheek. 'Cheer up, man. You might even enjoy it.'

The Lexus slowed to a halt at the edge of the runway fifty metres from the Gulfstream. Bald had to admit, the jet looked the business.

'You're looking at a G450,' said Cave. 'The best long-range business jet money can buy. Too good for you.'

The driver debussed, paraded around to Cave's side and opened the passenger door for him. Bald was left to clamber out himself. A smell of diesel and salt infiltrated his nostrils. He allowed himself a grim thought: at least the Firm are sending you off to your death in style. Shutting out further thoughts, he checked his surroundings. There were no other cars or people in sight. And that gave Bald an idea as Cave led the way towards the Gulfstream.

The jet filled their panorama. Bald could make out the signature oval windows and the 'G450' logo etched in stylish italics down the length of the tail.

'Hurry it up,' Cave said to Bald. 'Chop, chop.'

But Bald started pacing away from the Gulfstream.

'What the fuck do you think you're doing?' Cave shouted after him.

'I'm fucking leaving.'

Bald quickened his stride, heading for the blackness encircling the runway. He had no idea how he'd get back to London tonight. He hadn't thought that far ahead. All he knew was he wanted to get as far away from Cave and the Firm as fucking possible. No, he wasn't going to blow everything he had. Not even for five million quid.

'You can't leave!' Cave called after him.

I just have, mate, thought Bald.

He made it a few paces further when a cold circle against his nape made him freeze.

An unfamiliar voice said, 'Take one more step and I'll kill you.'

Bald was halfway through wondering who the fuck had shoved a gun into his neck when half a dozen figures emerged from the dark fields into the hot light of the runway. They were identically dressed in dark-grey suits, white shirts and black ties. They were identically armed too. Each guy packed a Sig Sauer P229 semi-automatic pistol.

The Firm's foot soldiers, realised Bald. He heard the click-clack of shoes on tarmac. The footsteps terminated immediately to his six o'clock.

'You really thought it would be that easy?' Cave sounded amused. 'John, the fact is you will do this job. Now get on the bloody plane. We're behind schedule.'

Bald figured it would be pointless to try to run. The foot soldiers would mow him down before he reached safe ground. He turned around and warily followed Cave towards the Gulfstream. By the time Bald reached the top of the airstairs he was struggling for breath. He stepped through the primary entrance door and found himself in the main cabin area. A smell of fresh leather hit him, walnutty and textured. He smelled something else too, something shitty, rank. He couldn't place it. He looked up and down the cabin. On his left was the starboard galley with a storage area stacked with cutlery and plates, a water-filter system and a coffee percolator.

Then Bald looked to his right at the main cabin area and dry-heaved.

nine

0100 hours.

The cabin had twelve seats. Or rather, it had clearly once catered for twelve passengers. Now only four seats remained. They were the four nearest to a second, aft, galley and toilet. Overhead cabin lights illustrated patches of darker carpet and screw holes in the floor where the other eight seats had been removed.

In place of these were a bunch of things that didn't feature in the Gulfstream corporate brochure. Strong points were secured to the cabin floor. Next to the chains there was a bundle of black hoods, and stashed in the aft galley were police batons and crocodile clips. Bald noticed a power cable snaking out of the galley.

Cave said, 'Excuse the mess. We're having to loan the bird off the Agency. Cutbacks and all that.'

'What's with all this shit?'

Clearing his throat, Cave answered, 'The Agency use this for the odd stopover. Normally they'll land in Tashkent or Warsaw, but the urgency of this mission required us to get the first plane they had available. They didn't clear up after themselves.'

'Extraordinary rendition,' Bald said.

'Yeah,' grumbled Cave. 'They call this little baby the Guantánamo Express.'

Bald had done his fair share of interrogations, and even tortured the odd bastard. But being in that cabin still made ants crawl up his spine.

Cave reached into his pocket and handed Bald a chunky black mobile that seemed as heavy as a brick, with a simple keypad.

'This is what we call a "burner". It's a pay-as-you-go job. The number isn't registered to anyone so there's no way of linking you or anyone else to it.' He also took out a mint tin. 'There's fifty SIM cards in here. After every call, be sure to replace the SIM card and crush the old one. That way no one can track the call or triangulate your position.'

Bald fiddled with the buttons. The burner was prehistoric, but then Bald didn't need a phone that could play Angry Birds.

'I'll take your phone, wallet and keys,' said Cave. Then, seeing the hesitation all over Bald's face, he quickly added, 'Don't worry. You'll get them back once the mission has been completed.'

Bald emptied his pockets and Cave produced a ziplock bag and sealed the iPhone, wallet and key fob inside. It reminded Bald of being booked into a police cell.

'Two more rules,' Cave said. Bald found it hard to stay focused. The meds and the booze had left him knackered. He could barely keep his fucking eyelids popped. 'One, we only talk in code. I presume you know the procedure from your days in the Regiment.'

Bald nodded angrily. '"Birthday cake" is the example they taught us at Hereford. The CIA use it as a codeword for a terrorist bomb. Every time someone makes a phone call in America and says "birthday cake" the call is red-flagged by the National Security Agency.'

'Correct,' Cave said. 'We know that the NSA listens in to every conversation, reads every email and text message that involves anyone in the United States communicating abroad. But there's a way round this.'

'How?'

'We'll communicate on Hotmail.'

'But you just said the NSA monitored emails.'

'Only what's sent through the ether. But we're not going to send emails to each other. We'll correspond through drafts. I'll write an email to you and save it in the drafts folder. You'll open it, read it and delete it, then write your reply and save it to drafts. We each check in daily. If I save a draft and then see it's been deleted, I know you've read it.'

'And the NSA can't see what we're writing?'

'No. It's 100 per cent secure.'

Cave glanced at his watch again, signalling that their talk was over.

'You'll touch down in Mexico City just after seven in the morning. A handler will be there to meet you. Don't look for her. She'll find you. She'll supply you with passports, cash and a route across the border. Once we've established a positive ID, you are to neutralize the sleeper. Make it look like an accident. The less suspicious the circumstances, the less chance you've got of getting yourself nicked.'

Cave gave his back to Bald and retreated to the entrance of the aircraft. A stewardess emerged from some unseen crevice at the starboard galley. Her tits were bunched up in the middle of her tight blouse, the top two buttons undone. Bald imagined himself digging a hand in there and cupping one of her tits in his hand. He had been thinking about Lena and right now his balls were looking like a pair of blue bowling balls.

'Looks like you got one thing right,' Bald called out to Cave. 'The in-flight entertainment.'

The stewardess smiled thinly and brushed strands of glossy hair behind her ear. Bald reckoned she was Thai, and that only made him even more horny. Lately he'd developed a thing for Asian women.

'Drink?' she asked.

'Rum and Coke,' Bald said, focusing.

She nodded and disappeared back into the galley.

Cave stopped, turned and looked back inside the plane. 'One more thing, John Boy. I'm sure I don't need to spell it out.'

'What's that?'

The jet engines whined, then rumbled. Cave had to shout to make himself heard above the drone. 'The stewardess is out of bounds. She works for the Agency.'

Then he breezed down the airstairs, his brogues clanking against the metal steps, and hurried towards the Lexus, his jacket and tie flapping wildly.

The stewardess shut the door.

Bald was sealed in.

ten

The moustached border officer caught the whiff of booze
on Bald's breath and nodded approval. Mexico, thought
Bald. Probably the only country in the world apart from
Scotland that approves of my drinking regime. The officer
stamped Bald's passport – it gave his name as James Grant
and birthplace as Belfast – and waved him through, pointing out the duty-free shop where he could stock up on
tequila. But Bald resisted the temptation to buy a bottle
of José Cuervo. He was feeling pretty loaded after the
flight. The look-but-don't-touch stewardess had plied
him with a stream of Heinekens and when the cans ran
out he'd gone to work on the bottles. Brandy, bourbon,
vodka. There wasn't much that Bald hadn't tipped down
his gullet during the eleven-hour flight.

He followed the sign which said '*Llegadas*', his limited
Spanish telling him this translated as 'Arrivals'. Bald
never ceased to be surprised by the airport. Most Central
and South American airports tended to be ramshackle
and cramped but Mexico City International was clean,
spacious, modern.

That was the first thing that Bald noticed. The second
was the number of cops. Officers of the Policia Federal, the

military branch of Mexican law enforcement, stood guard at every exit and patrolled the terminal in packs of three and four. They were clad in black and blue fatigues with riot helmets, elbow and knee pads, bulky utility belts and tactical vests studded with button clips. All of them were packing AR-15 carbine tactical rifles. Some had German shepherds tugging at their leashes.

Bald shoved his way through the crowd in the Arrivals lounge and ventured outside. Morning smog. He squinted up at the sky and the heat swamped him. It was greasy and close, like he was doing push-ups in a sauna. He traipsed into the parking bay and located the taxi rank, where fleets of VW Pointers and Hyundai Atos were jostling for trade on the three-lane blacktop. Bald couldn't see a queue, just a bunch of dumpy people, most standing a good six inches shorter than him. Then a family of four bundled past him and crammed into a taxi. A hand squeezed his bicep and a female English voice whispered into his ear, 'Don't look at me. Don't say or do anything that shows you know me. Cough twice if you understand.'

Bald obeyed. He caught sight of the woman's reflection in the passenger window of a parked Chevrolet C2. She had black, curly hair and the scent of expensive perfume wafted off her neck. Her skin was a shiny copper. Bald figured she was the Firm's local handler. They had one in every city in the world. The handler was somebody who knew the lie of the land, who had an understanding of the situation on the ground. A Mark One Eyeball, as they called it in the Regiment. Usually the handlers were semi-retired Civil Service gits who spent their afternoons getting drunk on gin and tonic and their evenings making racist jokes. The woman at his six o'clock was about as far from that description as it was possible to get.

'You're John, right?' Her accent was nasal, formal but somehow charming.

Bald coughed twice again.

'This way,' she said.

The woman walked quickly towards the short-term car park. Bald followed four metres behind. One look at her rear and his mouth was salivating. She had a first-class arse, the kind of arse that got featured on Internet forums. It was maybe the best arse Bald had ever seen. It swayed smoothly from hip to hip like a pendulum, neatly wrapped like a gift inside her abraded skinny jeans. A group of taxi drivers were smoking and playing cards on the top of a cab. They paused to eyefuck the woman. Bald followed her as she navigated her way through a maze of cars until she came to a silver Nissan Sentra. Bald smiled to himself. In Europe an MI6 agent could get away with shooting around town in a posh car. In Mexico you didn't want to stand out. To do so would only make you a target for the local kidnappers. In that regard the Nissan was a shrewd choice. The woman hopped in, reached over and opened the front passenger door.

'Get in,' she said quietly.

Bald ducked into the front passenger seat. The woman fired up the Nissan and accelerated out of the car park. The airport was unusually close to the city centre and after a few hundred metres the whine of aircraft had been usurped by the catcalls of traffic and street vendors. Palm trees and bare concrete apartment blocks ticker-taped past, the sequence only broken by vast billboards advertising Mexican mobile phones and Coca-Cola. Bald remembered reading somewhere that Mexico consumed more Coke than any other country in the world.

Bald grew tired of the scenery. He angled his head at the woman and said, 'You know there are easier ways of picking up a guy.'

'First time in Mexico City?' she replied.

'Second. I got posted here four years ago with the Regiment. We were helping train the local cops in close-quarters battle, building assaults – all that shit. Back then they were getting fucked big time by the drug cartels.'

'Nothing's changed.' She waved away an old woman who was stopping at each car and offering trinkets. 'The whole country is caught up in the war between the Gulf, Zapoteca and Sinaloa cartels. Forty thousand dead in the past decade and the number rises every day. Just be glad you're only passing through. I've been here three and a half years.'

The streets narrowed the further into the city they went. The pavements were festooned with rubbish.

'What's your name?' Bald asked.

'You don't need to know that.'

'Come on, lass. Fair's fair. You know mine.'

She rolled her eyes. 'Grow up, for God's sake.' Dead air passed between them for a moment. Bald sat there wondering how the handler could be so fucking humourless. Then she said, 'You're Scottish?'

'Dundee,' Bald replied.

The woman adjusted herself in her seat. 'Can't say I've ever been there.'

'Don't bother,' said Bald. 'Unless you like pub fights.'

The woman laughed politely, but the tension in her shoulders slackened.

'I'm Antonia. Daniel gave me your file,' she said, Bald noting that she called Cave by his first name. 'I know all about you.'

'Yeah,' Bald said, sliding down further into the seat. 'Well, I know fuck all about you.' He noticed the corners of her mouth flinch when he swore. Bald figured she'd had a posh upbringing but he couldn't quite place her. She spoke with an upper-class English accent but her skin was Mexican. He went on, 'What's your cover here?'

'I work at the British Embassy.'

'And before that?'

'I went into the Firm straight from university. I graduated from Balliol College with a first in Philosophy, Politics and Economics.'

'Fuck me,' said Bald. 'You're one of them.'

Antonia shot Bald a glance that could have bored through lead. 'I beg your pardon?'

'How many languages can you speak?'

'Four. Five if you include my rather modest Mandarin.'

Bald nodded like she'd given the right answer. 'And where did you grow up?'

'Harpenden, in Hertfordshire.'

'And what did your old man do for a living?'

'Daddy was Professor of Defence Studies at King's College, London. He was a very important man.'

'Yeah,' Bald grunted. 'Like I said. One of them.'

'One of who?'

'One of the posh twats who sail through life with a silver spoon up their arse.' He imagined messing her up a bit. 'I bet you never had to work for anything in your life.'

Antonia reddened, then fell into a stony silence as the car crawled around the edges of Zócalo Square, the beating heart of Mexico City. Bald remembered the place from his previous stay: the plaza the size of two football pitches, the vast baroque buildings hemming it in, the protest-ers camped out on the plaza and surrounded by trigger-happy cops. Finally Antonia said in her most professional and cold voice, 'Daniel said you have to get across the border tonight, and you have to do it illegally.'

Bald nodded. 'How hard is that?'

'Thousands make a run for it every day.' Antonia honked her horn at the locals, who seemed to take forever to cross the road. 'A handful make it across.'

Bald said, 'And the others?'

'If they're lucky they get caught.'

'And if they're not?'

'They get shot.'

'Makes you wonder why they fucking bother. Life doesn't look so bad here.' Bald eyed the crowds. The women weren't exactly stunners. Half of them might generously be described as pear-shaped. A lot of the men were decked out in Manchester United shirts with 'Chicarito' on the back. The footballer's face also beamed out from several billboards.

'Crossing used to be easy,' Antonia said. 'But now there are gangs of rednecks on the border. I'm sure you know the type. They patrol at night and shoot at anyone trying to get in. It's murder but the US government chooses to turn a blind eye.'

'Why?'

'Illegal immigration is a red-hot issue in America. Down here, people just want to make a better life for themselves and send some money back home.'

'Weird,' said Bald.

'What is?'

'That you can be so posh it's embarrassing, and yet you still feel sorry for the great unwashed. Where did that come from?'

'Maybe it comes from hanging around too many Scottish soldiers with chips on their shoulders.'

'Ouch,' Bald squealed.

'But, believe me, if you're caught crossing that line, the rednecks will kill you.'

They veered away from Zócalo Square and motored down Avenue 5 de Mayo. Kids, eight years old at most, hawked cigarettes and nachos.

'There's a man in a town about 100 kilometres north of here. His name is Nelson.'

'Who he?'

'The guy who will smuggle you across the border.'

Bald pulled out a miniature of Jim Beam he'd pilfered from the Gulfstream. He unscrewed the cap and tipped the bourbon down his mouth. It tasted honeyed and wooden. He wiped his mouth with the back of his hand and ignored the incredulous look on Antonia's mug.

Bald said, 'And what time are we meeting Mr Nelson?'

'Three o'clock this afternoon.'

'Great. That means we've got time for a drink.'

They had turned down the tatty thoroughfare of Luis Moya and ventured east onto Ayuntamiento. This was a sweaty, desperate neighbourhood. Battered houses lined the street, their side walls often missing, like dolls' houses with the hinged façades left open. Bald could peek right in and see podgy women washing and cleaning. Old men wearily climbed concrete stairs. Bald spotted a saloon-type bar twenty metres down from the Nissan on the opposite side of the road.

'Pull over here,' he said.

Antonia looked down the street, then screwed her face up. 'What on earth is that?'

Bald did a spit-take. 'You've lived in Mexico City for three fucking years and you don't know what a *pulqueria* is? Jesus, where do you go for fun?'

Antonia shrugged. 'I'm not a prude. And I'm not upper-class. But I do have taste – which you clearly lack.'

Christ, thought Bald. This bird's so prim she makes a primary teacher look like Frankie fucking Boyle.

'Join me for one drink,' he said, unbuckling his seatbelt. 'You never know, you might like a bit of rough.'

She thought about it for a long moment. Then she said, 'Just the one.'

They got out of the car. The air stank of maize and body odour. A wild dog pissed enthusiastically against rusty metal railings. A beggar was suddenly stepping into Bald's face. The guy had a face like a bowl of rotten minced beef and a stump for a right arm. He looked like some lame Hispanic version of Joe Gardner. He made some noises. Bald shooed him away with a simple 'Fuck off'.

Bald escorted Antonia through the *pulqueria*'s swing doors. He watched her arse and dreamed about slamming her in her bedroom while her parents sat at the dining table eating salmon and drinking white wine. Her old man trying to politely ignore the ecstatic screams as Bald drilled his precious daughter in the arse.

Something in his peripheral vision snapped Bald out of his fantasy. The beggar had stopped thirty metres down the street. He was lingering. Staring back at Bald.

eleven

It was a million degrees in the bar and the place stank worse than the changing room at Bald's gym. Some kind of shit local music was playing. Loads of fucking banjos and shouting. Brightly coloured murals covered the walls like graffiti. Bald half-expected the dozen locals at the bar to turn around in unison and draw their weapons, Western-style. But they didn't. They chain-smoked Marlboro Reds, motioned for more shots of pulque and minded their own fucking business.

Bald made a beeline for a table near to the bar. He waved two fingers at the drowsy bartender, indicating he wanted a couple of shots of pulque, and pulled up a chair. Antonia was standing behind hers, as if waiting for Bald to pull it out for her. But Bald wasn't programmed that way. He let her tuck herself in.

'I'll have a Diet Coke,' she said.

'Too late,' Bald replied. 'I already ordered.'

The bartender dumped two shots of pulque in front of them. The pulque was creamy and looked like dog sperm. Bald knocked his back in one swig. Spicy and hot in the back of his throat, it settled in his stomach like battery acid. He wiped his mouth with the back of his hand. Antonia didn't touch her drink. She stared at it like it was, in fact, dog sperm.

'Go on, lass. Drink up.'

'I'm not thirsty.'

Bald shrugged and said, 'What did Cave tell you about me? Apart from the fact that I'm a legend in the sack?'

Antonia pushed her drink away. 'He said that you used to be in Special Forces. One of the best, and one of the worst. That the other guys respected you but steered clear, because they couldn't trust you an inch. He also said that you're a bitter drunk living in the past and I should keep a close eye on you in case—'

Four chubby Mexicans at the bar laughed out loud at something. Antonia looked over her shoulder at them. 'In case what?' Bald said.

'Daniel said you're a combustible Scot,' Antonia said, speaking as if reading from an autocue, 'who's prone to violent tendencies, frequently expresses his anger with his fists and has a serious dependency on cocaine.'

'I agree with everything except the bitter part.'

Antonia didn't laugh. She didn't smile. Her lips were so straight you could paint road lines with them, and Bald was thinking the same thing he thought about every English bird. That she'd look a hell of a lot sexier if she didn't have a face like the world was taking a shit on her.

'You think you're a funny guy.'

'Nah,' said Bald.

'You know that humour is the first defence mechanism for people suffering from acute PTSD.'

'You know that psychobabble is the first line of defence for people who've never fired a gun.'

He suddenly realised how knackered he was. Mexico City was six hours behind London. Which made it almost 1500 hours back home, which meant that Bald had been awake for more than thirty hours. He hadn't slept a wink on the flight. He'd been too busy chugging back free beverages and eyeing up the stewardess. Now the jetlag had caught up with him. He needed something to juice his bloodstream. He pointed with his eyeballs to the untouched pulque in front of Antonia and said, 'You gonna drink that?'

'I think I'll pass.'

Bald sank Antonia's shot and gestured to the bartender for two more.

'Daniel's making a big mistake,' Antonia said. 'You're in no shape to do this job.'

'Still, he reckons I'm the best hope we have.'

'Then we are screwed.'

The bartender brought over the drinks and laid them both in front of Bald, who sank them one after the other. He waved to the bartender – 'Keep 'em coming' – then said to Antonia, 'You're just fucked off that I'm a Jock from a working-class town. That I don't have the posh accent and a public-school education. And I bet if I was James fucking Bond you'd be tearing your knickers off in a heartbeat.'

Antonia snorted.

'Not even in your dreams,' she said. 'Face it, John. We're different species.'

Bald had a comeback line but something else had stolen his attention. He was peering over Antonia's shoulder at a guy who had entered the bar. He looked like a beggar in his stained jeans, sandals and old duster jacket. A pair of blackened goggles were strapped around his eyes. In his hands was a battered eighties cassette player held together with duct tape. A microphone was plugged into the player and some old Sinatra song was dribbling out of the speakers. Then the guy started belting out the lyrics in a voice that sounded like a dying dog. The punters sitting at the bar heckled him but the man refused to budge.

Antonia said, 'I've got some things to take care of. Meet me at the Sheraton at ten o'clock sharp.'

Bald toasted Antonia's arse as she rose. The bartender was manhandling Sinatra out of the saloon, to the cheers of the punters. Bald drained another pulque.

'What's at the Sheraton?' he said.

'Our package is waiting for you there.'

'What kind of package?'

'It's a surprise.'

'Great. I fucking love surprises.'

twelve

Bald rolled out onto the street precisely one hour and twelve pulques later. White sunlight, hot and intense as burning sulphur, greeted him. He squinted and established his bearings. He was on Ayuntamiento heading east, so he needed to take the next left going north to get onto the main drag along Juárez. He was conscious of the fact that he was shitcanned. Each step was deliberate and required all his powers of concentration. He was focusing on the few inches of pavement ahead of his feet and wondering how he could sober up before his rendezvous with Antonia, when someone bumped into his shoulder.

The guy raised his hands in apology. He was a scrawny fuck with eyes that pointed in towards each other, as if staring at some invisible trinket being dangled in front of him. He tried to mumble sorry, but since he had no teeth, only shapeless, deformed sounds came out. Bald eyed the guy as he stumbled on up the street. What's with all the fucking bums in Mexico City? he thought.

As he watched Cross-Eyes shuffling down Ayuntamiento, he clocked Sinatra from the bar. The guy was fifteen metres away and lurking by a lamppost on the other side of the street. Six or seven metres behind him was the Hispanic Gardner. They were both staring at Bald.

Nah, Bald thought. Can't be. He shook his head clear and hurried on.

Eight minutes later he arrived at the Sheraton Centro Histórico and weaved his way towards the revolving glass door. He shot another glance over his shoulder and spied the homeless trio hobbling towards him. Like zombies raised from the fucking dead. Bald laughed to himself at the image of these fucking bums trying to get past the hotel's security. He made a wanker sign at Sinatra and entered the foyer.

Antonia was waiting for him there, flicking through messages on her iPhone. She locked it and said, 'You're late.'

'And your boss is a prick, but what can you do?'

Leading Bald through to the restaurant, she scanned the breakfast crowd, looking past the familiar mix of lethargic travelling businessmen and bloated tourists common to any five-star hotel anywhere in the world. Her eyes settled on a man at a table in the far corner. He was clean-cut, stick-thin, with side-parted brown hair and wearing loafers, shell-white linen trousers and a pink shirt with the sleeves rolled up to his elbows. A white jacket was draped tastefully over the back of his chair. Everything about him said Englishman abroad. He drained the dregs of his cappuccino, unhooked his jacket from the chair and made for the exit, blanking Bald and Antonia on his way out.

'A friend?' said Bald, nodding at the guy's back.

'A colleague,' replied Antonia.

She sidled up to the table. Bald plonked himself in a chair that gave him an unobstructed view across the restaurant to the foyer and the entrance of the hotel. He always chose restaurant tables that gave him a view of every other diner. Just as he always sat at the very back of an airplane and secreted a gun under his pillow at night. He told birds who were uncomfortable with the idea of sharing the bed with a fully loaded P229 that it was force of habit.

Bald noticed that the guy in the white suit had left a brown envelope at the table. He peered out to the street for any sign of the Three Zombies. Nothing.

Antonia ordered a skinny latte from the waitress in what sounded to Bald like perfect Spanish. He asked for a triple espresso in a Scots brogue that had the pretty Latino waitress frowning cutely at him. In the end Antonia had to order for him. Bald shifted his legs and ended up kicking something under the table.

He looked down and saw a black gym bag propped between his legs and Antonia's. 'Another surprise?'

'For later,' Antonia replied.

'I've got a surprise for you now, if you want,' Bald said sleazily.

'You need help.'

'I reckon if you let yourself go a bit, you'd enjoy it,' he said. 'You've just lived such a shy and rich little life that you're afraid of the real world.'

'No. I'm just not attracted to drunk old Scottish men.'

Antonia was still tightly coiled up and Bald got the impression that something new was making her uneasy. He couldn't help wondering if the Three Zombies had been paid to follow him, and maybe Antonia knew something about that. He thought about asking, but decided against it. She was Firm, after all. And as far as Bald was concerned, no one in the Firm could be trusted.

'We shouldn't stay here long,' Antonia said.

Bald looked mock-upset. 'But I thought we were getting a room?'

Antonia tipped her head forward slightly and dead-eyed Bald over the top of her sunglasses. 'You don't have a chance.'

'I like a challenge.'

She was still staring at him, but the smile had crawled back into its hole.

'I'm a lesbian.'

'That makes two of us.'

'I don't bat for both teams.'

'We'll see.'

The waitress brought their coffees. A guy had sat down at the next table and was tucking into a fajita. For breakfast. Fucking hell, Bald thought. All Mexicans ever seemed to scoff was some kind of maize mixed with some kind of meat. He decided it was time for his breakfast too. He took out another miniature he'd nicked from the Gulfstream – Chivas Regal this time – and tipped it into his triple espresso.

'How do you manage to stay alive?'

'I'm Scottish.'

Bald tasted his alco-coffee. It could fuel a monster truck across the Nevada desert. He reassured himself that his body clock was still running on London time and this was technically a mid-afternoon tipple.

Someone had turned up the volume on a big flat-screen TV hooked up to the wall behind the restaurant bar. It was tuned to one of the national news stations. You didn't need to know the local lingo to understand the headlines. The pictures told their own story. Eighteen headless corpses lying in a ditch near Acapulco, their hands bound with plastic cord and their bodies bloated from rigor mortis. Another spate of drug-related murders.

Antonia looked away from the TV. She slid out of her chair and dumped three fifty-peso notes on the table. 'Let's go,' she said. 'Nelson won't hang around.'

'Where are we meeting him?'

'The small town I mentioned north of here,' Antonia said, checking her iPhone again. 'San Hernando. It used to be a mining centre, but now it's run by the Gulf Cartel. Anything else you want to know? Good. Then hurry up. And don't forget the package.'

Bald tucked the envelope under his arm and slung the gym bag over his shoulder. It was surprisingly heavy. He wondered what the fuck was inside. They bugged out of the Sheraton. A silver-haired valet had Antonia's Nissan rumbling and ready to roll. Climbing into the front, Bald stowed the bag at his feet while Antonia greased the valet's palm with a hefty thousand-peso note, which Bald knew translated to around $100. The old bastard waved the cash at her and shouted, '*Gracias, chica.*'

Antonia arrowed the Sentra into the traffic that was steadily flowing east on Juárez, headed in the opposite direction from the Sheraton. After 100 metres they veered north on Eje Central Lázaro Cárdenas. Two kilometres down, Antonia took a left, then the first right onto Avenue Insurgentes Norte. The streets were lined with rundown Internet cafés and crumbling cantinas. Throngs of indigenous people were hawking trinkets, playing accordions and demonstrating crap magic tricks.

Bald ripped open the envelope and tipped the contents onto his lap. A sea of papers flooded out. Some pages were yellowed and wrinkled, others were black-and-white photocopies. The top one caught Bald's eye. It was a background report on an employee at Lance-Elsing Incorporated. A photo clipped to the top-right corner showed a guy in his late twenties or early thirties with thick-rimmed spectacles.

'His name is Shy Laxman,' Antonia said, eyes nailed to the road. 'And he's the sleeper.'

Bald flicked through the report. It was an inch thick. A man's life condensed into one inch. There was a photocopy of a graduation certificate, showing that Shylam K. Laxman had graduated from Harvard with a degree in Computer Engineering. A typewritten letter stapled to the certificate informed Laxman that he had been awarded a Special Mention in the Dean's List on account of his outstanding academic abilities.

'He was just sixteen when he got accepted at Harvard,' Antonia said.

'Yeah? Well, when I was seventeen I got an apprenticeship at a garage in Dundee.'

Antonia gunned the Nissan and skipped a red light. Car horns sounded.

'A Master's Degree in Chemical Engineering from Northeastern University, Boston, and a PhD in AI from MIT.' Bald thought, this guy's got more letters after his name than most people have got letters in their names.

Antonia interrupted his reading. 'By the time Shy Laxman left the university system he was twenty-four and had a reputation as one of the brightest young minds in his field. Companies were falling over themselves to hire him.'

'So he threw his lot in with these Lance-Elsing guys?'

'Defence companies have an ace up their sleeves. Access to the most cutting-edge tech, the stuff that no one knows about. The kind of stuff that makes nuclear submarines look like a relic from the Dark Ages.'

'So they're a big company?'

Antonia shook her head. 'Tiny. They're based in Clearwater, on Florida's west coast. Twenty-nine employees working out of a small factory in an industrial park.'

Bald was now skimming through a copy of Laxman's employment contract. It spanned forty-three pages. 'Jesus, this thing's longer than the Disclosure Contract they made us sign in the Regiment.'

They were breezing past a neighbourhood that bore the classic signs of grinding poverty. Dilapidated housing blocks, check. Old men with leathery skin rummaging through rubbish bins, check. Old women carrying babies on their backs and begging for change? Double fucking check.

'If you look at the signature and date on the contract,' said Antonia, driving through the slum super-fast, 'you'll see that Laxman joined Lance-Elsing four years ago. Around the same time, Congress awarded Lance-Elsing a $240-million contract to develop the next generation of military-grade weapons. The brief was to design weapons systems that would help the US military achieve its number-one goal by 2050.'

'Which is?'

'Zero per cent casualties in the combat environment.'

Bald was unimpressed. 'Lass, I tell you now. Whatever these boffins are cooking up is a load of bollocks. The head shed had us test-piloting all kinds of shit down at Hereford. Lasers that were supposed to melt tanks. Body

armour they reckoned was indestructible. The bottom line
is always the same: you win wars with men and bullets
and skill. Anyone who says otherwise has never done the
business.'

'This is different,' said Antonia.

'Oh yeah? So what exactly are they developing?'

'All I know is that Lance-Elsing have been working
on a top-secret new project and Laxman has been heavily involved in it. And if he smuggles out the technology,
things will get very ugly.'

Bald let the files fall to his lap.

'This is all very fucking nice,' he said. 'But I don't need
to know any of it. Look, lass, all I'm going to do is drop in,
slot the cunt and bug the fuck out.'

Antonia frowned with her lips. The neat brushstrokes of
her eyebrows almost met. Something up, Bald knew.

'What is it?' he asked.

Antonia said, 'Daniel hasn't told you the whole mission
yet, has he?'

thirteen

Avenue Insurgentes Norte transitioned into Mexico 85. The five-lane motorway forged its way between banks of clay and long grass. The road smoothed out and the crammed mass of Mexico City faded to a ghostly outline. Bald hardly noticed, pissed off that Danny Cave hadn't been straight with him.

'What else did that cunt have in store for me?' he asked.

Antonia studied the road very hard. 'Daniel wants you to monitor Laxman before you take him down.' She cleared her throat. 'With a view to obtaining information.'

'Why?'

Now she looked at him. Did a thing with her eyes that reminded him of his ex-wife. The look said, 'Are you really that drunk and stupid?'

'Intelligence,' she said. 'Daniel wants to know what Laxman's links are. Who he's working with. If the terrorists are trying to extract American technology, they'll aim to do the same at British sites too. The more intel we have from you, the more chance we have of uncovering sleeper cells in the UK.'

Bald felt his neck muscles tighten. The heat inside the Nissan smashed the mercury. He was working himself up into a rage. But rage had got Bald nowhere in the past and he tried to stifle it. He turned back to the front page of the file and studied the photograph in more detail.

'Laxman is Pakistani?'

Antonia said, 'Indian by birth. His parents emigrated to Boston from Delhi when he was three.'

'And now he's a good old American boy?'

'He has US citizenship, if that's what you mean.'

A road sign announced they were entering Tizayuca. Bald knew from studying maps of the area around Mexico City that the town was about thirty kilometres north-east of Mexico City. They were still an hour away from San Hernando.

Bald rested the file on the dash. Suddenly everything seemed out of focus. His breathing was getting out of control. He felt a searing pain, like someone was firing staples into his skull. He felt in his pocket for the amitriptyline.

The container wasn't there.

He closed his eyes. Tried to bury the migraine. 'Are you sure this is the guy?'

Antonia looked at him curiously. 'You're saying you have doubts?'

'He might be a specky twat.' Bald studied the face once more. 'But this guy's story . . . it's not ringing true, lass. I'm not so sure he's a fucking terrorist.'

'What makes you think that?'

'Grooming a sleeper takes years. For a start you need to find the right person. Right psych profile, right character, good fucking liar, smart, able to work alone without any contact for years, loyal. That's a lot of boxes to fucking tick. Terrorist groups aren't famous for their patience or forward planning. Danny says Lashkar-e-Taiba are more organized. A new breed. Anyway, Laxman is Indian, right?'

'Uh-uh.'

'India and Pakistani aren't the best of friends. Why the fuck would he do their dirty work?'

'Maybe he's a secret sympathizer. Maybe he's being bribed. Or maybe he's doing it for the same reason you're here. Five million of them, in fact.'

'I'm not doing this because of the money.'

'Of course you're not.'

Bald didn't pursue it. His efforts to squash the pain inside his head were futile. He figured he'd left the meds on the Gulfstream. In his boozy haze the container must have slipped out of his pocket and fallen down the side of the seat. No meds and no fucking booze. Bald was losing the battle. His skull was throbbing. Ever since the migraines had started, a week after returning to England, he had told himself that he could deal with them. The pain was crippling but as long as he was sitting behind a desk or playing a round of golf, it didn't fucking matter. But now he was back in action a voice chipped away at his brain like a pickaxe on a block of ice. What happens if you suffer a migraine in the middle of a firefight? What then?

Need to take my mind off my mind, he thought. He hauled up the gym bag he'd stashed at his feet, unzipped it and took a wee peek inside.

'Fuck me,' he said.

The bag weighed mostly nothing and was mostly empty, except for a single bundle of American dollars, Benjamin Franklin smugly looking at Bald from the face of each one. Bald dug a little deeper and found a pack of UK passports bound together with an elastic band. Like some kind of intelligence Secret Santa.

'Eight British passports, all courtesy of HMG and containing falsified biometric data, plus $7200 in clean bills,' Antonia said. 'That should cover any expenses. Although it'll be a miracle if you don't blow the lot on Southern Comfort.'

There was something else in the bag too. Bald picked it up.

'What the fuck's this?'

He was holding a stubby-nosed Smith & Wesson 637 revolver. It was 16.5 centimetres long and couldn't have weighed more than 450 grams. So far, so good. But Bald was pissed to see that the grip was pink. The revolver was the type of personal defence gun designed for a woman to fit snugly in her handbag. From the weight Bald understood that the revolver was empty, but he flipped out the stainless-steel cylinder anyway to check. There was also a box of .38 Specials in the gym bag.

'It's the only gun I could get at short notice.'

'Christ, I point this fucker at some cunt and they're more likely to die of laughter than a bullet wound.'

The road corkscrewed around the mountain corridor and began its rapid descent through the rugged terrain of Hidalgo State, snaking through a basin of mountains covered with a sprawling jungle of pine trees and holm oaks.

'You're drinking to get rid of something, aren't you?' Antonia said.

Bald rested his head on the headrest. 'That's something else we have in common.'

'What's that?'

'You're not just a pretty face.'

Antonia said nothing for longer than a little while. Then she piped up, 'What are the headaches about?'

'It was after I got shot to shit in Belgrade,' Bald said. There was a bottle of water on the dash and he took a long gulp. 'One bullet, the fucker bounced around my skull. Skimmed my cerebral cortex and exited my left shoulder.' He lowered the collar on his polo shirt and pointed to a patch of whitish skin on the apex of his shoulder blade. 'The docs said my motor skills were fine, but the damage to the cortex was permanent.'

'What kind of damage?'

'Memory loss, headaches, hallucinations, paranoia. The usual.'

'Does it give you Tourette's as well?'

'Some guys in the Regiment swear ten times as much as me.'

'Does Danny know about the migraines?'

Bald jerked his shoulders. 'Would he give a flying fuck?'

Bald drained the rest of the mineral water, rolled down the window and tossed the empty bottle out onto the roadside. Bald didn't do recycling, just like he didn't do yoghurt, Zumba fitness or pear cider. Far as he was concerned, the world was already fucked, no matter how big or small your carbon footprint was.

They drove deeper into Hidalgo on Mexico 105. The landscape was pockmarked by depressing shanty huts and beat-up old pickups. Bald didn't see any people milling about, just tired chickens picking at the soil.

Bald checked his Aquaracer. It was 1358 hours. Eighteen hours since he'd departed Lydd. Fifty-four hours to go. By the time he'd made it to the border, crossed into Texas and headed east to Florida, he'd have less than forty-eight hours to observe Laxman and report back to Cave. And then move in for the kill.

He thought, too, about the five million. Whatever he'd said to Antonia, he did care about the money. Money didn't make you happy, they said. Bald figured only penniless pricks believed that bollocks. He'd seen muckers from the Regiment pocketing tens of millions from selling their private military companies to the big defence contractors. Now they were living the high life in Abu Dhabi and California, and Bald was hungry for a piece of the action. Fuck it, when this mission was over the first thing he'd do was trade in the Aquaracer and buy himself a Porsche Design Indicator P6910. He'd seen one in *Forbes* magazine. It was built from titanium and finished in rose gold. Price tag $225,000. He wasn't much into cars. Didn't see the point of splurging eighty grand on a car only to see it lose twenty K in value the minute you drove it out of the showroom. Watches, on the other hand, tended to go up in value rather than down.

He reckoned it would look nice on his wrist. He'd be pulling birds like Antonia all over the fucking place then. Have them queuing up to blow him.

'Shit,' Antonia said, thumping her palms against the steering wheel. Bald looked at her and wondered what the fuck was wrong. Her pupils were wide as poker chips, her gaze fixed on the rear-view mirror. Bald looked too, and saw a white Dodge Charger dominating the mirror.

Engine growling. Racing towards them at full speed.

fourteen

1402 hours.

The Dodge was twenty metres away and closing fast. Bald watched it grow in the mirror. 'Unlicensed plates. Tinted windows.'

'In Mexico that means narco cops,' said Antonia.

But Bald thought back to the zombies in Mexico City. He wondered if somehow they were tied to his past, smuggling drugs and gunning down cops in Brazil. Maybe it was catching up with him. He decided against sharing this with Antonia.

They raced past a beat-up sign that said, '*Bienvenido a San Hernando. Población 7569.*' The town was a barely visible scattershot of specks amid the belt of reddish rock on the horizon. We're still four or five miles away, Bald thought. Not another fucking soul on the road. Perfect opportunity to take a couple of *gringos* hostage.

Now the Charger was ten metres from their rear bumper. They needed speed, Bald knew, and they needed it fucking now. 'Drive faster,' he said.

Antonia nodded quickly and shunted her foot all the way down on the accelerator. The Nissan's chassis began to vibrate. The speedometer clocked 130 kilometres per hour and the engine started making a strange rattling sound.

They were in the middle of Bumfuck, Mexico, with a narco-cop car closing in on them fast. Because even though Antonia was gunning the Nissan like hell, the Dodge was clinging ten metres behind them like a bad smell.

'Step on it,' Bald urged Antonia. She put her foot to the floor. The needle hit 140, then struggled to 150. It wobbled around the 155 mark and the chassis throbbing so violently that Bald could feel it echoing inside his skull. The Sentra's 200-horsepower engine was giving it absolutely everything. But Bald knew it wasn't going to be enough. The Charger was still closing the gap. Now it was less than ten metres behind.

Bald knew that the Charger had a beast of an engine capable of around 235 kilometres per hour. It did exactly what the name suggested. It charged. The Nissan Sentra, on the other hand, had a top speed of around 210. In a straight shoot-out, they were going to lose.

The Charger was almost parallel with the Nissan, and growling angrily. Bald adjusted his position so that he was side-on to Antonia. I need an eyeball on the occupants, he thought. Find out how many of these fuckers I'm up against.

With the two vehicles now parallel, the Charger's window tint was sufficiently light that Bald was able to peer into the murky interior. He ID'd two slate-grey shapes in the driver and front passenger seats. The back seats appeared to be empty.

Bald unzipped the gym bag and pulled out the Smith & Wesson 637, along with the box of ammo. Antonia glanced over at him and asked, 'What are you doing?'

He laid the box of ammo in his lap and pressed the release catch on the side of the weapon. Then he used his right thumb to push out the cylinder. He plucked a round from the box and loaded it into the first chamber. The .38 Special rimmed cartridge was the old faithful of the bullet family. Smith & Wesson had been churning out Specials since 1898 and had seen action in pretty much every war fought since then. Antonia may have made a dubious choice of handgun, but she'd redeemed herself by giving him a weapon that used such a solid, dependable and lethal round. There was a beautiful simplicity to these revolvers. Very few moving parts, no fancy safety mechanisms or cocking systems. You just slapped in the rounds, pulled the trigger and *boom*.

Bald finished loading the fifth and final chamber, then snapped the cylinder back into place. Antonia watched him with her eyes almost popping out of their sockets.

'This is your bright idea? Shooting cops?'

'You have a better one?'

'We'll have every federal cop hunting us—'

'I'll be across the border before these fucks catch me.'

'And what about me?'

The Charger was drawing ahead of the Nissan. Bald ran his hand over the 637's grip. The hammer was double-action only. You couldn't cock the hammer back and then discharge. You had to depress the trigger all the way. Which meant Bald would have to apply more pressure when firing. Which meant that the extra movement and recoil would make the round marginally less accurate.

In a firefight, every fucking inch mattered.

Antonia eased off the gas.

'What the fuck are you doing?' Bald yelled.

Then he saw it.

A Honda Civic Type R blocking the road ahead.

fifteen

The Honda Civic Type R hot hatch was thirty metres in front. Bald sized it up the way he sized up everything in this world, as a threat. No licence plate. Tinted windows. The spitting fucking image of the Dodge Charger.

'Classic kidnap manoeuvre,' Antonia said.

'That's what these guys are? Kidnappers?'

'Thousands happen every year in this country. If you're rich and have no personal security, then you're a target. This is definitely a kidnap attempt.'

What are you gonna do now, John? the voice at the back of Bald's head demanded. It was the voice of doubt. The voice he'd shut out with booze ever since he returned from Belgrade. The voice that said he'd lost the magic touch.

Bald and Antonia were now twenty metres from the Civic. The Charger had dropped back behind the Nissan and was killing its speed. Bald closed his eyes, then opened them again. The Civic was fifteen metres away. His hands were rattling the 637's cylinder. He drew in the world's deepest breath and said, 'Stop the car.'

'But—'

'Just do it.'

Antonia swerved to the side of the road. They stopped ten metres short of the Civic. Bald spotted a farm at their three o'clock twenty metres away. It was a humble thing. A couple of bare concrete buildings with corrugated-iron roofs, and a field of maze fenced off with wooden stakes and chicken wire. A few skinny goats were tethered to a post. A boy and a girl were playing in the dirt. The boy had a bouncing ball. The girl had some kind of a hoop. The Charger stopped ten metres behind the Nissan.

Engines died. Grilles hissed. Heat shimmered on the tarmac.

A pale-faced officer dressed in the universal narco-cop uniform of white pressed shirt, Ray-Ban Aviators and combat boots debussed from the Charger. The guy was so light-skinned he could have passed himself off as albino. Pale Face wasn't alone. Another man had emerged from the front passenger seat. He was stocky and tanned, with blue trousers, blue shirt, blue baseball cap. Pale Face and his mucker were both packing MP5Ks, the same weapons that Bald had seen the Policia Federal wielding at the airport.

Stocky approached the Nissan from the left, on Antonia's side. Pale Face made his way towards Bald. Antonia looked from the cops to Bald and back again.

'What are we going to do?' she said.

'Sit very fucking still.' Bald was working through the angles in his head. But it wasn't easy. The migraine was picking at the back of his skull.

'They're going to kill us,' Antonia said. Her eyes were welling up. Bald gripped her by the shoulders and dead-eyed her.

'They won't,' he said gently but firmly. He didn't do so out of sympathy. He didn't even do it because it was true.

He did it because the last thing he needed was some bird having a nervous fucking breakdown. 'Listen to me. Do exactly as I say. If you do that, we'll get out of this alive. Do you understand?'

Antonia swallowed her tears like they were foul medicine, and nodded.

'Good,' said Bald.

Pale Face and Stocky neared the Nissan. Nobody got out of the Civic up ahead. Logic suggested that there would be at least two guys in the Civic to supplement Pale Face and Stocky. So, at least four targets. Five bullets in the revolver. He had another thirty-five rounds in the box of .38 Specials, but reloading a revolver took at least seven or eight seconds and in the heat of a firefight he wouldn't have that kind of time.

Bald watched Pale Face in his side mirror. He was four metres away now. Bald stuffed the 637 into the top of his jeans and sat upright in his seat. Flexed his neck muscles.

Pale Face whipped off his Aviators. He had eyes the colour of bleach and lips so narrow they looked like a surgical incision. Pale Face stopped at Antonia's window and rapped his knuckles on the glass. Antonia did nothing. He knocked firmly again. Then he bent forward a little so that his face filled the view from Antonia's window.

Stocky had halted beside Bald's door. Folds of flesh encroached on his eyeballs, reducing them to black lines.

'Roll down the window,' Bald told Antonia, who was staring vacantly at some point in the middle distance. He kept his voice as steady and normal as possible, still trying to put the lid on her nerves. Half of winning any firefight was the ability to stay cool.

Antonia thumbed the window selector on the armrest. The glass whirred down and a whole lot of ugly leaned into her face. The right side of the cop's jaw was blistered and puffy.

'Get out!' Pale Face barked. Drops of his spittle sprinkled Antonia's arm.

Bald nodded at her. 'Do as the man says.'

Antonia slowly tugged on the door handle and began to climb out of the car. Pale Face clamped his hand around her wrist and hauled her out and onto the ground. She didn't have time to get to her feet. Pale Face shoved a foot onto the small of her back and forced her to lie face down while he tied her hands behind her back with plastic cord. She struggled, rocking her body from side to side and screaming for help. But the screams died at the mountains and Bald imagined the family at the farm sitting in their living room praying.

'Bitch! Stop fucking moving!' The way he said 'fucking', hard as gravel, told Bald that this guy was about as Mexican as Aberdeen Angus beef. He tried to place the guy's accent. American. Somewhere in the Deep South.

Pale Face thrust Antonia's face into the dirt with his foot, making her chew on the soil. Then he rolled her over onto her back, and couldn't resist groping her tits as he did so. Sick cunt, Bald thought.

Now Pale Face roughly manhandled Antonia to her feet and shoved her towards the Charger. She was choking, her face powdered with hot dirt. Bald was interrupted by a *tap-tap* at his window. He clocked the MP5K muzzle eyefucking him six inches from his face.

'You. Open. Too,' Stocky's twisted English leaked through the laminated glass.

Bald stayed put.

'Open the fucking door.'

Bald took three long breaths, filling his red blood cells with as much oxygen as possible so as to pump up the muscles in his shoulders and chest. Adrenaline was racing through his body. He lowered the window.

'Out the car, *gringo!*' Stocky shouted.

A third guy emerged from the driver's side of the Civic. He looked Native American. Five-five but almost as wide. Slicked-back hair the colour of Coca-Cola. He was also carrying an MP5K. Behind him Antonia had tripped on a rock a few steps from the Charger. Pale Face was helping her to her feet and copping another feel of her tits into the bargain.

Stocky to my three o'clock, Bald thought. Pale Face ten metres to my six. Third guy twelve metres to my twelve.

Five shots. *Make them count.*

He thrust his right arm out of the window and grabbed Stocky by the open neck of his sweat-stained shirt and tugged him towards him. At the same time he was digging the 637 out of his jeans with his left hand and bringing the barrel level with Stocky's rubber-tyre neck. Before the cop could react he had depressed the trigger fully, ten ounces of pressure cocking the hammer and springing it back into place and ejecting the bullet out of its brass jacket. The round travelled out of the barrel, perforating the flap of skin directly beneath the guy's chin. His pumpkin-shaped head slumped lifelessly over to the frame of the rolled-down window. Blood fountained out of his skull and glooped over the Nissan's interior.

Bald booted the door open, sending Stocky's corpse tumbling backwards. He dived out of the car and crouched behind the door, open at a right angle to the chassis. The door offered poor protection from bullets, and the MP5Ks were loaded with 9mm full-metal-jacket rounds, that could penetrate anything, making the metal plating useless. But shit cover was better than fuck-all.

Pale Face was dragging Antonia behind the boot of the Charger, but Bald couldn't get across to her. Not with the other targets to deal with first.

The driver of the Civic was holding his MP5K in a two-handed grip, his right hand clasping the trigger mechanism and his left acting as a fire-support platform on the underside of the barrel. Raising the weapon, he targeted Bald. The laser sight mounted on the submachine gun glared at the Nissan. Bald could see the red mil-dot on the windscreen.

Three stark *ca-racks* punctured the air. The Nissan's windscreen starred twice. The third round ricocheted off the hood.

Bald edged out from the right-side of the door and targeted the driver, who had neglected to seek cover. He lined the guy's head between the sights, keeping the front sight in focus. He relaxed his shoulder muscles. Shut out the rest of the world.

The revolver barked. A flame ignited at the end of the barrel. The driver's body spasmed. The first bullet smacked into his knee. Just twelve metres away, but Bald's aim hadn't been true. He didn't panic, simply took aim again and discharged, and this time he hit the fucking jackpot. The .38 Special tore a two-centimetre hole in the middle of his chest. The driver dropped his MP5K. Then he dropped too.

Two rounds left.

Bald scrambled to his feet and made for the Civic. Another glance at his six. Pale Face was hauling Antonia towards the maize field. The bass thump of a car door shutting drew Bald's attention back to the Civic. The fourth guy had slipped out of the passenger seat and was frantically unholstering his secondary firearm. A Glock 17 semi-automatic. Good weapon. Bald raised the 637 level with his shoulder. By the time the guy had his Glock out, Bald was putting down his fourth .38 Special. The bullet nearly split the guy's fucking torso in two. Red shit sprayed over the soil. His body slumped against the Civic hood as he tried to shovel his bowels back into his lacerated stomach. A minute or two, Bald thought, and that cunt would be heading over to the dark side with his mates.

Then a scream slit the air like a razor.

'Help!'

sixteen

Pale Face was scrabbling across a field of drooping maize, towards the farmhouse, one arm tight around Antonia's waist, his free hand pressing the MP5K muzzle against her temple. Bald followed, onto ground as arid and dry as ancient ruins. Each maize stalk stood well over two metres tall, and this height, combined with the fact that the dry leaves were peeling away like old skin, shrank visibility to a few measly metres. Bald was forced to rely on his hearing to get a position on Pale Face. Antonia was silent now but the rustling of leaves and the scuffing of shoes on rock-hard soil told him that Pale Face was somewhere at his ten o'clock. Bald set off in that direction, 637 in his grip and murder on his mind.

Sunlight broke through the leaves in hot packets. Bald felt nauseous from the heat and the exertion. Through a gap between the stalks he spotted some maize plants that were swaying back and forth. The air was otherwise dead still. Bald rushed towards the rustling stalks, a stinging pain in his quads and a stitch spearing his right side. He brushed aside the stalks with his elbows, snapping them at the stems. He blinked the leaves out of his eyes. Kernels crunched underfoot. He was closing in on Pale Face. The stitch climbed up his torso. He shut it out, like he'd been trained. He was coming to the end of the field. Beyond it he could spy a small field of bare soil leading up to the farm buildings.

Then the migraine exploded in his skull.

The pain. It was fucking intense. Bullet-ant pain, he called it. Once, in the jungle in Belize, a colony of *Paraponera* bullet ants had bitten his ankle. A single bite from one of those fuckers induced twenty-four hours of excruciating pain. But that was nothing compared with the burning, throbbing sensation Bald felt now. He sank to his knees, the 637 clattering a few inches in front of him. He couldn't move. The sun painted his neck and the back of his head, boiling the blood inside. The buzzing noise in his skull returned.

Then the migraine cut him some slack. He knew it would come back again. It always did. But he had a small window left in which to act. He realised he was curled up in a foetal position on the ground and every bone in his body was telling him to remain where he was and ride out the pain. But the operator part of him preached a different gospel. It was the voice that had urged him on during the roughest days of Selection and combat. Get the fuck up and stop feeling sorry for yourself, it kept telling him.

Bald put one palm flat on the ground and extended his elbow, as if prepping himself for a one-handed push-up. Then he planted his other palm the same way and pushed. And pushed some more, until he was lifting himself up off the ground. He climbed to his knees, scooped up the 637 and staggered towards where he'd seen the kernels swaying.

He emerged onto the open field and saw Pale Face twenty metres away, dragging Antonia towards what was clearly the inhabited one of the two miserable buildings. They were three metres from the rear porch, which was in shadow. Pale Face was good. He stayed behind Antonia, using her as a shield, and didn't present Bald with a clear shot. Bald started to give chase when the whooping of police sirens carried through the air. He jerked his head back to the road. He could make out four different sirens. That meant at least eight more cops. Could be as many as sixteen.

Pale Face backed into the farmhouse, dragging Antonia inside. Another woman screamed. A man shouted.

The sirens were getting louder, ripping through the air. Bald couldn't see them beyond the maize, but the cars had to be close now. He was forty metres from the road. If he pursued Pale Face into the farmhouse the guy's mates would have him pinned down in the time it takes to make a brew. Or he could just bug out of this shithole, fuck off in the Civic and get on with the mission.

As much as he'd got to like Antonia, she didn't come with a £5-million reward. And anyway, he had no chance of nailing that arse, no matter how badly he wanted to. She was too posh for her own good.

Bald lowered the Smith & Wesson. He turned his back on the screams and raced towards the Civic. What they would do to Antonia was unthinkable. So Bald decided not to think about it. He didn't stop.

He came to the roadside. Pools of blood stained the dust. Burned lead and brass particles tickled his nostrils. He knelt down beside the bastard he'd slotted. Still fucking breathing, blood sloshing about in his lungs like he was sucking with a straw at the bottom of a milkshake.

'*Mátame,*' the guy said through the crack in his lips. 'Kill me.'

Bald fished the car keys out of the prick's pockets and left him weeping into the dirt. Then he sprinted to the Nissan and fetched the gym bag. The sirens had shape as well as voice now. Bald ID'd the cars on the horizon. Their lights were cracking and popping. Less than a hundred metres distant. Bald marched back to the Civic, dumped the gym bag in the passenger seat and gunned the motor. The Civic could hit 100 kilometres per hour in under seven seconds. And that was all it took for the bodies to shrink to cockroaches and the sirens to fade into the sky. Bald cranked the Civic all the way to 160. Five kilometres down the road he was entering San Hernando when the burner shook angrily into life.

Cave was calling.

seventeen

1512 hours.

San Hernando was in full-on siesta mode. Bald passed ramshackle villas painted pink and turquoise and red. Stacks of old tyres lay in overgrown front yards. The gardens were tangled knots of weeds. Wild dogs roamed the streets, licking at sweet wrappers and steaming puddles of raw sewage.

Bald let the phone ring a few times before tapping the answer key. He liked the idea of that cunt Cave sitting behind his polished oak desk, unable to get hold of him.

'John.'

'Danny, old boy,' Bald replied.

'Don't take the piss, you Scottish bastard. I've just received a distress signal from Antonia. What the bloody hell's going on down there?'

'She walked into a trap. There was nothing I could do.'

The line broke up for a second, amid furious crackling. 'She was one of the best handlers we had. Jesus fucking Christ,' said Cave.

'I tried to save her,' Bald said, 'but—'

'Where are you now?' Cave cut in.

'In San Hernando. Where the fuck do I meet this Nelson guy?'

'Head to San Bernardo church. He'll be waiting for you there.'

Nicolas Guerra fed into Xicotencatl and then Emiliano Zapata. Street names aside, Bald couldn't tell the fucking difference. Each slab of road told the same pitiful story of breeze-block homes with black-box windows, rusting chain-link fences warped by the relentless sun. Long-haired greaseback weasels scurried among the garbage. Every street carried a canal of litter. The stench was vicious. Christ, thought Bald. Ten minutes in this fucking hellhole and he could understand why everyone was so desperate to try their luck in America. Washing dishes for some rich arsehole in California had to be better than this.

He looked at his watch. 1530 hours. Fifty-one hours to go to kill the sleeper.

'There's something else that's come up,' Cave continued.

Bald looked down at his jeans, spattered with blood. Drops of it were on his arms too. He could feel it on his neck, dried like scabs. He felt a powerful need to wash it off.

Cave hung up.

'I'm all ears,' said Bald.

'The Agency want in on this.'

Bald said, 'I thought they wanted their hands clean.'

'They do. You're still the one who has to take Laxman down. But they want a pair of eyes on the ground while you're there. To make sure nothing goes wrong.' Cave paused, then quickly went on, 'Now before you get all premenstrual on me, listen. Her name is Rachel Kravets. She's one of the best the Agency has to offer.'

'Great,' Bald deadpanned.

Cave ignored the comment and went on. 'She used to be Miss Florida. Actually entered for the Miss World competition last year. She'll rendezvous with you in Clearwater. She has some extra intel on Laxman that you may find useful. Do me a favour and check your email when you get the chance.'

Bald listened to the vanilla drone of the dial tone. Fucking great, he thought.

A strange thing had happened to Bald since he'd come back from the dead in the backwaters of Central Europe. It wasn't merely the migraines. It was something more troubling. At certain moments he had started to see things that weren't there. He hesitated to call them hallucinations, because that's what crazy people had. And whatever fucked-up shit was going on in his head, Bald was sure he wasn't crazy. They were more like echoes. Echoes of the violence he had witnessed. The first time it happened, six months ago, he'd been sitting in a bar in Pimlico enjoying a beer with a Russian stunner he'd pulled, when out of nowhere he experienced a strange buzzing noise in his ears. He looked up and saw that half her head was blown off. Bits of brain matter were bobbing on the surface of her Long Island iced tea. Another time he was in the back of a black cab ferrying him across town when the driver turned around and asked where Bald wanted to be dropped off. His lower jaw was hanging off, attached by only a few thin cords of muscle, his upper teeth leaching blood.

The echoes would last for a few seconds or a few minutes. Then they were gone.

He had never mentioned it to anyone. Didn't feel that he could. He was a Blade, and Blades didn't talk about their problems. They talked about the relative merits of the

.45 ACP round and they laughed about the time Warrant
Officer Paul Mundy terrified a stripper by whipping out
his horse-length cock and telling her to finish the job.

Bald spied a crumbling Spanish Colonial-style church.
Barren fields to the north, mountains of rubble and metal.
To the south a bunch of excavated homes that looked to
have long been abandoned to the weeds. San Bernardo
church, he figured.

Slinging the gym bag over his shoulder, Bald approached
the doors of the church. They were constructed from alder
and stood four metres tall. Bald tugged at the black iron
lever. The door was heavy and Bald had to pull hard to
open the fucker.

The church looked derelict on the outside, but the interior, with its tall white columns breaking up the star of
aisles, seemed well looked after. The only people present
were an ancient man and woman sitting side by side on
the rearmost left pew. They whispered prayers to the gold-
leafed Virgin Mary adorning the pulpit.

Bald wandered up the nave, veered right where the
aisles crossed, and entered the transept. He found
himself in a six-metre-square enclosure facing a richly
decorated statue of Jesus Christ. A man was praying
on his knees in front of the statue. The man stood up.
He was shaven-headed and not exactly fat, just big all
over: big head, big shoulders, big hands. He wore black
vestments and from his neck half a dozen gold neck-
laces dangled, beneath which a white clerical collar was
visible.

'I'm Nelson,' he said, turning to greet Bald and speaking in the lowest of whispers. 'You must be the one called
John. I have been expecting you.'

The priest was six inches taller than every other Mexican Bald had seen, and about six inches wider too. His forehead was lacquered in sweat and he looked like Marlon Brando after he piled on the pounds. He thrust a nicotine-stained hand at Bald and said in a voice that was so thick it could tarmac roads, 'Do you believe in the light and word of Jesus?'

'I believe in the light and word of a Colt Commando,' said Bald. 'After that, everything's up for grabs.'

'Perhaps I can show you the Truth.'

'The route across the border is good enough for me.'

Nelson peered at Bald's face the way posh wankers study a piece of art in a gallery. He looked concerned. 'Yours is a troubled soul, my son.'

'I'm not your fucking son.'

'I see violence in you. And trauma. You seek peace. Let me help you.'

'Is that what you say to all the boys?'

Nelson smiled at Bald, showing that the jibe didn't bother him. He wiped sweat off his gleaming dome with his chubby fingers.

'We must leave now,' he said.

He darted out of the transept and back down the aisle leading to the entrance of the church, beckoning to Bald to follow. Despite his girth the man was fleet-footed. 'The transport is at the market three blocks north of here. Everyone else is waiting,' he said.

'Everyone else?'

Nelson gave a sinister chuckle. Bald suddenly worried that Antonia had hired the wrong fucking man. This guy was like a snake-oil salesman.

'There are other *migrantes* waiting to cross,' Nelson said, looking at Bald across his shoulder, his gold-ringed hands making gestures the Scot couldn't fathom. 'You're not the only one trying your luck in America tonight, my son.'

Outside, they hurried round the church and entered the graveyard at the rear. Suddenly Nelson slowed his steps until his fat feet were making a heavy pitter-patter on the dry earth. They were now picking their way through ornate tombs and gravestones.

'A woman was supposed to be accompanying you here,' Nelson said without turning round. 'Where is she?'

'Don't know,' Bald lied.

'I was expecting—'

'If you're expecting a fuck, forget it. She doesn't put out.'

The priest had stopped in his tracks. Bald could hear the man's breath, gravelly and slow.

Nelson swung round and Bald found himself staring at the business end of an ageing M1911 single-action semi-automatic. The priest's eyes boiled as he aimed the handgun at Bald's forehead and rasped, 'Now, you tell me where my daughter is.'

eighteen

The Ruby Ridge indoor gun range announced itself with a ranch-style billboard in the shape of a cowboy hat, off the I-10 near Sunny Slope on the east side of town. 'GUNS & OUTDOOR. KIDS WELCOME,' the billboard promised. Hauser parked his GMC Yukon Denali in the gravel parking lot and retrieved an orange Pelican box from the passenger seat. It was forty degrees in the open and twenty-two in the air-conned bliss of the Ruby Ridge Armory and Survival Store. The store manager, a guy with a rustbelt beard and a beer gut with its own gravitational pull, greeted Hauser as he walked up to the counter. There was an impressive array of Glocks and Sig Sauers on display in the counter and a stuffed moose head framed on the wall behind the manager. The guy was forty or thereabouts. All that fat, it was hard to tell.

'I'll take a booth,' said Hauser.

'Sign here,' the manager said, gesturing to a pad of blank forms next to a stack of paperbacks entitled *The Essential Texas State Gun Law Handbook*. Hauser wrote down a false name, address and social security number.

'And here.'

Hauser ticked a box declaring that he was not mentally ill. With the State of Texas satisfied that he wasn't going to randomly kill anybody, Hauser was free to spend a half-hour on the range.

'See anything you like?' The manager waved a hand at the Sigs and Glocks. 'Got a special on the Rugers at the moment, if you're looking.'

'I'm not.'

Hauser patted his Pelican box.

'Brought my own piece.'

'Change your mind, let me know,' said the manager, his voice the colour of mild disappointment. He handed Hauser a pair of protective glasses and earmuffs. Hauser strapped on the glasses but didn't bother with the muffs. He lugged the Pelican box down an egress corridor to an airlocked door at the end. Limped into the gun range.

The air stank of lead. The newer ranges had sophisticated ventilation systems that blew smoke and lead particles down the range to the sloped bank. Not here. Hauser could feel a greasy film of lead powder forming on his face and neck. He chose the second booth from the end. On his right a forty-something woman with a shock of peroxide-blonde hair was popping rounds out of a ridiculously big revolver. Hauser couldn't make out the brand.

Three rednecks were having themselves a whale of a time at the booth to his left. They were all wearing a uniform straight out of the Ranger Joe's catalogue. The youngest was decked out in an ACU pattern T-shirt and desert-brown fatigues. With his flat-top crewcut and bowling-ball biceps he looked like a lifesize Marine Corps action figure. The second guy was thin as a strip of beef jerky, with a face that looked like it had been marinated in

Jim Beam. His ponytail poked out like a skunk's tail from underneath his Texas Rangers baseball cap.

The two dumbfucks looked on approvingly as the third guy unloaded a clip from a Ruger SR40 semi-automatic. Emptying the last round at the paper target hoisted fifteen metres ahead of him, the guy lowered the firearm as Rangers hit the red button on the wall mount and the target whirred back towards the booth.

Marine Corps plucked the target off the clips. 'Hell of a punch that point-forty packs. I mean, look at this shit, Rudy.' Marine Corps was poking his pinkie through one of the bullet holes ripped through the target. Wiggled it about like a little dick.

Rudy, the shooter, laid the Ruger flat on the booth table and examined the hits for himself. He was wearing digi-cam combats and a pair of weathered combat boots. A black T-shirt hung down over his moobs with the words 'OPERATION IRAQI FREEDOM VETERAN' humped over his neat little beer belly. Hauser figured the closest this guy had got to Iraq was looking it up on fucking Google Earth.

Rudy rubbed his grizzly-bear jaw and nodded at the target.

'Like I told you, dummy. You put Hector and his fajita-eating buddies down with one of these babies, and he ain't for getting up. And you know what you call a dead beaner?'

'One step in the right direction.'

'One step in the right direction,' Rudy concurred.

Marine Corps, Rudy and Rangers snickered like three schoolkids who'd just discovered a hole in the wall of the girls' changing room.

'Not bad,' Hauser said.

Rudy pulled the plug on his laughter. Rangers and Marine Corps fell into line and did their best to look severely pissed. Rudy turned around. Slowly, as if giving his rage time to properly boil up inside of him. Hauser whistled 'When Johnny Comes Marching Home' as he busied himself with springing open the Pelican box.

Rudy said, 'What did you say, friend?'

'I meant what I said. You're not a bad shot. But you're not a good one either.'

Rudy pointed a finger at a spot between Hauser's eyes and said, 'And who the fuck are you?'

'Someone who shoots better than you.'

Rudy blazed up like petrol. He shaped clumsily to swing a punch at Hauser but Marine Corps and Rangers wisely grabbed hold of him and held him back. Rudy looked like he was shitting out a cannonball. Hauser removed the components of his gun from its box and laid them on his booth table. The weapon's smooth polymer surface had four light-grey buttons dotted above the trigger mechanism and an anti-friction layer tapering at both ends of the grip. In the middle of the grip was a seal encircling a regal 'N' and 'F'. Running down the side of the barrel were the engraved words 'FN HERSTAL BELGIUM'.

'An FN Five-Seven,' said Rudy, folding his arms across his chest. 'Big fucking deal. Those things have been on the market for years.'

'The civilian version, sure,' said Hauser. 'But not this model.'

Now Hauser removed a box of ammo from the Pelican box and placed it on the table in clear view of the rednecks. He began thumbing rounds into the clip. Each cartridge was roughly the height of two quarters and bottlenecked at the tip like a spear. Rudy swapped glances with Marine Corps and Rangers.

'This is a 5.7x28mm FN round. Notice the lack of the hollow point on top of the round. As I'm sure you know, you can't buy these rounds commercially.'

Rudy said, 'I hear them things can punch a hole through forty bulletproof vests.'

Hauser said, 'You heard right.'

He loaded the last cartridge into the clip, then slid the clip into the pistol grip. Now he fastened a red-mil-dot laser sight to the underside of the barrel and punched the numbers '5' and '0' into the target range-setter. The fresh bullseye target whirred away and came to a halt a few metres short of the rear bank.

Rudy was about to say something but Hauser discharged the first round from the chamber. Flames spewed out of the muzzle. The recoil was barely notice-able. With some guns the recoil was so bad it was like wrestling the hind legs of a dog. But not the Five-Seven. Hauser kept his grip steady and his support firm and casually emptied all twenty rounds of 5.7x28mm ammo. When he was done he palmed the red button on the controls. The target zipped back to the booth. Hauser left it clipped to the rail while he removed the laser sight and ejected the spent clip. He could feel the rednecks closing ranks around him.

'Holy shit,' said Rangers. 'That's some fucking shooting.'

Twenty holes were crowded around the bullseye in the centre of the target. Every single bullet had struck within a quarter of an inch of the bullseye.

Rudy nodded with his bottom lip. Grudging acknowl-edgement of Hauser's shooting skills. He looked at him in a different light. 'You know, a man who can shoot shouldn't let his talent go to waste. He ought to put it to good use.'

Hauser continued packing his Five-Seven into the Pelican box.

'Lemme ask you a question,' said Rudy.

'Ask,' said Hauser.

'Do you love America?'

Hauser's eyes pinballed from Rudy to Marine Corps to Rangers. All three were staring at him. 'That depends,' he said.

'On what?'

'Which part you're asking me about.'

'How about I'm asking you about the whole damn thing?'

'I like free speech and low taxes. I like my fuel cheap,' Hauser said. 'But I don't much care for big government. Or Arab-loving, pro-lifer faggots. And I sure as hell don't like having a president who's not even American.'

'Fuckin' A.' This from Marine Corps.

Hauser gently clipped the Pelican box shut while Rudy broke out into a full-on smile that fractured his skin, like a dried-out riverbed. He gave Hauser an ironclad handshake. 'Name's Rudy.'

'Greg Tilson,' said Hauser.

'Pleasure, Greg.' Rudy patted Hauser on the back like they were friends from way back in the day. 'I knew from the moment I saw you. I thought, now there's a guy who knows what's really going on in this country of ours.'

Hauser looked down the booths, waited for a lull in the gunfire and dropped his voice. 'I hear you boys like to go out of a night. Stopping those wetto motherfuckers from crossing the border.'

Rudy grinned and revealed a set of teeth that were mostly coffee-brown and bent except for one silver tooth on the upper ridge. 'Well, someone's got to stop those sneaky sons of bitches coming over here—'

'Taking our jobs—' said Hauser.

'And our women—' said Rangers.

'Freeloading off honest taxpayers,' said Marine Corps.

'Know what?' said Rudy, slinging a bare arm around Hauser's shoulders. It was coated in sweat and Hauser could feel it sticky and cold against his neck. 'We're heading down to the border tonight. Word is, it's gonna be a big crossing tonight. I'm talking beaners coming out of your frigging asshole. Why don't you come along? Have some real-life target practice for a change.'

Hauser smiled.

'I'd love to,' he said.

nineteen

Texas-Mexico border. 2332 hours.

Too easy, thought Bald as they reached the northern bank of the Rio Grande and he hoisted himself up onto American soil. The swarthy illegals broke the waves and cheered and cried at making it over to the other side. Bald reckoned their celebrations were premature. His training told him it was unwise to relax.

Texas looked despondent. A full moon over a stubbled desert, receding dry grass and scrawny mesquite shrubs impervious to the heat. Bald took his first steps in Uncle Sam territory and sucked in the night air. It was freezing. The kind of cold that had no taste, no texture, no scent, because wherever the hell it came from was too cold for life.

For a moment Bald watched the illegals trot east along Ranch Road 1472, a stretch of blacktop linking one hotpotch of distant town lights to the next. Then he slung the gym bag over his shoulder, gave his back to them and started pacing north towards the desert plain. He made the first ten metres in eight strides and clicked the clicker he was visualizing in his head. His clothes were drenched through. Icy water needled his bones. Bald was midway to twenty metres, his second mental click, when a voice called out to him from the pack.

'Let me come with you, *ese*.'

Bald stopped the clicker in his head on six strides, and turned around. The voice belonged to Felix, a grubby-faced sixteen-year-old with even grubbier hands and a face like a burnt matchstick. During the six-hour drive from San Hernando to the border he'd been the only one to strike up a conversation with Bald.

'Got shit to do, lad. Watch yourself.'

'But I've got nowhere to go,' the kid said.

Bald didn't reply. He was already setting off again. Seven, eight . . . ten metres. Felix started along the trail. The kid had a stride like he was doing the run-up to a triple jump and he kept up with Bald effortlessly, much to the ex-Regiment man's annoyance.

'What about the others?'

'Fuck them,' said Bald.

He didn't add that the other eleven illegals were doing him a massive favour by handrailing the Ranch Road. By sticking so close to the border they would attract the attention of any nearby patrols. Leaving Bald free to carry on undetected along his planned route. The nearest town was ten miles east but Bald decided he'd hike it north to Eagle City, twice as far away. Figured the locals in Eagle would be less attuned to the movements of illegals.

'You're just gonna leave them like that?'

'They wouldn't understand a word I fucking said anyway.'

'They all speak English. They heard you killed Padre Nelson in San Hernando.'

San Hernando, Mexico. Twelve hours ago a guy in a white dog collar by the name of Nelson had pointed a gun at the back of his head and asked in his diesel voice where his daughter was. The short answer was, Bald didn't fucking know. But Bald didn't bother telling the guy this. He had simply jerked his head to the left and reverse-jabbed his elbow into his solar plexus. Put the gun to the fat priest's face and ignored his desperate pleas not to kill him. Sent that son of a bitch on the fast track route to join his Jesus buddies up above.

Now he was trampling through a patch of thick buffalo grass and trying to get Felix off his fucking case.

'It was me or him. His fucking mistake,' Bald said. Then he spun around and grabbed Felix by his spindly neck. 'And you'll end up the same way if you don't fuck off right now.'

'Please, *ese*. I got no one.'

'I don't give a shit. You're on your fucking own.'

He left Felix trailing in his wake and had made another two clicks north when an ocean of white light flooded the desert floor. The grass and the rocks disintegrated into a blinding lather. Bald stopped dead in his tracks and looked across the bow of his right shoulder at his three o'clock.

Two mounted spotlights were careering down the road and heading straight towards the crowd of illegals eighty metres away. The spotlights were accompanied by the growl of two pickup trucks and a much stranger noise. A *yee-haw* that sounded like a cross between a battle cry and a wolf's howl.

Rednecks. He remembered what Antonia had told him in Mexico. 'If you're caught crossing that line, the rednecks will kill you.'

Bald clocked a muzzle flash from the passenger window of the truck on the left. The whiplash of a rifle shot came a split second later. Then an old man dropped simply in the middle of the road, like a sigh. The rest of the illegals screamed and scattered.

'Get the fuck down!' Bald said to Felix, hunkering the kid down beside him in a shallow scrape. Gunshots *ker-rumped* through the night around them. Sounds generally carry faster and clearer at night and Bald could make out two different weapons being discharged. One was a rifle. The other was a pistol. He could hear the *clink-clink* of spent brass bouncing on the ground. The pickup on the left, a blazing-red Toyota Hilux, encircled a group of five illegals. Dust plumes spiralled behind it like a mini-sandstorm as the shooter leaned out of the passenger window and picked off his targets one by one. Three of the illegals quickly went over to the dark side. The remaining two, a chubby bloke in his forties and maybe his old man, began fleeing north.

In the direction of Bald and Felix.

The pickup on the right was a black Dodge Ram with a quad-cab body, raised suspension and a spoiler. Kind of thing you might spot at a rodeo. The driver was clambering out of the Ram. He was dressed like a combat veteran in camo trousers, black T-shirt and Texas Rangers baseball cap.

His eyes locked on a heavily pregnant woman faltering off the road onto dusty ground, beating a retreat back to the Rio Grande. He casually took aim with his pistol. His upper body jerked. The muzzle starred. Blood erupted out of the woman's belly, like champagne out of a heavily shaken bottle.

The driver returned to the Ram, cranked up its turbo-petrol engine and accelerated towards the chubby guy and the old man, the twenty-two-inch Pirelli tyres eructing dust clouds over the dead illegals. Directly in the vehicle's path were the two men, scrabbling over the flat, barren land as fast as their stubby legs could carry them. But the V10 Ram was one of the world's fastest pickups, with a top speed of 154 mph, and the twenty-metre gap between it and the men was rapidly shortening to nothing.

'Not this fucking way,' Bald hissed to himself as the two illegals frantically raced towards his position. The gym bag was lying next to Bald, between him and Felix. Peering above the scrape, he noticed a figure standing on the back of the Ram. He was clutching an FN Five-Seven pistol with a red-mil-dot attachment. The mil-dot traced lines over the chubby guy. Two quickfire shots and he was pawing at the penny hole in his Adam's apple. The old man made it a few steps further before the figure double-tapped him in the back of the head. He dropped fifteen metres shy of the scrape. Thirty-five metres behind it the Hilux was encircling the remaining four illegals. Picking them off one by one.

The Ram stopped.

Bald froze.

The spotlights lit up the area surrounding the scrape. Bald killed his breath. Felix was whimpering prayers in Spanish and suddenly Bald regretted losing the Smith & Wesson revolver he'd acquired in Mexico. Meaning he had no weapon.

The mil-dot abruptly vanished. Like an eye blinking shut.

The rednecks still haven't spotted us, Bald was thinking.

Then Felix's head exploded.

Blood and gristle slicked over Bald. Bits of mucus-like eyeball slopped down what remained of the kid's jaw. Bald shoved him away. The body rolled lifelessly onto its side. Bald picked himself off the ground, grabbed the gym bag by the strap and darted towards a patch of cactus twelve metres away at his eight o'clock.

He ducked to make himself as small a target as possible. With the peripheral vision of his right eye he caught another glimpse of the figure from the back of the Ram. The guy had debussed. He didn't look like a redneck. Too thin around the neck and shoulders. His hair was grey. He was dressed in a plain white shirt and grey trousers. And he seemed to be limping heavily on his right leg. He was packing a Knight's Armament Company Stoner SR-15 semi-automatic assault rifle. He tucked the Stoner into his right shoulder and aimed directly at Bald.

Three rounds slapped into the dirt a few centimetres from his feet. Bald was ten metres from the cactus. Now eight. Another three-round burst cut through the air, fizzled into the ground. Just wide of Bald. Getting closer. Now Bald darted to his left, moving away from the cactus. He was putting more distance between himself and the guy shooting at him.

The shooter took a time out. Bald glanced over his shoulder. The Ram was revving its engine, the guy with the Stoner struggling back onto the rear cargo bed, his right leg dangling uselessly as he hauled himself up. Bald looked forward again. He could feel the electric heat of the mounted spotlight tanning his back. The Ram was gaining on him.

No cover. No weapon. No fucking way out.

Then he spotted a rock a couple of metres in front of him. It was the size of a kettle bell, smooth and round. Bald ducked lower as he ran, his chin touching his chest.

He scooped up the rock in his right hand and in the same move spun around to face the Ram. He could see the shooter on the back of the Ram. Now he sprang up from his crouching stance and threw the rock overarm at the front of the pickup. It skimmed through the air and landed smack on the spotlight. The light dulled. The left headlight was busted and the other one cast only a weak beam of light across the desert floor.

Bald broke to his left, north, running into the dark. The shooter unleashed three rushed shots. Bald heard them thwack into the ground metres to his right. He ran along a winding route across the sand, careful to steer clear of the road. After a hundred metres he looked back across the undisturbed desert: the Ram was reduced to a pair of faintly glowing buttons.

He carried on a northward bearing towards Eagle City. He didn't feel bad about the illegals getting it. There were more important things to worry about. Like staying out of trouble. And finding himself a gun and a set of wheels so he could get the fuck across to Clearwater and link up with the CIA handler. He pulled the gym bag, containing the fake passports and $7200, over his right shoulder. In forty-eight hours' time, he would be £5 million richer, and the cash in the bag would seem nothing more than beer money.

No one could fucking stop him now.

twenty

Eagle City was hardly a town, let alone a city. It was a carcass of deadwood houses and a few humdrum stores stalling for time, trying to ignore the foreclosure signs that hung from every third property on Main Street. There were no street lights. A stifling backdraught blew across the street. Bald's clothes were still drenched through. Not with river water but with sweat.

It was the dead zone, the time when every decent tax-paying civvie was sound asleep, leaving Bald free to roam Main Street like he owned the fucking place. He guessed less than a thousand people lived in Eagle. He counted two gun shops, both heavily padlocked, three repair garages, two mom-and-pop diners, a pharmacy and a thrift store. No library and no vegan shop. If the place had included a couple of strip clubs, Bald might even have been tempted to relocate.

His burner buzzed in his jeans pocket. He flipped it out and hit the answer key without looking at the display. There was, after all, only one prick who had this number.

'There's a message waiting for you,' said Cave. 'Check your email when you get a chance. Some interesting facts about our birthday boy.'

'Great,' Bald said dryly as he paced up Main Street.

'Have a bit of enthusiasm, John Boy. Rachel can't wait to meet you.' Cave sounded fucking smug on the phone. That was the act, Bald knew. When agents talked in code in the movies they were always so fucking serious and fake, but in the real world you had to sound authentic. You had to sound excited about a birthday party that only existed in your head.

'I think you're going to like her,' said Cave.

'She can't be as big a cunt as you,' said Bald.

Cave laughed weakly and said, 'I hear she's got a thing for Scottish men.'

Images of a Miss Florida with a fetish for kilts played out in his head.

'She'll be waiting for you.'

Bald killed the call. He arrived at the northern end of Main Street. To his right was an army surplus store and to the left the Alamo Bar N Grill, a simple red-brick structure built like a military compound, with a flat roof and a rusting metal door with a shutter at eye level. A couple of neon Budweiser and Coors signs lit up the darkened windows. Three cars stood in the parking lot. A Cadillac with a warped hood like a crushed Coca-Cola can, a prehistoric Lincoln and a white Buick '93 Roadmaster.

Bald trudged past the Alamo and did another circuit of Main Street. Confident that there was nobody about to ID him to the cops, he trudged back to the Alamo and crept up to the Buick. The rear bumper was stickered with Dixie flags, GOP elephants and a photo with the slogan 'SARAH PALIN FOR PRESIDENT'. Bald didn't do politics but now he thought about it he'd definitely smash Palin.

He drew level with the driver's side door. Then he pushed himself up on the balls of his feet until he could see through the window into the cab. There was a bunch of junk inside. Pack of Lucky Strikes on the dash, Gatorade bottles littering the footwell and a silver ocean of quarters and dimes in the storage space by the gearbox. Toll booth money. There was something else on the dash. Bald pressed his nose against the glass and scoped out the stainless-steel semi-automatic proudly on display. He recognized the weapon as a Colt Delta Elite. Next to it was a box of HSM bulk 10mm ammo. Cops favoured the shortened-down .40 S&W round, but the 10mm still did a lot of damage. Bald said a silent prayer to whichever genius had invented the Texas state gun law that stipulated that firearms must always be overt rather than concealed. Then he stood back, lifted his right leg and launched his boot through the window. No protective sheet over the glass. Just glass. One kick was enough. The window obliged; glass fountained onto the seat, shards piercing the worn fabric. Bald loved old cars. No alarms. No computer-chip locking systems. No voice ID. Just a boot and a knack for hot-wiring engines, and you were away.

He reached in and grabbed the gun. Then he heard the Alamo's heavy door swing open with a crash.

Laughter erupted from the bar. Hoarse and rustled. Bald squatted low behind the front wheel of the Buick, which was parked twenty metres from the bar. He heard the uneven scrape of shoes on gravel. The faint afterglow from the flashing beer signs revealed a couple of mottled shadows in the doorway. One of the guys was pretty lit. He did that drunk thing of walking like he was balancing on a high wire, every movement deliberate. He was dressed in holed jeans, a logger shirt and scuffed trainers.

The guy hiccupped. A bottle smashed on the ground.

'Jesus, Pete, you drunk son of a bitch.'

'I ain't drunk,' Pete slurred.

'Aw, hell,' his mate joked. 'How stupid of me. Course you ain't drunk. You way beyond that, fella.'

'Fuck you.'

Pete dumbly assessed the shattered glass around his feet. He blinked, then stooped low, as if trying to touch his toes. He was trying to pick up his broken bottle of beer. His face was illuminated by the red and yellow rays from the beer signs. Then he straightened up and staggered uneasily towards the Buick.

Bald flexed his fingers around the grip of the Colt. He gently slid back the barrel and inspected the extractor hole. Could see the brass nugget of a chambered round. The drunk was now five metres from the Buick. Bald hadn't reckoned on things getting messy this quick. This could fuck up his plans big time. But if the guy came one step closer he wouldn't leave him with any choice.

'Hey!' the other man shouted to his mate. 'Uh-uh, no way.'

'What?'

'You planning on driving back home tonight?'

'Don't you fucking tell me what to do,' Pete drawled.

'Come on, you big dumb asshole. I'll shout you a ride.'

Pete mumbled something that Bald didn't quite catch. Then he about-turned and wandered off down Main Street with his buddy. Bald relaxed his finger on the trigger. He opened the door of the Buick, swept glass off the seat, sat down, then reached under the steering wheel. There he located the wires he needed to strip to hot-wire the engine.

Tap-tap-tap.

Bald froze.

Someone was rapping their knuckles on the window. Bald stared dead ahead.

'Hey, Pete,' the guy slurred. 'You gonna give a buddy ride home?'

Bald continued eyeballing the road. He could make out the guy out of the corner of his left eye. He was grizzled, unshaven, pupils glazed.

'Fuck's sake, Pete. Open the goddamn door.'

The guy looked again.

He did a spit-take and beer dribbled down his shirt as he said, 'Hey. You ain't Pete.'

twenty-one

Bald took a detour off the I-90 between Devers to the west and Nome to the east. He was eighteen miles from Beaumont, just over thirty from the Louisiana border. Abandoned oil gushers towered over the salt domes like ancient edifices. The sky was grey. Bald arrowed the Buick down Farm to Market 365, a crappy single-lane road that bulldozed its way past blistered farmhouses and sunburnt Fresno trees. After a couple of minutes he pulled over beside a bleached field and slammed on the brakes. He left the engine running.

He stepped out onto the cindered asphalt and went round to the boot. Pete's friend had stopped thumping his fists a couple of hours ago. Now Bald cranked the boot open. Bleary daylight spooked the guy. He went to shield his face, but Bald was already grabbing his shirt and hauling him to his feet. His skin had paled during the seven-hour ride from Eagle. The cuts on his lips were wide enough to slide the side of a quarter through. His nose had been smashed into the approximation of a nose, like a five-year-old's sketch. Bald had dragged him into the Buick back at Eagle and beaten the living shit out of him, and the dead shit too. Now he shoved him roughly to the side of the road. The guy's eyes were on the grip of the Colt jutting out of the front of Bald's jeans.

'Please,' he said. 'Don't kill me.'

Bald pulled out the pistol and walked up so close to the guy that he could smell the sweat and booze leeching off his pallid skin. He reached into the man's pocket, pulled out his crocodile-leather wallet, removed his driver's licence and tossed the wallet into the field. 'Duane Kurlansky. Now I know your name and where you live. And if you tell anyone – and I fucking mean *anyone* – that you saw me, I'll kill you. Do you understand?'

'Y-yes,' the guy stammered. 'I won't say a word.'

His cries were interrupted by the sound of piss hissing down his leg.

'Now fuck off,' said Bald.

Bald watched the guy walk off down Farm to Market, urine streaking and misting on the asphalt. Then he fired up the Buick and raced back onto I-10, heading east. He passed Beaumont and the Louisiana border. He passed Lake Charles and Lafayette and Baton Rouge. At 1311 hours, having covered 620 miles on I-10 and I-12 since he'd left Eagle City, Bald could feel himself starting to flag, like someone had sewn hockey pucks under his eyelids. Ten hours on the road, and he still had another 560 miles to go before he would hit Clearwater.

He took a rest-stop at a nothing hole called Superior. Ditched the Buick down a side street on the outskirts of town and changed from his muddy T-shirt to a lumberjack shirt he'd found lying on the back seat. He retrieved a DVD disc from inside the gym bag. The disc had been an extra treat from Land. The sleeve plastic was cracked from the border crossing. Kind of a miracle something that delicate had survived the journey intact. Then he made his way into the town centre and paid $5 for a half-hour at the Xpresso Internet café and $3.75 for a large Americano. Between heavy swigs of his coffee Bald accessed the Hotmail.com web page and typed in the details Cave had given him. Username 'birthday-boy19@hotmail.com, password 'whisky1503'.

He flicked his eyes to the drafts folder. Two saved items were marked for his attention. Bald clicked on the first and the text sprang up in the main window.

The draft email contained personal information about Shylam Laxman. According to the Florida voters' registration database Laxman lived at 11 Gladeview in eastern Clearwater. He drove a black Infiniti G37 four-door, licence plate 504 XKW, and he was employed as Chief Research Officer at Lance-Elsing R&D Inc. He lived with his wife, Sameena, and two children, Gurvinder and Sunny. He earned $127,544 a year and had no convictions against his name.

There was no information from Cave about how they had identified Laxman as the sleeper, or what he stood to gain. That didn't come as a great shock to Bald. He was a soldier. Never once in the Regiment had a rupert stood up and said, 'This is why we need to kill X.' The Blades were just told where a guy would be, and why, and how many X-rays were lying in wait for them on the ground. The rest, as his old Major Pete Maston was fond of saying, was none of their fucking business.

Bald drained more of his milky Americano. The size of the cup was monstrous. No wonder everyone seemed so fucking fat. He clicked on the second draft email. This one had no text; its subject header was labelled 'RK'.

There was a .jpeg file embedded in the HTML text body. It was a photo of Rachel; the kind of thing you might find in a passport or a driver's licence. Bald sat upright. Rachel had smiling eyes and mischievously straight lips, like she was trying hard not to laugh at a crude joke. Red-apple cheeks, chlorine-blue eyes. Bald shook his head and reminded himself that as an employee of the Agency, Rachel Kravets was about as trustworthy as an email from a Nigerian farmer. Either way, she was hot and definitely beat having to deal with a shit-flinger like Cave.

There was a phone number below the picture. Bald saved it to the burner's memory. Then he deleted both drafts to indicate to Cave that he'd read their contents, logged out of the Hotmail account and waited until the manager was distracted. Bald removed the DVD disc and inserted it into the machine drive. Windows auto-ran the program on the drive. Then the screen went blue, then white, and Bald ejected the disc and placed it back inside the cracked sleeve. The program on the disc was designed by the Firm's tech crew, and it fried a computer to shit and turned the drive contents into garbage. A highly effective way of covering his tracks.

And he needed to cover them, and cover them well. He was on a non-attributable operation. Fuck this one up and he was entirely on his own.

Bald left the café.

He didn't head back to the Buick. Instead he walked north for six blocks, stopping at a hardware store to pick up a crosshead screwdriver. There seemed to be an abundance of hardware stores and shops selling booze or buying gold, and not much else. He pressed on north for a couple of minutes, looking for a Buick similar to the '93 Roadmaster. Having crossed state lines, he'd decided that he would be far less conspicuous if he swapped the Roadmaster's Texas licence plate for a Louisiana one. Another hundred metres and Bald reached the fag end of Superior. He found himself cutting through a warren of tired, Depression-era wooden houses with boarded-up windows and front yards full of scrap metal, where the people looked like they lived off the dollar menu at McDonald's. A fat old guy was dozing on a rickety chair on his porch. He looked like he'd been asleep since 1997. At the end of the street Bald clocked a white vehicle with the distinctive trishield badge and fender vents of a '96 Buick Regal coupé. Louisiana plates.

Bald checked the coast was clear, then knelt down beside the rear bumper and unscrewed the licence plate with the screwdriver. He removed the plate, tucked it down the front of the lumberjack shirt and diligently gathered the screws. Then he walked quickly back south to the Roadmaster, took off the Texas licence plate and replaced it with the Louisiana one. The two cars were made by the same manufacturer and from the same era, so the screw holes on the licence-plate frames were a perfect match.

Bald dumped the Texas plate in a trash-filled alley next to a boarded-up house. He was climbing back into the Buick and preparing for the long haul along I-10 when his burner vibrated.

It was Cave. 'I've got a problem,' he said.

'Try Viagra,' said Bald.

'The birthday party's been moved forward. It's going to happen tomorrow at 2000 hours your time.'

Bald slumped behind the Buick's wheel and felt his bowels splicing and tensing. Thirty metres ahead a bum was pushing a lopsided shopping trolley down the road. The trolley was piled high with sheets of crumpled aluminium.

'That's not enough time,' said Bald. 'I'll be going to the party half-cocked. It'll be a clusterfuck. I need time for planning and preparation and all that shit.'

Cave breathed heavily down the line. 'Tough shit, John Boy. That's just the way it is.'

Click.

Bald watched the trolley trundle past. Then he slammed a fist against the wheel. His plans had been thrown out of the fucking window. He'd planned on observing Laxman for a while, carefully making notes on his routines and assessing a good strike-point. Now he'd have to virtually kill him the moment he reached Clearwater. It would be messy, unplanned and risky.

His mission had suddenly become a whole lot more dangerous.

twenty-two

Bald rolled off the Courtney Campbell Causeway feeding into Clearwater and gunned down Gulf to Bay Boulevard, heading west. He'd covered the last five hundred metres clocking a cautious 55 mph, not wanting to veer above the miserly state speed limit and attract unwanted attention from Florida's finest. It was 2000 hours exactly when a road sign enthusiastically announced, 'WELCOME TO CLEARWATER, SPRING TRAINING HOME OF THE PHILLIES.' Twenty-four hours to find Laxman, check out his routine, kill him and fuck Rachel Kravets. Then Bald was distracted by a double-dozen of border-line-ten blondes milling about the Clearwater Mall. Peroxide blonde, tanned skin the colour of butterscotch sundaes and D-cup tits. Bald thought about Rachel again. His balls felt like they were about to burst.

He thought, too, about how his life would look this time tomorrow. Laxman would be dead. And he would be on his way out of the country to pick up his reward. Some people might take that five million and invest it in stocks, real estate, government bonds. Bald had other plans. He pictured himself cashing in on the Spanish property crash, snapping up a villa and a bar on the Costa del Sol for rock-bottom prices, the local whores busting lines of coke off his chest. Lena, his Russian part-time PA with the tits that demanded full-time devotion, would be his permanent mistress. He wasn't so sure about the bar. Bald and alcohol didn't exactly sound like good business partners. But his future was looking bright; brighter, anyhow, than Joe Gardner's.

Bald fished out his burner and called the number he'd saved from the draft email. There was a scratchy beat while one carrier tried to establish contact with another across a network of cell towers. Finally he got a long, sonorous ringing tone. Someone picked up on the fourth ring and said, 'You're in town?'

'Just arrived.' Bald tried to sound as much like Sean Connery as possible.

'There's a slight change of plan,' Rachel said. 'I'm caught up with some other stuff here at the moment. I can't meet you until later tonight.'

'So what am I supposed to do until then?'

'Keep an eye on birthday boy.'

But Rachel had hung up before Bald could get a word in. He flipped out the SIM card, destroyed it and threw it away. Then he stashed the phone in his pocket and figured he'd pay Laxman a visit at Lance-Elsing's offices. He drove another third of a mile down Gulf to Bay Boulevard before hanging a left onto Edenville Avenue. Then he took the first right onto Druid Road East and drove past a gang of bikers whose bikes were pelting out a pneumatic bass. A quick right guided him onto an unmarked road that coiled around the Everglades. Cable lines hung slackly from utility poles. There were no homes here, just a tangle of sawgrass marsh and slash pines. The road curved sharply to the right for two hundred metres until it finally broke free onto an isolated length of blacktop.

An elegant sign announced Gladeview.

Bald hit the brakes, stopping the Buick ten metres shy of the entrance to the estate. Either side of a wrought-iron gate, three metres tall and five wide, was a two-metre-high brick wall with spikes on top. On one of the gate's pillars there was a camera and a metal sign warning passers-by, 'DO NOT TAMPER WITH GATES. RISK OF DEATH.' Gladeview looked like a fortress.

Rolling gently past the gate at five per, Bald checked for cameras and guards. There were none. Through the bars he could see spruce lawns and people carriers in the driveways and whitewashed villas with terracotta roofs. He drew to a halt thirty metres beyond the gate. Sundown, and the heat was still merciless. Bald could feel beads of sweat gluing his back to the seat. Warm air wafted in through the broken driver's side window, carrying the excited rattle of crickets.

He couldn't risk patrolling the perimeter on foot. People who lived in gated communities naturally tended to be paranoid about strangers hanging around. If some-one spotted Bald climbing over the walls he'd have half the fucking Clearwater PD on his case in the time it took him to set foot on the manicured lawns. But then he got to thinking that if another car came out of the gates, he might be able to wing his way inside. 'I'm visiting a friend. He's not answering.' Then he could drive right up to Laxman's house. Knock on the front door. Double-tap the cunt on his doorstep. Effective.

Bald checked his Aquaracer. 2100 hours. Twenty-three hours to go. He watched the sun burn up on the horizon.

Drummed his fingers on the steering wheel and slapped himself on the face to stay alert. He hadn't slept for more than forty-eight hours, ever since he first touched down in Mexico City. His body was sending him warning signals. Telling him that unless he got some shuteye soon he'd be putting the mission at risk. And his payday.

Thirty-six minutes after Bald arrived at Gladeview a whirring noise disturbed the crickets. He flicked his eyes to the rear-view mirror. The gates were fanning open. Bald strained his neck to get a look at the car emerging from the estate. He noticed the badge on the grille. Suddenly his luck was taking a turn for the better. The car was an Infiniti. The licence plate matched the one Cave had given in the email.

Laxman was on the move.

The Infiniti slithered out of Gladeview. No sooner had the gates closed than Laxman was speeding off in the direction Bald had arrived. Bald quickly fired up the Buick and K-turned. Then he hit the gas and sped after the Infiniti. A breeze blasted through the window and he felt the tiredness lift from his shoulders.

He was closing in on the sleeper.

Laxman hung a left onto Prosper Avenue and passed a church the size of a shopping mall and a golf course with the texture of marzipan. The sun had slipped under the horizon. Five hundred metres down the road Laxman turned into Gateway Industrial Park.

Gateway was pissing distance from the Gladeview community. Bald figured that the employees were all required to live on the doorstep so their paymasters could keep a close eye on them. Whatever the reason, it didn't look like some top-secret research facility. The unguarded entrance widened into a deserted parking bay and a series of Lego-block lots. Bald decided against tailing Laxman into the industrial park. He figured there had to be a heavy security presence. Slotting Laxman on the doorstep of Lance-Elsing's offices was too fucking risky. Cameras, microphones, infra-red sensors. Instead he slowed the Buick to a fast walk and took the next right onto County. He drove around the perimeter of Gateway. Midway down County he found what he was looking for.

A blind spot.

Bald noticed that most of the buildings on the edge of the industrial park had cameras on their rooftops that faced out across the street. Good idea in principle. But whoever had contracted out the work had screwed up. The cameras were fixed, not set on rotatable mounts, and there was a gap where two of them failed to criss-cross a certain angle overlooking the street. As long as Bald stuck to his current position at the side of the road he would be invisible. He killed the engine and studied the industrial park. A wire-mesh fence screened several rows of Humvees. He spotted stacks of radar equipment too.

The lots were basic. The only distinguishing marks were the businesses' names displayed beside the doors. These were all unimaginative, like Acme Dental and The Tiling & Flooring Co Inc. Except for three lots further down. The two signs closest to the street indicated Forensic Intelligence Services and Ballistic Development Inc. The third lot belonged to Lance-Elsing. Laxman's Infiniti was the only occupant of the eight parking spaces out front.

The company's offices were much smaller than Bald had been expecting. He scanned the immediate area several times. No sign of any sophisticated intruder-detection system. Just a basic ADT alarm, the kind of thing that's fine for securing a small private house, but not a multi-million-dollar military research facility. Whatever security Lance Elsing had was discreet and well hidden.

Ten minutes later, at 2130 hours, Laxman exited Lance-Elsing's offices and headed for his car. He looked edgy. Under his right arm he was carrying a briefcase. He thrust this onto the front passenger seat, gunned the Infiniti and sped out of Gateway. Bald tailed him south down South Keene Road. Laxman took a right onto Jackson Street, heading west. Downtown.

Neat rows of white-picket-fenced bungalows gave way to shabby-looking slum dwellings. Gangs of kids hung around outside porches and stared at Bald as he passed by, their arms hanging low and their baggy jeans hanging lower. A hundred metres west on Jackson and suddenly the homes were pleasant again.

After just over a mile Laxman turned on north onto South Myrtle Avenue, then west onto Chestnut Street. Now they were in downtown Clearwater. It was almost 2200 hours and the stores were all closed up for the day. Traffic was sporadic but Bald hung three cars back from the Infiniti at all times. Like any sleeper or terrorist, Laxman would be getting more agitated and paranoid the closer he got to accomplishing his mission. With less than twenty-four hours to go he was probably expecting to be tailed.

Laxman took a right onto South Fort Harrison Avenue, the main drag along Tampa Bay. Four- and five-storey whitewashed buildings lined either side of the smooth blacktop. Laxman continued north. Soon they hit downtown Clearwater and Laxman dropped to forty per. Bald did likewise. He noted that every third or fourth building along the road was anonymous. Blacked-out windows, no store signs, nothing to indicate any human activity. Then he saw half a dozen men file out of one of the buildings, dressed in pristine white shirts and grey trousers. They clutched colourful textbooks and walked down the street with their eyes fixed ahead. No one was talking to anyone else. Like kids on a school trip to a museum.

Then Bald saw something else. Fifty metres up ahead were a pair of tall, white buildings, one on each side of the street, like two giant wedding cakes. A corridor suspended over the road connected the two buildings. The birthday cake on the right was a discreet luxury hotel. The one on the left was wildly ostentatious. Like a Colombian drug dealer's pad. Each of its fifteen storeys had a symmetrical façade. A tower was built into each of the building's four corners, with the central part of the building surmounted by a taller tower capped with a golden dome. On top of the dome stood a giant metal cross with four diagonal rays slashed across the horizontal and the vertical arm. Eight points. Bald recognized the symbol of the Church of Scientology.

The Infiniti's tail lights flared for a moment. Then Laxman carried on for another two blocks at a slower speed before hanging a right onto Pierce Street, then a left onto South Garden Avenue. One hundred metres down this street the Infiniti eased into a parking lot outside a four-storey building set back twenty metres from the road. The architecture looked out of place amid the cheesecake-smooth, gabled buildings set neatly along the main drag. The ground floor was a band of white-painted stone. It was punctuated by a pair of rudimentary glass doors, the frames black, the glass painted off-white. The three floors above it were of mottled red brick with eight windows on each.

Bald pulled over. Shunted the Buick into park. He saw Laxman climbing out of the Infiniti. Now he got his first real look at the sleeper. Laxman was fucking skinny, maybe nine stone with his clothes on, five seven tall, with ruffled black hair, rimless glasses and dressed in a beige suit with a two-button jacket, white shirt and shiny black brogues. Look at this cunt, Bald thought to himself. Prancing around looking like he should be trading shares on Wall Street.

Laxman glanced furtively across his shoulders before walking to the doors of the building. He reached for the handle but was caught off balance when one of the doors was thrust open in his face. A couple of portly Arab men in bulging dark suits stepped out onto the street. Bald watched as the Arabs warily sidestepped Laxman without saying a word to him and quickened their stride towards a Lincoln Town Car parked at the other end of the lot.

Fuck this, Bald thought. He ditched the Buick in the lot next to the Infiniti and made for the building. Was this where Laxman handed over high-tech secrets to terrorists? A warehouse stood next to the building, with a giant sign saying 'FORECLOSURE. FOR LEASE OR SALE' draped across the front.

To one side of the doors there was a battered intercom, seemingly held in place by a single screw. The name of the business occupying the ground floor was smudged. The other floors had names that suggested accountants or law firms. Peebles and Wood. Mason, Grey and Schulmann. Bald thumbed the buzzer for the ground floor. And waited.

Bald made out a voice amid the intercom's popcorn crackle.

'One moment, please.'

Female. Foreign. Young.

Three things Bald approved of.

The crackle died out.

Something didn't seem right.

The intercom squawked again and the door lock was released. Bald pushed the door open and entered a long corridor, dimly lit but extravagant. Red carpet, white walls and deep-red velvet curtains over the windows. Classical music playing in the background. This isn't a fucking office, he thought.

The voice that had cawed over the intercom belonged to a Chinese woman. She looked frigid and charmless and was dressed in a button-down white shirt and a short skirt designed to show off all the good bits. Except she had none. Her breasts were flatter than an iPad and her arse non-existent. One look at her and Bald figured that boning her would be like fucking a dead fish. She offered Bald her delicate hand. He shook it and thought, maybe this is a Scientology hangout? Maybe Laxman's been brainwashed?

Then he glanced past the woman's shoulder. A group of four Arab men were standing at the end of the throat-like corridor. Laxman was with them, his back to Bald. He was clutching the briefcase in his right hand. Dollar signs danced in front of Bald's eyes. I've caught the cunt red-handed, a voice in his head said.

Then the Chinese woman said, 'Me fuck you for dollar, Mister. Fuckee for big dollar.'

twenty-three

'You want fuck?'

He'd had better offers. Bald stared beyond the woman's slender shoulders at the layout of the place. He was looking into a reception area where there were half a dozen booths with leather-covered seating. Buddha candleholders were on the walls and in front of the seats stood tables made of glass and filled with exotic fish. Three of the Arabs Bald had seen were now being led by hot blonde women up a staircase at the back of the reception. The fourth was seated in a booth facing Bald. Two Latino beauties dressed in satin corsets slid into the booth, one either side of him. A brunette joined them. She was wearing a fishnet bra, G-string and garter belt that reminded Bald of Lena. A dog leash was hooked to a spiked collar around her neck.

The Chinese woman tried to grab Bald's attention. 'Me do ass, me do mouth.'

Bald scanned the rest of the booths. It was pretty much all foreign guys getting their rocks off. A couple of Indian-looking businessmen in gaudy suits sipped cocktails at a further booth while a pair of blonde-haired twins in G-strings made out in front of them. A Japanese guy was entertaining two black women who stood a good head taller than him. He was topping up their champagne glasses with thousand-dollar a pop Cristal. The gangsta's tipple of choice.

In the far corner of the room stood Laxman. The sleeper was sitting alone and tapping an unlit cigarette on the table top at a frantic speed, over and over, like he was tapping out Morse code. He was facing the stairs and hadn't yet glanced over in Bald's direction. He seemed like he was waiting impatiently. Maybe he's got a regular prossie here, Bald figured. He weighed up slotting the guy right now. Send Laxman over to the dark side and bug out via the fire exit: it could all be over in under a minute. In and out. But there were problems. The Chinese woman had an ID on his face. Several others in the booths could have noticed him. And for all he knew there might be CCTV in this damn place.

'Me do other woman.'

The Chinese woman ran a hand down his chest. 'One hour. I give you special fun time.' She did a thing with her tongue. 'Me give best blowjob in all USA.'

'Hold that thought,' said Bald as he answered an incoming call on his burner.

'Yes?'

'Do you know the Monkey Bar?'

Rachel. Scot-loving Rachel.

'No,' Bald said. 'But if it serves Wild Turkey and Stella it'll do just fine.'

The Chinese woman was still trying to get his attention. He waved her away.

'A Scottish guy who likes a drink? What are the odds?' said Rachel. 'So. Like I was saying, the Monkey Bar, it's on

East Shore Drive, west of the Causeway. Meet me there in thirty?'

'Sure.'

'Don't be late. I've got a little surprise for you.'

'I fucking love surprises.'

twenty-four

Four and a half miles due west of Gateway Industrial Park, Bald was cruising over Tampa Bay on the Clearwater Memorial Causeway. The sky glistened. Bald nosed the Buick off the Causeway and onto the Clearwater Beach resort. First right off the Causeway took him onto East Shore Drive. He saw the Monkey Bar. He saw nowhere to park. But seconds later he brought the Buick to a halt by a parking meter. He stepped out onto the blacktop and inserted six quarters, then strode back to the bar.

Inside, the place was a confusion of bright lights, wild colours and aggressive voices. A widescreen plasma TV fixed to the wall was showing a gridiron game. The barmaids were dolled up like cheerleaders. The air was redolent with the smell of hamburger grease and Sambuca. Nickelback's 'Rockstar' thudded out of the speakers. Bald felt at home.

The counter was a stand-alone thing in the centre of the room with a wide choice of whiskeys on offer. About two dozen people were seated around the counter, most of them as couples. The men were all in their fifties or sixties with faces like landslides and decked out in floral-print shirts and khaki shorts. The women were mostly in their thirties or late twenties. Their bored faces betrayed too-early plastic surgery and Botox injections. Money and Viagra were the sticking plasters keeping these couples together.

Bald spotted Rachel at the end of the bar. She carried herself in that way only certain American girls can, brash but sprinkled with a sweetness that was almost naive. She wore a black knee-length skirt that hitched up slightly at one side and a sleeveless top with a deep-scoop neckline. Her long, beach-blonde hair draped like a wedding-dress train across her slender shoulders. The shot Cave had emailed didn't do her justice.

She was downing a large glass of white wine. Bald made his way across the bar towards her. He ordered a Stella from the barmaid and took the seat next to her.

'That was quick,' Rachel said.

'I don't like to keep women waiting.'

Rachel laughed into her wine and said, 'In my world, waiting is all part of the game.'

'In my world, it's all about who shoots first.'

'From those scars on your face, I'd say someone shoots faster than you.'

'I was outnumbered.'

Silence. Bald drank to fill it.

'I heard you like a bit of Scots,' he said.

'Not really.'

Bald frowned. That fucker Cave lied to me, he thought. Then Rachel was smiling teasingly at him and saying, 'I'm just fucking with you. I love Scottish men.' She leaned in closer to Bald. 'You know, I could *totally* fuck your accent.'

'So what's the surprise you have for me?'

'In a little bit,' Rachel said, necking the rest of her wine. She studied the bottom of the glass for a moment, then looked Bald in the eye. He was hypnotized by her lips, glossy and parted just enough to give a glimpse of her teeth.

'Did you have fun trailing our birthday boy?' she asked, 'He's a fucking weird one.'

'How so?'

Bald shrugged. 'Al-Qaeda terrorists don't usually have much time for whorehouses.'

'Bin Laden had a porn stash in his hideout.'

Their chat was interrupted by the grating of metal against the tiled floor to their left. A guy was easing himself onto a barstool three seats along from Bald. He ordered a bottle of Bud and another glass of wine for Rachel, giving the guy a nod to reassure him that he was here to mind his own business. A static roar from the TV rippled like a shockwave through the bar. Florida State linebacker Tyson Tomlin had levelled things up.

'You have to make it look like an accident,' Rachel said, staring intently at the screen, as if she gave a fuck about the game.

'What? Meeting you?' Bald sank the rest of his beer and winked at her.

'You know what I'm talking about.'

'Like a car accident?'

'Like a robbery gone wrong.'

'No fucking problem.'

Rachel raised her eyebrows. 'You don't want to know why?'

Bald shook his head. 'Look, if you want me to cut his fucking balls off and write his name on the wall in blood, I'll do it. As long as I get paid, it's all the same to me.'

'Is that who you are? A guy who's in it just for the money?'

'A new low,' said Bald with a mock groan.

'Why's that?'

'I have a CIA agent lecturing me on morality.'

Rachel was silent for several seconds, then she said, 'Our hands are tied until tomorrow on this whole Laxman thing.' Her eyes were looking right into Bald. He felt himself harden. 'So why don't we have ourselves a little fun tonight?' she said.

'What did you have in mind?'

Rachel licked her lips and ran her finger around the rim of her glass. It made a soft, squeaky sound. Then she looked up at Bald. 'Well. There is one thing. I shouldn't say, but—'

'What?'

'Look, I'm gonna level with you. We're gonna fuck tonight. That voice is driving me crazy. But before then, I wanna drink a shitload of tequila, dance and snort a couple lines of coke.'

'Jesus,' said Bald.

'What? Too much detail?'

'No,' said Bald, shifting in his seat. 'We have so much in common.'

Rachel's eyes lit up. She edged closer until she was a few inches from Bald's face. So close he could smell the almond and jasmine perfume coming off the smooth expanse of her neck. Without averting her eyes from Bald she ordered four shots of José Cuervo. The barmaid promptly poured four generous measures and lined up all four in front of Rachel like a pool rack. Rachel then passed two to Bald and sank one of hers.

Bald tipped the first one down his throat. The liquor mainlined his bloodstream, sending waves of heat into his skull. He was already halfway lit by the time he downed the second shot. Rachel motioned to the barmaid again.

'Bottoms up,' she said to Bald, downing her second shot. 'You're doing a good thing, you know. Laxman is dangerous.'

Bald felt the booze fogging his mind. He closed his eyes and said, 'I don't care.'

'You don't mean that.'

'There's an old mucker of mine. He was one of the good guys. Whatever the fuck that means.' Bald was thinking of Joe Gardner.

'What happened to him?'

'He died doing the thing he loved the most. Being a fucking loser. He had no money, no prospects. Being a good operator doesn't count for much on the outside. Nah, I look out for number one. Everyone else is on their own.'

'So you really don't care if Laxman smuggles military technology into the hands of our worst enemies?'

'The only thing I care about is how many zeroes my cheque has on the end of it.'

Bald necked his third tequila. The alcohol slicked his throat like crude oil.

'Besides,' he went on, 'your average terrorist has got fuck-all training. Tenner says the tech will be worthless in their hands. Al-Qaeda spent years trying to build a dirty bomb and they couldn't do it. So some jumped-up Paki militants get their hands on a hot new missile. Big deal. They won't be able to use it.'

Rachel said, 'What if I told you that the technology Laxman has his hands on is way, way more secret than some slick new missile?'

Bald said nothing. He was suddenly feeling light-headed. A combination of the booze, the lack of sleep and the fact he hadn't eaten since rocking up in Clearwater.

'Danny didn't tell you the full story, did he?' said Rachel.

'I'm just a fucking soldier,' Bald replied.

Rachel waved her purse at Bald. 'Now how about we take this party someplace else?'

Rachel downed her third tequila quicker than Bald had, which impressed and troubled him in equal measure. She wiped her lips and said, 'I need to make a quick trip to the bathroom. Meet me out front in five?'

She slinked off her seat, pecked him on the cheek and sauntered across the bar. The guy three seats away was tipping the last drops of something down his throat. He finished, replaced the empty bottle on the counter and laid eight crisp one-dollar bills on the tip tray. Something about him struck Bald as vaguely familiar. He was in his late forties with a face like a chalk cliff. He was dressed in a shirt and trousers, his suit jacket draped over the stool next to him.

Then the guy stood up and limped towards the restroom. Once he had disappeared, everyone else was absorbed by the college game. Bald slid off his stool and rooted through the guy's jacket. He drew a blank. No wallet, no ID, no keys. But he did find something in the left pocket. It was a green ticket stub. The kind of thing you get at a church raffle. Printed on the stub were the words 'RUBY RIDGE RANGE & ARMORY. SAN ANTONIO, TX 78205'.

The date and time were the previous day, late afternoon.

No fucking way. Bald felt a cold rage inside him. Now he knew where he recognized the guy from. Rio Grande. The border.

The rednecks.

twenty-five

2350 hours.

Outside the Monkey Bar, an orange-scented breeze swept like a whisper across the parking lot. Rachel emerged thirty seconds after Bald, looking flustered. She smiled briefly at him and then brushed past, heading for a Chrysler 300C sedan parked twenty-five metres away from the bar. Light from the main drag illuminated the dozen or so cars in the lot. There were almost as many cars as there were patrons. Drink-driving wasn't perhaps as frowned upon in Florida as it was in England.

Unlocking the Chrysler remotely, Rachel removed her key fob and slid into the driver's seat. Bald eased himself in beside her. He made himself comfortable while she reached into her purse, removed a twenty-gram plastic bag of cocaine and laid it on the dash. Then she took out a Bank of America credit card and a $100 bill.

'Shouldn't we be doing this somewhere a bit more private?' Bald said.

'Relax,' Rachel said cheerily as she began chopping up the coke with the card. 'No one's gonna bother us. Jesus, everybody round here does coke anyhow. In Clearwater, you're weird if you *don't* bust lines. You know?'

Bald didn't, but he kept his mouth shut and his eyes on the door of the Monkey Bar while Rachel went to work

on the cocaine. He had the tequila shots and beer sloshing around his system, and his stomach felt like a cave,
but even the booze couldn't stifle the unease about the
redneck. He dimly realized that the guy could have tailed
him all the way from Texas. Bald experienced a brief pang
as he wondered if that really was possible. He had changed
licence plates, had been cautious and stayed low-profile.
Any lower and I would've been underground, he thought.

Rachel interrupted his thoughts. 'Laxman is planning
to steal Intelligent Dust,' she said.

Bald rubbed his eyes. 'Dust with brains?'

Rachel got rid of all the small lumps until the cocaine
was uniformly fine. Then she began dividing it into six
trim lines three inches long and an eighth of an inch wide.
'That stuff is cutting-edge,' she said. 'It's like a gas. You can
put it in a can. Or load it in a bomb. Or a syringe. You can
even release it through a ventilation system. Each burst of
ID is made up of millions of tiny robots. Nanobots. The
dust enters your body and puts a permanent trace on you,
wherever you are. They can report back to a central server
with information about your vital statistics, your movements, even your fingerprints.'

'Doesn't sound like a military application to me.'

'That's where you're wrong.'

'Like how?'

'I'm not at liberty to say.'

'I've heard that one before.'

'Trust me, if the bad guys get their hands on this, we're
all in big trouble.'

'I've heard that one before too.'

Rachel shrugged, then rolled the $100 bill so it formed
a tube a quarter of an inch wide and three inches long.

Then she placed one end of the tube to her nose and the other at the beginning of the line. She inhaled, but not too strongly. Just enough to entice the powder up the tube and into her nostril. She hit the top of the line, then slumped back on the leather seat. Her nose was leaking blood. That meant that the purity was fucking good. Rachel smiled dreamily at Bald, pushed her face close to his. Their noses were touching. He could feel her breath tingling his lips.

'Now it's your turn,' she said.

Bald went to crack a smile and felt his jaw muscles lock up. He'd been putting off this moment. He'd smuggled drugs, sure. But using them was a mug's game far as he was concerned. He believed in supply and demand, not cut and snort. Bald had only shoved Bolivian marching powder up his hooter on two occasions, and on both times he'd been operating undercover. Back then, it had been necessary to complete the mission. Now doing a bit of toot was necessary if he wanted to end up with his head buried between an ex-model's legs.

Rachel handed Bald the rolled-up bill and he ran it over his line. He felt the tiny grains funnelling into his nostril. But instead of melting in his nasal passage the coke sprayed the back of his throat. As soon as the coke hit Bald it sucked the moisture out of his mouth, like a vacuum. He suddenly had a hard-on that could drive a hole through a brick wall. A wave of euphoria rushed up inside his stomach, sent butterflies flapping inside the wall of his chest. He was super horny. He craved a shag. He coughed to try to clear his throat. The coke was melting under his tongue like sugar.

Rachel laughed at him. 'I guess you people do stuff differently in Scotland.'

She snatched the hundred from Bald and snorted another line. Tilted her head back. She looked even more fuckable now.

'So how about that surprise?' said Bald.

Rachel reached out and touched his wrist. He looked up at her. Her eyes were wide and wired like a pair of spark plugs.

'Not just yet, cowboy. I'm still up for partying. Then you get your surprise.'

She reached into the glove compartment and fished out a bottle of Wild Turkey. She adjusted her blouse, fiddled with her hair and looked at him breathlessly.

'Walk with me to the beach?' She was talking quickly. Bald realized where this was going. Coke made some people horny as fuck; it turned others into marathon chatterboxes. He'd have to endure a few hours of Rachel talking bollocks before the coke wore off and he could drill a hole through her. Good job she's got the Wild Turkey, Bald thought. His mouth was dry as the arse-end of a dog and he figured the booze would wet his tongue a little. Still, his balls were aching and he fully intended to get his fuck on with Miss Florida tonight.

The beach lay 300 metres east across the closely mowed grass of a park. Rachel guided Bald towards the beach. Palm trees were racked up along the walkways, pleasure boats moored at a brightly lit pier, Mediterranean-style penthouses painted soft shades of pink and blue and stacked like chimneys along the coastline. A cool wind fanned in from the bay. They stopped at the edge of the beach. Rachel unscrewed the cap of the Wild Turkey and handed the bottle to Bald. He took a long swig. It singed his throat and left a honeyed, spicy dew under his tongue.

'You saw him go into that brothel, right?'

'It looked like an office from the outside. But, yeah, I did.'

'We have some intelligence. Laxman is a regular there.'

'How regular?'

'Clockwork. Monday to Friday. Same time, same woman. According to our sources, Laxman is closer to this prostitute than his own wife. Here.' Rachel dug a photo out of her purse. Bald studied it. He was expecting to see a babe but it was the Chinese woman he'd met in the brothel.

'Sounds like he's in a happy marriage.' Bald took another hit of Wild Turkey. Big mistake. Drunkenness hit him like a one-two-three combo. Somewhere through the booze he realized he was fucking tanked. A voice in his head warned, take it easy, John. Big day tomorrow. But a stronger, louder voice boomed, one more drink and she's all yours. Bang Rachel tonight. Kill Laxman tomorrow.

Bald took a third gulp and was mildly surprised to find that half the bourbon had already transferred from the bottle to his liver. Now he felt the reverse effects of the coke. His dick started to shrivel up. Rachel started nibbling his ear and said, 'All this talk of killing is making me horny.'

Bald sobered up a little. He was about to kiss her again when a voice at his back, male, officious, said, 'You OK there, ma'am?'

Rachel pulled away from Bald.

'Yes,' she said. 'I'm fine.'

Bald steered himself 180 degrees. It was like trying to get off a spinning roundabout. He clocked a pair of cops. The nearest guy was white and shaven-headed, his calloused hands resting on his utility belt. He was wearing Ray-Bans and Bald wondered how the fuck the guy could see anything in shades at this time of night. His partner was a Hispanic guy. Buzzcut, small eyes and a BMI in the high thirties. He had residual muscle around the shoulders and neck, and Bald reckoned he had probably been a gridiron footballer or boxer in high school.

'What about you, sir?' Ray-Bans said to Bald. 'Been drinking, huh?'

'Just a couple of beers,' Bald tried to say. His gums and lips were numb, a side effect of inhaling the coke too deeply into the back of his throat rather than leaving it up his hooter. His lips were bulbous and unwieldy. Ray-Bans swiped the bottle from Bald and shot it a disapproving look. He handed his partner the bourbon and stepped into Bald's face.

'Where are you from?'

'Scotland.'

'Is that a joke?'

'It's a place north of England.'

Ray-Bans and Hispanic swapped glances. Then Ray-Bans looked back at Bald and said, 'You look intoxicated, sir. And from the look in your eyes I'd say it's not the only substance you've been abusing tonight. Am I right? Sir?'

Bald acted like he had lockjaw.

Ray-Bans lowered his shades and stared at Bald.

'If there's one thing I hate more than a drunk asshole in my town, it's a drunk foreign asshole. You've got ten seconds to get the fuck out of my sight or I'm booking you for being drunk and disorderly.'

Bald was about to say something he'd regret when Rachel was thrusting an arm around him. 'It's OK,' she said to Ray-Bans. 'I'll take him home. Sorry for bothering you, officer.' She sounded sober. Sensible. Bald asked himself how the fuck that was possible. She'd downed as much booze as Bald and she was half his fucking size.

Ray-Bans raised his shades. 'Keep him out of trouble,' he shouted to Rachel. 'I'll remember his face.' The cops departed, Ray-Bans muttering under his breath.

Rachel escorted Bald back up the beach, towards the Chrysler. A hundred metres from the Monkey Bar parking lot he stopped short and shrugged off her arm. The Fear was taking hold of him, digging its claws into his bowels. What if the redneck at the bar wasn't a redneck after all? the Fear asked.

What if all this time he was someone sent to kill you?

'Something the matter?' Rachel said, concern playing on her face.

'I'll be fine.'

'I don't believe you.'

Bald didn't reply. Couldn't. His world was suddenly blurred and distorted. He shook his head. The giddiness didn't clear up. Actually, it made things worse. He fumbled through his lopsided world in search of Rachel.

Then he tripped up, and everything went vertical.

Then black.

twenty-six

Bald woke to a harsh, relentless drilling noise somewhere close by. He had no idea where he was, or why. He rubbed hard, waxy balls of sleep from his eyes and got his bearings. He was lying on a double bed. Bollock naked. For a second he figured he'd got lucky with Rachel. But then he looked at the space beside him in the bed. The pillow was smooth and undisturbed. He felt a slow release of confusion through his system.

Where the fuck am I?

The mattress stank of urine and had cattle wire for bedsprings. His eyes adjusted to the light seeping through a single curtain thin as an old pair of tights. A fourteen-inch cathode-ray TV squatted in the corner of the room, snow static scrolling down the screen. A voice cut through the drilling: you're in some kind of low-grade motel. His wrist bones ached. He rubbed his wrists and tried to remember last night. It was like someone had clicked on his short-term memory and dragged it into the trash bin. He couldn't recall anything after blacking out near the Monkey Bar.

The coke, a voice pickaxed at the base of his skull. Mixing blow and booze had been a bad fucking move.

The drilling was now so loud and piercing he couldn't be sure if it was coming from inside his head or somewhere outside. He crawled out of the bed and staggered into the bathroom. Sink unit, toilet, shower stall, all fitted into a space so tiny you'd have to leave just to change your mind. Generations of pubic hair clogged the shower's plughole. Something brown and viscous had congealed in the basin. Bald ran the cold tap and sloshed water over his face.

A memory rushed back at him. Last night.

He filled a chipped glass with water and drained it in three gulps. Then two more glasses. He seemed to have an unquenchable thirst. He remembered puking up onto a lime-grass verge. He examined his hands in the sink. His fingers were painted in dried blood. Not his own.

The drilling quietened in the bathroom. A little more of the fog cleared from behind Bald's eyes, and he recognized that distinctive drilling noise.

The burner.

Bald stumbled back into the bedroom. There, lying on a carpet so worn it looked like goats had been chewing on it, was a pile of clothes. Bald knelt beside them and groped at the T-shirt and jeans. He found the burner in the back pocket of his jeans. The battery was low: two crappy bars. He had six missed calls, all from Cave. Bald sat on the edge of the shitty mattress. A sharp pain was announcing itself in his right hand. He stared at the display and let the phone ring. The display darkened.

He sat there in the semi-darkness. Then the burner trilled again, and this time he took the call.

'Where the fuck have you been?' Cave snorted between each word, barely able to suppress his rage. 'Everyone here is going fucking ballistic. It's almost time for the birthday party.'

'I overslept,' said Bald. 'Haven't slept for two days.'

Another snort came down the line and blasted Bald's eardrum. 'Bollocks. You've been out on the piss, John Boy. I know.'

'Rachel?'

'Yeah. She said you were in a proper state. Got into a fight with a bouncer. The cops are looking for you. That motel you're in was her idea. Better make sure you stay out of trouble, unless you want to spend the next thirty years of your life in a steel cage.'

Bald was gasping for more water. Felt like someone had Scotch-taped his tongue to the roof of his mouth.

'Just over five hours to go,' said Cave. 'That's all you've got. If I were you, I'd get off the line and pay a visit to birthday boy before it's too late.'

Cave ended the call. Bald sat on the edge of the bed, listening to dead air. He didn't move for longer than a little while. He was angry with himself for pissing away all his preparation time.

Five fucking hours.

His training voice kicked in over the pulsing between his temples. No margin for error, pal. One chance to slot the prick, or you kiss a painful goodbye to your retirement fund and your villa on the Riviera.

The pain in his right hand was getting worse. So was the throbbing in his head.

A knock at the door. Three heavy, urgent raps of knuckle on hardwood. Bald froze. He was about to search for his Colt Delta Elite, then remembered that he'd left it in the Buick outside the Monkey Bar.

Rap-rap-rap.

A familiar voice said, 'It's me.'

Relief flushed through Bald's system. He unlocked the door – he couldn't recall locking it, but old habits die hard – and jerked the handle. Rachel barged her way inside. Bald expected her to look the worse for wear. He was wrong. She looked like she did last night. Waxy and spankable. She was clutching his gym bag. She ran her eyes over his naked torso.

'We need to leave. Now,' she said.

Bald grabbed his jeans from the pile. 'You don't look so bad this morning.'

'Compliment me later,' Rachel said. 'The cops are on their way here.'

'Someone tipped them off?'

'I don't see how. I paid the motel manageress to keep her mouth shut.'

'Maybe you should have paid her more.'

Rachel slow-burned at Bald as he slipped on his T-shirt. 'Well, maybe you shouldn't have put a bouncer in a coma.'

'I'm sure on some level he deserved it.'

She sighed her disapproval and dropped the gym bag at her feet. Reached around to the back of her skirt, and for a second Bald thought she was going to show him her birthday suit. But instead she whipped out his Colt and chucked it to him.

'You really don't get it, do you?'

'Get what?'

'The world doesn't play by your rules any more, John. Jesus Christ, you could've jeopardized the entire mission.'

'I don't seem to remember you stopping me from hitting the tequila last night.'

Rachel turned away and left the room. Bald followed, hoisting the bag over his shoulder and stuffing the Colt into the top of his jeans.

They emerged into an apron of blacktop parking lot flanked by an L of universally depressing rooms. Seventies-style architecture that hadn't been renovated since Jimmy Carter got elected. The motel looked like the kind of place where sex pests and serial killers lived out their sick fantasies. Bald spotted Rachel's Chrysler 300C gleaming in the middle of the lot. He heard the howl of police sirens.

'They're almost here,' Rachel said, doubling her stride towards the Chrysler. Bald upped the pace too. The afternoon sun was lasering white-hot light over the blacktop. Sweat rolled down Bald's forehead and into his eyes, blurring his vision. Rachel started the Chrysler and filed into traffic. In the rear-view mirror she saw the police cars screeching into the motel lot. Cops crawling out of them like insects, piling into the room they had vacated thirty seconds earlier.

Rachel headed west, darting through the traffic, switching lanes at speed. She bust through a red light at a junction, narrowly skimming past a truck rushing along in the other direction.

'Mind telling me where we're going?' Bald asked.

'Lance-Elsing.'

'What's there?'

'Laxman.'

'So?'

'You can kill him there. When he leaves work.'

Bald made a face. 'Shooting the cunt outside the Lance-Elsing office is suicide. The place is riddled with cameras.'

'You got a better idea, now's the time to share.'

Bald fished out the Colt from the waistband of his jeans. 'Just follow the prick. We still have a few hours to play with.'

Rachel worked her face into a slant. 'And what if we don't have a chance before the handover? What if we've already missed our window of opportunity? What then, John?'

Bald didn't dignify the question with a reply. He grabbed the gym bag and removed the cardboard box of HSM bulk 10mm ammo. Then he hit the eject button on the side of the Colt. The clip sprang loose from the underside of the pistol's grip and he rhythmically thumbed rounds into the empty clip. He gently loaded the clip into the bottom of the pistol grip. The Colt made a definite *click*. Now he abruptly pulled the slide mechanism back then forward again, to chamber the first round. He performed this action quickly, because if you shunted the slide mechanism back and forth too slowly the first round would get jammed in the chamber, and you'd have an instant stoppage. The mechanism jerked back to its original position.

They drove on in silence, both half-listening to a local radio station. The forecaster excitedly warned that the Tampa Bay area would get blitzed later that same night by a nearby hurricane. There were a few perfunctory words about the civil war in Libya. America, thought Bald, always intent on making the rest of the world a footnote.

'You know, it's a shame you got so wasted last night,' Rachel said.

'Why's that?'

'I really want to fuck a Scottish guy.'

'You know what they say. Aim high.'

'Maybe later you can make it up to me.'

'Later sounds good.'

But Bald pushed thoughts of sex to the back of his mind. They reached Prosper Avenue and Gateway Industrial Park. Rachel slowed the Chrysler to twenty per as she neared the entrance. Bald's neck muscles tightened like tension rope. They were forty metres from the entrance and craning their necks beyond the fence when a black Infiniti, licence plate 504 XKW, bounced over the speed ramp and rocketed into traffic.

'Shit!' Rachel said, upping the Chrysler to seventy-five and racing after Laxman. The speedometer flicked past eighty-five. They were going so fast that every other car on the road seemed static. 'We cut that pretty fine,' she said. 'A minute later and we would have missed him.'

'He must be on his way to the handover,' said Bald.

'But there's still four hours to go. It's way too early.'

'Unless he's heading out of town?'

Only Laxman didn't head east, out of town. Instead he threw a curveball by flying west on South Keene Road in the direction of downtown Clearwater and Tampa Bay. Rachel followed him onto South Myrtle Avenue and Chestnut Street and after six blocks the Church of Scientology HQ was mushrooming out of the horizon.

Now the Infiniti skipped right onto South Fort Harrison Avenue. Bald suddenly understood where Laxman was headed. Nine blocks on South Fort Harrison and the Infiniti eased off the gas and joined Pierce Street for three blocks, then slid onto South Garden Avenue. Two blocks down South Garden Laxman pulled into a parking lot.

'Fuck's going on?' said Bald.

Rachel said nothing.

They were both looking in the direction of the brothel.

It wasn't there.

twenty-seven

1809 hours.

In its place stood a burned-out shell of a building. The windows were all blown out, the red bricks above and below all charred, like giant fists had given the windows black eyes. The front doors slanted off to one side, giving Bald a line into what had been the brothel. He could see the corridor, a lake of ashes. The top two storeys had melted into each other. There was no roof. Lumps of broken plaster littered the ground like mortar shrapnel.

'Maybe someone didn't want Laxman coming back,' said Bald.

'Could be coincidence. There's a lot of hookers in Clearwater. A lot of pimps. Competition can get out of hand, you know what I mean?'

Then Laxman did something that confused Bald. He stepped into the smoke-blackened corridor.

'What the hell's he hoping to find in there?' said Rachel.

'Only one way to find out.'

'I'll wait here.'

A perfect place to finish the job, thought Bald. He got out of the Chrysler and walked briskly towards the shell. Raindrops sporadically chopped at the air and sluiced water across the blacktop. The handover was scheduled for 2000 hours. That gave Bald an hour and fifty minutes to settle it for real. He felt the reassuring pistol grip of the Colt Delta Elite stashed under his T-shirt, its finger-grooves lightly pressing against the wall of his once-hard abs. He felt the violence in his fingertips.

Bald now noticed a second car in the parking lot. An SUV he recognized as a GMC Denali. It was way over at the other end, in the shadow of the warehouse.

Ten metres from the brothel Bald heard a loud growl at his six o'clock. He spun around. Rachel was pelting off towards the main road. Bald stared angrily at the tail lights. What was going on? Now he was alone, with no getaway vehicle.

He entered the corridor a minute after Laxman. Calmly withdrew the Colt from under his T-shirt. He used both thumbs to cock the hammer so he'd need to apply less pressure to the trigger for the initial shot. A gentle squeeze on the trigger mechanism and the round would tear out of the barrel and put Laxman out of business. He pulled back the slider just a fraction and checked the chamber to make sure there was a round inside. He caught that reassuring slither of chambered brass. The gun felt solid and cold.

The corridor reeked of charcoal and burned fabric. The air was heavy with damp. Bald felt moisture drizzle his face, his shoulders. There was a couple of inches of water on the floor, a gunmetal flotsam of nails and papers and glass. One of the smoke detectors had fallen from the ceiling. Now it was lying on the floor half submerged, its wires exposed and its red alarm light glaring amid the debris. Bald crept into the reception area and mentally readied himself. Took in deep breaths that flooded his body with oxygen and pumped his muscles, preparing them for the task ahead.

The leather on the seating in the booths had burned away, exposing yellow foam innards stained black in patches. The Buddha candle-holders had shattered in the heat, sprinkling the floor with shards. Bald didn't see Laxman. The staircase was fundamentally intact. Bald walked towards it.

He was ten metres from the bottom step when he spotted a shadow coming down the stairs, coming his way. He ducked into one of the booths, crouched behind the seat, and observed the Chinese woman. She stopped at the foot of the stairs and lit a cigarette. Then she picked her way towards the reception, her high heels cracking debris underfoot, taking long drags on her cigarette and checking her BlackBerry. Bald manoeuvred around the seat so she wouldn't catch him in her peripheral vision. He watched her stop again by the entrance to the building. Thought for a second she'd seen him. Then he clocked her BlackBerry screen. The woman hit the green key and spoke to the person on the other end of the line in snappy, aggressive bursts that sounded to Bald like someone being stabbed repeatedly, but he guessed was her native tongue. The call lasted around thirty seconds. Then she hung up. The screen dissolved. The woman dashed her cigarette in a puddle and walked out into the night.

Bald started to count to thirty. His Regiment training taught him to always consider that the enemy was smarter than you. That way, you never get caught off guard. Maybe the woman had gone outside just for a moment? Perhaps to meet somebody? Bald could feel his eyes beginning to water, could feel smoke particles swirling in his throat.

Thirty.

He stood up, saw Laxman descending the stairs and shot back down again.

Laxman seemed in more of a hurry than the woman. He walked fast across the reception area and along the corridor, headed outside. Bald moved out from his cover cautiously, deliberately, careful not to make a splash or tread on glass. He stilled his breath in his burning throat. Now he was at the entrance. No sign of the woman. Laxman was making his way towards the Infiniti. Bald was fifteen metres away from Laxman ... then less than ten metres from his target. His body was working on muscle memory now. That was what training was for. Not to make you perfect, but so that in the middle of a situation about to go fucking noisy, you didn't have to think about what you were doing, or how, or when.

He brought the Colt level with Laxman's head.

Five metres.

Fucking finish it, he thought.

Bald's index finger was pressed halfway down on the trigger when he felt cold metal on the back of his neck. He froze. Laxman carried on unaware towards the Infiniti. Four metres became eight, then twelve. The metal dug harder into Bald's flesh and rubbed against his upper spine. Sixteen metres now, and Bald watched the Infiniti's lights flicker as Laxman hit the unlock button on his key. He was getting away.

An American voice, hard as rock, whispered, 'Move and I'll fucking kill you.'

twenty-eight

1907 hours.

Bald didn't move. He watched Laxman hop into the Infiniti in blissful ignorance. Five million quid catapulted into the Florida night. Just like that. Bald and his new best friend were left in the lot.

'Drop the piece,' the American said.

With his arm outstretched and finger clearly off the trigger, Bald bent to his knees and placed the Colt flat on the ground. The American swung a foot and side-kicked it. The pistol spun as it skated across the blacktop.

'Get in the fucking car,' said the American.

'Which one?'

'The Denali, dumbass.'

The American again jabbed his pistol into the knotted flesh at the base of Bald's neck. Bald got the message and started for the SUV, forty metres away. The sun was making a slow loop down towards the guts of the earth. Sunset wasn't far off. This time of year, autumn, it came around eight o'clock. Bald was getting to grips with the idea that no one could help him now.

'What's your name?' he said.

'I wouldn't bother to ask.'

'Why's that?'

'Any plans you got beyond the next thirty minutes, cancel them.'

They reached the Denali.

'I have money,' said Bald.

'You think I'm a criminal? Turn around,' the American said.

Bald did a one-eighty and came face to face with the guy. First thing he noted was the gun. An FN Five-Seven semi-automatic. Not the weapon of choice for a mugger. The Five-Seven was a military-grade weapon and had the evolved look and feel that were the hallmarks of its Belgian manufacturer. It was like the Aston Martin of guns. The Five-Seven was used by the US Secret Service and law-enforcement agencies, but had been on the civilian market only since 2004. Guns were like dogs, Bald believed. They told you a lot about the owner. The gun told Bald that the shooter was a firearms fanatic, someone who appreciated the finer aspects of weapon design.

Then Bald noticed the American's face. The same one he had seen in the Monkey Bar. The redneck who had tried to kill him at the Mexican border. But of course he didn't really look like a redneck. He lacked the cross-eyed look. Redneck or not, Bald felt an urge to smack this dick-licker so hard he'd be pissing blood for the next ten days.

'Your name's Bald,' the American said.

'What's yours?'

'I don't have one.' Definitely not redneck. Texans talked slow, they drew words out like clothes on a line. This guy spoke fast and had an accent on him. East Coast. Too harsh and mellow for New York. Upstate, maybe. Or Maine.

Bald hauled himself into the Denali. The cab was big enough to host the fucking Oscars.

'Budge over. You take the wheel,' the American said. 'Now drive.' He held the Five-Seven below the dash, out of sight, the business end six inches from Bald's chest. 'Keep her under fifty. Try anything stupid and three hours from now a paramedic will be scraping your brains off the sidewalk. *Comprende?*'

Two cop cars bombed past. For the first time in his life, Bald wished the police would pull him over. But they carried on, oblivious to the shit unfolding in the Denali.

'Head east on Jackson,' the American said.

Bald studied the guy in the rear-view mirror. Early forties. Possibly late thirties. His skin had a rugged texture and he had hands that worked fields rather than lifted weights. A jaw shaped by frosty nights and rough sleeping. His eyes were flat and black and dull. He didn't have an ounce of body fat. His face was unreadable. Bald remembered from somewhere that the human face has around fifty-two muscles. The American wasn't engaging more than one at a time.

'Who the fuck are you?' Bald tried again.

'I'm the guy you wish you'd never fucked with. I'm that guy.'

Suddenly Bald felt ants crawling along the surface of his brain.

Shit. Not now.

Ever since he'd crossed the border from Mexico, he'd managed to keep a lid on the migraines. The adrenaline, the mission, the alcohol and the prospect of shagging Rachel. Now he knew all they had done was bury the migraines. Not kill them. They'd been biding their time in the background. Sharpening their teeth.

'If you want to do what's right, then let me go,' Bald said.

'And leave you free to terminate a vital intelligence asset?'

The migraine jolted through Bald. Like someone had clipped a pair of crocodile clips to his temples and flicked the juice switch. Electricity surged through his jawbone.

'Shylam Laxman isn't an asset. He's a fucking terrorist.'

'Be that as it may, my orders are to protect him at all costs.'

'Look, mate, I don't know who you work for. But it's not just me who wants to do in that fucker. It's your people too. The CIA want that cunt dead.'

The American chuckled. 'I *am* the fucking CIA,' he said.

twenty-nine

1948 hours.

They descended into the slums. Unseen dogs yapped. Unseen voices hurled drunken insults at each other. The America no one saw, and no one wanted to see, a square mile of crackheads, welfare families and desperation. A warren of alleyways intersected the streets. Shadows scurried up and down the alleys.

They passed a bungalow where five black guys were squatting on the porch dressed in the gangbangers' uniform of loose, low-hanging jeans, hair in cornrows and trainers white like bleached skin. The bungalow was wood-framed with a corrugated metal roof and a porch that wrapped around it like a moat. It looked a bit like the shotgun houses Bald had seen in Louisiana. The windows were boarded up. The boards were sprayed with gang tags. The gang tags were partly obscured by rival gangs' IDs. A crack addict in threadbare slacks stumbled out of the bungalow.

'Pull the fuck over.'

'You're out of your fucking mind.'

'And you're a washed-up British fuck who's about to find out what it's like to have a bullet shot up his asshole. Now pull over.'

Thirty metres beyond the bungalow Bald hit the brakes. The five guys who'd been squatting in front of the crack house stood up as one. The American pressed the Five-Seven into Bald's chest.

'Ladies first,' he said.

Bald clambered out. The gang guys were swaggering towards him. One of them was decked out in a Miami Heat replica basketball jersey. He was wielding a Beretta 92 semi-automatic, the old hard-chromed version, not the more modern polymer type. He waved it dramatically in the air. On the back of his jersey '3' and 'WADE' were emblazoned in big gold letters.

'Yo, nigga!' 'Wade' shouted at Bald.

The American debussed. Bald had the unmistakable sense that things were about to turn ugly.

'Nigga! I'm talking to you. Answer me, bitch.'

Wade paraded around the Denali until he was standing shoulder to shoulder with Bald, and flashed a gold-toothed grin. Two of his mates were brandishing guns, ageing but effective 1911 single-fire semis. Introduced in 1911 by John Browning, and used in every war up to the mid-eighties, they were possibly the only firearm in the world that had seen more action than Bald. The fourth and fifth guys seemed unarmed. They were a good four or five years junior to Wade. Fifteen, sixteen. Not yet trusted by the elders to pack a piece.

'You ignoring me, son?' Wade asked Bald.

'Back off,' the American said. 'This doesn't concern you.'

'Sure it does.'

'How'd you figure that?'

'You trespassing.'

'It's a free country.'

'Not here it ain't. You got to pay the toll, muthafucka.'

'Fuck your toll.'

Wade pulled a screw face at the American. 'Fuck my what?'

'You deaf as well as stupid? Get out of my fucking way.'

Bald's abductor had a blank expression that suggested he was capable of anything you might imagine, and more than a few that you might not. He looked like he would butcher a family if the job called for it, and only pause for a moment if the family was his own. Wade lost the stare-down. Gave his back to Bald and the American. Wade and his gang buddies strolled macho-like back to the bungalow, chanting cuss-words as they retreated.

'Cracker-ass bitch.'

'Honky piece of shit.'

'Bitch-ass.'

The American stared at their backs. 'Black bastards. Can't get them to work, can't get them to stay out of trouble,' he said.

'This way.' He prodded the Five-Seven into the small of Bald's back. He forced him down an unlit alley sandwiched between a couple of crack houses. The passage wasn't clearly defined but was no more than a strip of grass worn down to a nub. The only light came from the half moon, and overhanging pines and palms obliterated most of its rays. Bald couldn't see more than eight or nine metres in front of him. The world was a cola fizzle of blackness pockmarked by distant house lights.

'Where are you taking me?' Bald demanded. But, deep in his coiled guts, he knew the answer.

'It's a bad idea for white folk to venture into this neck of the woods,' the American said. 'Especially Brits. They don't much care for Brits around these parts. All that slave history leaves a bad taste in the mouth.'

Pain rippled through Bald's skull. What a fucking shit way to end it.

'Last British guy that came down here? They fed him to the dogs.' Bald was having a hard time tuning in to the American. 'Weren't nothing left of the poor son of a bitch except some hair and bones. Folks said he was looking to score some dope, asked the wrong guy . . . *bam.*'

Twenty metres down the alley, the American said, 'Here is good.'

Bald stopped.

'On your knees,' said the American.

Bald sank to his knees.

'Open your mouth.'

Bald opened his mouth.

'You should have stayed in Scotland.'

'I didn't like the weather.'

The American shoved the Five-Seven's muzzle into Bald's open mouth. Put it in deep and at a fifteen-degree angle, so the tip of the muzzle was pushing into the roof of his mouth. He tasted the stainless steel. He eyeballed the American.

Closed his eyes.

thirty

2019 hours.

He heard the shot before he felt it. A split second later he could smell it. Smoked gunpowder and hot brass, flaring in his nostrils. Another half second after the shot and Bald could still feel his face, and he wasn't dead.

He opened his eyes. He could see moonlight on the edges of the palm trees. He could hear the thunder of distant traffic. The American was glancing across his shoulder. Back down the alley, to the direction of the shot. Bald put the shooter at fifty metres. Maybe a little more.

The gang, Bald thought.

'On your feet,' said the American.

But the gang was converging at the dark lip of the alley, fifty metres away. Three of them. The American turned to run. He reached out to drag Bald with him, Bald grabbed the Five-Seven with his left hand, turning his palm facing up and directing the pistol away from him. But the Yank still had his fingers wrapped around the grip and Bald countered with a bunched fist that landed solidly in the American's balls. Air windrushed out of his mouth, slack with shock. The blow had knocked him off balance. His bad right leg was throwing him backwards. He automatically relinquished the Five-Seven. It fell to the ground with a metallic clatter. The American dropped to his knees. Now Bald properly seized the Five-Seven.

Wade and his two mates were thirty metres away, the Beretta 92 glinting under the moon. Then the muzzle barked and flamed. Two rounds swooshed past Bald. Missed. Bald scrambled to his feet and broke into a sprint. Another shot broke the air. Bald heard the American grunt at his six o'clock.

Bald glanced over his shoulder. Dark liquid was oozing out of a ten-pence hole on the American's right arm. He toppled forward, smacked against the dirt. Blood fountained onto the scrubby grass. Three more shots. At Bald's six o'clock. Rounds hailed down. Bald turned away from the American. He had to get the fuck out of the slums. Stick around and he'd soon have a hundred more angry locals searching for him. Itching to tear him a dozen new arseholes.

'Shitting fuck!' the American yelled. His breathing was erratic, his face varnished in sweat. 'Don't leave me here.'

Bald ignored him and set off down the alley.

'Please,' the American said, his voice jumpy and desperate. 'I know what's really going on.'

'Bullshit.'

'They're lying to you.'

Fuck this, thought Bald.

Wade and a mate were twenty-five metres away, but the third gangster was the immediate threat. He was eight metres short of the American. Wade unloaded three more rounds from the Beretta. They zipped through the air and slapped into a fence four metres to Bald's right. The fence spat wooden mist in his face.

Now the nearest gangster was four metres from the American.

Bald dropped to one knee. Gripped the Five-Seven with both hands. The gangster was wielding a knife and arrowing it down at the American. Ready to give him the good news.

Two metres.

Bald unleashed two quick-fire rounds from the Five-Seven. Precious little recoil, to the point where he wondered if he'd actually discharged rounds, but they tore viciously into the guy's chest, one after the other. He tumbled silently, without protest, like he was grateful this business of living was over and done with. Bald rushed back to the American.

But Wade was still racing towards them at speed, his long-legged gait allowing him to leave his mate in his tracks. He moved in a zigzag fashion, making it harder for Bald to get a fix on him with the Five-Seven's sights. Now he was fifteen metres from the American, eighteen from Bald. He rushed diagonally across the alley, left to right. He had the barrel level with Bald.

Pulled the trigger.

White light flickered in front of Bald. Blinded him. Hot pain lacerated his left ear. Something hot and sticky was weeping down his ear and onto his neck. Now Wade was moving right to left. Still hanging low. Still moving diagonally. He was ten metres from Bald. Beretta still level with Bald's head.

But Wade had made the fatal mistake of not properly zeroing in on his target. You go to shoot somebody, make sure you have something small to aim for on their body. A necklace, a logo on a T-shirt. Aim for the small target and you're more likely to strike the big target surrounding it. That was weapons training basics, fundamental to an operator. But not to a street tough. The round thwacked into the ground to the right of Bald. Dread etched itself across Wade's face, like he'd been bitch-slapped. He realized he had blown his big chance.

A *ca-rack* and Wade's ankle shattered like a fucking Jenga block. Bits of ankle bone and ligament muscle dolloped out. His leg kept moving but his foot stayed where it was, nearly detached from the rest of the limb. Veins and muscle strung like goo between the two joints. Wade howled. Then he fucking stacked it.

Bald scrambled to his feet. The third gangster was bounding towards them. Bald levelled two luminous green dots on the Five-Seven's rear sight. The guy ducked for cover behind a dumpster. Bald squeezed the trigger. The moving parts inside the Five-Seven stressed and tensed.

He squeezed harder. The chambered bullet sprang its jacket out of the side ejector and ruptured the air. Struck the dumpster and went straight through it. The guy screamed. Bald put down three more rounds. The Five-Seven bullets were piercing through the dumpster like it was a wet paper bag. Blood pooled out from behind the dumpster, a black hole opening up. The screaming ceased. The guy had got his fucking ticket punched.

Wade was writhing on the ground, pawing at his ankle. His leg was in fucking rag order. He was whimpering like a dying dog. Bald kicked the Beretta and shoved the Five-Seven into the side of his head and trod on his busted ankle. Wade squealed like a stuck pig. Bald got a weird kick out of watching Wade's eyeballs bulge in their sockets.

'Looks like you're all alone, fuckface,' he said.

A voice came back to him. The one he could never silence. The one that he had heard more and more since he left the Regiment. Just because Laxman got away, doesn't mean I have to go home empty-handed.

He trod harder on Wade's ankle. Like he was grinding a cigarette butt. Wade gagged and choked. Bald applied a degree of pressure to the trigger.

'You got a fucking stash somewhere. Where is it?'

Wade flashed his most defiant face. But the giveaway was in his eyes. They were big and frightened. Bald pulled the Five-Seven away from Wade's head. The guy keeled over and alternated between choking to death and taking deep, greedy breaths of air. Now Bald grabbed him by his cornrows and said, 'Fucking tell me.'

A beat of silence in the alley, stippled only by the shouts of angry neighbours, the hyperactive squawk of a car alarm. Then Wade locked eyes with Bald and said, 'In about five minutes you're gonna have half the neighbourhood coming down on your crackerjack bitch-ass.'

'Wrong. In about five minutes I'll be fucking long gone.'

Bald hauled Wade to his feet and shoved the Five-Seven into his mouth again. This time he cocked the hammer with his right thumb. Tempted the trigger back a little. He could feel the resistance in the weapon, the various moving parts ready to snap and discharge the chambered 5.7x28mm round. The gangster's tears and saliva were binding at the barrel and forming a soapy foam. Bald removed the Five-Seven.

'Where is it?'

'Shit! Cool the fuck down, nigga.'

'Where can I find the stash?'

'I ain't telling you shit.'

Something made Bald look round at the American.

Then he spun around. Saw several Rorschach splotches of blood across the ground. Saw the alley unfolding up ahead: strewn trash and weeds and darkness. But he did not see the American.

He'd disappeared.

thirty-one

'Lost your friend, bitch?' Wade's voice hacked.

Something flipped inside Bald. It had been burning slowly, cloistered in his guts for days, fuelled by every drop of alcohol and missed opportunity for a fuck. With the sleeper now gone and taking Bald's five-million-quid payday with him, the rage exploded.

He smashed the Five-Seven's butt down on the back of Wade's head. The blow left a groove an inch and a half wide and a quarter of an inch deep. Wade mouthed his pain into the dirt. Bald grabbed him by his cornrows and thrust him upright. Wade's fucked-up foot touched the ground and he howled again. Without painkillers the agony would quickly become unbearable.

'Where's the fucking stash?'

'OK, OK.' Wade couldn't get the words out quickly enough now. 'There's this place across the block. A connect. Goes by the name of Leon.'

'On your feet. We'll pay Leon a visit.'

'He don't deal with strangers.'

'He's not going to see me, fuckface. Just you.'

Sniffing now, his eyes watering, his lips shivering, his nose sticky with snot, Wade meekly picked himself off the ground and hopped at gunpoint down the alley. Bald kept the Five-Seven six inches from the back of his head. After fifty metres they emerged from the other end of the alley onto Pike Street. It was eerily vacant. The lights on every house were extinguished. Everything that could be locked and latched and shut, was. The porch seats abandoned. Bald guessed the residents in this neighbourhood were familiar enough with gang violence to know the drill. Stay indoors and keep your fucking head down. It'd be a short while before someone plucked up the courage to call the cops. Until then Bald had the streets to himself. Well, himself and Wade. The gangster had given up the tough-guy front. He whined and rasped with every draw of breath.

Wade hopped ahead of Bald down Pike until they came upon a modest single-storey home flanked by a column of stripped-back palm trees and foregrounded by a weed-scarred lawn. Empty Coca-Cola cans and malt beer bottles rolled on the steps of the flaking white porch.

Bald pushed Wade up the porch steps. They stopped in front of the door. A chicken-wire screen covered the main door. Bald flipped the screen door open, shoved Wade up to the main door and knocked briskly. Footsteps decanted through the door.

'Who is it?' a voice echoed.

'Me, yo,' Wade said. 'Open up for your boy.'

The door cracked open a couple of inches. Whoever was inside lived a life fuelled by paranoia and fear. The guy inside clocked only Wade's face. Didn't see Bald.

'Who the fuck bitch-slapped you, son?'

'There's a white—'

Bald thrust Wade through the gap and booted the door wide open with his left foot. Wade nosedived into the corridor, the guy inside backed up, and in the same motion Bald was training his Five-Seven on the guy. He instinctively raised his hands. He was twenty-five or thereabouts with a buzzcut shaven down to the scalp at the front in the shape of a 'G'. He wore a long white vest and silver San Antonio Spurs basketball shorts that curtained down to his ankles. The guy hung in the doorway for a second, his eyes flicking from Wade's wounded leg to Bald.

'No offence, bro,' the guy said, shifting on the balls of his feet. 'But you don't know who you're fucking with. This is Red's stash, yo.'

'Give me the coke,' said Bald.

The guy grimaced.

'Fucking do it.'

The guy weighed up his options. Bald tightened his grip on the trigger to show he meant business. The guy took another look at Wade. Then he reluctantly edged back from Bald, stepping in reverse down the corridor. He almost tripped up over Wade's prone figure. Regained his balance and ducked into a kitchen bathed in UV light. Bald looked back out of the front door and across the street. The warning signs in his head told him that Wade's gang mates would be here any minute. He looked back at the kitchen. Cockroaches scuttled across the laminated wood floor.

'I'm a find you, I'm a put a fucking bullet in you,' Wade said.

Bald said, 'Don't make promises you can't keep.'

'Nah, fuck that. Me and my boys, we gonna hold you down, cut you up with an axe.'

'These boys friends of yours? Like your mates in the alley?'

The sound of a safe being unlocked reached Bald. Music to his ears.

A Rottweiler burst out of the kitchen door. Pure muscle. It throttled towards Bald, and he pumped four rounds into its belly. The dog yelped. It didn't die, but worked itself up into a frantic, lurching growl, swiping its heavy paws at thin air. Its right ear was blown completely off. Its nose was like a plum chopped in half and drooled blood over its teeth. Bald couldn't believe the fucking thing was still alive. It was just two metres from him now and launching itself into the air, snarling and giving him a view of its saliva-coated teeth. He pumped a round into its mouth. That did the trick. The Rottweiler whimpered and dropped. Its jaws slackened; the rump of its belly inflated and deflated like a bellows. It whined, lamely pawing at the bullets stitched across its belly.

'My fucking dog,' the guy screamed from the kitchen.

'Get out of here now with the shit, before I give you and Rover a premature reunion.'

The guy trudged tearfully back down the corridor. He was carrying a brown paper bag and two bricks of coke, each one shrinkwrapped and the size of a hardcover book. He stopped beside Wade and slid the bricks and the paper bag along the floor towards Bald. He bent down, eyes never veering from Wade and the stash guy, and scooped up both bricks with his left hand. Stuff looked pure. Had to be a sell-on value north of fifty thousand dollars. Bald looked inside the paper bag. It was choc full of wads of hundred-dollar bills. Bald thumbed one of the wads. Had to be two hundred Benjamins to each wad. Twenty gees per wad. Four wads in the bag. Eighty large. He dumped everything in a Nike sports bag propped up by the side of the front door. Zipped it up and shouldered the bag.

'We'll find you,' the stash guy said.

'Chop you up,' Wade added.

'I doubt it,' said Bald.

'Shit, man, you're taking my livelihood. This is my business,' stash guy said.

'You won't be needing it any more,' said Bald.

He put a single round through the guy's head. He dropped like gravity had doubled under his feet and landed side by side with Wade, who screamed like a little bitch. Bald put a round through Wade's skull too. No witnesses. Cleaner that way. Then he bugged out. Closed the door. Four minutes later he was pacing along Vine Street and putting a healthy distance between himself and the slums. His burner vibrated in his pocket. He checked the display. Hit the answer key. His fingers reeked of gun smoke.

'Is it over?'

Rachel.

Bald struggled to hear her above the police sirens approaching the ghetto. Bald doubled his pace. 'It's over,' he lied. He still had his eyes on that shag.

A sigh of relief breezed down the line.

'Where are you now?' Rachel's voice was perking up.

'Vine Street.'

'Wait there. I'll come pick you up. I think it's about time you unwrapped your present now, don't you?'

thirty-two

Rachel had a room at the Hilton St Petersburg Carillon Park, about twelve miles south and east of Clearwater and pissing distance from St Petersburg International Airport. Bald didn't say a word during the drive. He was fucking knackered. He thought of the drugs concealed in the Nike bag currently nestled between his feet, and how good it would feel to finally nail Rachel. Things were working out after all. He gazed out across Tampa Bay. The sky was percolating its charcoal blackness into the water. Moonlight shards lay like spent brass on the still water.

They parked in the underground lot. Rachel excused herself and stepped out of the car to take a call. Bald reached into the back seat and retrieved the gym bag loaded with cash and passports. He waited until Rachel's back was turned, then he transferred both coke and the paper bag into the gym bag. He had mates in Miami, contacts he'd made on the Circuit, and he knew they would definitely be interested in snapping up the gear wholesale. Once Bald was done ploughing Miss Florida he'd drop those guys a line.

He was zipping up the bag as Rachel returned to the Chrysler.

'All set?' she asked. Bald nodded and eased his exhausted frame out of the car. Each muscle seemed to have been taken apart and clumsily put back together. It hurt to walk, it hurt to breathe.

It was gone 2245 hours when Rachel slid the card into the door of room 221. Vanilla light flushed over soft-focus, inoffensive furnishings and smoothed-out cream sheets adorning a double bed. The room smelled of detergent and pot-pourri.

Bald shut the door and drew Rachel close to him. Wasted no time getting to work on her clothes. He ripped off her blouse and felt something hot spill open in his guts.

'You like to play dirty?' she said. 'I like dirty too.'

Bald cast off his T-shirt and let Rachel lock herself around him. She took turns tonguing him and chewing his bottom lip like it was a piece of gum. She dragged her fingernails down his back. Bald leaned in to kiss her. She shoved him back onto the bed. She peeled off her skirt and kicked off her shoes and pounced onto the bed. She slid his jeans off and crawled up him until her nose was touching his.

She breathed violently into his ear. She smothered his face in the warm fold of her tits for a long and blissful moment before pulling herself up straight and sliding her thighs across Bald's arms so that she was pinning him down at the elbows. She pressed her lips against his and breathed hot, almond air over him.

'I like to be beat,' she whispered. 'I like to be told I'm a bad girl.'

She lifted up her right knee, giving Bald just enough space to manoeuvre his left arm. He reached around to her arse and spanked it. She froze for a moment. Then she did something he didn't expect. She spat on his cheek and followed it up with a harsh slap across the same spot.

'I said *beat*.' Rachel's voice was laced with aggression. 'Not *spank*. Jeez, fucking hit me.'

For a second Bald figured she was play-acting. But the look in her eyes told him otherwise.

'Hit me, you fucking dick. Hit me so hard I bleed. I wanna feel the pain.'

She slapped Bald on the pecs. 'You wanna fuck me?' she said. 'Then do it.'

So Bald struck her on the face. His knuckles connected with the triangle of her cheekbone. A soft, high-pitched scream escaped from her mouth. She shied away from Bald and for a moment he thought he'd gone too far. That maybe she had been fooling around. Then she slowly angled her head back at Bald. The soft-focus lights coloured in her features and gave the purpled bruises on her face a pretty sheen. Her cheek had swollen up like a rotten pear. She seemed – not angry. Not even upset. More like – disappointed.

'I know you can do better than that, John.' Her eyes hardened. 'Hit me again. Harder this time.'

Bald slugged her across the chin. His knuckle joints were on fire. That told him he'd given her a proper smack-up this time. Job done, he shaped to tear off her bra and get down to the serious business of fucking. But she interrupted him and said, 'Choke me, John. Put your hands around my neck and squeeze tight. I want to feel like I can't breathe when you're inside me.'

Now Bald locked his hands around her neck and applied a degree of pressure to her air passage. Her mouth evicted a peculiar sound into the sheets. Not quite a groan and not quite a pained noise. More like a satisfied moan.

'Yeah, that's it. Come on, big boy. More. I want you to fucking choke me.'

Bald squeezed harder. Her skin blued.

Then she started beating with her fists at his hands and her eyes were almost popping out of her skull and she was retching and kicking at him with all her strength. Bald released his grip from her neck. She had new bruises either side of her throat, deep and dark, like he had pressed his fingers into a piece of bruised fruit. She crawled out of bed and nursed her neck. Said, 'Jesus, that fucking hurts. You asshole.'

Bald looked at her quizzically.

'But you said you wanted it.'

'God, that really fucking hurt,' Rachel said. She stumbled out of the bed and took her clutch bag and disappeared into the bathroom. Locked the door behind her. Women confused the shit out of Bald at the best of times, but Rachel's flip-out had him scratching his head. He pulled the duvet over his balls and listened to the noises coming from the bathroom. Running water. Probably washing off some of the blood. Something in the trash can caught Bald's attention. Amid the empty wrappers and tissues there was a vial. The kind of thing a doctor prescribes. It struck Bald as odd.

He scooped the vial out of the trash and inspected the label on the front. Then his guts did somersaults. He suddenly understood why Rachel hadn't been drunk in the bar last night, even while she matched him drink for drink, shot for shot.

The vial contained ephedrine.

The bathroom door unlocked. Bald quickly dumped the vial in the trash can. Rachel hovered in the bathroom doorway. Her face caught the fluorescent bathroom light. Strands of her blonde hair were glowing white-hot, like flames peeling off the surface of the sun. The light picked out Bald's handiwork: every bruise and welt, every cut and graze.

There was a gun in her hand. A pistol. A Browning Hi-Power. A weapon Bald was instantly familiar with, because for a long time it had been Regiment-issue. But the Browning wasn't so popular in America. It wasn't the kind of firearm you could pick up in your local Wal-Mart or gun show. It was more of a specialist, collector's piece. Part of him wondered where Rachel had managed to acquire the Browning. The other part of him went limp at the waist and wondered if she had the strength to pull the fucking trigger. He hoped not.

Rachel said, 'Get up.'

Bald stayed put. 'Stop pointing that fucking thing at me.'

'I'm not playing games, John.'

She cocked the hammer.

Said, 'I'll ask you one last time. If you like your balls, you'll get up.'

Bald liked his balls. Bald stood up.

Then she warily shuffled closer to Bald, the Browning trembling in her hand, her lips copycatting. The discomfort at walking was written deep into her face. Into the frown bunched up on the bridge of her nose, and the delicate wincing noises that escaped from the corners of her badly swollen mouth.

She stopped a metre short of Bald. Hand extended, the Browning barrel tip was less than half that distance to Bald's forehead. A simple slip of the finger, a little too much pressure. That's all it would take.

Bald said, 'Can we fuck now?'

She smiled at him through the blood and the bruises.

'No. I'm going to kill you, baby. Just like you killed Laxman.'

thirty-three

Rachel Kravets sniffed blood. It bubbled under her nostrils. One was bigger than the other. Not a natural disfigurement, but one that John Bald had moulded into her face with the clenched knuckles of his right hand.

She cocked the Browning Hi-Power. Springs and coils and all sorts of pistol machinery made metallic clicking noises. Bald stayed absolutely still. The way Rachel handled the gun told him she was an amateur, despite working for the CIA. Maybe Agency cutbacks meant field agents didn't get time on the ranges any more. But an amateur with a weapon to your head is a bad thing.

For a slippery second Bald had figured that Rachel's stunt was all part of the game. Of the fantasy that she'd ditch the Browning and get down on her knees and start giving him the BJ from heaven. But the second greased Bald with a surprise. Rachel's eyes were fixed on the TV, where the local Fox News affiliate was reporting on the shooting incident in Ghetto Central, Clearwater. A far too excited and happy reporter gave the lowdown on what they described as a gangland shooting. They listed four dead gangbangers, complete with photo IDs. Bald had been too far away to recall the faces of the guys he shot, but the police seem to have got the basic facts straight enough.

Then Rachel screwed up her face at the screen. Her eyes slowly returned to Bald.

She said, 'What happened to Laxman's body?'

Confession time. Bald had been hoping he could get away with the lie, at least for long enough to jump Rachel. But the report had driven a train through his story.

'There is no body,' he said.

Rachel dug out a face that Bald had seen on too many women down the years. Black with anger and looking at him like he was dirt. Like he'd just admitted to smashing her best friend behind her back.

'There's no body, because I didn't kill Laxman. He got away.'

Rachel's expression unwrapped like a crumpled ball of paper and turned straight and pale and vacant. She lowered the gun. Then she warily edged across the room, scooped up her iPhone from the desk and called a number. Bald could make out the voice of Danny Cave, coughing and warbling down the line from London. Almost four o'clock in the morning UK time. Rachel took the call out to the corridor, telling Bald, 'Wait here.'

Five minutes later Rachel returned. Colour had drifted back onto her face and she had an uneven smile. Like one side of her was trying to smile and the other wasn't putting in the effort. She held the face and said, 'Cave says you have to fly to Libya.'

'Fuck off.'

'He says you have to track down Shylam Laxman and finish the mission.'

'Fuck off twice.'

'He says you do this or you can wave goodbye to your freedom and your pay cheque.'

Bald realized he had no choice but to agree. Someone had you by the balls, either you did what they wanted or they squeezed tight until they burst.

'Oh, and another thing. You'll like this, baby. Cave says I'm coming with. The Agency wants their own set of eyes on the ground on this one.'

Bald nodded absently, then said, 'You were just playing back there, right? With the pistol?'

Rachel smiled sweetly at him. 'Sure, baby. I was playing.'

thirty-four

The first thing Bald saw in Libya was a plume of smoke. It slow-motioned down a bombed-out two-lane stretch of asphalt. Could have been a kilometre; could as easily have been two, or twenty. There were no other features against which to judge the distance of such an object. Just a basin of finely ground sand and a limitless sky. Bald gripped the wheel of the Land Rover Defender 90 as it hopped and pitched and lurched over a million craters and divots – the legacy of NATO air strikes – the 2.4-litre diesel engine *grrring* like a cornered dog.

The smoke plume spiralled lazily into the sky. Bald was doing a hundred kilometres per hour but he didn't seem to be getting any nearer. It remained stubbornly suspended on the horizon. Always out of reach.

Rachel was cursing at her iPhone in the front passenger seat. She had a pashmina shawl scarf wrapped around her head to cover up her hair. The Arab Spring gangs were ready for democracy, but not the exposed female form which still caused them problems.

He said, 'Any luck reaching Cave?'

'Still no signal.'

'Typical for the Firm. They spend millions on lampshades,

but then they go and give you a phone that can't get a fucking signal.'

Rachel attempted a smile, then quickly retracted it, her sore face paining her to move. 'I'll keep trying. His message said it was important.'

'It'll have to wait,' said Bald.

'Why?'

'We've got company.'

Insects on the horizon. Four of them. No bigger than cockroaches. Heat flourished off the asphalt and blurred their outlines. They came from the same direction as the smoke plume. From where Bald was sitting he couldn't yet see their faces. One hundred metres from your enemy, you can make out distinguishing features such as noses and hair. At three hundred metres, you can tell whether a guy is white or black, whether he's broad in the shoulders or heavy in the gut. At six hundred metres, all you get is a roughly human smudge. Bald counted four shapes and concluded they were six hundred metres distant. They were on foot, but next to them was a vehicle. Likely a Toyota Hilux. Mid-nineties edition. There was a large object mounted on the rear bed. Thing was shaped like an oversized party popper.

'Who are they?' Rachel said.

'Rebels or loyalists. It's a fifty-fifty call.'

'What do we do?'

'If it's the rebels, we'll be fine.'

'And if it's the loyalists?'

'We fucking leg it.'

The insects grew as Bald kept the Defender at a steady hundred per and steered towards them. Three hundred metres. They were static and arranged across the road, blocking traffic in both directions. A checkpoint.

Two hundred metres. Now he could see their clothes. The band around his chest began to loosen. The guys were wearing beige and dark T-shirts and stonewashed jeans and trainers that had been white in a previous life.

'Definitely rebels,' said Bald.

'How can you be sure?'

'They're not in uniform. They look like they're going to Magaluf.'

She worked her brow into a frown and said, 'What's Magaluf?'

'It's a place where Brits go to get drunk and fight and shag.'

'Oh, right. Because you guys don't do enough of that in your own country.'

Her quip helped slacken the tension a little. At a hundred metres the rebel faces coloured in and the rifles each man was holding took on the distinct, lethal outlines of AK-47 assault rifles.

At fifty metres Bald wound the Defender down to thirty-five k per, to indicate to the guys that he didn't plan on smashing through the checkpoint. But they raised their AK-47s at the vehicle.

The Hilux's bodywork was spotted with rust but the colours striped around it were clearly visible. Bands of red, green and black. The colours of the new Libyan flag under the National Transitional Council. The windscreen was starred and the roof had a dent in it like a crushed drink can.

Forty metres now and Bald was able to put a name to the party popper mounted on the cargo bed. It was a UB-32 57mm rocket launcher. An air-to-ground weapon normally fitted to Soviet SU-20 fighter planes and helicopters and capable of firing thirty-two unguided rockets at ground targets. It was pointing skywards at forty-five degrees.

At thirty metres Bald made out the features of the four men. They all wore the same tense, animated look. They could smell victory in the air but they were too green and high on adrenaline to appreciate, as he did, that the peace would be more difficult than the war. One guy was older than the rest, in his late thirties or early forties. Black hair matted and greased, eyes beginning to show the strain. Barrel chest, arms like slabs of beef. He didn't possess an AK. Just a holstered pistol, his right hand resting loosely on the exposed grip. He had a beard that looked like something a cat had coughed up. Former army, Bald figured. Probably the leader of this ragtag crew.

Then Beard stepped forward, held up his palm at Bald. *Stop.* Bald brought the Land Rover to a halt fifteen metres from Beard and his buddies. He kept the engine ticking. He felt his delt and lat muscles stiffen and contort, like metal twisting around metal.

The smoke on the horizon slimmed to a thread.

Beard held his ground.

Bald removed his hands from the wheel and leaned across and pulled out a Union Jack flag from the glove box. The flag would alert the freedom fighters that Bald and Rachel were friendlies and not hostiles.

Then he saw a wave of colour in his rear-view mirror. White. The edges were all out of focus. It drew along the road at a good speed, eighty or ninety k per, sunlight rebounding off the bodywork. A flag flew at mast from the antenna. Rebel colours. At a hundred metres Bald could see a .50-calibre heavy machine-gun mounted on the rear cab, a couple of weedy guys manning it. At fifty he could make out the overlapping ovals of the Toyota badge. It was screwed to a grille big enough to roast a pig on. At a distance of forty metres the Land Cruiser ground to a halt and three guys, dressed in the same get-up as the crew at the Hilux, armed likewise with AK-47s, debussed.

Bald realized he was surrounded.

Then Beard strode purposefully across the asphalt and closed the fifteen-metre divide to one. In the same quick-draw motion he whipped out the pistol from his holster. Bald was close enough to see the fine, individual details on the weapon. It had a short barrel and a polished wooden grip and a run of slanted grooves at the base of the barrel arranged in a //////////// pattern.

Makarov semi-automatic.

There was a pause of near silence. The engine ticked. Bald felt his heart ticking inside his chest too. He was conscious of several angry voices shouting in Arabic at his twelve o'clock.

'Hands in the air,' Beard said.

Bald ditched the flag and told Rachel, 'Do as he says. No sudden movements.' Beard and his buddies were hopped up, looked like the kind of soldiers who were trig-ger-happy. Bald didn't plan on doing anything that would give them reason to open fire.

Spent brass glinted on the asphalt. The other three guys from the Hilux were walking steadily towards them. AK-47s still raised, stocks tucked into their shoulders, dark eyes peering down iron sights.

Beard looked at Bald. 'Where are you from?'

'Scotland.'

'What about her?'

'America,' said Rachel.

Beard's men stopped ten metres from Bald and Rachel. He acknowledged them and waved to the guys still inside the Land Cruiser. Then he said, 'Step out of the car.'

Bald said, 'Don't do anything stupid.'

Beard sneered. 'I know exactly what I'm doing.'

Bald delicately moved his left hand down to the door latch. Or as delicately as is possible for a guy who peaked out at six-three and weighed fourteen and a half stone. He tugged on the latch. The door gave a sigh as it released. He pushed it open and swivelled around ninety degrees so his legs were hanging over the edge of the vehicle, then he eased himself off the seat and dropped to the ground. Rachel followed moments later, equally slowly.

The heat quickly made itself felt. Now Beard was prodding the Makarov at Bald's chest. Spit flew out of his mouth as he said, 'This way! This way!'

He was pointing at the desert.

Bald said, 'This is a big fucking mistake.'

'No, my friend,' said Beard. 'The mistake you make is invading my fucking country.'

There was no point putting up a fight. There was even less point trying to run for it. Four freedom fighters at the Hilux and another five at the Land Cruiser. Six guys packing AK-47s. Two guys behind a machine-gun with rounds so big and powerful they could sever a fucking limb with one quick blast.

They were marched off the road. The ground was dusty and loose. The heat wriggled its way into Bald's trainers and singed the undersides of his feet. They walked across the desert. Bald glanced across his shoulder. The Land Rover had shrunk to the size of a remote-controlled car.

They stopped, finally. Bald didn't know how far they had come. Far enough that the road was a lizard's tail on the horizon, thin and curled.

Beard had the Makarov by his side and said, 'Who first?'

Bald said nothing.

Rachel said nothing.

Then Beard thrust the tip of the Makarov against the side of Bald's temple. A circle of cold on his sunburnt flesh. Bald kept his eyes on Beard. On his index finger, tensing around the trigger.

'You die first,' Beard told him.

thirty-five

0701 hours.

'They're watching me,' Bald said. 'If you do something stupid, they won't be fucking happy.'

Beard hit the pause button on his trigger finger. 'Who is watching?' he demanded.

Bald sensed a seed of doubt and said, 'NATO, you fucking idiot. I'm here to help you.'

'Liar! You are both spies.'

Bald rolled his eyes for effect. 'For fuck's sake. I've got orders from the top brass at NATO to come here. They told me you guys needed my help.'

'Help?'

'Training. Explosives. Counter-sniper tactics. How to kill people. That's my game.'

'No one told us you would come.'

'We're here now. Deal with it.' Bald concentrated on giving a world-class performance in bullshit. The more convinced you looked of your lies, the more likely you were to get away with it. He eyefucked Beard and did his best to look pissed off.

Beard shifted his feet uneasily.

'What about her?' he nodded at Rachel.

'Human rights observer,' Bald said before Rachel could

open her mouth. 'She's here to make sure *I* don't do anything stupid.'

Bald had heard all the rumours about the CIA rendering hundreds of Libyan dissidents in the paranoia-fuelled years after the Twin Towers came down. Half the fucking NTC leadership had spent time flying Torture Class on a Gulfstream. Everyone in the private security gig knew it, and Bald figured that revealing that Rachel worked for the Agency wasn't likely to go down well with Beard and his mates.

Beard shook his head. 'We don't need help. This is our fight.'

'Then why would they fucking send me?' said Bald. He could see the Makarov faltering in Beard's hand. 'Your fucking war, not mine. You've still got about a hundred fucking towns ready to bring out the bunting for the Gaddafi-welcome-home party. It'll take you months and cost thousands of your men to secure them all, but fuck it.'

Beard ran his eyes up and down Bald, as if seeing him for the first time. But he kept the Makarov level with Bald's head.

'If NATO sent you, why you don't wear uniform? You don't have gun?'

Bald glanced up at the sky. The sun was nowhere and everywhere. Heat fireballed down over the desert, licked at his face. Sweat drenched his arms and back and his balls.

Bald said, 'I'm ex-British Army.'

'Why they send someone retired?'

Bald said, 'Blame the fucking politicians. They promised no boots on the ground. Guys like me, strictly speaking, we're not soldiers – just hired hands. So the suits get to keep their bullshit promise, and I get to teach dickwads like you how to beat Gaddafi.'

'We were in the army,' Beard said. 'We know how to fight.'

'But I can teach you how to *win*.' Bald laughed scathingly. Took a step towards Beard. Then another. 'You want to win the war, don't you?'

Bald was standing six inches from Beard now. Could smell the foul body sweat and tobacco clinging to his skin. He noticed a scar on the guy's neck. Similar to the one Carlos Tévez had. Beard said, 'You have no paperwork. You are not in uniform. There is no one to back up your story.' He gestured to his men. 'How can I trust you?'

Bald pointed to the sky. 'Right now there's an unmanned spy drone 20,000 metres above us. There are cameras on board looking down on me now. There are people in London and Washington keeping tabs on those cameras. Live feeds.'

Beard paused and said, 'Spy drone?'

Bald said, 'Like I said, I'm here to help you.'

'Gaddafi is a bad man.'

'Yes, he is.'

'A very bad man.'

Beard wavered for a moment longer. Then he made a cutting movement with his left hand, and his men lowered their rifles. Bald's bluff had paid off. Beard started grinning. His mouth was a black hole, his teeth mostly missing. The few he had left were brown stubs, like cashew nuts.

'My name is Younes,' he said, offering Bald his ample hand. Bald accepted it. Firm grip, rough palm, brief. 'We come from Benghazi. We were the first to rise against Gaddafi.'

'John,' said Bald. 'This is Rachel.'

Younes gave Rachel the traditional warm Arabic greeting from man to woman, and pretended she didn't exist.

He plucked a Turkish cigarette from a crumpled packet, which partly explained to Bald the rank smell coming off the guy, and said, 'We are *Kateeba*.'

'What does that mean?'

'*Kateeba* are the most experienced brigades of all the rebels. But there are not so many of us. We are overstretched. You say you are Special Forces. Then you are worth ten soldiers. A man like you could make a big difference.'

'Our orders are to get to Tripoli.'

'Then you are just in time. Our brothers are taking control of the city right at this moment. We will take you there.'

'Won't be necessary. Just tell me the way.'

'You won't make it alone. The Brother Leader still controls many towns and villages. Only we can take you and your friend across safely.'

Younes barked at his men in Arabic and they shot towards the Hilux in loose formation. Bald watched Rachel head back to the Land Rover, then said, 'You still call Gaddafi the fucking Brother Leader?'

Younes smiled apologetically. 'I mean "that piece-of-shit tyrant". Forgive me. It is hard to lose habits after forty years. Even when they are bad ones.'

The rebels led the way. The Hilux took the lead, with the Land Cruiser a constant twenty metres behind. Bald and Rachel, in the Land Rover, tail-end-Charlied the convoy. The vehicles gunned down the highway, never dropping below 90 as they pushed through the land. At Bald's east, over his right shoulder, was undulating desert the colour and texture of rawhide. Flat, hot, dust-laden. In the far distance he could make out a wash of mountains lengthening out into a plateau. West and north-west, across his left, was the Mediterranean. Endless blue. Imprisoning the land, rather than freeing it. The few towns they did pass through were brutal, sunbaked backwaters, with a mosque here and a Gaddafi monument there. Each town was as empty as a shopping-mall parking lot after closing time.

Bald was in a foul mood. He'd not had time to hook up with his Miami connect before departing St Petersburg, meaning he had to leave two bricks of coke with a wholesale value of more than fifty large left in the hotel room, and the money too – he couldn't fully well secrete eighty thousand bucks on his person without alerting Rachel, who would no doubt bitch up the food chain to Daniel Cave about his side business. He left the coke and the cash with a heavy heart, and the consolation that if he completed the job, the size of the reward on the table would make the $130,000 drug stash look like pocket shrapnel.

Zawiyah was the last major town before Tripoli. The highway suddenly degraded into a black smear, like a tar pit. They were travelling through Bomb Central. Before, the landscape had been mostly flat. Here it was just flat, pounded that way by hundreds of thousands of pounds of munitions.

Bald glanced at his Aquaracer. 0845 hours. A little over three hours since they had left the refugee town of Allouet el Gounna in Tunisia and raced for the border. Gaddafi's regime was in its death throes, but the border crossing at Ra's Ajdir, on Libya's northernmost tip, was still closed. So Bald had decided to risk crossing open land outside

Allouet el Gounna, eight kilometres to the south. He'd
figured that Gaddafi's loyalist homeboys had more important shit on their minds than running border patrols.

They nudged past Zawiyah and were now forty kilometres from Tripoli. Rachel finally got a signal on her
iPhone, a fact announced by an irritating ringtone that
made Bald want to eat his own face. Rachel hit Answer.
A voice warbled something or other, then Rachel handed
Bald the phone and said, 'He wants to talk to you.'

Meaning Cave.

Bald reluctantly accepted the iPhone. Steered with his
right hand, spoke with his left.

'You're a lucky man, John Boy.' Cave's voice was flecked
with static.

'A bunch of rebels almost fucking killed us,' said Bald.

'Yet you're still alive. And guess what? You're going to
get to Tripoli just in time for the big show.' Cave took
Bald's silence for ignorance and went on, 'Operation
Mermaid Dawn is happening as we speak. In a few hours
Tripoli will have fallen.'

There was a sudden rush of air. A Boeing F-15E
Strike Eagle whooshed high in the sky, drowning out
the engine growl and Cave. Bald glimpsed the fighter
jet scudding overhead, impossibly small against the
sky, like a dust mote.

Cave went on, 'A short while ago we made contact
with people on the ground. In Benghazi. They disguised
themselves as fishermen and entered Tripoli by sea.
They've been waiting for the signal. We had our own
sleeper network right in the heart of Gaddafi's empire.'
He sounded pleased with himself. Bald imagined Cave
in his swanky office, dainty feet perched on the edge of

his expensive desk, smug grin plastered over his much too cleanly shaven face.

'Most of the city has fallen by now,' Cave continued. 'Fucking great, isn't it? Gaddafi's boys saw the writing on the wall and melted away, just like that.'

Bald heard Cave click his fingers for effect, then said, 'But why do I care?'

'Parts of the city are still dangerous,' Cave answered. 'Lots of snipers. Running battles with the hardcore mob. You must get to Laxman first. Foreigners aren't safe in Tripoli right now. If Laxman gets kidnapped, the technology will fall into Gaddafi's hands. He might see the dust as the only way of winning the war.'

'So where do I find Laxman?'

'That's why I'm calling. He flew out of Tampa on a fake passport. It's just been red-flagged on a hotel reservation system. The Mansour Hotel. He's posing as a journalist. Name of Moussa Al-Nasr. You'll enjoy the company at the hotel. All those journos are based there. BBC, CNN, Sky.'

'Who's he making the handover to? Rupert fucking Murdoch?'

'There might be a future for you in stand-up,' dead-panned Cave. 'No. Of course, the journalism thing is just a front. But we believe the handover will happen tomorrow: 1420 hours on the dot.'

'But you won't tell me who he's smuggling the dust to.'

'He's in Libya,' Cave reminded Bald. 'Who do you think?'

Bald came up blank.

'We think it's Gaddafi,' Cave said. He paused, but not long enough for Bald to get a word in. 'Now get to Laxman before the Colonel's heavies do. Do it right, mate, and we'll do all right by you too. Remember. The Firm takes care of its own, John Boy.'

Cave killed the line and Bald handed the iPhone back to Rachel, who was still pretending not to overhear. She stashed it away and settled back into her seat. She looked as tired as Bald felt. She'd crashed out the moment they had stepped off the Gulfstream in Remada, a garrison town on the south-eastern tip of Tunisia, and hit the road. She'd also slept the moment they had stepped onto the Gulfstream on a private airfield in Kathleen, east of Clearwater. Eleven hours on the flight, another two on the ground. Thirteen hours' sleep, all told. All that ephedrine in her bloodstream, it was going to catch up with her sooner or later.

Two kilometres beyond Zawiyah they arrived at a rebel checkpoint. Plastic barriers blocked both lanes of traffic. The checkpoint had been set up in the shadow of a monument venerating Gaddafi. It was covered in Arabic writing and looked like a smaller, lamer version of the Arc de Triomphe. A pair of rebel soldiers stood between the barriers, AK-47s dangling at their hips.

Gunfire crackled in the distance. Celebratory or hostile, it was hard to say. Younes and his men got out of the Hilux. The three soldiers hung around the checkpoint while Younes lit another tab and gestured for Bald to join him.

'Wait here,' Bald said to Rachel, nudging the Land Rover to a halt four metres to the rear of the Hilux. His gaze was drawn to half a dozen wounded rebels slumped against the body of a bombed T-72 tank. Their legs and arms were in fucking rag order. One guy's nose had been blown apart. Flaps of charred skin were peeled open down the middle, and he had a serrated black triangle where the bone used to be.

Bald approached Younes through the cloud of Turkish cigarette smoke. It was spicy and at the same time smelled like a goat's arse, and it got him asking himself what crap the manufacturers were putting in them.

'I have news from Tripoli,' said Younes. 'It is good. Our brothers have taken most of the city. Only a few pockets of resistance remain. They are planning to attack the compound at Bab al-Azizya today.'

'I don't care about the compound. I need to find a guy.'

Younes flashed a face at Bald. He'd allowed him passage, but his demeanour suggested that was where his friendliness both began and finished. 'This is Tripoli. Everyone is trying to find someone.'

Bald worked his body into a combative stance. 'This guy' – his voice was low, gravelly and lethal – 'he's a NATO contact. If I don't get to him, your bosses will hang you from the nearest lamppost.'

Younes cleared his throat. 'What is his name?'

'That's none of your business. Just tell me how to get to the Mansour Hotel.'

Younes suddenly developed a painful itch on his elbow. He was scratching it as he said, 'I will speak with my comrades. They know the situation on the ground better than me. But I can promise nothing.'

'Tell that to the NATO chiefs, pal.'

Younes nodded and hurried over to a senior-looking guy standing to the left of the checkpoint some ten metres from where Bald was standing. The man was of a similar age as Younes, had tousled hair and was dressed in a much more obvious uniform. Higher up the food chain, Bald presumed. The man and Younes immediately began an excitable conversation, taking turns to point furiously at the sky and then towards Tripoli on the horizon.

Bald kicked dirt and chewed tarmac and waited impatiently for Younes and his mucker to finish their lovers' tiff. Younes folded his arms and said something the other guy didn't like. He spat on the ground, gave Younes his back and walked towards Bald.

'What's the score?' Bald asked.

'The hotel you wish to go to . . .'

'The Mansour?'

'It's in the east of the city. Not far. But the route is very dangerous. Many loyalists are roaming the streets.'

'I'll take my chances.'

Younes had joined them. He shook his head. 'We are supposed to take over the checkpoint here. But I insisted that we go on to Tripoli. So I will personally show you the way.' Bald recognized the tone of voice from his time in the Regiment. A soldier taking shit from a superior, relaying the order to someone else, barely disguising his anger. Fuck these Arab ragheads, Bald thought. Soon as the guns stopped firing they and every other Abdul in the country would discover that the West was king, and if they didn't suck up to Washington and London they'd soon find themselves at the bottom of the fucking pile.

Younes was silent for a second. Then he went on, 'There is something else. You said you arrived with the woman, Rachel? No one else travelled with you?'

'No,' said Bald. 'Why?'

'My friend says you are not the first SAS soldier to pass through here today.'

thirty-six

The Second Ring Road sucked them deeper into Tripoli, like a heroin user mainlining that second, addiction-creating hit. Rachel stared silently ahead. A battered road sign indicated that they were ten kilometres due west of Green Square. Bald could see several tall fires fizzing out of the city centre and dispensing tar-black smoke into the sky. Car tyres being lit up by loyalists to blanket the skies and obscure NATO fast air. Bald could smell the burning rubber from the car.

The road was wide as a berthed cruise ship, and Bald was able to easily navigate pockets of shrapnel and chunks of twisted metal that had once been cars. The road was lined with palm trees and lampposts of equal height, and fresh soil lay in great heaps on each side. Bald spotted several gated mansions set back from the road. No cars inside the gates. Abandoned, and probably in a rush. Giant posters of Gaddafi were stuck to the fronts of several light-brown apartment buildings. Several of them were sprayed with graffiti and bullet holes.

Past the June 11 Memorial Stadium, three kilometres deeper into Tripoli, the landscape changed. Whitewashed, flat-roofed city dwellings were arranged in neat lines.

There was grass, and greenery, and trees other than palms. Dozens of three- and four-storey buildings stood half-finished, some with rough brickwork on the lower floors, others just steel bones draped in tarpaulin, all around them cranes and diggers left abandoned. Burned-out cars lined the road, its surface flecked with shrapnel and spent brass. Now Bald could make out the *tak-tak-tak* of distant gunfire and the *crump* of mortar rounds. The air was tamped with the smell of gunpowder and burning flesh. Bald felt his muscles harden.

For the first kilometre and a half they managed to steer clear of the fighting. They clung to the Second Ring Road as it contoured around the southern edge of the city, past the ribcages of apartment blocks and the jigsaw shrapnel of mortar rounds. The Hilux was ten metres ahead of the Land Cruiser and the Cruiser fifteen ahead of Bald and Rachel in the Land Rover.

The Hilux stopped forty metres shy of the turn-off from the Second Ring Road. The Land Cruiser too. The distant gunfire was now immediate, urgent. Three of the rebels vaulted off the back of the Land Cruiser. Heads down and clutching their AK-47s, they scrambled for cover by its sides, two guys to the right side, the third on the left, all looking frantically at the surrounding buildings, clueless as to where the shooter was firing from.

But Bald had seen the direction immediately the rounds had strafed the Hilux. The easy money was on the shooter coming from somewhere at his twelve o'clock. He'd looked up and spied a silvery glint beaming from a concrete over-pass thirty metres down the road. And where the gunman was positioned gave him a clear line of sight over all three vehicles.

Stay here a second longer and the guy might plug us both full of holes, Bald figured. He grabbed Rachel's wrist, kicked open his door and yanked her across and out of the Land Rover. They dropped onto scalding asphalt. Now Bald pushed himself up into a low run, ducking and speeding along the road to cover behind the Land Cruiser, pulling Rachel with him. He flung her behind the left rear wheel, making sure her head was fully below it. The two remaining rebels on the rear bed of the Land Cruiser were decked out in woodland-camo ponchos and baseball caps, and wore ear muffles and thick woollen gloves. They were angling the .50-cal at a row of buildings to their three o'clock. Not that they had any clue where the shots were coming from.

Rachel screamed, and Bald looked past her shoulder – at the rebel who had taken cover on the left side of the Cruiser. The guy's body was a fucking mess. He was slumped against the front cab door, his head tucked into his chest. His guts were ripped open like an overcooked sausage that has split down the middle. His right hand was fastened around the grip of his AK-47; his left was wrapped around a spiral of intestines. He had voided his bowels, and the blood and excrement had congealed into a thick brown pool around his feet.

The .50-cal erupted. The earth shuddered. A thunderous sound assaulted Bald. Spent shells the size of screwdriver grips dinked onto the road.

'Move, move!' Bald shouted, dragging Rachel out from behind the Land Cruiser. They hurried, low, around the right side of the vehicle and made for the Hilux. Ten metres. The machine-gun continued to thunder at their backs. *Thump, thump, thump.* Six metres to the rear of the

Hilux. Now five. Now four. Younes was crouched behind the right-side rear wheel of the Hilux. He saw Bald and Rachel and motioned for them to hurry over.

'Your man's at the overpass,' said Bald.

Younes looked beyond the Hilux, in the direction Bald was pointing. Two figures were displacing from a spot midway along the overpass. They were clad in grey combats, black boots and grey jackets. Balaclavas over their heads.

No thank you from Younes. He yelled orders at the guys on the .50-cal. It whirred on its axis as the fire team swivelled it to the twelve o'clock position: directly at the overpass. The gunner unleashed round after round. Bald could feel the waves of heat burning the hairs on his neck. He watched as the overpass was pummelled into a cinereal mist. Dust and mortar waterfalled from its middle section onto the highway. Younes and his men cheered.

The Libyans didn't involve Bald in their celebrations. And that was just fine by him. He needed to ditch Younes and his muckers before they figured out he wasn't here on NATO's dime. He spotted a grove of olive and orange trees 150 metres away, next to a left turn-off leading away from the Second Ring Road and in the direction of the Mansour Hotel. Bald grabbed Rachel and bugged out towards the trees, scuttling across open, exposed ground. He checked his six: Younes still had his back turned. So did his mates. But any second they'd realize that Bald had pulled a fast one, and somehow he doubted they'd be happy about it. A hundred metres to the grove now, and Bald glanced over his shoulder. Younes was turning around. Fifty metres to the grove. Bald was certain that a bullet was going to slap into his back at any moment. But then he was bursting in among the branches, putting Rachel behind cover of a cluster of orange trees. He looked back towards the Hilux, but Younes was nowhere to be seen.

Bald could see the Mansour up ahead on the left. Moving fast, he led Rachel by the hand, out from the trees. They hugged the side of the road, where abandoned cars provided cover against any snipers lurking in the blocks of flats opposite. His limbs moved stiffly, under protest; the key muscle groups in his quads, upper arms and calves felt pained and tired. His body was overdrawn.

They saw a freshly slotted rebel slumped against the twisted wreckage of a taxi. Nineteen or twenty. Just a kid. A kid with a white vest top drenched in blood and a neck that had a hole in it big enough to drive a flagpole through. But his guns were still intact. Bald knelt by the guy and grabbed his AK-47. The weapon was the fast food of the gun world. Quick, cheap and no frills, but it did the fucking job. The kid's wasn't the Soviet original. A Chinese copy: the Type 56. But pretty much the same tool. Equally effective. Bald pushed the magazine release latch. Full clip. Thirty rounds of 7.62x39mm short. He also took the kid's secondary, holstered weapon. Another Makarov semi. Lot of Russian and Chinese guns for a North African state, thought Bald.

One Type 56, one Makarov. Assault rifle and pistol. That was all he needed.

The Mansour was smaller than Bald had expected, but then again he supposed tourism wasn't big in Libya. There wasn't much to see, unless you were interested in oil, Islam and state-sponsored terrorism. The hotel was shaped like a car battery. Four-storeys tall across the middle, with a fifth-floor annex fixed like a stump on the right and left corners of the building. Each floor was a symmetrical bank of dark glass panels held together by steel. A canopy the colour of recycled cardboard was draped over the marble-floored entrance. A garden separated the hotel from the road, so prinked up it looked to Bald like something from a fucking gardening show on TV. Strange, he thought, in the middle of all the rubble and bloodshed.

A dark-blue Chevrolet Impala was parked out front. It caught Bald's eye, as every other motor he'd seen in Tripoli was either a pulverized mid-nineties saloon or a pickup just about ready for the tow truck. The Impala, on the other hand, was all new and shiny, with heavily tinted windows.

A heavy, all Ray-Bans and steroid smile, blocked their entrance.

'You can't come in,' he said, nodding at the Type 56. 'No weapons.'

Now Rachel flicked on her anger switch. She stepped into the heavy's face, doing her best to show off her impressive rack. 'This is my personal security. Where I go, he goes. If you have a problem with that, let me speak to your commanding officer. I'm sure my audience on CNN would love to hear about how you put the lives of female news reporters in danger.'

Ray-Bans stewed for a moment. He rolled his tongue around his mouth and spat on the floor and stepped a half-metre to the side. 'OK. This time. But in the future, he can't bring that kind of weapon into here. Personal defence guns only.'

'Sure,' Rachel said.

They brushed past the guy, walked under the canopy, and then, as casually as possible, through a set of tinted-glass doors. The glass was scratched and flecked with mud. Inside the lobby the floor was polished marble, the atmosphere placid, refined. Arab-style muzak seeped out of unseen speakers.

A middle-aged white guy in a crumpled linen suit sat cross-legged on a leather armchair, flicking through the news on his white iPad 2. A podgy woman in an ill-fitting suit sat on a sofa opposite him. She was jabbering into an iPhone 4. A waiter moved among the crowd, serving tea. The Mansour looked like any hotel in the world.

'I'm impressed,' said Bald, nodding at her chest.

'I work for the Agency. They teach you a lot of things, but rule number one is, if you've got it, don't be afraid to use it.'

'They're your secret weapon?'

'Is that your idea of a compliment?'

'Get this right,' said Bald, 'and you'll get plenty more. Now go and do your thing.' He lingered in the lobby while Rachel sauntered over to the ladies' restroom. She emerged a minute later with her face cleaned up and her hair loosened, each blonde curl like a finger encouraging you to come a little closer. She approached the main desk. A guy stood behind it, wearing a faded white shirt and a harassed look.

Rachel leaned across the desk and brightened up his day. She presented the guy with the best close-up of a miraculous rack he was likely to see outside of RedTube. He suddenly looked less harassed. Meanwhile Bald couldn't help himself from checking out Rachel's arse. One look reminded him how desperate he was to sling her one.

The guy said something to Rachel. She laughed teasingly and gave him a smile. Then turned away and retreated to Bald.

'Well?'

'You're right. My secret weapon is pretty damn effective.'

'And?'

'Laxman checked in this morning.'

Thank fuck, thought Bald. He was still on course for his five million. 'Room number?'

Rachel smiled at him with her eyes, offshore-blue, and said, 'Two-one-two.' Bald half-turned but stopped when he realized that she was staring at him, the smile smoothed into her delicate features, her face straight and serious and itching to share something else with him. He turned back and she said, 'He's not in his room.'

'How do you know?'

'Our friend,' she said, thumbing at the manager. 'He says the guy flunked out about an hour ago. Handed in his keys for safe keeping. He told the manager he wouldn't be back for a couple of hours.'

'I'm going to check out his room. He might have left the Intelligent Dust up there.'

'Unguarded? Hard to believe.'

'Sometimes people do stupid shit.'

She winked. 'You're the expert.'

'Wait here in the lobby. If Laxman comes back, stop him from going up to his room.'

'Got it,' Rachel said.

Bald started for the lift but decided to take the stairs instead. A lift usually opened out into the middle of a corridor, and a threat could be lurking in either direction. Stairwells ran up the sides of buildings. You could push the emergency door ajar and take your time to assess threats, rather than risk jumping out into the middle of a clusterfuck.

No one was around, and Bald took the stairs three treads at a time. Each stride took him one step closer to the promised land: five big ones and a chance to build a new life somewhere, away from the shit and the bullets and the Firm. The stairway was basic: concrete steps, metal railings that were coming loose from the concrete, cracks in the walls. His muscles were pumped. His blood was up. Adrenaline needled his spine like a burst of electricity. He reached the second-floor fire exit, pushed both palms down on the crash bar and peered into the corridor. Empty. He scanned it for twelve more seconds, his eyes alert to the smallest detail. An open door, a tray left outside a room. A smell of smoke in the air.

He entered the corridor, softly closing the door behind him.

Almost there.

His eyes flicked left to right: room 201 to his left, 202 to his right, 203 . . . A knackered air-con system spewed out reheated air, like someone permanently breathing in your face. Bald slowed his pace, his trainers cushioned by the geometric-patterned carpet. He counted the doors on the right, at his one o'clock. The next door was 204. After that 206 at ten metres. Then 208, 210 and the door which had to be 212, twenty metres ahead. The Type 56 was slung over his shoulder on its strap.

He didn't want to go into a close-quarter battle situation with a weapon as clunky and awkward as an assault rifle. In a confined environment like a hotel room you needed speed. Speed of movement, speed of thought. So he went with the Makarov. He gripped the pistol in his right hand and flicked his thumb to the slide-mounted safety catch and pushed it down to the 'fire' setting. The Makarov bore all the hallmarks of a Soviet firearm. An elegantly simple design, features way ahead of its time, and a reliable assembly. But, like other Russian guns, it was heavy and loud as fuck. The Russians specialized in functionality. They didn't care much for elegance. Normally the noise would be an issue. Not here. Bullets were cracking off in the distance every few seconds, interrupted by the occasional wall-shattering thud of incoming mortar rounds. A couple of shots being unloaded in a hotel room would go unnoticed. You wanted to murder someone and get away with it, a war zone was your ideal fucking location.

Bald tightened the screw on his breathing. Then he edged closer to room 212.

A few more careful strides and he was at the door. He pricked his ears. A hollow, wooden noise: the sound of a drawer being opened or shut. Bald froze. Shit, he thought. Laxman's home after all. I've hit the jackpot. *This is it.*

He assessed the lock. It was an old-fashioned thing with a doorknob and a keyhole, not one of the modern keycard-operated things. He gave the knob a try, his fingertips lightly touching the brass. He slowly twisted the knob clockwise, and it turned a lot more than a locked door would do. Satisfied that he could enter without forcing the door, Bald adjusted his stance so that his right leg was half a foot's length behind his left leg, and bent his knees slightly. He took in three deep breaths and tensed his ab muscles, so that his core was stable.

Makarov in his right hand. With his left hand he rotated the knob again, slowly and soundlessly, until he heard the tiny click of the latch releasing. Now the door was loose, and he gave a final twist and pushed it inwards. It opened quietly.

Bringing his left hand up, he wrapped his fingers around the ridgeline of his right hand to give himself a solid firing platform for the Makarov. The door stilled, almost fully open, giving Bald a complete view of the hotel room. Operators are trained to assess every potential threat inside a contained environment in 1.5 seconds. The room was six metres deep and three wide. To his left was the bathroom. To his right was a trouser press and a wooden desk with a small flatscreen TV mounted on top, plus the usual hotel facilities of mini-bar, room service menu, phone and hairdryer. A king-sized bed stood against the left wall and consumed most of the floor space. At the far side of the room was a sliding door – closed – leading to a balcony.

A figure was in front of the bed.

Bald was ready to give Shylam Laxman the good news.

Then he clocked the face. A single thought pickaxed his skull.

No. Can't be . . . Fucking impossible.

The man in the room was Joe Gardner.

thirty-seven

1144 hours.

They stood apart for what felt to Bald like a long time, but in reality was only five or six seconds. Bald studied the man six metres from the business end of his Makarov. The man who had once been a mucker, then an enemy, and finally a washed-up bag of shit. As if to prove he wasn't a ghost, Gardner bore the scars of his recent encounter with the Thames. The front of his face was stamped with bruises. His cheekbones were misshapen lumps, as if someone had sewn peanuts under the skin. The skin around his eyes was coloured all sorts of putrid yellows, purples and browns.

Gardner didn't say anything. He kept his hands by his side. His eyes were big and wide. His left one, anyway. The right was puffed up and the eyelid drooped down over half his eyeball. He looked startled, like a kid caught mid-wank by his mother.

Bald kept the Makarov trained on a spot between Gardner's eyes. He pictured a round pencilling his forehead, spitting brain matter over the furniture and the cream walls, the round yawing through soft flesh and hard bone, his body going limp.

Then he let his eyes run across the room, more slowly this time. It was a fucking mess. Drawers had been ripped

out of the desk and upturned on the floor. Clothes were
scattered all over the place. The sheets had been ripped off
the bed. A knife slash like a 'Z' had been carved into the
mattress. The edges of the carpet had been rolled up and
the ventilation grille had been torn off. Everything that
could be removed had been. The room looked like it had
been hit by Hurricane Katrina.

Like Gardner had been looking for something.

Like the Intelligent Dust.

Bald's eyes returned to Gardner. He opened his gob to
ask about the ID but cut himself off before he got a word
out. Maybe Gardner knew about the stuff. But maybe he
didn't, and Bald wasn't in the business of giving out free
fucking int.

Then Gardner spoke up. 'John—'

His voice was suffocated by the flushing of a toilet filter-
ing through the bathroom door. Bald turned to his eight
o'clock. Eyes on the door, Makarov on Gardner. The water
gargled and swilled and then petered out, replaced by the
hiss of the cistern refilling. Bald flashed a look at Gardner.
His old mucker was eyeballing the door and grinding his
swollen jaws. As if trying to send a thought message to
whoever the fuck was the other side of the bathroom door
not to come out.

The door was a plain slab of wood with a dozen black-
ish smears and a brass handle. A half-inch gap between
the bottom of the door and the carpet.

The handle tilted down. Halogen light seeped out. The
door pulled back fully and revealed a guy standing in the
doorway. Slim build, but not puny. Angular, bony. Like a
flyweight boxer. Mid-forties. He wore just stonewashed
jeans. The belt buckle hung loose and his flies were

undone. A Sig Sauer P228 was tucked into the waistband. His chest was one giant fucking tattoo, depicting an eagle grasping the Irish Republican flag between its talons and the letters 'NO SURRENDER' below, surrounded by shamrock leaves.

The guy stepped out of the bathroom. Hands in the air, a pungent smell of shit in his wake. The wire-mesh shadows on his face dissolved, and Bald found himself staring face to face with a man he hadn't seen for a very long time.

'John fucking Bald,' the man said.

Gardner's eyes played eeny-meeny-miny-moe with Bald and the guy in the bathroom doorway. 'You two know each other?' he said.

'Yeah, I know Bill fucking Fourie all right,' said Bald. His stomach muscles tensed. His index finger ran up and down the trigger mechanism.

'But he quit the Regiment before you'd even joined.'

'He had his fingers in a lot of pies in Hereford,' said Bald. 'Our paths crossed.'

'They more than fucking crossed,' said Fourie. 'We worked together. On the Circuit. Two proud Scots, doing what they do best. Drinking and fighting.'

'That was a long time ago,' said Bald. 'Then I realized you were a cunt.'

Fourie pantomimed a pout. 'Jesus, John, you say it like you really mean it.' Fourie took a step closer to Bald. Two metres between the men. 'Put the gun down, lad,' he said.

'Stay where you are. Both of you. Either one of you cracks so much as a wet fart and I'll slot you.'

Bald arced the Makarov at Fourie and gave him a close-up look at the barrel, to emphasize that he was dead serious. Fourie got the message and stopped in his tracks.

Shoved his hands into the air. His skin had a marinated look to it, like rust, and wrinkled with it, a quality peculiar to Scotsmen who've spent too long in the sun. His eyes were locked in a permanent squint. It got Bald thinking. It looked like Fourie hadn't graced Hereford or his native Stornoway for longer than a little while.

Bald traced the Makarov from Fourie to Gardner and back again. 'What the fuck are you doing here?'

'Me? Why, I'm enjoying the weather, John.' Fourie sniffed and wiped his nose with the back of his hand. 'But I heard you got rich. Big drug deal down in Rio. Is that so? But hold on, John. If you filled your boots down south, what're you doing here?'

'None of your fucking business.'

Fourie exaggerated a shrug at Gardner. 'Then I guess you didn't get that rich after all.'

'What's it to you, Bill? You're forty-fucking-eight. An old cunt with a shit face and a shit life. All you've got to show for it is a security company you bankrupted and a load of other Blades who'd love to skin you alive. It won't take two guesses to figure out who the loser is in this room.'

Fourie suddenly worked his face into a snarl, as if the expression had been lingering under the surface of his skin all along and the flick of a switch had brought it out. He said, 'Fuck you, John. Remember who you're talking to.'

At five feet five, Fourie had been the shortest guy in the Regiment. The other lads had relentlessly ripped the piss out of his height. But the man had always given off an air of great confidence. His beard was reddish-brown and bristly like an old broom, and his small black eyes and distance-runner frame made him seem even smaller than he actually was. Some joker had nicknamed him

'Inch' and the name stuck. Bill 'Inch' Fourie had been the human illustration of the law that says the smallest dogs have the worst bite. During his time in Boat Troop he'd had so many complaints against him he made Bald look like fucking Bono. Then he'd handed in his papers and fucked off on a security contract, and no one had heard from him in more than five years.

Fourie's world was black and white. He called his mates 'son' and everyone else was 'prick'. Bald spotted a brand-new Breitling on his wrist. Chronomat Evolution. Stainless-steel case, sapphire-crystal display. Whatever Bill Fourie had been up to, it hadn't been scrimping around the fringes of society like Gardner.

Fourie caught Bald glaring at the Breitling. 'You like it, son? I can get you one, if you want. Plenty more where that came from.' He smiled uncomfortably at Bald, like someone was shining a torch directly in his face.

Then it jumped Bald. The migraine. It came without warning this time. No slow build-up. Just a crack like his skull splitting in two, like a hand grenade had popped off inside his head. The pain plunged all the way down to his toes and for a second he thought he was going to lose control of his body and pass out. Then, as quickly as it had arrived, the pain and dizziness and numbness subsided.

He tensed his wrist flexors. Get a grip, John.

'What about you, Joe? What brings you to this corner of the world?'

Gardner ignored the question and said, 'Drop the gun.'

Bald laughed. 'Or you'll hurt my feelings?' He shook his head in pity. 'I see you're still making the same old mistakes, Joe. Thinking you're smarter than everyone else. When are you gonna learn? This didn't work out too well for you last time out, mate, and it won't be any different this time.'

Gardner wrinkled a smile out of his bruised features. His prosthetic left hand lightly rested by his side. He seemed to be in pain. He shifted his stance and moved his left hand to his ribcage, and his smile deformed into a wince.

'You look like shit,' said Bald.

Then he shot a glance at Fourie. 'You both look like shit.'

To Gardner he said, 'What the fuck are you doing here? Who sent you?'

Gardner didn't answer.

Bald cocked the Makarov's hammer. He was already thinking about what he'd tell Cave. *The guy just jumped me. He had a gun in his hand. I fired first. Tragic, but these things happen.*

'Fucking tell me.'

Gardner still didn't answer.

'Last chance, Joe.'

He was about to introduce Mr Hot Lead to Mrs Skull when Fourie piped up. 'Cave hired us. He told us you're not up to the job.'

thirty-eight

1211 hours.

The migraine hit Bald for the second time in three minutes. It donkey-punched him in the back of the head. A million different pains announced themselves. The ground seemed to tilt and shift under his feet like an earthquake simulator. He clocked Fourie in the corner of his eye. Shuffling closer towards him.

'Another hangover, John? Aye. Can I get you an aspirin?'

Bald tried shaking the pain out of his head and said, 'Why would the Firm post you halfway across the world?'

Cobwebs of the migraine clung behind his eyeballs. Gardner didn't answer.

'You're no good to Cave. You're just a loser with a hand from a fucking crash-test dummy.' He swung around ninety degrees and pulled a screw-face at Fourie. 'And you, Bill? Fuck me, the Firm wouldn't touch you with a barge pole. Not after the way you took Whitehall money and subcontracted the Kabul jobs to a bunch of Chinkies.'

Gardner said, 'He wanted us to keep an eye on you. He said he couldn't give the gig to some jumped-up field agent with a PhD in being a cunt. Said that he wanted people who knew how you worked.'

'So he chose a fucking Regiment crackhead and a guy with one arm?'

Fourie said, 'I'm clean these days, John.'

'Bollocks.'

Fourie did a thing with his eyes that gave Bald a fair idea of what he'd like to do with him. Bald went on, 'Why would Cave think he needed two guys to keep tabs on me?'

'You're a danger to the mission. He couldn't take any more risks. That's what he said.'

Bald couldn't help notice that Gardner's false hand was brand-new, not the piece-of-shit NHS job he'd been sporting the last time Bald had seen him. This one looked fucking real. The fingers moved fluidly, like real fingers. The texture of the skin was eerily close to the real thing.

Gardner went on, 'See, the way Cave saw it, you made such a cock-up of the Florida job that he couldn't trust you with this one. He visited me in the hospital. Said, did I fancy a job? I said yes.' Gardner had his smile on full beam now. He was enjoying this.

'And guess what, John? It's your name that's dirt inside the Firm now. That's you. Mate.'

'I couldn't give a toss what Cave thinks,' Bald said, taking a step back and manoeuvring closer to the door, to put more distance between himself and Fourie. Gardner, Bald knew, was too smart to make a move on him. But Fourie smoked crack and was prone to doing something stupid, and Bald trusted him less than a Chinese human rights pledge.

Bald said, 'Put the Sig on the bed, Bill.'

'Come on, lad. We're all grown-ups here.'

'Fucking do it.'

'Bollocks to it, then,' Fourie said, digging out the Sig, emptying the chambered round, then the clip and the spare. He tossed the items onto the mattress. Bald scooped them up. Tucked the Sig into the waistband of his jeans. Pointed the Makarov at the blind above the balcony door and said to Gardner, 'Take the cord off and tie up your new best friend.'

Gardner hesitated.

'This is stupid,' said Fourie.

'I'm waiting, Joe,' said Bald.

Gardner did a super-slow one-eighty and reached up to the blind. He yanked the cord free, causing the blind to fall in a heap on the floor. Then he skirted around the bed and put Fourie's hands behind his back and started to bind them.

'Turn him around,' said Bald. 'I want it tight enough that it hurts.'

'Prick,' said Fourie.

Gardner finished securing Fourie. Bald gestured for him to patrol Fourie around to the other side of the bed and make him squat on the floor.

Then he said, 'It's time, Joe.'

Gardner blinked his confusion. 'Time for what?'

'To finish what I started on the bridge.'

A half-second. That was how long it took for Bald to close the gap on Gardner, and for Gardner to unknot the confusion on his face and realize it was all over for him. Bald lunged at him side on, to present a smaller target, leaning forward with his right foot and pressing on the ball of that foot, feeling the energy transmit all the way up from his leg to his right shoulder muscles. The shoulder was the most important part of a punch. Because punches weren't really thrown from the fist or even the forearm. A real punch, one that could flatten a fucker in a single blow – that truly began at the shoulder. That's where you had the biggest muscle groups and could generate the maximum force.

Bang.

He lamped Gardner on the side of his head with the butt of the Makarov. Hardwood hammered the vulnerable aspect of the skull between the corner of his eye and his ear. Really fucked him up. The blow made an explosive thud, like a car door slamming shut. The sound was quickly gobbled up by a grunt spilling out of Gardner's mouth. He fell to his knees. Clamped his hands over the wound. Blood percolated through the dark gaps between his fingers, ran down his wrist and stained the sleeve of his white polo shirt. He dropped to his knees like a Muslim late to the call of prayer and now Bald was on top of him, locking his fingers around his neck while the cunt's face leaked blood. He dragged Gardner across the floor. Gardner shook his head frantically left to right, wriggled free of his grip and rolled onto the floor and curled himself into a ball. Now Bald kicked him in the balls, then the shins, the most vulnerable parts of his exposed body. This forced Gardner to uncurl himself. And when he did, Bald launched another kick at his face. The tough sole of his trainer connected with the sensitive nasal and frontal bone structures. The blow was devastating. Gardner howled and jerked his head back. His neck muscles tensed. He was stunned. If this had been a boxing match the referee would have been slapping the floor now, counting Gardner out.

Bald hauled Gardner into the bathroom. Blood oozed out of Gardner's nose and dripped onto the cool tiles of the floor. The bathroom was four metres long by three wide. Bath to the right with a shower rail and dirty-white curtain draped over it. Porcelain washbasin to the left, tiled surface, mirror, extractor fan fitted to the side, the blades coated in dust. The toilet was located at the far end. Gardner lay just in front of it, breathing hard. Every time he exhaled the blood on his face bubbled and hissed.

Bald stepped to the side of Gardner and filled up the bathtub with water.

'Drown, you cunt,' he said as the cold water filled to the halfway point. From the bedroom Fourie called out, 'Think about what you're doing, for fuck's sake.'

But Bald *was* thinking. In fact right now he was perfectly lucid. And he was enjoying it, too. He enjoyed watching Gardner fight to yank his face away from the tub. But Bald had a firm grip on his neck and simply concentrated all his upper-body strength into his forearm. Gardner's room for movement was limited to twisting his neck an inch to the left, an inch to the right. Not enough to avoid contact with the water.

Bald applied more pressure.

The fight in Gardner's muscles collapsed, and now Bald thrust his head down. Bathwater sploshed up and sluiced over the rim and cascaded onto the tiles. Gardner hurled his screams into the water, and they echoed in the bathtub. His hands flapped and pawed at Bald's legs. But Bald had a wide, firm stance and he wasn't about to let go. He did a three-count in his head, then he shoved Gardner's head deeper into the water, and his screams became garbled and frothy and gagged. Bald did a second three-count. Then a third. On the count of nine he hoisted Gardner's head up and out.

'Still thirsty, Joe?'

Gardner sucked in a breath, hoarsely. His face was glistening. A crescent-shaped purple bump had announced itself on his forehead. Beads of water dripped from his bushy eyebrows and the tip of his nose. He blinked droplets out of his eyes and dead-eyed Bald.

'You're soaking wet, Joe. Let me clean that up for you.'

'Cave will kill you for this,' Fourie called out.

Bald plunged Gardner's head back under the bathwater, deep as it would fucking go, until only the nape of his neck was visible from where Bald was standing. Gardner's right hand thumped furiously into Bald's thigh. Bald locked him in that position for twelve seconds. Gardner's legs flailed wildly. His combat boots scuffed the tiles. On thirteen seconds Bald hoisted him up again. The ex-Blade gasped and dry-heaved. He folded forward loosely, and violently emptied his guts into the bathtub.

Bald listened to the sound of Gardner retching, and positioned himself directly behind Gardner, shaping to push his head back under the water.

'Wait!'

Gardner spat the word out between clawing at the humid, close air. Bald released his fingers from his neck and took a step back. He watched Gardner crawl away from the bathtub on all fours. Spittle and stringy vomit dangled from his cracked lips. A pungent smell corrupted the bathroom. Acidic and rancid. Like pressing your nose to a pint of gone-off milk. Gardner wiped his mouth and hack-coughed.

'I can help you,' he said.

'Bollocks,' said Bald. 'You can't even help yourself.'

'Don't.' Fourie's voice boomed off the walls. 'Don't fucking tell him, Joe.'

'Shut up,' Bald called out, kneeling down beside Gardner. His head was hanging low. A defeated man. Gardner looked dimly at the blood streaked across the floor.

'What is it?' Bald asked.

'I swear, if you say a word . . .'

Bald kicked the bathroom door shut. The door was thick, and Fourie's voice faded to a muzzled, throaty growl.

'I know where he is,' said Gardner.

'Who?'

'Laxman.' He paused a beat. 'He's not coming back here. I can take you to him.'

thirty-nine

They rode in the Chevrolet Impala Bald had spotted on his approach to the Mansour. Turned out Gardner had the keys. Bald had marched Gardner and Fourie out of the room and down the stairs. They took the back exit from the hotel and crossed the garden to the Impala. It was a brand-new LT four-door sedan with light-grey leather seats and a metallic silver-trim dash and seventeen-inch aluminium wheels. It got Bald thinking that perhaps the Impala had once belonged to a Gaddafi loyalist, someone with a good job and high up the food chain.

Bald pushed Fourie in the back, Gardner into the driver's seat, and took the front passenger seat himself. He kept a hold on the Type 56.

He'd spotted Rachel waiting in the hotel restaurant, nothing but a cup of muddy coffee for company. He told Fourie and Gardner to wait outside while he made a quick trip to the shitter. Then he approached Rachel and told her to sit tight. He didn't hang around to listen to her protests. He left her there. Right then he only had eyes for the money. He also thought about the fact that Cave had brought Gardner into the fold. If Cave had hired Gardner and Rachel, then maybe Rachel knew about Gardner?

Which would mean she had kept that from Bald. Which would make her a lying fucking bitch. Which would make her like every other woman Bald had ever known.

A splinter of thought had lodged in his brain. He was thinking, fuck Rachel and fuck her coke-snorting arse. Experience had taught Bald that the best way to get over pussy was to bang more of it. All he needed was to ice Laxman and pick up the five million and he'd be knee-deep in it.

Gardner took the wheel. He drove fast. Gunfire echoed all around them, bodies were festering on the ground, and you didn't want to be driving slow enough to present yourself as another target. Bald held the Makarov in his right hand. In his left he clutched another length of cord from the blind. Once they'd reached their destination, he'd bind up Gardner too.

And maybe he'd do more than that. He was of a mind to slot Gardner and Fourie once he had sight of Laxman. There was no good reason to keep the fuckers alive, and even less when he started grilling Gardner.

'Where exactly are you taking me?' he asked.

Gardner didn't answer.

'Come on, Joe, don't be a cunt.'

Gardner glared at Bald. 'I'm not fucking dumb enough to tell you where Laxman is now. Shit, if I do that, what's to stop you popping me and Bill?'

Bald decided against telling Gardner that he was right on the money.

They threaded south through four kilometres of chaos and celebrations. Sometimes it was difficult to tell which was taking place and where. Near the Second Ring Road a throng of locals had gathered in their thousands. They looked angry and shouted and unloaded entire mags from their AK-47s into the air. Thin lines of unshaven, malnourished loyalists trooped past. Most of them stared forlornly at the ground. Their faces were darker, their features more weather-beaten than the average Libyan. Tuaregs, Bald figured. Gaddafi's hired toughs.

South of the Second Ring Road they hit Al-Hadhbah Road. Less a road, more a scarred dagger of asphalt that was scattered with shrapnel, the leftovers of recently dropped Paveway and Mark-82 bombs. Democracy hurled down from the skies. Acrid smoke rose slowly out of a row of blacked-out buildings. Liberated Tripoli looked to Bald a lot like rioting London, only without the hoodies.

'How many years since you left Hereford?' he said to Fourie.

'Two.'

'Everyone thought you were finished after the Mauritania job.'

'Aye, that story's plenty true. I got in the shit down there big time. Up to my fucking eyeballs in it.' The smile disintegrated. 'Ever been to there, son? No? Lucky prick. Let me tell you something about Mauritania. It was the last country in the world to make slavery illegal. Only a few years back. Hey, Johnny, be a lad and open the glove box, won't you? There's a little something I could do with right now.'

Bald popped the catch. Vials of white powder tumbled out, along with a hip flask.

'Just give me a bit of the toot, cheers,' said Fourie.

Bald scooped up the vials in his left hand. He counted eight in total. Inside the glove box there was also a crack pipe, with a small ball of steel wool shoved in the mouth end as a filter and a pebble of crack cocaine wedged in the lighting end. There was also a plastic baggie containing several ecstasy pills and a syringe loaded with morphine and sealed inside a hygienic packet. Sweet Jesus, there was enough gear there to keep a Hollywood bad boy happy for a week.

'Come on, John,' said Fourie, widening his eyes at the vials. 'Just a wee sniff.'

Bald rolled down his window and chucked the vials and the crack pipe out of the window. Fourie pulled a face and dropped his jaw, like someone had just shoved their dick in his mouth. He frantically rolled in his seat, craning his neck at the window. His eyes were fit to burst.

'You cunt,' he said to Bald.

But Bald ignored Fourie and unscrewed the cap of the hip flask. He wafted the flask under his nostrils. The sweet, slightly peaty aroma of single-malt whisky said hello to the olfactory receptor cells at the back of his nose. He took a long sip of Scottish medicine and *aah-ed*.

Then he said, 'What happened in Mauritania?'

Fourie slumped back on the seat.

'It was a close-protection job. Big deal. I'd seen that in Baghdad and bought the fucking T-shirt in Kabul. Prick by the name of Ould Cheikh Abdallahi. First elected president those fucking barbaric pricks had ever had. The money is top dollar. I'm talking, you know, big money. Capital B. Enough to make Simon Cowell blow a load in his pants. Anyway, I'm down there with that Welsh faggot from Mountain Troop. Jimmy Coyne?'

Bald nodded. He vaguely remembered the guy.

'Life was easy. For the first six months, anyway. Then, out of fucking nowhere, the army launches a coup. Abdallahi gets his marching orders, and Coyne gets thrown in the slammer. Me? I bugged out of the fucking country in the middle of the night and escaped to Algeria. Had half the army on my case the whole way. Coyne spent the next three years in a jail cell with twenty other blokes. Fucking bucket to shit and piss in and mouldy bread and maggoty rice twice a day. Poor bastard got taken out to the yard each morning and had the guards run a train on his arse. Last thing I heard he was released and had AIDS. Prick died homeless in London.'

'What about you?' Bald said.

'I hooked up with some contacts in Algiers. They found me some work in Libya. They said the pay would make me piss myself. Which I nearly fucking did. Then the ragheads start rebelling, and I'm out of a job. I'm telling you, son, I can't fucking take a dump without a revolution kicking off. Luckily I linked up with Joe here, and now I'm back in the money. And let me tell you, Johnny, I'm rolling in more cash than ever before.'

'How long have you been in Tripoli?'

'A year, give or take.'

'Doing what?'

'Son, that's none of your fucking business.'

'Why did Cave hire you as well as Joe?'

'I know the lie of the land. They wanted a Mark One eyeball. That's me.'

But in the periphery of his vision Gardner was twitching and sweating like a Yardie at a Job Centre. Something didn't feel right to Bald. He took another deep gulp of whisky. It flooded his system, and the migraine subsided. Bald had made a discovery in Mexico City. The drugs had only a limited effect on his migraines. But booze silenced them. As long as he kept his bloodstream juiced with alcohol, he wouldn't have to feel like his head was nailed to a tectonic plate.

After four kilometres Gardner hung a left and shunted east. The palm-fringed city avenues were replaced by cramped streets lined with modest, flat-roofed houses. They soon found themselves in a sweaty, humdrum neighbourhood. An unmanned MQ-8 Fire Scout drone swept over the rooftops. It captured little on its infra-red camera; the streets were empty except for the occasional T-shirted soldier flip-flopping from one corner to another. This part of Tripoli, Bald figured, hadn't yet thrown its lot in with the rebels.

'How far?' he said.

'We're nearly there,' Gardner replied.

Loose stones and dirt crunched and spattered under the Impala's tyres. Fourie gave a low groan and began dry-heaving. He said to Gardner, 'Pull the fuck over. I'm gonna be sick.'

'Swallow it,' said Bald. 'We're not stopping here.'

'Oh, Jesus.' Fourie was breathing hard. He curled himself up into a ball and clamped his eyes shut.

While Fourie fought his gag reflexes, Bald turned to Gardner. 'Why'd you do it?' he said. 'Working for Cave to spy on another Blade?'

'He promised me a job at the end of it,' Gardner said, twisting his head left and right and relieving some of the tension in his neck muscles. 'Back on the frontline. Full pay and pension, John.'

Bald laughed. 'You stupid cunt. You really believe him? Cave will stab you in the back, just like Land stabbed you in the back. Just like he shafted me too.'

'Land was forced out of the picture. Things are different there now.'

'Bullshit. The Firm never changes.'

Gardner said, 'This is it.'

Bald scoped out the street as Gardner slowed the Impala. They were in a deserted back street. A row of whitewashed houses were riddled with bullets. One house at the end of a row had collapsed, its front avalanched across the blacktop. Flames lapped from the engine of an overturned pickup. In the middle of the road lay a hand, unclaimed. A stray dog approached it. The vehicle startled the dog and it glanced warily at the Impala. Turned its back and scampered meekly off with a thumb.

Bald took in little else of his surroundings. His focus was split fifty-fifty between Fourie and Gardner. The thought scratched at his skull: they might be leading you into a trap.

No. Fourie's tied up. I have a gun to Gardner.

But there might be a third man. Did you consider that? He might be lurking here.

Waiting to slot you.

Fifty metres further along, they hit the end of the street. It simply stopped. A carpet of desert unfolded in front of them, with banks of palm trees and wispy grass looking odd against the sand, like an old Hollywood movie lot. A dead end. At their eight o'clock was a dirt field with a mosque set a hundred metres back. The field was punctuated by electricity pylons. At their three o'clock was a half-finished compound. Work on foundations for a wall to surround a building in the middle had begun but abruptly stopped at ankle height. Twenty metres inside the planned perimeter was a flat-roofed, two-storey building with dirty, bare concrete walls. A bank of satellite dishes gazed out from the rooftop to the sky. Pots of wilting palm trees surrounded the building. Two things struck Bald. First, the front door was metal and substantial-looking. And second, there were no windows.

Without Bald prompting him, Gardner hit the brakes and brought the Impala to a halt forty metres from the gate. The silence was disturbed only by the rattle of the car's overcooked engine and the thrum coming from the electricity lines strung across the road. Bald looked over his shoulder at the street behind them. The houses were bullet-riddled. There was an absolute absence of people and cars and noise.

Bald looked at Gardner and said, 'This is it?'

'This is it.'

'What the fuck is this place?'

'It's an opium den,' Fourie said.

forty

Bald did a spit-take.

'An opium den, in the middle of Tripoli?'

Fourie said, 'Plenty of them around now the slant-eyes have moved in. Look around you, lad. We're no longer the big power in Africa any more. All the contracts are with the Chinese these days. They bring in the manpower and the industry and the influence. All the oil and the mineral rights. The Chinese have those sealed up too. Everyone else is left fighting over the scraps.'

Bald scanned the compound. Part of him wondered why an opium den would need a reinforced door. The other part of him was already thinking about the assault. It would be hard to approach the building unannounced. To its east and south was nothing but desert and exposed terrain. To its north was the dirt field and the mosque. To its west was the road.

Bald flicked his eyes down at his Aquaracer. 1419 hours. The handover's happening at 1420 this afternoon, Cave had said. Those words made Bald swell with confidence and adrenaline. This had to be the right place.

Bald said, 'How'd you find out about this place?'

Gardner shrugged.

Bald turned his gaze on Fourie. 'Did Cave tell you?'

Fourie kept his mouth zipped. Bald didn't press the issue but he was wondering about the amount of int that both his fellow Jock and Gardner seemed to have. Cave had briefed them on Laxman and the Intelligent Dust? Maybe, Bald thought, the two of them had been offered the same five-million-quid reward. Speculation. He scratched his balls. He was thirsty as fuck.

Bald asked Fourie, 'What's he coming here for?'

Fourie coughed up a hoarse laugh. 'Sipping tea and doing yoga. It's an opium den. You go inside and get off your bloody nuts. You prick, what the fuck do you think he's doing here?'

'So he's not making the handover here?'

Fourie shrugged his ignorance. 'Maybe he just fancies doing some Big O with a bunch of slant-eyed pricks? Your guess is as good as mine.'

With the engine turned off the temperature in the Impala quickly skyrocketed. Bald felt the heat creep and crawl over his body, like an anaconda. He studied the layout of the building again, and decided that he'd have one good chance to slot Laxman, and that was when he arrived. That front door looked pretty impenetrable, and with the building lacking windows, it was probably badly lit inside and host to an unknown number of people. If they were running a hop-shop it was more likely than not that they'd be armed, and if they were off their fucking faces on poppies then they'd be ready to use their guns as well. Which made busting inside the building an altogether bad fucking idea.

No. Bald would wait for Laxman to rock up to the building and double-tap the cunt in the back of the head.

He was warming to the idea. And killing a man in Libya had certain advantages over Florida. There were no cops here any more, for starters. He wouldn't have to worry about his photo being sent to every police department and airport in the country. Fuck it, with the war rumbling on he doubted anyone would find Laxman for several days. And when they did, they'd assume he'd simply run into the wrong mob.

Crude. But effective.

Bald grinned at Gardner. 'How about we make you more comfortable, mate?' He dangled the length of cord in front of Gardner and said, 'Give me your hands.'

Gardner turned side on to Bald and scowled. The gaping wounds on his right temple and nose had formed sticky welts that had hardened at the edges like black tar. Bald dug the Makarov's muzzle hard against the head wound. Gardner hissed in agony.

'Give me your fucking hands, or I'll paint the dash with your brains,' said Bald.

'You're making a big mistake,' Gardner said.

'The only mistake I ever made was not properly cunting you in London.'

Gardner reluctantly twisted in his seat so that he was looking out of the side window and his hands were tucked behind his back and presented to Bald above the gear shift. Bald bound the cord a dozen times around his wrists, forming it into a strangle knot. He pulled the cord tight enough to cause Gardner discomfort. Then he slipped out of the car and went round and flipped open the driver's door. He made Gardner step out onto the boiling asphalt and then dragged him to the passenger side and roughly shoved him into the seat.

'John, for fuck's—'

'Shut up and start choosing a fucking religion. Because once I've done Laxman, I'm gonna do Fourie, and then I'm gonna do you.'

Gardner fell silent. Fourie was silent too. Bald slammed the passenger door shut. Then he settled into the driver's seat and fired up the Impala. Beautiful cool air flushed out of the air con and gushed over his face and iced his sweat. A moment's relief from the business of taking a human life.

Then he waited.

He didn't have to wait long.

Bald heard it before he saw it. The unmistakable shotgun throttle of a Jeep Grand Cherokee. Silver bodywork. Bulky chassis. An on-road people carrier masquerading as an off-road SUV. It was big and brutal. It bubbled into view on the horizon and bounced recklessly down the road, beating the most direct line to the compound, the V8 engine working itself into a rage. Bald blinked cooled sweat out of his eyes. It was now just a hundred metres away.

He squeezed his fingers round the Makarov's wooden grip. Safety engaged, hammer cocked for a single-action shot. Violence was brewing in his blood. He felt his ears throbbing with the sound of his own breath and the terrific thump of his heart. An image in his head fuelled him. Bald slotting Laxman and telling Cave the good news. He pictured himself on a business-class flight to Monte Carlo, shitcanned on Laphroaig single malt and losing count of the zeros in his bank balance and the women on his arm.

Fifty metres.

So close now.

Just seconds.

Bald felt various parts of him contort, like a boa constrictor around a rat.

The Grand Cherokee's wheels sneezed dust and spat out rocks, and its bodywork winked reflected rays at Bald, momentarily blinding him. The growl reduced as the Cherokee slithered to a halt beside the opium den, twenty metres ahead of the Impala and facing in the opposite direction. Its engine snorted and promptly stuttered and died. Bald had one hand on the Makarov. The other on the wheel of the Impala. His foot on the pedal. He was ready. He looked ahead as Laxman climbed out of the Cherokee. The Indian was small and frail. His hair was matted and his suit more crumpled than an old man's face. Bald couldn't see his face, only the back of his head.

Laxman stretched his legs and arms. But otherwise he didn't move. Bald's hand lingered on the door catch. He watched as the door of the den yawned open and a figure emerged, a wire-mesh of shadows. The figure stepped tentatively out into the sunlight. Paced the ten metres to Laxman at the Cherokee. Bald recognized the Chinese prostitute from the brothel in Clearwater.

Bald stayed in the car, his face obscured by the forty per cent tint of the window. Fuck me, he thought: Laxman likes this whore so much he's brought her along for the ride. Only she wasn't dressed like a hooker any more. Gone were the high heels and the short skirt. Now she was wearing a pair of tight blue jeans, white blouse and wraparound shades. She flashed a seductive smile at Laxman, leaned into him and kissed him on the lips. Then she dipped a hand into a black grab bag slung over her shoulder and pulled out a phone. Looked like an iPhone. Checked her messages, slipped the phone back into her bag. Then she took him by the hand and began leading him towards the door.

Bald went to get out of the Impala.

Fourie said, 'You shoot Laxman now, you're making a big mistake.'

Bald froze his hand on the door catch.

'I'm being paid to kill the guy. End of.'

'It's not as simple as you think, John.'

Bald looked to his right at Gardner. The guy was leeching sweat.

'It's true,' Gardner said. 'There are things you don't know about.'

Laxman was ten metres from the door. Five million quid strolling away from him. He pushed at the catch and said, 'I'm not listening to any more of your shit.' Eight short metres between Laxman and the opium den.

'It's not a load of shit.' Gardner's voice was strained and flat and serious. 'You want to know the truth? We weren't sent here to spy on you.'

Cold air blasted out of the vents at Bald. The kind of cold that burns up your flesh. He watched the Chinese woman usher Laxman into the building. He watched the door close.

He watched his big chance disappear.

Gardner said, 'We were sent here to kill you.'

forty-one

Bald had been hanging on by a very thin thread ever since Mexico. Now he felt the thread snap, and the whole of him tumbled loose and went into freefall. It was like HALO-ing into deep space. Nothing solid under his feet – only blank, uncertain blackness. A Chinese man pulled the door of the opium den shut and to Bald the landscape somehow felt more isolated. A thought assaulted him like a cold, bracing wind.

I'm in the middle of nowhere.

Gardner looked at his lap, grimacing like he'd just pissed himself. 'Cave told me about the Intelligent Dust,' he said. 'He said that Laxman had arranged to make a handover to the Pakistanis, and you were supposed to slot him in Florida.'

Bald chewed glass.

'He said you needed to be taken care of. Once you'd done the mission.'

'Why?' said Bald.

'Tying up a loose end.'

'His words, or yours?'

Bald felt a voice spear his brain. A voice he had heard before, and one he never wanted to hear again. Danny

Cave. Smug and chummy and fake as a pack of Serbian smokes. Bald remembered something he had said on the phone earlier. 'The Firm takes care of its own, John Boy.'

But Bald wasn't part of the Firm. Never had been. He said, 'So he sent you both here? To tie up a loose end.'

'No. Just me.'

That made Bald jump in his bones. He swivelled around at Fourie. The guy was slouched low on the back seat. He looked sapped of energy, like he'd just given blood, and way too fucking much of it. He was grinding his teeth; Bald could hear the squeak of enamel rubbing against enamel.

'Cave doesn't know about Bill?'

'Of course not,' said Gardner. 'Like you said, he's cancer to the Firm.'

'Then why's he here?'

Fourie hocked up something gobby and gross in his throat. He played with it in his mouth before swallowing it again. 'I got word from the lads at the checkpoint that Joe had rocked up in town.' He spoke sluggishly, barely parting his lips. 'I thought, fucking weird. Because all the other lads had already been here for a while.'

'What lads?'

Fourie rolled his eyes, as if he was explaining a simple maths problem to the thickest kid in the class. 'The Firm had a bunch of guys over here. Ex-Blades, like you and me. We'd all been hired to train Gaddafi's personal security.'

Bald choked on air.

'It was part of the oil deal struck between Libya and the UK,' said Fourie. 'They'd give us first dibs on the oil interests and in return we'd help train the guards for the Gaddafis. The Colonel, he likes his bodyguards to be from the same tribe as him. It's an Arab thing. So we'd train them and teach them the ropes.'

'Putting your training to good use.'

Fourie laughed. 'Welcome to the real world, John.'

'Blades helping a tyrant. Brilliant.'

'Pah. It ain't the first time and it won't be the last, so stop getting your knickers in a twist. We're just soldiers, Johnny. We don't get to make big fucking moral judgements or wonder about the politics. We do what we're told, and at the end of the day we cash our cheques and we go and get pissed.'

Bald was facing forward. Eyes on the building twenty metres away at his one o'clock. Then he spied movement at the mosque on the other side of the road from the den, at his eleven o'clock. A huddle of figures dashing across the dirt field away from the road, away from the den and Bald, in the opposite direction. A dozen of them, maybe more. Civilians. Women and children. Unarmed. Not a threat. Bald relaxed a little. He watched them trudge across the dirt field. It tapered towards a series of low buildings in the middle distance.

Now Gardner spoke up. 'Bill found me in the hotel. Early this morning.' He paused. Eyed the hip flask in Bald's lap. Bald passed it over to Gardner. He took a long sip.

Fourie said, 'I knew he had to be here for a special mission. One ex-Blade flies in by himself, with no support, just as Tripoli goes to hell in a handcart? It had secret op written all over it.'

'And then?'

'We hatched a plan.'

'What kind of a plan?'

'We weren't going to kill you. That would go against the code of ethics for operators.'

'Spare me the fucking sermon. What was the plan?'

'Gardner was told to slot you once you had taken care of Laxman. But we had a better idea.' Fourie looked out of the window. A forlorn face, gazing out on a forlorn landscape. 'We'd stop you killing Laxman and take the ID off his hands.'

Bald swallowed hard. The whisky was sticky and harsh in his throat.

'And do what with it?'

Fourie looked at Bald in the rear-view mirror. 'Take a wild guess.'

Bald ran a hand over his scalp. His few strands of hair were slicked with sweat and grease, and his fingers were covered in a greasy film of gunpowder. He was hanging out of his arsehole here, and now he felt a thumping in his temples again. Like hammers tapping against the sides of his head.

'Think about it, lad,' Fourie said, sitting up, suddenly animated, suddenly excited, suddenly talking super-fast. 'My contacts are willing to pay fucking big money for this technology. What's the alternative? You kill Laxman and give that cunt Cave the satisfaction of another promotion in Whitehall? They'll only send some other cunt to kill you next. Who knows, maybe he's got others on the case already.'

Bald watched the silhouettes hurrying towards the horizon. He stayed quiet for several seconds. Then he said, 'How much?'

Gardner and Fourie swapped a glance. Fourie nodded.

'Forty million,' said Gardner.

Fourie leaned forward, pushed his head between the front two seats.

'We'll cut you in, lad. You'll get a good share. Think about it. Twenty for me, because it's my connect. Ten for you. Ten for Joe. Can't say fairer than that. Look, I don't know how much Cave is paying you for this job. But I'll bet that what I'm offering blows it out of the water.'

Ten million. Double my fucking money, Bald was thinking.

'Am I right?' Fourie said.

But Bald was also warming to the idea of pulling a fast one on Cave. The Firm had, after all, plotted behind his back to slot him the moment he stiffed Laxman. In the world of John Bald, forgiveness ranked up there with recycling and *Glee* at the top of the list of pointless crap. He believed that if your enemy took an eye, you had a duty to rip both his eyes out and piss in the fucking eyeholes. He allowed a pleasing image to enter his thoughts. Cave, somewhere further down the line, once he'd lost his job due to the Laxman fuck-up, once his girlfriend had left him and his house had been repossessed. The cunt sitting behind the wheel of his car on the hard shoulder of an anonymous stretch of the M25. Weeping like a fucking kid and pressing rounds into a snub-nosed revolver.

Bald parked the image and said, 'Who's the buyer?'

'A close contact of mine.'

'Not a government?'

'No.'

'Forty mil is a lot of money for one man.'

'He's good for it. This guy is richer than Abramovich.'

'But you won't tell me his name.'

'Look,' said Fourie. 'I just need to know, are you fucking in, or what?'

Bald thought about it for a moment longer. He didn't like the idea of an anonymous buyer. But he liked the idea of ten million more. So he nodded at Fourie and nodded at Gardner. And they both nodded back.

'Fuck it. I'm in.'

Easy sighs all round. The atmosphere in the Impala started to unwind. Gardner even managed an awkward smile.

'Good man,' Fourie said. 'I knew you'd see the light, John.'

But Bald didn't reply. He was canvassing the opium den again. It was a bland structure in a sea of scrubland. He noticed several other features within the unfinished perimeter. There was a stack of car tyres fifteen metres to the west of the building and the shell of a pickup deposited some twenty metres to the rear. The thought had suddenly struck Bald: what's wrong with this picture?

He downed another mouthful of the single malt and shook off the thought. Eyed Fourie in the rear-view mirror and said, 'So now what?'

'You untie me. We wait. My contact said Laxman was meeting someone here. Someone high-level. A terrorist.' Fourie craned his neck at the building, to get a better look. 'He finishes up here, we go in, kill everyone and take the ID. Then we get the fuck out of here and head to Sirte.'

'What's in Sirte?'

'My contact. Now, for fuck's sake untie me, John.'

Bald let his silence answer for him. He went back to OP-ing the building. There was a dull thought at the back of his head, like a flint trying to strike against steel, wondering why the folk in the mosque had been so eager to bug out. But the whisky and the prospect of ten million quid drowned it out, and Bald settled into a routine of running his eyes around the opium den, then doing the same to the mosque, then the surrounding land.

He waited.

Gardner waited.

Fourie waited.

They didn't have to wait long.

Four minutes later the heavy door was flung open and Laxman stepped out into the parched, bleached desert. He squinted and looked at the Chinese woman at his side. They started to walk towards the Cherokee.

Fourie said, 'There he is. Untie me.'

'Me too,' said Gardner.

'How about neither of you?' said Bald. 'Just because I'm in on your plan doesn't mean I trust you cunt-lickers a short inch. No, you two wait here and read each other bedtime stories. I'll take care of business.'

Bald flipped open the door and scrambled out of the Impala. Laxman had reached the Cherokee and was pacing around the vehicle to the rear, now with his back to Bald. Bald was running on muscle memory as he walked towards the Indian. His body recalled the thousands of hours of training in Hereford and the variables from the hundreds of missions he'd carried out. The kill would be quick, he knew. It had to be. He'd slot Laxman and sweep into the den, clearing the rooms. Slotting any X-rays he encountered. Then take the ID package. The building wasn't big, two storeys, perhaps twenty metres square. If he was surgical, the whole operation could be over in two or three minutes.

Bald's stride was fast, his breathing controlled, his nerves steady. He was now fifteen metres away from

Laxman. Laxman was flipping open the driver's door and had his back to Bald. But the woman had stopped beside the passenger door and was whirling round.

Facing Bald.

Ten pissy metres. Too late to abort. Bald raised the Makarov level with Laxman. Sighted the big target of his back. It didn't matter if the first shot didn't kill him. As long as it put him down, then the double-tap to his head would be one hundred per cent guaranteed to send him over to the dark side. Now Bald was six metres from Laxman and the woman. Now Laxman noticed that the woman was looking towards Bald. He followed her eyes, and his own settled on the Scot. Laxman looked vaguely surprised, like he had suddenly recalled where he left his car keys. It was the look Bald had seen in dozens of fuckers, right before he gave them the good news.

'Hands in the fucking air,' he said.

Laxman pulled the woman close to him. 'Please.' His voice was cracking like popcorn, and the thought entered Bald's head that people always offered such shitty excuses for sparing their lives.

Bald stopped two metres from Laxman. The Indian was numb, stared dumbly at the Makarov. The woman seemed perfectly calm. She was looking at Bald, not the Makarov. No surprise or shock on her face. As if she'd been expecting this.

Bald blanked her. 'Where is it? Give me the ID.'

Laxman didn't seem to hear. 'You have to help me,' he said. 'They're coming.'

Bald was about to ask, who? But he didn't need to. The earth rumbled at his six o'clock and he got the answer to his question. He knew what that sound advertised, even before he half-turned and fixed his eyes on the same spot that Laxman was hypnotized by. A kilometre back. Pickup trucks. The hum of four turbo-diesel engines swelled to a rock-crunching, soil-churning swarm. He counted three vehicles. All looked like they had been through the wars. The lead pickup was a Toyota Land Cruiser. The vehicle to the rear and left was a Hilux, painted red, green and black.

Laxman said, 'They are rebels.'

'Thank fuck for that,' said Bald.

'No.' The panic was rising in Laxman's voice. 'They're going to kill all of us!'

forty-two

Bald shoved Laxman and the woman towards the Impala.

'Fucking hurry,' he shouted at them.

Twenty metres back to the vehicle. He walked in brisk, urgent strides. The Land Cruiser and two pick-ups to its immediate six o'clock were heading down the road as fast as their knackered engines would allow. Not very fast.

Bald reached the Impala ahead of Laxman and the woman. He yanked open the rear passenger seat. Fourie shot him a stink-look and said, 'What do you think you're doing, John?'

'Getting us out of here before the rebels tear us a fucking new one.'

'The dust!'

Bald spun around and pointed to Laxman.

'Where is it?'

Laxman swapped glances with the woman, then looked beyond her at the building.

'It's in there. I will give it to you. I swear. But you have to protect me from them,' he said, pointing with his eyeballs to the pickups. The convoy was now two hundred and fifty metres distant. They had slowed to navigate around a corpse lying face down in the middle of the road. 'They have orders to shoot me on sight.'

'In and out.' Bald said. 'You get what we want and that's it.'

Then he opened the front passenger door, seized Gardner's T-shirt and dragged him out and onto the dirt. He loosened the knot in the cord enough for Gardner to wriggle his hands free and soothe his wrists.

The convoy was now sixty metres away. Six seconds until they reached Bald. Seven at most.

Bald said, 'Where's your flag?'

Gardner dug folded a Stars and Stripes flag from somewhere out of the Impala glove box. Some British PMCs carried American flags because a lot of Yank soldiers didn't recognize the Union Jack. Gardner unfolded the flag in a hurry and began waving it at the convoy. But the convoy didn't stop. It kept rumbling towards them.

Gardner ditched the flag and said, 'Fuck this, I need a gun.'

Bald chucked him Fourie's Sig Sauer P228 from the waistband of his jeans. He fished the spare mag out of his jeans pocket and chucked him that too. The weapon was equipped with a SIGLITE night sight, and was chambered for the 9x19mm Parabellum instead of the more powerful .40 S&W. But the pay-off was more rounds to a clip. The chrome-plated clips Fourie had been packing carried twenty rounds. That gave Gardner a total of forty rounds to play with, and evened up the odds a little.

Fourie said, 'What about me?'

Bald said, '*What* about you?'

'Fucking prick. You have to let me go too.'

'Who made that rule?'

'I can help.' The anger was rising in Fourie's voice.

'I don't trust you,' said Bald.

'That's bullshit.'

'It is what it is.'

'What if they fucking jump me, John? How am I supposed to defend myself?'

'Use the power of prayer.'

At forty metres the Land Cruiser's engine toned down to a mechanical buzz. At thirty metres it pulled up at the left-hand side of the road. The two pickups further back were veiled by the dirt clouds the Land Cruiser had been snorting from its rear tyres, but they were back there somewhere, Bald knew. Figures began debussing from the lead vehicle. Three of them. All clutching AK-47s. Bald spotted a .50-cal unit mounted on the cargo bed. Two more rebels manning it.

Bald said, 'Joe, you go with Laxman. Nab the fucking dust. The bitch stays with me.'

Gardner headed for the opium den, Laxman alongside him. Bald watched them for a moment longer, sixteen metres to the building, now thirteen, now ten. Then he lowered himself into a squat and reached into the front of the Impala and retrieved his own Type 56, from the dash. The assault rifle was already fully loaded. Kill-time was merely a selector-switch and a trigger-pull away. Bald hadn't used a Type 56 before, but he had plenty of experience with the AK-47, and they were basically the fucking same.

The three guys at the Land Cruiser formed a line. They adopted kneeling fire stances, each man sure that there was five metres between him and the next guy. Not bad, Bald thought. Not geniuses, but these guys weren't amateurs either. They flicked the selectors on their AKs, just like Bald did on the Type 56. Tucked the wooden stocks tight to their shoulders. Unlike Bald, who kept his weapon lowered, not wanting to panic one of these sand wankers into an accidental discharge. Nobody moved. No one fired. There was still a chance this could end without getting noisy. Bald ushered the woman around to the front of the Impala, where she would be best protected against incoming fire. Pushed her down to her knees, like she was sucking dick.

The two guys on the cargo bed of the Land Cruiser were standing at the operating end of the .50-cal, one gripping the handles, the other loading rounds into the feed tray. For a split second Bald thought they weren't going to open fire.

Then they disappointed him.

The first rounds drilled past him. A tight grouping of three shots that pelleted the soil twelve inches from his feet. Bald reacted quickly. He dropped to one knee behind the driver's door of the Impala and listened as two three-round bursts hammered through the bodywork and shredded the engine block. Metal clanged. Glass crinkled. A tyre offered a lung-cancered wheeze. The Chinese woman screamed. In the back seat Fourie's head was buried in his lap. The rear window shattered, showering his hair. Bald lost count of the number of rounds being discharged.

Bald glanced over his shoulder. Gardner and Laxman had reached the opium den. The ground at their six o'clock coughed up burnt sand and hot brass as a volley of rounds slapped into it. Three rounds studded the Cherokee. Voices yelled in Arabic above the clattering gunfire. The guys in the other two pickups had finished gathering either side of the Land Cruiser, completely blocking off the road and the one exit from this clusterfuck. Bald peered out from the side of the door and quickly assessed the number of threats he was up against. He counted four guys debussing from the pickup to the left of the Land Cruiser. Another three on the right. Add that lot to the five guys at the Land Cruiser and he was facing down twelve rebels in total.

A dozen guys tooled up with AK-47s. Probably a few mortars and grenades in their arsenal too. Bald had his Type 56 and the Makarov. Gardner had the Sig, which was good for slotting targets up to a range of fifty metres but beyond that was about as effective as hurling insults.

Not good odds.

Not good at all.

On the Land Cruiser the two-man team had finished reloading the .50-cal. The guy on the left held the belt of .50 BMG cartridges at the feed tray. The guy on the right had his right hand on the trigger mechanism, his left hand propped against the rear of the weapon for support.

Another series of AK bursts shredded the air. Nine of them, in clusters of three, *rap-rap-rap*, spitting at and cleaving the ground around him, turning the Impala into a fucking homemade colander. Can't run, Bald told himself. You don't have the manpower or the firepower to perform any evasive action. Face it: you're in the shit. The only thing you can do is keep them pinned down. Three more rounds whipped and zipped and fumed past Bald. One smacked into the side window and spider-webbed the glass four inches from his skull.

'For fuck's sake, lad, get me out of here,' Fourie shouted.

'Save your breath,' said Bald.

'Wait,' said Fourie.

Bald waited.

'I can cut you something extra,' Fourie said. 'A week ago I had some Libyan general literally begging me to get him out of Dodge. I said I'd drive the prick to Niger.'

'This isn't the time for your fucking stories, Bill.'

'Listen, you dopey cunt. The general paid me for safe passage. I'm talking forty kilos in gold bullion. You know how much forty k's worth, John? One point three million pounds. But I didn't drop the guy off. I told him to hide in the boot. Then I drove to the middle of the desert, emptied the gold and set the car on fire. Cunt cried his way to a fucking early grave.' He laughed at death, did Fourie. Then he said, 'I have the coordinates, John. Right here in my pocket. I can give them to you. More than a million quid. All yours. All I'm asking is for you to let me go.'

'I'll think about it,' Bald said. Still ducking, he moved to behind the front wheel of the Impala, next to the woman. She was curled up on the ground. Bald pushed up to a three-quarters standing position so that his head, but not the rest of him, was above the vehicle. He aligned the iron sights with the two guys manning the .50-cal.

There was a truism people accepted readily about the AK-47, which was equally true for its Type 56 sister, and it was this: when it came to accuracy, its aim was about as good as a drunk guy taking a piss in a nightclub. It splashed all over the fucking place. But in Bald's experience it wasn't the gun that was wildly inaccurate, but people's perceptions. With a typical grouping of AK shots, at a hundred metres there would be a maximum of four inches between the two shots farthest apart. Technically speaking, that was inaccurate. But four inches was less than the width of a human face. And if you could nail a guy's face from a hundred metres, that made a weapon effective in Bald's book.

He had the selector on the Type 56 switched to single-fire. Single-fire was more surgical. If you fired three shots on the hop, the second would be less accurate than the first, and the third less accurate than the second. And so on. Bald kept it stupid-simple and went for two quick but separate shots at the guys on the machine-gun.

Ca-rack.

Ca-rack.

His aim was true. The guy on the left jerked like he'd just been given the defibrillator treatment. Blood arced out of his pulverized eyeball. He turned to his mate, spraying blood into his face. His mate had just enough time to register his shock when the second round pierced the right side of his neck. A great place to hit someone, if you wanted to really fuck them up. There's the big carotid artery to puncture there. The guy jerked and flailed and slumped across the barrel of the .50-cal. Torrents of blood gushed from his neck, slicking the barrel in a red grease. His hands spasmodically pawed at his face, slapped at his cheeks and clawed at his throat. Then he went all heavy and slack and died. Just another cunt who chose the wrong man to pick a fight with.

Bald watched him die and felt nothing.

A lull in the shooting.

The dead guys' three mates pulled back to the sides of the Land Cruiser. To seek extra cover, Bald assumed. But also because they were thinking what every soldier thinks when he sees a mucker buying a one-way ticket to the graveyard: what if it's me next? They were doing the maths in their head. They'd fired more than a dozen shots and killed nobody. Bald had fired two shots and chalked up two KIAs. It might make them think twice. For a few seconds. But their second thought would be, let's nail this fucking bastard. Bald used this pause of uncertainty to cast a look at his six. No movement at the den. It had been fully two minutes since Gardner and Laxman had gone inside.

'What's taking them so long?' Bald asked nobody.

Fourie said, 'Laxman is a fucking liar. It ain't here.'

Bald didn't have time to play games with Fourie. In the corners of both eyes he clocked movement. Right and left. Simultaneous. Coordinated. Silhouettes shuttling across the sides of the road. Four to the right. Three to the left of Bald. The four at his three o'clock concerned him the most. They were encircling him. Closing the net. Smart for third-world squaddies. They grouped by the corner of the north- and east-facing walls of the mosque, dropped to one knee and started putting rounds down on him in three-round bursts.

Now Bald swivelled round and from his kneeling fire stance unloaded a trim succession of rounds at the rebels. Shoot, breathe, shoot. *One-two-three.* The ground coughed up dirt in their faces. The mosque wall spat mortar over them. The rounds didn't hit, but that wasn't Bald's primary aim. He wanted to keep them pinned down, make them shitless and run for cover. *Four-five-six.* Brass tumbled and clinked around Bald's feet. He felt one round flick back in his face and leave a hot mark on his eyebrow. The ankle of the rebel furthest to his left first buckled and then folded in on itself. *Seven-eight-nine.* The other three guys retreated to the rear of the mosque. To cover. They left their mate howling at the bone and gristle exposed at the raw end of his leg. Piss and shit darkened the soil around him. A tenth round from Bald's Type 56, unaccompanied, a lonely shot, nailed the rebel in the sweet spot, right between his eyes. Another cunt put out of his misery.

Ten rounds at the mosque. Plus two at the guys on the .50-cal. Twelve spent, eighteen rounds of 7.62mm left. No spare clips.

He saw two more guys scrambling onto the Land Cruiser's cargo bed. The .50-cal. He had to choose between putting rounds down on them and the three guys at his nine o'clock. They were headed for the opium den. Bald concluded these were the more immediate threat. Gardner had the Sig, and he was a big boy, but he was outnumbered and outgunned. So Bald arced the Type 56 against the three guys and unloaded eight rounds in a rhythmic burst. He chopped down the guy leading the assault sixteen metres from the den. Rounds one and two dipped and dived and hit the dirt. Round three slapped into the guy's gut and sent him into a balletic whirl. Round four was the money shot. Scalped the cunt. Brain matter sprayed across the ground. Bald could make out the coconut outline of his exposed brain, sloshing around in his skull like a meatball in a pan of water. The guy stacked it.

Ten rounds left.

Bald turned his attention to the opium den.

Still no sign of Gardner or Laxman.

Then he heard the sound he had dreaded the most.

The .50-cal.

The two guys had managed to climb up while he'd been taking one of the three guys heading for the den. Now they opened fire. The first three rounds impacted into the rear end of the Impala. The chassis squealed as the rounds opened up new craters in the bodywork and flung pieces of metal, leather and glass into the air.

'Fucking cunting fuck,' Fourie said as the rounds corkscrewed past him. Bits of shrapnel pinballed around the interior.

A smell of burning rubber assailed Bald.

He whirled back around. The den. Toxic black smoke was pouring from the building. The smoke was so thick he couldn't tell whether it was coming from inside or from the stack of tyres he'd seen to one side of the den. He caught the spectral glimpse of two silhouettes rampaging through the smoke. The rebels. Tongues of fire sparked at the door. The Sig Sauer barked. A guy howled. Another guy shouted. The first guy howled again.

Fuck, thought Bald. The plan's going down the shitter.

Bald put down fire on the Land Cruiser and shut the .50-cal up for a few precious seconds, peppering the vehicle with hot lead. Eight rounds. Then he got the dreaded *click-click*. Empty mag. Bullets ricocheted off the bonnet of the Land Cruiser and glanced off the .50-cal. Bald looked back to the den.

Through the smoke he saw a figure breaking through the door.

Laxman.

He was on fire.

forty-three

1659 hours.

Flames licked at Laxman's wild arms and legs. He was howling. The smell of burning human flesh festered in the air. Bald was powerless to do anything as Laxman fled towards the mosque. Powerless except to watch the .50-cal rounds pump away at Laxman and speedball through the air and slice and dice his torso in half, blood wellspringing out of his legs at the severed hips, all kinds of stringy shit evacuating from his stomach cavity. Fresh out of ammo, Bald couldn't even put the cunt down and end his pain.

He could only watch his five large, and his villa in Monte Carlo, going up in smoke.

Bald stayed low by the Impala. The Chinese woman was cowering by his side. Her face was buried in the ground and she was breathing heavy, snotty breaths, like she was snorting sand. Now Bald was focused on survival. Not winning. Just getting out of this situation alive. He saw the three remaining rebels at the mosque emerge from cover. A second later he saw the two rebels from the opium den running towards him. He was trapped on both sides, with the .50-cal blocking off his only other exit corridor.

The guys at the mosque were thirty metres away. Then twenty. Then ten. Bald considered the inescapable shitness of his situation. He was out of rounds, out of escape plans and out of hope. His best plan was to look dead. So he splayed himself face down on the sand, his legs and arms worked into the odd sprawls of the dead, and pressed the woman down beside him, making her play dead too. Then he waited, hoping to bollocks that Fourie didn't make a noise.

The smell of burnt flesh dissipated. Or rather, it was consumed by a stronger smell closer to Bald. Something tangy, spicy, but retaining the after-taste of an overflowing dumpster. He heard the slow grind of gravel trodden underfoot. The sound came from his six o'clock.

A familiar voice said, 'Give me the gun.'

Younes.

Bald stayed dead.

'I know you are alive. You can stop pretending now.'

Bald looked up. Younes towered over him. He had his Makarov lined up between Bald's eyes. He took a long, satisfied drag on the smoke between his lips. His features were caked in a layer of mortar dust. His fatigues were dusted the colour of alabaster. He blew smoke at Bald and offered his hand. Bald didn't accept it, but he handed the Type 56 to him, stood up and surveyed the damage. The ground was sprinkled with spent brass. Battle's crop, waiting to be harvested. The fire raged inside the opium den. The rebels were heading back to the pickups. Younes nodded at them; he wanted Bald all to himself.

Bald said, 'So why were you after Laxman?'

Younes shrugged with his bottom lip.

'The Americans told us to protect him.'

Bald coughed. Burnt air scorched his lungs.

'What Americans?'

Younes smirked. 'CIA.'

Bald immediately thought, Hauser.

'But if you were told to protect him, why the fuck is he dead?'

Younes threw his tab to the floor. It fizzled out in the sand.

'Just because the CIA helped us, it doesn't mean we are their slaves.' Younes stepped right up to Bald and traced a dirt-flecked hand over the scar on his own neck. 'You see this? The CIA and MI5 abducted me. Two years ago. I was in Frankfurt. For a medical conference – I used to be a doctor. They stopped me at the airport, put me in handcuffs. They took me to a private jet and flew me to Bangkok. I was taken to a prison somewhere outside the city. They introduced me to a man from Libyan intelligence. He tortured me for three days. If you or your American brothers think we have short memories in Libya, you are wrong.'

He spat on the ground.

'Enough bullshit,' Younes went on. 'You are a dead man. But I can do it slow or do it fast. It's up to you. If you tell me what you're really doing here: fast. If not: slow. And please, no lies. I know your NATO cover story is lies. I asked my superiors. They know nothing about you.'

'I'm offering you a treasure,' said Bald. 'I'm talking gold bullion. Buried in the desert. I have the coordinates.'

Younes laughed at the ground, his corpulent belly jellying up and down, his double-chin wobbling.

'Treasure. Buried in the desert. Now we are in a children's story.' He looked back up at Bald. The smile was uncurling itself into a plain and simple rage. 'You think I am a peasant? Or worse, a fool? It must be one or the other, since only a fool or a peasant would believe such a tall story.'

Fucking Fourie, Bald thought. The cunt played me.

'Of course,' Younes went on, 'this is not the first time you have lied to me. Just like you lied about being sent here by NATO.'

The words hit Bald like a fist. He felt the rebel's raw, intense stare-down. The man's black poker-chip eyes searched the lines of Bald's face. 'I don't know what you're talking about,' Bald said. 'I'm here on NATO business. Go check if you don't believe me.'

'I already did.'

Bald stiffened.

'None of our NATO contacts has ever heard of you.'

Younes flipped the Type 56 around and pointed it at a spot between Bald's eyes. The black hole of the muzzle stared indifferently at Bald. His life whittled down to one pissy second or perhaps two. No way out this time, the rifle seemed to be saying to him. No last fucking words.

Bald waited to die.

A grinding noise trembled across the air. It was back-draughting from up the street, beyond the rebels' pick-ups and towards inner-city Tripoli. Now Bald and Younes traced the sound with their eyes. A dust cloud was spurting up behind the gleaming frame of a Mercedes Benz C-Class, cocaine-white, brand-new, unscathed by the conflict unfolding around it. Each of the front wings carried a flag: a navy-blue field with a central white compass rose emblem and four white lines radiating from the rose. Bald immediately recognized them as the NATO flag.

The Merc swerved to a halt next to the pickups. Two men got out of the rear. The guy on the left was an Arab dressed in military fatigues. The one on the right was European-looking, grey-haired, wearing a suit, sunglasses and a stern expression.

'John!' the guy in the suit shouted at Bald, waved at him too, like a long-lost brother. 'Christ, I've been looking for you all over.' He marched confidently over to Younes, while the Arab folded his arms and stayed back by the Merc. The suit whipped off his sunglasses and pointed them accusingly at the rebel.

'What the fuck is going on here?' he said.

Younes wasn't looking at him. His eyes were on the Arab, a puzzled look sewn into his features. He shot the same look at Bald, the Scot just as thrown by the guy in the suit as he was.

Then, his voice laced with uncertainty, he said to the suit, 'Who are you? And what business does my general have here?'

The man flashed Younes his most evil expression. 'Brad Stromback, NATO liaison. General Safiyah tells me you have one of my contacts hostage.' He nodded sagely at Bald. 'It looks to me very much like you were planning to put him in an early grave. And that would be a grave mistake.'

Younes grimaced. 'I thought he wasn't NATO.'

Stromback jabbed his sunglasses at Younes's chest. 'Well, do us all a favour and un-fucking-think. Christ, we're here to help you win this bloody war and all you're doing is trying to execute my men.'

Then he turned to Bald, put an arm around his shoulder and said, 'It's bloody good to see you again, John. How's the wife?'

Bald hoped the confusion he was feeling wasn't billboarded all over his face. He tried to keep his features straight and blank, but he was slow to respond to Stromback's question and the NATO man quickly filled the awkward silence. 'Oh, I'm sorry. I forgot. You're separated these days. My memory.'

'Something is not right here,' Younes said, shaking his head.

'The only thing not right is your kidnapping of an ally.' Stromback was suddenly sneering at Younes, looking so authentically pissed off that Bald found himself half-believing it too. 'Hand my guy back over to me before General Safiyah puts you before a firing squad. Your choice.'

Younes hesitated. General Safiyah gave a slight, impartial nod.

Bald wondered why the general wasn't joining Stromback and talking to his man Younes. He figured it was a pride thing. Stromback was in control here; he had his dick wedged up the general's arse, and the general knew it.

Younes slowly lowered the Type 56. Stromback put his sunglasses on, eyefucked Younes for a moment longer, then told him, 'Your business here is finished, sir.'

Younes trudged back towards the Land Cruiser with his head down. He stopped after ten metres, looked back at Bald and said, 'They say the CIA helped Bin Laden against the Soviets. Now they help us. It's a good thing that the Americans are so naive.'

Then he walked on.

Stromback curled a long finger at Bald. 'You're to return to the Mansour sharpish. Your guest is waiting there for you.'

What guest? Bald thought. 'Uh, yeah. My guest. Got it.' He looked back at the burning building and called to Stromback, 'I'll catch you up.'

The NATO man was already spinning around as he said, 'Don't take too long. There's still pockets of loyalists around here. Wouldn't want you to catch a stray bullet.'

Bald was left with the woman and a pounding headache like a grenade had gone off next to his ear. He watched the fire lap over every last inch of the opium den. The building was almost razed to the ground. Two dead guys to the right. One was the rebel Bald had slotted. Another rebel lay ten nearer to the den, his jeans burnt away by the fire, his exposed flesh all flaky and charcoaled, like dark walnut.

The dust, Bald thought.

He started for the den. He didn't give a fuck whether Gardner was dead or not. But he still figured he could make his fortune off the dust. Even better, if Gardner was out of it he could cut a more pleasing split with Fourie. And he reasoned that a top-secret technology like ID wouldn't be carted around in a standard briefcase. No. It would be sealed up inside a Pelican-style box, engineered to be fireproof and waterproof and bombproof and everything-proof. Bald got to within ten metres of the place before the heat suddenly became intolerable. It scalded his skin and singed the hairs on his face. He took another step forward and felt like someone was holding a Zippo lighter under his eyes.

Bald stopped. The heat was sending his sweat glands into overkill. Through his blurred vision he surveyed the damage to the opium den. He saw collapsed concrete and twisted metal and the outline of a body fused to some kind of warped plastic. The features had been burnt to shit, but Bald figured it was Gardner.

'Fucking cunt. Couldn't even do a simple little thing right.'

He peeled away from the blaze and strode back towards the Impala, his face lit up with determination. Telling himself that since Laxman was dead, his mission had been achieved. It didn't matter that some rebel chancer had put him down. Who the fuck was going to know? And one dead Laxman meant five million quid. Which wasn't anywhere near as good as twenty million, but it was better than a kick in the teeth.

He spotted the Chinese woman scurrying away from the Impala. She was headed in the same direction the pickups had taken. Bald withdrew the Makarov from his jeans and cocked the hammer. The sound was distinct and crisp in the air. The woman stopped running. He watched the slim line of her shoulders sag. Then she did a little pirouette. A smile vacillated on her face beneath the dirt.

'Where the fuck do you think you're going?' he said.

'Home,' the woman said.

'I didn't say you could go anywhere.'

The smile thinned out.

'Why you keep me?'

'Because you were with Laxman.'

She tried to conjure up the smile again, but this time it just looked sad.

'He paid me for sex. That was it. I didn't know him any better than you.'

Bald said nothing.

'I'm just a call girl.' The woman folded her arms impatiently. The black pearls of her eyes stared at Bald.

'You know something, don't you?' he said.

She didn't get a chance to reply. The pickups were suddenly coming under heavy fire from a thin line of loyalists pitched fifty metres further up the street. Incoming rounds dashed around the vehicles. A couple of strays bounced around Bald and the woman. She managed to shake herself free in the confusion and made for the dirt field, in the same direction as the civilians who'd earlier fled from the mosque. Bald moved to chase her. Then he caught a sound coming from his immediate right.

Inside the Impala.

Fourie.

Bald edged towards the back of the car. Fourie was still inside, head in his lap, hands by his side. Just like the illustration from the airplane safety sheet. Except that Fourie's brains were splashed all over the place, ruining a perfectly good interior. His head was tilted at a slight angle and his right eye was prised open and hooked on Bald. Blood, gummy and mixed up with bits of brain matter and chipped bone, was leaking out of the hole.

He'd been hit by a stray .50-cal round.

Fuck this cunt, Bald thought. If he'd had the chance he would've slotted Fourie himself. He reached into the back seat and padded Fourie down for his GPS navigator, thinking that he could nab the coordinates to the treasure and take it all for himself. He found it in his jeans pocket. He dragged it out, blood and shit spilling out of Fourie onto the leather interior, splashing over Bald's hands. Finally he pulled it free.

'Cheers Bill,' Bald said to Fourie.

But he could swear Fourie was smiling at him.

Bald inspected the navigator. A round had smashed through the middle of it. The device was inoperable.

The coordinates were lost.

It took him an hour to get back to the hotel. He'd had to make the journey on foot. The route back had been treacherous. Snipers were holed up all over the place, dead bodies providing their own cautionary tales about what happened to you if you weren't sharp of ear and fleet of foot. He stuck to the shadows and the backstreets and stayed behind cover. At last he reached the Second Ring Road, the rebels' inner security cordon, and he was able to relax. The atmosphere switched from bullets and screams to bullets and cheers. Men were kissing each other in the street. Statues of Gaddafi were being torn down.

Banks of excitable journos had assembled outside the Mansour Hotel. Bald had a theory that all journalists were born pussies and his belief was reinforced by the fact that the majority of them were delivering their reports while decked out in bulletproof vests and blast helmets. Standing in the middle of what was probably the safest patch of land in Tripoli at that moment. He threaded his way past the throng and into the lobby.

Bald was looking forward to three things. He was looking forward to smashing Rachel's arse. That was the third thing. He was looking forward to calling Cave and telling him Laxman was dead, and then reading out his bank sort code and account number. That was number two on his list. But most of all he was looking forward to a cool beer. Libya was mostly dry, but the hotels were known to accommodate Western tastes. Even during a civil war, they were bound to have a few lagers on tap.

He made a beeline for the hotel bar.

As he barged through the double doors he saw a barman pulling a tall glass of something golden and refreshing. Minutes later he was slaking his thirst when he noticed a guy sitting at a corner table. His legs were crossed. He was wearing a white linen suit and sipping from a glass tumbler filled with some kind of a mixer and ice. He looked like a gay version of The Man from Del Monte.

The man looked up from his copy of the *Daily Telegraph*. 'What a coincidence,' he said.

The man was Leo Land.

forty-four

1900 hours.

Bald was rooted to the spot. Land removed his jacket, revealing a pink shirt beneath, silver cufflinks. He undid the collar button, carefully draped his jacket over the chair and gestured to the free seat opposite.

'Why don't you come over and sit down, John?' He folded up the *Telegraph*. 'You look like you could use a seat. Get your breath back.'

Bald eyed the chair like there was a bomb secreted in the seat.

'Oh, don't be like that. I just saved your bloody life.'

Bald was frazzled and exhausted and hungry, and it took him a few fuzzy seconds to work out what Land was talking about.

'You mean Stromback? The NATO guy?'

'MI6, actually. That was my idea. I knew you'd used NATO cover to get past the border patrols. So I thought it would be in the best interests of us both if I made sure that the rebels believed you. If they knew you were lying, well . . . we wouldn't be having this delightful conversation.'

Land looked pleased with himself. Bald didn't offer him even the hint of a thank you. Instead he said, 'I thought you'd retired.'

Land seemed to find this funny. Bald didn't laugh.

'On the contrary.' Land played with his cufflinks. 'They had to make a big show of putting me out to pasture after that ugly business in Turkey. But the top brass recognized I had a particular set of skills they admired. Skills that most men lack, I should add. So, in the end, I was promoted.'

If Bald had been drinking at that moment he would've spat it over the carpet. 'Promoted?'

Land laughed again. It was a smug, self-satisfied laugh, a guy finding his own jokes hilarious. 'You see, this is precisely why the meek shall *never* inherit the earth. You're too plain and crude. You lack the nous to work yourself into a position of strength. I mean, you do have certain . . . skills, yes, that is the word, isn't it? But you're always doing someone else's bidding. Aren't you? Whereas me, I make other people do mine.'

Bald clenched his fists. His nails dug graves into the palms of his hands. He seriously considered giving Land the tasty end of a knuckle sandwich. Land seemed to pick up on this and said, 'There are agents everywhere, John. You wouldn't even make it out of this hotel. Now be a good chap and sit down and have a drink.'

Bald held his ground for a moment longer. Then he drew up the chair opposite Land and sat down.

'I heard about Bill Fourie's plot,' Land said.

Bald didn't answer.

'We bugged the room Laxman was staying in. And the car Gardner rented too. You should know by now never to underestimate us.' Land crossed his legs the other way. 'I also want you to know, the deal that Fourie talked about, between us and the Gaddafis, it wasn't real.'

Bald still didn't answer.

'But it turns out that Fourie had his own plans. When it came to Gaddafi he was actually currying favour. Particularly with the sons. It's my fault. We should've known better than to send him on that mission. Bit of a menace, that chap.'

'Not any more,' said Bald.

Land expressed no emotion at this news. He paused and searched Bald's eyes. 'Once he had acquired the dust, he was going to kill both Gardner and yourself and keep the money himself.' He paused again. 'But of course, I'm sure you knew that too. What's your poison, John?'

'Beer.'

Land waved to the bartender. Then looked back at Bald. 'One lager coming right up.'

Bald nodded at Land's tumbler.

'You should lay off that stuff,' he said. 'You're gay enough as it is.'

Land raised his glass as Bald's pint arrived. 'Cheers,' he said. He sipped at his drink and licked his lips. 'Nothing makes an Englishman feel like an Englishman quite like a gin and tonic in a foreign land.'

The waiter placed Bald's lager in front of him. He drained a third of it in one gulp.

Land was silent for a moment. Then he said, 'You're probably asking yourself why I'm here.'

'I'm asking myself why you're such a prize cunt,' said Bald.

'I believe you know Daniel Cave? I'm his superior at Six.' He took another sip of his G&T. A cube of ice slipped between his lips. 'I'm most people's superior there now, actually.'

'I couldn't give a fuck what you are.'

Land crunched the ice and let the comment slide.

'You're expecting to get paid for killing Laxman. Am I right? What is it again? Three million?'

'Five,' said Bald.

'Oh. Nice work if you can get it, John. Well, here's the bad news. Cave has made a royal mess of this. You see, the CIA were aware of the sleeper cell and the plot to smuggle out Intelligent Dust from Lance-Elsing quite some time ago. Before we'd been aware of it, in fact.'

'There was a guy from the Agency,' said Bald. 'Hauser. He tried to stop me killing Laxman.' He sank another third of his pint. 'Guess he failed.'

'Well, actually, you are wrong about that.'

Bald felt a dense pressure building in his skull.

'The Yanks wanted to see where the sleeper would lead them,' said Land.

'But why? They already know it's for those Pakistani pricks.'

'Well, no. That's who we *believed* was behind the sleeper cell. But that was a smokescreen. The real brains behind this operation comes from elsewhere.'

'This isn't making any fucking sense.'

Land suddenly shot forward in his seat and grabbed Bald by the wrist. His bony hand had a surprisingly tough grip. Land sneered at him. 'Then you'd better start engaging that fine brain of yours, because this mission as it stands is screwed.'

He released Bald's hand and slumped back in his seat and pulled a disappointed face like a spoilt child.

'Your mission, John, was to prevent Lance-Elsing technology from reaching its destination. And in that context, you have utterly failed. You won't receive a penny until you bloody well do.'

Bald shook his head. 'I killed Laxman. Send your boys across town if you don't believe me.'

'Oh, I know Laxman is dead. But the rub of it is, you didn't kill the right person.'

Bald blazed up. He went hot and cold and numb and pained all at the same time. He managed to say, 'Then who the fuck was it?'

'She was operating under deep cover as a prostitute. Her name is Xia Wei-Lee.'

The Chinese woman. Bald thought about the way she had dressed. The way she had kissed Laxman on the cheek, like at the end of a first date. The black grab-bag over her shoulder.

'She works for Chinese intelligence,' Land said. 'And you let her get away.'

forty-five

Leo Land peered down from the balcony at the street forty metres below and frowned. He tucked a Montecristo cigarillo between his lips. Patted down his trouser pockets for a light, came up short. He left the unlit cigarillo drooping from his mouth. A white Toyota Hilux was driving at a slow walk at the head of a procession of weary pickups. The new Libyan flag was draped over the Hilux's bonnet, bands of primary red and green with a wedge of black thrusting through the middle. Half a dozen rebel soldiers were hanging from the cargo bed; half a dozen more jogging either side of the truck. The driver was honking his horn and shouting above the blare, 'Libya, Libya!', like a football chant.

Land rolled the cigarillo with his milky hand and scoped out the crowd parading outside the Mansour Hotel. A poor turnout, all things considered. Perhaps a thousand gathered on the pavements. Another thousand walking around in a heady daze. The other 998,000 Tripolians were probably huddled around television sets and radios, preferring to celebrate inside. Perhaps, thought John Bald, they'd already worked out that democracy wasn't all it was cracked up to be.

Land wetted the cigarillo leaves with his tongue. Further down the road and behind the procession, aid workers were stockpiling a dusty lot with body bags. All the time AK-47 muzzles were flashing at the night sky. Assault rifles, defaced icons of a deposed dictator, not a woman in sight; this had all the makings of an Arab street party.

As Land turned away from the street, Bald was propping himself up against the hotel wall and taking a piss while swigging from a bottle of Wild Turkey. The sound of his glugging was matched by the furious stream of urine hissing on scorched brickwork.

'John.' Land folded his arms. 'It's almost time. The plane is waiting.'

Bald had a full tank to empty. He pissed some more. Then he saw Land scrutinizing his cheap plastic watch. On top of everything else, Bald loathed Land for being a tight cunt. Only he could wear the kind of watch you'd find in Poundstretcher.

'It's an eight-hour flight from here to western China,' Land said, his voice superior. 'Xia is en route to the rendezvous. You must catch her before she hands the Intelligent Dust to the Chinese military. I'm sure you realize what would happen then.'

'We all sing the words to "Imagine"?' Bald shook the last few drops from his dick, zipped himself up. 'Get some other prick to do it.'

Land said, 'I know of only two people with the skills for this job, and the other chap is so badly burnt that we'll have to use dental records to make a positive ID.'

'Joe's death wasn't my fault.'

Land cocked his head at Bald. 'I'm getting sick of your excuses.'

The gunfire was basslined by a low and steady *phom-phom-phom*. Anti-aircraft assemblies were jettisoning phos rounds into the sky. The bellies of the clouds glowed synthetic reds and purples and greens. Land grimaced at the sky, then looked back at Bald. 'Don't suppose you've got a box of matches on you, old boy?'

'Don't smoke.'

'No, you just get pissed and screw things up instead.'

Bald shook the last few honeyed drops of Turk out of the bottle and down his throat. Then he turned back and made for the lobby.

Land said, 'Where do you think *you're* going?'

'You're sick of excuses. I'm sick of you. I'm out of here.'

'Fine,' said Land. 'But if you leave now, you can forget about getting paid.'

Bald paused. The hotel room's light was blinking on and off, splitting the balcony into schizoid light and dark. Bald said, 'I did what you asked me to do. Laxman is dead. End of fucking story.'

Land guffawed. 'I'm afraid it's not that simple, John. Your mission was to stop the sleeper and intercept the technology. You failed on both counts.'

Bald clamped his fingers around the door so hard his fingertips went purple, then white. 'We had a deal. I shook hands with Cave. You have to honour it.'

Land plucked the cigarillo out of his mouth.

'I've got some news for you, John. Young Cave has been taken off the case. I'm in charge now. And I'm in control of the purse strings at the Firm these days. If I decide there is no deal, then *voilà* – no deal.'

The sporadic bursts of gunfire suddenly swelled to a drum roar. Bald spun and seized Land by the lapels of his jacket and pushed him back until his head and upper body was suspended over the balcony's edge. Land yanked his head away from Bald as far as his muscles allowed. The veins on his neck were stretched and prominent.

Bald said, 'You're gonna pay up.'

'Or what, John? You'll throw me to my death? What do you think would happen then?'

'I'd get a warm, fuzzy feeling.'

Bald found himself releasing his fingers. Land scrabbled away from him, until his back was against the glass sliding door leading into the room. Time had pulled a fast one on Land, thought Bald. A year had aged the guy ten. His face was gaunt and worn.

'The Chinese are behind everything,' Land sighed. 'We weren't trying to deliberately shaft you, but now they're involved and the goalposts have moved. Why else do you think we helped the rebels? We're trying to protect our interests here. We have contracts for oil and gas, bloody good contracts for Britain.'

Bald still said nothing.

Land went on, 'Our friends in the rebel forces have discovered documents in the security service's offices. Documents that describe meetings between Gaddafi's inner circle and representatives from Beijing.'

'Talking about what?'

'Arms sales. The Chinese reckoned they could ship the arms to South Africa, then route them north into Niger and across the border to Libya. And we're not talking AK-47s here, John. We're talking about state-of-the-art surface-to-air missile launchers, data encryption devices, advanced sniper rifles.'

'I thought there were sanctions?'

'You really think the Chinese care? They were cosying up to Gaddafi because he held the power and thus the oil. Now the uprising has gained momentum they've switched sides and thrown their lot in with the rebels. And what do you suppose happens if the Chinese offer the rebels the dust in exchange for a good deal on the oil?'

Land popped his top collar button, pulled a handkerchief from the pocket of his trousers and began to dab his forehead.

'What with the recession and Afghanistan, our Oriental friends think it's their turn to sit at the top of the table. They believe the dust will help them achieve that goal.'

'And the Yanks? That guy who put a gun to my head in Florida was CIA. He said his orders were to keep Laxman alive.'

'Maybe they wanted to see who Laxman was ultimately dealing with?' Land frowned, then went on, 'Maybe the Agency was willing to let the dust fall into the wrong hands if it meant revealing the chain of command.'

'So they know about the Chinese sleeper?'

'Xia? No,' Land said. 'I don't believe they do. And we'd like to keep it that way.'

'Why not tell them?'

Land ran his tongue around his mouth. 'We came to an arrangement with Lance-Elsing, via Rachel Kravets.'

Bald said nothing.

Land said, 'We agreed that if we managed to snare the sleeper and prevent the handover, they would give us first refusal on their R&D. We'd have access to cutting-edge technology. I'm talking about stuff that even our American cousins wouldn't have.'

'I don't give a fuck about your dirty deals.'

'But you do care about getting paid.'

Bald closed his eyes. Lukewarm sweat was slicking down the sides of his face and slipping through the crevices at the corners of his mouth.

'Ten million,' said Land.

Bald popped his eyes open.

'Double your money, John.' Land's voice prodded at the base of Bald's skull.

'Why should I believe you? You fucked me over before.'

'Christ, man, I just told you: the situation on the ground has changed. This is critical. We need Xia Wei-Lee taken out before she gets the dust to her bosses. At this stage of the game, our paymasters in Whitehall are willing to do anything to make sure that doesn't happen.'

As Land spoke spittle flecked Bald's cheek.

'So here's how it's going to play. You're going to stop being a miserable Scottish drunk, for just one day. And you're going to get on that plane to China.' Land glanced at his naff watch again. 'It's now three-twenty in the morning Beijing time,' he said. 'Xia is due to rendezvous with the Chinese military chiefs at nine-thirty tomorrow evening. We have a company Gulfstream waiting at a secure runway twenty kilometres south of here. Leave now and we can have you on the ground for midday tomorrow. That gives you nine hours to complete your mission.'

'Ten million?' said Bald.

'Ten million,' said Land. 'Payable on completion of the mission.'

Ten million. Bald chewed the number around in his mouth. With that kind of wonga he could start dreaming bigger than the bar and the villa in Monte Carlo. He could relocate to Panama or Colombia, buy himself a whitewashed mansion and a harem of beautiful Latino women. He was starting to see the mission in a whole new light.

He said, 'Where's the handover happening?'

'Jinchun. It's in Xinjiang, an autonomous region located in the north-west interior. Shares borders with Kazakhstan, Mongolia and Russia. It's the city farthest from any sea in the world. Getting out won't be easy.'

'When is it ever easy?'

'You'll extract across the western border with Kazakhstan. We'll have a team waiting at an RV spot in the border town of Kargol. Just make sure you get across there by midnight. If our team hasn't heard from you by then, we'll assume the mission has been compromised. This is a non-attributable operation, naturally.'

'Does the Firm do any other kind?'

Land ignored this. 'We'll fly you in on a diplomatic visa. Be careful, and be discreet. China is the second-most heavily monitored country in the world.'

'Who's number one?'

'Britain, of course. We have almost twice as many CCTV cameras as China in a country a fortieth of the size.' He paused and inspected something on the sole of his Oxford brogue. 'The point is, there will always be eyes on you. Cameras, spies, informants.'

Land looked at his watch for the tenth time in a minute.

'Now, I know what you're thinking. How can you stay discreet when everyone else is the best part of a foot shorter and six shades yellower? You can rest easy on that count. Jinchun is just thirty kilometres east of the Kazakh border and not far from Russia either. A white face isn't unusual. I suppose, given the average Russian's penchant for vodka, they won't be too alarmed by your drinking either.'

Bald said, 'Who's the contact on the ground?'

'Sorry to disappoint your libido, John, but it's a he, not a she. And a rather old he at that. But a company man. Loyal. He's been monitoring communications between the military top brass.'

'Where do I find this old fart?'

'English Translation Services Ltd.'

'Another one of your little fronts?'

Land pulled a much-too-straight face. 'English Translation Services provides a valuable tool for assisting Chinese companies with the task of transcribing their texts into the language of business.' He paused, ditched the face, said, 'And also provides us with valuable intelligence about counterfeiting within Chinese industry.'

'I would've thought the Firm had more important things to do than worry about dodgy tabs.'

'We do,' said Land. 'But the Chinese are counterfeiting much more than a few cigarettes. They're the world leaders in forged goods. Currency, electronics, Viagra, car parts, Harry Potter novels. You name it, the Chinese fake it. They butcher domestic dogs to make fake Ugg boots. They export thousands of containers of counterfeit goods every day. A report landed on my desk a few days ago. Aeroplanes, John. Two per cent of the parts on every single commercial airplane in the world are Chinese counterfeits.'

'I don't give a shit. This contact, I'll find him at the translation company's offices?'

Land nodded and took out a passport from his inside pocket. He opened it in the middle. A diplomatic visa was paper-clipped to the left-hand page. Under the clip was a slip of paper folded in half. Land pulled out the paper and unfolded it to reveal a handwritten mobile phone number.

Land said, 'After you've destroyed the dust and neutralized Xia, call this number.'

Bald took the passport and the slip of paper.

'Now remember,' Land continued. 'Xia doesn't have the dust – only the schemata for developing it. So you need to be on the lookout for papers, dossiers, folders. Not weaponry. Not even the Chinese can reverse-engineer a technological breakthrough that fast.'

The cheers in the street below mutated into blue screams. The gunfire ceased. People were shouting and crying. Bald and Land rubbernecked the crowd. The procession was grinding to a halt. In the middle of the chaos a man was cradling the limp and bloodied body of a young boy.

'What if I say no?' said Bald.

Land directed his gaze at him and tightened his face into an angry ball. But Bald wasn't intimidated. He returned the look with interest and said, 'Don't bother trying to threaten me. You've done that too often. It's getting boring listening to the same old track.'

But the closer Bald looked at Land the more he started to think that it wasn't anger hardwired into his face, but something else.

Land said, 'We can't fail, John. If you don't kill Xia and destroy the Intelligent Dust, there'll be repercussions.'

Bald cocked his head at Land, looking into his well-bred blue eyes. And he dimly realized what he'd been seeing in Land since they had met in the hotel bar.

Fear.

forty-six

At six-five Bald towered over the crowd streaming down
the street. His height granted him an unobstructed view of
the electronic shops and Western coffee shops lining both
sides of the wide road, as well as the ash-grey office blocks
and brown new-built apartments chaotically arranged
on the horizon. Bald stood out in his informal clobber
of olive-green, loose-fit T-shirt, dark-blue zip-up hoodie,
desert-coloured combats and Timberland Earthkeepers.
The locals opted for the harassed businessman look. Drab
grey suits and white shirts, many of them with a Marlboro
Red hanging from their bottom lip. They were the perfect
match for the city itself, with its monotone skyline, septic
smells and brick-dust air.

'Mister, you want?' an old woman broken-Englished at
Bald. Four-foot nothing and perched on an upturned food
crate, she was hawking some kind of deep-fried foodstuffs.
They smelled good and reminded Bald of home. A closer
look served up disappointment. It wasn't pizza she was
frying, but what looked like scorpions.

'Mister, you try.'

Bald waved her away.

Someone nudged into his back. He spun round, working his hands into fists. Found himself chin to forehead with a road sweeper. The guy wasn't much taller than the woman selling deep-fried shit. He didn't look a whole lot younger either. He was decked out in sky-blue overalls and cap, and a pair of worn grey sneakers. The broom in his hands had a long stick that was almost as tall as the guy himself, and attached to the end was a thick pad of bristles.

The guy dead-eyed Bald.

'You want to say something?' said Bald.

Road Sweep didn't answer. The big Scot thought about punching him into two dimensions. He thought better of it. He was in a foreign country, and he was supposed to be covert. He uncurled his fists, let go the tension in his spine and gave Road Sweep his back.

He set off towards the apartment block housing English Translation Services. The block was easy to spot for Bald above the bobble of Chinese heads.

Bald remembered what Land had told him back in Libya. 'There will always be eyes on you.' Now he noticed a young woman to his right. Short black hair, dressed in a red cheongsam with a phoenix pattern splashed across the front. She was glaring at Bald. So was a plump, forty-something man in shades and a cheap black suit. Hard to tell whether they were government agents monitoring his movements, or merely locals giving him the famously warm Chinese welcome. He upped the pace. Checked his six o'clock again, searching out the street cleaner. Bald was starting to wonder whether Road Sweep had been dead-eyeing him for a reason other than a casual hatred of foreigners.

The guy had disappeared.

Bald reached the apartment block. The entry door had been wedged open and he stepped inside.

No lobby. No security guard. No intercom beside the door. Just a naked concrete floor, equally bare walls, and a staircase. Place looked more like a prison. Each door had a metal letterbox, and flyers were trapped in these, jutting out like colourful tongues. Bald looked at the business listing fixed to the wall. Helpfully it told him in English that English Translation Services was on the third floor. Bald started climbing. The temperature was cool in the block but he quickly worked up a sweat.

The third-floor landing was L-shaped with a single door to the right. Green paintwork was flaking off the door, revealing scabs of rusted metal beneath. The metal between the lock and the door frame had been reduced to a molten splodge like wax. Bald immediately recognized it as the handiwork of a Hatton breaching round. He stilled his body for a moment, trapped his breath in his throat and listened for movement.

Nothing.

He pushed the door open and edged inside. Entered a room that appeared to be a reception area. About five metres by three, with a linoleum floor that smelled vaguely of antiseptic, it contained an uncomfortable-looking leather sofa and a bank of grey filing cabinets. At the far end another door led into a bigger office. Bald moved cautiously towards it. His breathing was low and his movements were deliberate. At the door he did a quick sweep of the room, and quickly established there were no threats inside. A wooden bookcase to the left was filled with ancient-looking books. Centre stage was a walnut desk.

There was a globe on it, and a guy behind the desk. He was slumped forward in his executive swivel chair. Head down, like he'd fallen asleep going over some paperwork.

Hole in the back of his head.

The hole was fresh and prominent and deep, like a surgeon had been performing brain surgery and had forgotten to sew the guy's scalp up. Blood swamped down from the back of his head and his forehead before dripping off the tip of his nose and settling into a still-moist gel on the desk. The hair surrounding the entry wound had been burnt away. Nothing but singed, charcoaled skin. Smoke still whispered off the surface of the hole.

Bald manoeuvred around the desk to get a solid look at the guy's profile. Gears clicked and aligned themselves in his head into a single thought.

I know this guy.

Bald froze for a long moment. He spied a bottle of Bowmore twelve-year-old quietly maturing on the book-shelf. He seized it and unscrewed the cap and made a silent toast to the body slumped over the desk. It had been three hours since he'd last had a sip. Long enough that now he thought about it, he could feel another migraine coming on. Since he'd started this op in Mexico and been cut off from his supply of amitriptyline, he'd been relying on alcohol to ward off the migraines. And so far his experiment in self-treatment was working out all right. As long as he juiced his bloodstream with alcohol every six hours, he could keep the lid on the migraines and get on with his life.

Bald necked a half-thumb measure of the Bowmore, mentally reset the timer on his internal booze clock, and asked himself where he went from here. Land had instructed him to link up with the old guy. The old guy knew where to find Xia. But judging from the hole in his head, someone had found Edgar Mallory first. Bald needed a Plan B.

He decided to call Land.

Bald had been equipped for his mission with a BlackBerry Bold modified by the Firm's tech-heads to operate on a dual-frequency receiver. It had the necessary security hardware and software to encrypt phone calls and text messages in code similar to the encrypted GPS signals employed by the US military. In a country teeming with paranoia like China, you didn't want to take any chances. Bald tapped in Land's mobile number and tapped the call button. The line crackled. Eight long seconds later he got a ringtone – fuzzy, three beats long. On the fifth ring the mobile redirected him to voicemail. A corporate female voice told him to leave a message.

Bald said, 'Stop sucking dick and pick up. The back half of our contact's head is missing.' He drained another measure of Bowmore and went on, 'You didn't tell me Edgar Mallory was working for you guys. He was the worst rupert ever to disgrace the Regiment. The lads tried to frag him in Iraq.' He wiped his lips with the back of his hand. 'Just thought you should know.'

Bald pushed the kill button and stashed the BlackBerry in his jeans pocket.

Edgar Mallory. 'A company man,' Land had said. 'Loyal.'

Bald eyed the dead guy and looked at exactly where loyalty got you in this fucking life. He took a last swig of the Bowmore, screwed the cap back on and replaced the bottle on the shelf. There was nothing else for him to do here, and he didn't want to run the risk of whoever had murdered Mallory coming back, so he jogged back down the stairs and emerged onto the street, checking his BlackBerry every five seconds. The signal bars had declined from five to zero and there was an SOS icon in the top-right corner. The BB had lost its signal completely. That didn't make much sense, even to someone of his limited technological smarts. He was bang in the middle of a brand-new city in China. There had to be a dozen mobile-phone masts within pissing distance of his current location.

Suddenly Bald realized how isolated he was.

A lone man in a city of one million, in a country of one billion, with a slotted contact and no way of reaching out to the agent who'd sent him on the op in the first place. Bald hung a right down the main drag. He constantly checked his BB for a signal. Nothing. Bald felt his ten million quid slipping away, pound by fucking pound.

He walked a further fifty metres, then turned right onto a side street. He wasn't headed anywhere in particular, concerned only with getting a signal on his BB. The narrow street was deserted. Office blocks the colour of smoke-screens, gum-stubbled pavements, flaking adverts and a single dark electronics shop hawking counterfeit iPads and iPhones. A Lamborghini Gallardo hurtled down the road towards Bald, the engine booming out its unmistakable growl. People stopped and stared. Bald watched the Lambo flash past his shoulder, slow down fast, then grind to a halt in the distance.

And that's when he stopped too, and felt a band tighten around his chest. Road Sweep was standing forty metres to his six o'clock. He was clutching his broom but he wasn't busy sweeping up Coke bottles and McDonald's wrappers. He was pushing his way through the crowd.

Gunning straight for Bald.

forty-seven

1339 hours.

Bald threaded further up the side street. Away from Road Sweep. Fast. After a hundred metres, he veered left onto a residential street swarming with the sweet-and-sour smell of noodle bars and body odour. Bald checked his BB. The SOS icon remained doggedly in the top corner. Road Sweep was now thirty metres behind. Gaining. Bald took the first right and found himself arrowing down a tiny street. He was hit by a smell of raw sewage. Piles of bin bags were torn open at the seams. Bald wormed past a squabble of Chinese beggars with faces like unwiped arses. Three fuckers had runny noses and clusters of skin lesions on their faces and hands. The tell-tale signs of leprosy.

Sixty metres down the backstreet, Bald ducked into the first left turn. Road Sweep stuck to his tail. Bald hurried past a stretch of dwellings that looked like hangovers from pre-Communist times. The timber on the ramshackle houses was weathered and the roof tiles were discoloured various shades of ill-brown. Tattered talismans were fixed to the front doors. Nobody was outside.

Bald was twenty metres down the street when Road Sweep swung round the corner. Bald broke into a run and darted into an alley at his nine o'clock. It was deserted but cramped. Twelve metres deep, three wide, the back end of it sealed off by a chicken-wire fence three metres high. Dead end. Bald headed for the fence; a rat squealed and scurried out of an open dumpster midway down the alley. Then suddenly there were a dozen of the fuckers streaming around his feet. He kicked them away, sending three or four of them flooding back to the dumpster and the discarded noodle boxes and yellow-bean sauce pots. A thought formed in the back of his brain. Why am I running from this midget?

Then he got his answer as the first blow struck his back.

The pain epicentred at the base of his spine and expanded up into his shoulders and lat muscles. It sent Bald flying forward, like the ground had tilted down at a steep angle and now he was crash-landing. The blur of pain took on definition and form. It became something sharp and vicious. Bald tried rolling onto his back. The second blow came mid-roll. He glimpsed the broomstick swinging down. Too late to block. It smashed into his shoulder, hard wood greeting the bony blade of his shoulder. This new pain was instant and intense. But if he wanted to survive he needed to fight through it. He packaged the pain. Sealed it up and FedEx-ed it to the dark recesses of his brain.

Now he looked up to see Road Sweep bringing the broom handle down at his face.

In Bald's mind the best operators weren't the toughest, or the smartest, or even the best with an assault rifle. Those guys were the ones who usually got killed first. The operators who survived were the ones who could think on their feet, even while multiple X-rays were putting heat down on them and they were low on ammo. Bald had less than a second to react to the blow coming at him. He wasn't able to block the shot; something had snapped in his left shoulder. Felt like his blade had cracked into a half-dozen shards. And he didn't have enough time to roll out of the way. But he had another idea.

He shot up and forward with his head low and his chin tucked into his neck, and he thrust the hard shell of his cranium into Road Sweep's midriff. He hit the little prick hard. The guy grunted, backstepped unsteadily, the force of the blow tipping him off balance. Bald kept charging into him. The guy tumbled onto his backside. The fight was turning in Bald's favour. In the same fluid motion Bald sprang fully upright. Badly winded, Road Sweep generously presented his torso for a free hit. Bald gratefully took up the offer. He fired a Timberland at Road Sweep and winded him for a second time. Road Sweep made a weird sound. Creased his face into a ball of pain. Bald went to kick him again. He was vicious for such a stumpy fucker, thought Bald.

But now Road Sweep was moving his left arm, and Bald realized his left hand was still gripping the broomstick, and he was sweeping it across his front in a fast and low arc. The stick thwacked into Bald's right ankle with such immediate force and power of delivery that he was knocked clean off his feet. His ankle exploded with pain. Like someone had shotgunned his foot clean off. He fell sideways, bumping his head against the rim of the dumpster on his downward trip. Road Sweep was scraping himself off the ground, swinging and twirling his broomstick again. The stick made a whooshing sound as it chopped and diced thin air. Road Sweep was building up the momentum for a final, fatal strike. Bald picked himself up. Road Sweep twirled the stick inches from his face.

Then it stabbed him in the chest.

The blows came in a rapid-fire burst. One, two, three jabs. Road Sweep's hands moved with bewildering speed. This guy's had some serious training, Bald was thinking. Himself, he hadn't spent a solitary hour of his life studying martial arts and now he felt something hard crack in his ribcage. He formed his hands into an X in front of his chest to try to deflect the incoming shots, but Road Sweep simply directed his jabs lower, at his stomach and groin. He jabbed repeatedly. He went lower, at Bald's ankles and shins. The pain formed a ball of vomit in Bald's throat. Suddenly Road Sweep took a step back on his right foot and kept his left planted firmly in front of him, then raised the broomstick high over his head and brought it down in a diagonal arc, slashing it across Bald's chest. He drove the stick like a golf wedge into the side of his face. That was the blow that did for Bald. He dropped to his knees. His body was limp and numb. He tried moving. His muscles felt like bags of slag cement. He was losing the fight.

Road Sweep was still for a moment, watching Bald drop. Then he gripped the stick in the way a martial arts expert grips a samurai sword, the stick seeming to just lightly rest on his open palms, as though he was empty-handed. Bald tried to keep his eye on the stick. He had two immediate problems. One, he was unarmed. Two, the guy he was facing was faster than him and more agile.

On the bad days Bald had a million voices pinging around his head. On the good days he just had the one. The voice of a dozen years in the Regiment and lessons learned at the sharp end of life as a Blade. The good one came to him now. It said, get yourself a weapon.

The broomstick was spinning above Road Sweep's head like a chopper blade.

Bald spotted an empty Chang beer bottle by his ankle, amid the trash. Foamy dregs of beer rested in the bottom.

Road Sweep brought the broomstick down. Bald took evasive action. Scooped up the bottle and shunted to his right. Road Sweep swiped at nothing. From the look on his face he realized Bald had manoeuvred himself into a perfect counter-attacking position. The confusion turned to blood and serrated flesh as Bald slugged the Chang bottle directly into his face. The bottle neck snapped on impact. Bald ignored Road Sweep's screams and gave the bottle a hard twist, churning up the skin on his face, engraving spirals of blood into his forehead and embedding bits of glass in his flesh. The guy's screams went a couple of notes higher. Then Bald dragged the broken bottle across his neck. Road Sweep's left hand released the broomstick, but he wasn't done. He managed to bring his hands up, and he clamped them around Bald's neck and squeezed. As though the little prick was dumb enough to believe he could strangle him. As if he really believed he could still win this fight.

Bald clinched his left hand around Road Sweep's chin and used his thumb and forefinger to prise open his jaw. Then with his other hand he shoved the broken-off bits of the bottle into his cakehole. Forced his mouth shut again and quickly hammered a fist into his cheek. The glass made a wet crinkle as it crumpled inside his mouth. Bald slugged him again. Same spot. Road Sweep started choking on the fragments of glass. He was trying to cough them up, but Bald applied the full strength of his wrists and fingers and forced his gob to stay shut. His legs kicked furiously. His eyeballs were popping out of their sockets.

He stopped kicking.

Bald let go of Road Sweep. He collapsed, a pile of shit and bones, gargling and foaming at the mouth.

Bald was congratulating himself on a job well done when he felt a vibration in his pocket. He dug out his BlackBerry. He felt good about fucking up Road Sweep. Good, too, to finally get a signal on his BB. Three beautiful bars of reception. Land was calling. Bald answered. The line was blitzed by static.

'What the hell is going on? Where have you been? Where's Mallory?' Land fired off his questions in a burst, his diction posh and arthritic.

'Somebody killed him.' Bald was breathing slow and heavy, pumping oxygen back into his overworked muscle groups. 'Didn't you get my message?'

'Shit,' Land said, the word hissing down the line like a snake. Bald pictured Land rubbing his temples, furrowing his brow.

Bald said, 'Since when did Edgar start cashing your cheques?'

'Edgar Mallory was a war hero.'

'He was a fucking joke in the Regiment.'

Land gritted out the words slowly now, 'He left because of internal politics. He had other qualities.'

'If you call being a fag a quality.'

Land paused. Bald glanced at Road Sweep. His skin was whitening. Veins bulging on his neck. Bald figured that bits of the glass had filtered down his throat and punctured his lungs. The cunt was bleeding to death internally.

Bald said, 'Mind telling me how I'm supposed to find Xia now?'

'We're working on finding an alternative intelligence source. But it may take a while. We can't just magic these things up, you know. In the meantime just hold the fort. And watch your back. We have satellite pictures indicating a heavy Snow Leopard presence in your area.'

'Snow Leopard?'

'Chinese Special Forces.'

Bald casually strolled out of the alley and moved down the road, not walking fast enough to draw unwanted attention, checking the faces around him. He manoeuvred between the mobile noodle bars and street stalls and homeless people with no teeth and said, 'Someone was on my case. But I took care of him. He's not a threat.'

A banshee hail of police sirens cried out in the distance, growing louder all the time.

Six thousand kilometres away Land said, 'You bloody fool, John.'

'What?'

'Chinese Special Forces have GPS trackers sewn into their clothing . . .' Land shouted.

The sirens were now harsh and close.

Bald stopped dead. He was staring at the end of the street. Four VW Jettas in Chinese police livery were pulling up ten metres away. Three more bounded down the street at his rear. A dozen guys flew out of the cars. They were dressed in olive-green jackets and trousers. They looked more like squaddies than cops. They were reaching for their holstered pistols.

Land said, 'As soon as you killed that chap, the tracker broadcast a red alert to every Chinese security agent in an eighty-kilometre radius. They know where you are. Get the hell out of there.'

But it was already too late.

forty-eight

1442 hours.

Three cops shoved Bald into the back seat of one of the
cars. They bagged his BlackBerry and gave him stone-
faced looks and a pair of silver-coloured bracelets. The
Jetta was small. Bald had to fold his legs tight against
his stomach in order to squeeze inside. The cops hopped
inside and the car rushed west. Soon they left behind
the American computer stores and Italian fashion empo-
riums and entered a teeming sprawl of grey factories
belching smoke into a white-feather sky. The whole
area was cordoned off with barbed wire and security
cameras. This was backstage China, where factory workers miscarried in the morning and went back to work
in the afternoon, where they worked in enforced silence,
and ingested toxic fumes to make cheap trainers and
smartphones.

Eight kilometres west of Jinchun city centre civilization
abruptly ended. There had been concrete and steel and
glass. Now there was just desert plains and hunchbacked
mountains.

'Where the fuck are you taking me?' said Bald.

'This place very bad for you,' the guy in the front
passenger seat said in jerky English. His uniform jacket

carried more coloured insignias than his mates'. Senior officer, thought Bald.

'China is home of torture.' This from the guy next to Bald. He had a bumfluff moustache and flabby jowls. 'Water torture, slow slicing, tiger bench.' Bald didn't react but the man went on anyway. He began laughing and Bald saw he had a dreamy look in his eyes. 'We put your legs on bench. Strap belts around legs. Then put bricks under your legs. One hour, one brick. Two hour, two brick. Then three brick, and four, until it is very high, and all the bones in your legs break.'

Bald shot the cops an angry look courtesy of the rear-view mirror. 'I'm here on a diplomatic visa. You lay a fucking finger on me, you'll have to answer to the British FO.'

The senior officer in the front turned side on to Bald. 'You killed a Chinese soldier.'

'It was self-defence,' said Bald.

No one said a word.

Traffic on the motorway thinned out. The road sluiced between two mountain ranges. The mountains were low and long and the colour of sandbags. Twenty kilometres due west of Jinchun and the Jetta was the only vehicle on the road.

The silence was punctured by the trilling of Bald's BB. The senior officer made Bald hand it over, and frowned at the screen with his bottom lip. He held the screen up in front of him so that Bald was able to read the digits for the Unknown Number. The number was for Leo Land.

'A friend?' the guy asked Bald.

Bald said nothing.

The officer flipped out the battery, the SIM card and the 4GB memory card. He deposited both SIM and memory card in the left breast pocket in his jacket. He said, 'You are busy. He can leave message.'

Seven kilometres west of the mountains the driver hung a right off the motorway. The road degraded into a single potholed lane that ploughed through cold, dry and desperate land. The Jetta was going at a steady fifty kilometres per hour. The chassis absorbed most of the jolts and jars as they bounced down the road. Bald still had no idea where he was being taken. Now the Jetta began shedding speed. The desert land suddenly breathed into life and became verdant fields. Four hundred metres up ahead Bald could make out a deserted square with a building either side of it, and a third, much bigger one a hundred metres further back. The square was filled with cypress and magnolia trees and dotted around were statues of dragons and lions and camels. The buildings stood in a perfect symmetrical arrangement in the square, and this intrigued Bald. The China he'd seen so far amounted to little more than a smoggy industrial hellhole. But this place looked like the China of martial arts movies. Bald thought the large building might be some kind of a temple.

The driver pulled the Jetta to a rest twenty metres short of the square. The driver and the senior officer climbed out, leaving Bald lodged in the back seat with Bumfluff for company, the two of them just listening to the *tick-tick* of the cooling engine. Bald had the growing suspicion that the cops were going to slot him out here. He briefly wondered whether they had vultures in China.

The door to his right unlocked. The senior officer peered in at Bald and gestured.

'Get out,' he said.

Outside the Jetta, Bald sucked in a lungful of gritted air. A gentle breeze was blowing dust into his nose and lips and eyes.

Any second now, he was thinking, he's going to march you away from the car. And he's going to put a bullet between your eyes.

Bald tried to cook up an escape plan. His hands were locked behind his back. He was not armed. The three cops were. During the ride Bald had got a close look at the weapon Bumfluff, next to him, was holding. The logo on the grip told him it was a Norinco-manufactured nine-mil. It could chamber five rounds, and since the other two cops were packing the same, that made a total of fifteen rounds of 9mm Parabellum. If he tried fleeing he'd get nailed in the back.

Then a low rumble reached his ears, like a thunderbolt hammering in slow motion. It came from his six o'clock. A car on the horizon. White bodywork, headlights shaped like cat's eyes. A Lincoln Town Car. Curved bonnet, shortened grille. Bald watched the Lincoln lumber towards them – doing no more than thirty per, he reckoned – and crawl to a stop five metres or so behind the Jetta. A chauffeur hopped out, opened the rear door and helped his passenger out of the car. The legs came first, then the rest of her followed, and last her head, caressed by short, glossy black waves of hair. She straightened up and nodded at the cops. A sign that she was in charge.

The cops stood erect as Xia Wei-Lee walked towards them – a stand to attention minus the salute. Bumfluff and the driver held Bald by the arms as she approached.

Xia marched towards Bald, stopping a metre short of him. She nodded and said, 'I know you came here to kill me.'

She was wearing a serious-looking Mao suit. The top half was a stiff tunic the colour of pomegranate with four pockets and five gold buttons running down the front and another three on each cuff.

Xia smiled a strange kind of a smile at Bald. He could see stresses in the corners of her eyes and lips as she froze it for five long seconds, then it crawled back underneath her skin like a snake slipping into the long grass. She shouted something at Bumfluff, then snatched his weapon from his hand. There was a lot of sudden motion around Bald. Bumfluff breaking to one side, the senior officer backing off to beside the Jetta. Xia shoving the Norinco's muzzle between his teeth.

Bald felt the cold metal digging into the roof of his mouth. His eyes flicked from the cocked hammer to her finger on the trigger. Her index finger was slender, almost fragile. Not a lot of strength in that finger. One small inward curl of her forefinger was all it needed to activate the trigger mechanism. Bald went from not sweating at all to swimming in the stuff.

Xia laughed and unplugged the pistol from his mouth. She reset the hammer and handed the gun back to Bumfluff. Bald opened his mouth, but Xia put her trigger finger to his lips and winked at him.

'*Shhh,*' she said. 'It's OK. It's over now. You don't have to worry any more.'

She removed her finger from his lips. Brushing her hand across his, she whispered moist, electric breath into his ear. 'Tell me everything you know soon and there doesn't have to be much pain for you.'

Bald didn't answer.

Xia gestured to the senior officer. He brusquely nudged Bald at gunpoint in the direction of the square, and he,

Xia and Bald started walking. The buildings on the left and right of the square were fifty metres away. Their timber fronts were painted white and red, and they had brilliant yellow tiled roofs that curved up in a sweeping motion. Figurines decorated the roofs. All the figurines, Bald noticed, were facing south-east.

Directly ahead was the larger building. At forty metres Bald was able to pick out more details. It was painted an immaculate white with an octagonal roof that peaked some sixty metres above the ground. Two sets of white stairs led up to a main entrance formed by a pair of five-metre tall double doors. Bronze statues of ancient Chinese warriors stood guard either side of these.

Bald said, 'What is this place?'

'Li-Fen Chuen Memorial Hall,' Xia said. 'I could tell you about its glorious history. Or I could just tell you that this is where you are going to die.'

Xia guided Bald up the steps, the senior officer at his back, vigilant with the nine-mil. Bald counted the steps. Thirty in total. The officer heaved open the door at the top. It gave a loud, dense groan.

At a gesture from Xia, the officer handed her the Norinco and turned back to descend the steps. Xia led Bald into the main hall. It was gloomy inside and it took him a few moments to adjust his eyes to the granular half-light. Xia pushed at the door and it closed definitively behind them. A bronze statue, twenty metres tall, occupied the central part of the hall. Some guy sitting on a throne, dressed in traditional Chinese clothes. The walls were built from bulky, shiny bricks and decorated with Mandarin inscriptions. Giant stone columns supported the roof. A design was engraved onto a spider-web-shaped panel sunken into the ceiling. Its colours glowed: it depicted dragons and elephants and a bunch of other shit.

Bald said, 'Can I get a take-away?'

Xia ignored him. She led him further into the hall, past the statue. The far wall was fifty metres from the main entrance, and a small wooden door was set centrally in the wall. When they reached the door, Xia opened it. Strokes of brilliant light flashed in through the gap, briefly blinding Bald. Artificial light. Bald cleared his vision and looked again. A set of stone steps led down into what he assumed would be a courtyard of some kind. Cypress trees, stone statues, carefully maintained lawns.

Instead the steps led down a brightly lit staircase. Holding the Norinco to his back, Xia ushered Bald down the stairs. He lost count of the number of stairs, but knew they were leading away from the building. The air grew increasingly stale and humid and when they reached the bottom of the stairs it felt like they had descended a long way below ground. In front of them was a solid metal door with a keypad to the right, and above the door a single light burned brightly. Xia punched in a four-digit combination and the door hissed and yawned heavily open. She pushed Bald through the doorway. He couldn't see much inside, except for distant lights, hooked high up above like stars.

Then he took a few steps more, and the lights revealed a vast, open area the size of eight football pitches. He saw teams of guys in white coats frowning at banks of computer screens, engineers assembling metal components on work benches, and black-suited, black-haired Communist Party bureaucrats nodding seriously at various hi-tech bits of weaponry. He spied racks of weapons stacked up on the far wall. The weapons were experimental, Bald guessed, because none of the designs looked remotely familiar to him. And Bald knew his guns. There were bullpup assault rifles shaped like dolphins' heads, pistols with flexible barrels and machine-guns kitted out with antennae. There was an assault rifle with thirty-six barrels in a simple yet elegant pod-like configuration at the muzzle end, the whole arrangement roughly the size of a hardback book.

Bald said, 'What the fuck is this place?'

Xia said, 'Welcome to our underground city.'

forty-nine

1720 hours.

A large steel lift dominated the middle of the bunker. The size of the thing suggested it was designed to take heavy loads: machinery, parts, even vehicles. There was a basic sliding door with a grille in it. On top of the lift a series of steel cables fed into an overslung gearbox and motor system. That told Bald it was designed to travel down, not up. The lift was manually operated by a button on a panel to the right of the door.

'Project 779,' said Xia, leading Bald towards the lift. 'That's the official codename for the city. It was built in the sixties, when the Communist Party ordered the construction of a hundred underground cities to protect us against nuclear attack by the West. There are shopping malls and factories in these cities, and gardens and housing blocks and schools. There is everything here people need to survive and flourish.'

Bald was still looking longingly at the weapons rack.

'You like what you see?' asked Xia. She nodded at the gun with thirty-six barrels at the end. 'That one fires a hundred thousand rounds a minute.'

'You designed this gear yourselves?' Bald kept up the small talk as he tried to assess how he could escape from this fucking place. But it looked airtight.

Xia laughed. 'An American company did. We made a very generous offer to them to build new designs for us. They refused. So our National Knowledge Infrastructure team stole the technology instead. And it's not just guns we're developing. We have hyper-velocity systems to intercept ballistic missiles. Space weapons.'

She shoved Bald into the lift with surprising force. He felt sorely tempted to punch the bitch but with his hands still locked behind his back he was helpless. Xia stepped in after Bald and the door whirred and slid shut. Now they were sealed inside, on an six-metre-square platform. The space was lit by amber lights on the metal walls, and a big yellow sign graphically illustrated the dangers of riding the lift without a hardhat. Xia thumbed a red button and the lift stammered. Gears clicked and clanked. A motor churned into life. Then the steel cables began feeding up into the loop.

The lift rumbled on its descent. The sounds tumbled down faster than the lift and were regurgitated as echoes that flooded Bald's ears. He tried to figure out how far down they were going. Most lifts dropped at a rate of around 150 metres per minute. But freight lifts were much slower, owing to the heavy loads they were designed to carry. They sacrificed speed for sturdiness. They averaged more like 100 metres per minute.

Bald noticed his right hand was shaking. He stilled it with his left. Felt the tremors twitching in his left wrist. The needle on his booze clock was hitting the three-hour mark. The migraine was whispering in the base of his skull. Then Xia talked over the voice in his head.

'Do you like Asian women?'

'Depends,' said Bald.

'On what?'

'On whether she's got a gun pointed at my fucking head.'

Xia tittered like a schoolgirl seeing her first cock. 'I heard you like beating up women.' She wiped her hand across her face and said, 'I think you will find you've never met a woman like me.'

Bald sniffed. 'Where are you taking me? To show me your dildo collection?'

'I read your file,' Xia replied, blanking the question. 'Chinese intelligence has files on everyone who has worked for Western intelligence. CIA, MI5, MI6, FBI. Mostly they are thin. Like this,' she said, forming a centimetre gap between her thumb and forefinger. 'Yours was more like *this*.' She widened the gap to an inch.

'What can I say? I make good bedtime reading.'

Xia gave Bald her back.

He'd been counting. Thirty seconds. Fifty metres.

Xia turned back to Bald. 'They send you to this country just to kill me. And they think I'm the only sleeper who's managed to smuggle technology out of their back yard.'

'So there's a few of you. Big fucking deal. You all get caught in the end.'

'A few thousand. Ten years ago the Chinese military decided it needed to upgrade its weapons.'

Invisible drills bored holes into the sides of Bald's skull. The migraines were coming back. He snorted at the ground.

Xia said, 'The nineties was a good moment to carry out the operation. China was becoming more open. Beijing relaxed travel restrictions; we knew that the Europeans would return the compliment. We sent out thousands of our brightest minds to operate in all the major industries, for all the major players. Communications. Space. Defence. Chemicals. Heavy industry.'

'And do what? Steal their shit?'

Xia wrinkled her lips. 'If you wish to put it like that – yes.'

Bald faked a yawn. 'I don't know why you're telling me all this bollocks. I'm just here on a diplomatic visa to meet a few contacts. That's it. I don't know anything else.'

'You killed a soldier. You're here to kill me. I know everything.'

'That wanker went for me first. Like I said, it was self-defence. And my diplomatic visa guarantees immunity.'

Xia evened out her lips into a wry smile. 'Not down here it doesn't.'

One minute. A hundred metres.

Xia said, 'Nearly there.'

'Where are you taking me?'

'Somewhere you will continue to have problems with your phone reception. But I think you will find it exciting.' Now her smile broadened as she said, 'This is the great project that you've been helping us with.'

Clang. Just over a hundred metres. Throw in the descent from the courtyard down to the bunker, and they were a long way below ground level.

Xia opened the door and a long corridor unfolded in front of Bald as she stepped out of the lift. Halogen lamps above them beamed jaundiced light across walls lined with grime-coated tiles like old teeth. The floor was linoleum and slicked with pools of damp. Four fuel pipes, mottled with rust, snaked along the ceiling. Bald heard the distant hum of a power generator. Frayed posters were peeling off the walls, depicting Chairman Mao and heroic Communist Party workers. Bald squinted. This section of the underground city was a world away from the futuristic, expensive set-up he'd seen in the main bunker. There were no hi-tech computers or scientists down here. The corridor appeared to gouge its way far into the distance.

The two of them passed a series of metal doors on either side, marked with yellow signs and mounted cameras. Bald peeked through the few open doors to see dormitories crammed with metal-framed bunk beds. Empty.

Xia said, 'The actual city is more than eighty-five square kilometres. What you see in front of you is just a small part of it. Most of the city has been cordoned off, but when the Cold War ended the Party decided we could use our cities to carry out our work, without our enemies spying on us.'

'You hide nukes down here?' asked Bald.

Xia laughed. 'Once, yes. But not now. We research.'

'Into what?'

'New weapons. You see, the true path to power is through technology. Innovation. Science. This is why the West was more powerful than us in the twentieth century. But starting now, things will change.'

They had travelled three hundred metres along the corridor when Xia abruptly stopped at an unmarked metal door. She turned to her right and flashed her security pass in front of a card reader to one side. Bald felt his bowels tighten. Sweat coursed down his back and onto his anus. The air was thin and stale. He glanced up and spotted air vents punctuating the length of the ceiling. The card reader blinked green and the door unlocked. Xia tugged it open and pushed Bald forward. The top of the door frame was too low for Bald and he had to duck to step through.

The room was basic. A metal table in the middle, two metal chairs. A mirror covered one wall. Overhead a fluorescent bulb filled the room with harsh white light. The place was some kind of interrogation room. Bald was willing to bet good money that the mirror was two-way and the door and walls were soundproofed. On the plus side, he didn't see any torture instruments. Maybe they'd just beat the fuck out of him and try to intimidate him.

'Have a seat,' Xia said. An order, not a welcoming offer.

Bald drew up one of the chairs and sat. Xia left the door ajar and set herself down on the other chair. Silence. She cold-stared at Bald across the table. A fly buzzed invisibly around the room. It zipped and hovered and darted. Bald wondered how it had got down here.

The fly stopped buzzing. Xia slapped her left palm down on the table with a bang. She held it there for a few seconds, her eyes not wavering from Bald. Finally she peeled her eyes away from him and lifted her hand to reveal the crushed insect.

She studied her palm, then said, 'You were meeting someone in Jinchun.'

Bald said nothing.

'The two of you were going to stop me handing over the plans for the Intelligent Dust.'

Bald still said nothing.

'I have a friend of my own,' Xia continued. 'He's on his way. A specialist. I know what he is capable of, and if you're smart, you'll tell me where your friend is. Then maybe I'll tell mine to make it quick.'

Bald laughed inside. A weak, ironic laugh. He laughed because Xia wanted Mallory but it sounded like she didn't even know the guy had been slotted.

He said, 'I can tell you that, no problem.'

'Good. Where can I find him?'

'Try the morgue.'

Xia maintained her blank expression, but it cracked a little at the edges. She snorted, then eased out of her chair and stepped towards the door.

Bald felt anxiety brewing in his guts.

'It's the truth,' he said. 'I went to meet him. He was already dead. Someone had killed him. That's everything. Jesus.' His arms, still restrained behind his back, were beginning to hurt. He took a deep breath and felt the pain in his shoulder blade and ribcage coming back with a vengeance.

'You're lying,' Xia said to the door. She pushed a buzzer and it clicked angrily. 'We know that your partner is alive. And you're going to tell me where to find him.' She paused. The door opened. 'I will come back later,' she said as she slipped into the corridor.

A second later Bald saw a figure lingering in the door-way. He was leaning against the metal frame and chewing gum. He stood in a kind of stoop in his hundred-dollar suit; the crumpled trousers and faded white shirt making him look like a used-car salesman. The right arm of his jacket was hanging free, and wrapped tight around the upper part of his right arm was a bandage.

He was carrying a rusting metal toolbox.

The American.

fifty

'You should have taken my advice,' the American said as he entered the room. 'Back there in Clearwater. It was good advice. Free, too. Yep.' With a big heave and a clang, he lifted the toolbox onto the table. 'You should've gone back to Scotland.'

Bald said, 'Thought I'd see the world first.'

The American chuckled. 'And how's that working out for you?'

His voice was scratchy and blunt, like an unsharpened shard of flint. 'I mean, any other guy would get the message after what went down Stateside. You know? They'd pack their bags. Call it quits. Go home, screw their wife. But you? You're a shit that won't flush.'

The American hocked something up in his throat, and shuffled around to get a good look at Bald's face. His limp seemed more pronounced than it had been in Florida. The bullet wound in his arm probably didn't help much.

'Hand on heart,' he said, 'I couldn't give a solid fuck about you. Twenty years in the game, all I know is that assholes like you end up one of two ways. Either you blow your own brains out or you drink yourselves into an early grave. That's fine by me, either way. But there's one thing I can't get my head around.'

Bald said, 'You still have doubts over your sexuality?'

The American shook his head wistfully and said, 'Why are you doing this?'

Bald didn't answer.

The American continued, 'To be this committed to stopping us, you must be mentally retarded, right?'

Bald said, 'I just wanted to get rich and get laid.'

The American belted out a laugh and sounded like he was choking on a bag of rusty nails. He reached out and patted Bald on the shoulder and said, 'Amen to that, my old friend.' He grinned. 'This was my idea, by the way.'

'What was your idea?' Bald said.

'Bringing you down here. Xia, she figured she could squeeze the necessary int out of you up there. On the surface. But I told her, no way. This guy ain't just good, he's also out of his goddamn mind. To get information out of a guy like you, we need to bring out the heavy artillery.'

'We? I thought you were working for the Agency.'

'I am.'

Hauser pushed his face close to Bald's, a smile playing across it. He didn't look like he smiled much. He had the hard, gristly look of someone who had lived an outdoors life. Not the artificial veneer of a life spent at the gym and consuming tofu salads.

'Sweet Jesus, you don't know, do you? I'm thinking, you must truly be dumb as a shit sandwich without the bread.'

Bald turned away. Hauser staggered around and locked onto his eyes again. 'The Agency set you up. Shit, you really had no idea? They played you, brother. All those ass-kissers in the Firm.'

Bald didn't answer. He was too busy trying to put the lid on the migraine. The pressure was building between his ears again. He could barely hear Hauser.

'We brought the Firm on board to help kill the sleeper. We had only one criteria: that the shooter needed to be hand-picked by us. Your man Land shared your file with us. I read about all the goddamn shit you've been involved in. Christ! Drug trafficking. Arms dealing. Assault. Murder. Alcohol dependency. PTSD. You're a work of art, John.'

'How's the fucking arm?' Bald said.

Hauser ignored him and went on, 'With all the shit you had under your hood, we knew we could control you. Then it was just a matter of making sure you fucked things up. Gotta say, that didn't require a whole lot of input from me. You seem perfectly capable of doing that all by yourself.'

Bald said, 'If you wanted my number you could've just asked.' His voice was cracking now and his brain splitting. He was on the edge.

'What about Xia?' he asked.

'What about her?'

'She works for the Chinese government. She's the enemy.'

'The rules have changed, friend. Keep up.'

'And Rachel?'

'That bitch is your problem.'

Hauser walked to the table and pulled open the tool-box: three trays folded out on either side of the lower compartment. He rummaged through an assortment of tools, before taking out a pair of straight-cut snips from the uppermost tray. He held them up to the light and rehearsed the snipping motion. They were the compound-action type with a leveraged handle to cut through thicker, more durable materials. Such as knuckle joints and finger bones. Hauser gently replaced the snips in the toolbox.

His fingers searched out a pipe wrench from one of the lower trays. It had a red handle over a foot long and looked like it was made of steel or aluminium. The adjustable, toothed head was coated in ginger rust. Hauser studied it under the hot light for a few moments, toying with the business end. He didn't seem satisfied by what he saw, so he dumped the wrench back in the box too.

Then he reached into the main compartment. This is better, his face said. This is the fucking tool for the job.

The tool was heavy. Hauser hauled it out with his left hand and set it down in front of Bald. At first glance it looked like a cordless power drill. The casing was made of orange plastic and at the base there was a handle with a chunky trigger mechanism. But there was no drill bit protruding from the head. Instead Hauser fished a strip of 1.83mm-diameter finish nails from the toolbox and loaded them into the unit. With his left hand he picked up the tool and waved it in front of Bald.

'Know what this is?' he said.

Bald hardened his features. 'A nail gun.'

Hauser stroked the top of the tool. 'Damn right it is. Powerful one, too. The propulsion engine inside this baby can punch a nail through solid rock. What do you think it'll do to your knees?'

Hauser began circling Bald.

'Xia asked you a question. Your partner. Where is he?'

'Like I said, he's dead.'

'Quit lying, or I start making you look like Jesus Christ on the Cross.'

'I'm telling the truth. I found the guy murdered.'

Hauser shrugged at the walls, like he was playing to an unseen audience. 'You expect me to believe that bullshit?'

'Believe whatever you want,' Bald said. 'It's the truth.'

Silence.

Then Hauser nodded. 'I was kinda hoping you'd say that.'

He moved with surprising speed. His right arm thrust across the table and his fingers gripped Bald's chin, while his left hand simultaneously drove the nail gun down onto his cheek. Bald braced himself for the shot. But it didn't come. Not yet.

'Fact: the nail gun injures about thirty thousand folk every single year.' Hauser was sweating hard. Air blew out of his nostrils like espresso-machine steam. 'That's almost the exact number of people killed by firearms in America. So nowadays they fit nail guns with a contact trip trigger.'

He pressed the tool harder into Bald's cheek.

'That means you can't just fire a nail by pulling the trigger. First of all you got to be pushing the head against the surface you want to nail.' He stopped, smiled at Bald and said, '*Then* you pull the trigger.'

Hauser pulled the trigger.

The nail punch was so fast Bald didn't even feel it go in. His cheek was intact one second and the next a long thick nail had surgically pierced his flesh and now he could feel the tip of the nail scraping against his molars, could feel the sting of its cold metal stem. Hauser pulled away the nail gun. It hurt like fuck, but at least there were no vital arteries in the cheek. The wound wouldn't kill him.

'How's that for you, John? That feel good? You want me to give you a matching one for your other cheek?' Hauser was leaning across the table. He pressed the tool's head down on Bald's left cheek. 'Or you want to tell me where we can find your partner?'

'I don't fucking know.'

'Fine,' said Hauser.

He halfway depressed the trigger.

'Wait . . .' Bald said.

Hauser rested his finger.

'. . . I need to tell you something.'

Hauser leaned in closer.

Bald jerked his head forward and bit Hauser's right ear. He chewed through gritty cartilage and bit the lobe clean off, spitting the flap of skin at the wall. Hauser pulled back to the door, clasping a hand over his mangled ear and hissing under his breath. He'd managed to scoop up the nail gun.

'All right, asswipe. You want me to get all Afghanistan on your ass? You got it.'

Hauser looked like he wanted to punch Bald full of holes, regardless of whether he got his int.

Bald said, 'How does it feel? Turning your back on your own tribe?'

Hauser looked quizzically at Bald. He still had a hand pressed to his ear. Blood rivered down the gaps between his fingers and forged red trails down his hand all the way to his white sleeve.

'What are you talking about?'

'I'm talking about you and Xia. I'm talking about you going behind the backs of your bosses at the Agency to do some dodgy deal with the Chinese.' Bald paused. Hauser was lowering the nail gun. Bald continued, 'You're selling your own kind down the river.'

Hauser pulled his hand away from his ear and pointed an accusing finger at Bald. 'I read about what you did in Serbia.'

'This is different,' said Bald. 'You're out here on a fucking limb, doing dodgy deals behind the CIA's back. Betraying your country.'

Hauser shook his head and said, 'You got the wrong end of the stick, *hombre*. Everything was cut by people way above my pay grade.'

'You expect me to believe the CIA is in bed with the Ching-chongs?'

Hauser glared at Bald and said, 'This goes above the Agency.'

Bald went to reply but Hauser broke him off and plunged the nail gun against his forehead. 'You know what, I'm done with this shit already. Last chance to tell me where to find your partner.'

Bald didn't answer.

'Fuck it, then,' Hauser said.

He was interrupted by the stern *clank-clank* of knuckles rapping on dense metal. Both men looked to the door. Hauser grudgingly set the nail gun down on the table and limped over to the door, cursing under his breath.

He cracked the door ajar.

fifty-one

1902 hours.

The doorway framed the bleached-out corridor. Nobody was waiting the other side. Now Hauser pulled the door open fully. He stood uncertainly in the doorway, trying to work out who had just knocked. Then he took a single curious step outside. He stopped. Looked to his right. Nothing.

Looked to his left.

Phttt.

A sound from nowhere, a flinch of movement in the corridor, a flash of black. Hauser swatted at his throat, like he'd been stung by a wasp. As he peeled his hand away, blood spurted out and Bald saw a black bolt sticking out of his throat just above his collar. The Yank seemed about to collapse in the doorway. Then a shadowy form collided with him and barged him back into the room. Hauser tripped, did a giddy pirouette and tumbled against the empty chair. His legs gave way gracelessly and he half-dropped to the floor, his head slapping against the wall and painting it in lustrous red blood. Bald directed his gaze at the figure in the doorway, his frame rinsed in fluorescent light.

Joe Gardner bent down over Hauser. He gripped the screwdriver spearing Hauser's neck and pulled. He was pulling emphatically with his left arm, the fingers of his prosthetic hand fastened tight around the handle. The veins and muscle in Hauser's trachea squirmed and squelched. Finally Gardner managed to extract the screwdriver and now the blood really got pumping: it looked like gallons of it gushing out of the hole in Hauser's neck. Gardner tossed the screwdriver onto the table. Mucus-like bits of muscle were hanging from the tip.

Bald looked at Gardner looking at Hauser. The Yank wasn't going over to the other side at speed. He was crawling to that dark place on his hands and knees. A wet, flopping noise escaped his mouth. Someone had cut the power cords behind his eyes, rendering them dull and blinking and lifeless.

Gardner spoke first.

'Screwdriver in the throat, and the wanker is still breathing,' he said. Gardner was wearing dark-blue construction overalls, combat boots and a utility belt equipped with several pouches. He caught sight of the nail head sticking out of Bald's cheek.

'Looks like I got here just before the party got into full swing.'

'I had it under control,' Bald said.

Gardner looked him in the eye.

'I just saved your shitty life, John. You owe me big time.'

'You're forgetting all the shit I've pulled you out of in the past. Consider us even.'

Hauser was pawing uselessly at the blood fountaining from his neck. Making all kinds of weird, throaty noises. Gardner patted him down. He had a pistol in a shoulder holster under his jacket. Gardner removed it, pulled back the slider and checked the chamber. An FN Five-Seven.

'How did you find me?' Bald said. 'And this place?'

'I followed Xia.'

Gardner stood upright. He had the universal cuff key in his hand, fresh from Hauser's trouser pocket.

'What the fuck's going on, Joe?'

'Land sent me here, you fuckwit.'

Gardner looked disbelievingly at Bald. 'Land didn't tell you? He arranged for me to RV with you in Jinchun. Said that he couldn't afford for this op to go down the shitter and two old Blades are better than one.'

'Bullshit. You were gonna kill me in Libya, first chance you got.'

Gardner shook his head vigorously. 'That was Bill's idea. It had nothing to do with me. Believe me, John, I would never kill another Blade. Never.'

Bald looked into Gardner's eyes. They were nominally green, but in this pit of darkness and harsh glowing lights they took on a greyish hue. His brain told him that Gardner was telling the truth. That Joe Gardner was a yes man, and when you cut down to the nub of it, lying didn't come naturally to him.

'Land didn't say a word about you being on this op,' Bald said. 'Why would he keep that from me? And the opium den? You were inside when it burned down.'

'I hid in the basement and waited for the smoke to clear. Then I escaped.' Gardner studied the cuff key in the palm of his hand. 'I saw what happened to Bill.'

Bald gritted his teeth. 'Fourie had it coming.'

'I met Land at the hotel. We talked.'

'Something's missing. You're not on the level with me.'

'Think what you want. If I wasn't here, you'd be fucked.'

Then it hit Bald, like a slap across the face. 'Xia. The Chinese bitch. She was asking about a friend.'

Gardner lingered by the table.

'I thought she meant Edgar Mallory.' Gardner shrugged at this. Only *he* wouldn't pull a disgusted face at the mention of that tosser, thought Bald. His hatred for Gardner was building minute by minute. He went on, 'Someone did a bit of DIY surgery on Mallory's skull.'

They both turned as Hauser made a gurgling sound, like a blocked wastepipe. He spat out shit and said something, but his voice was whispery and mangled and gasping, and Bald couldn't understand a word.

'Time to leave,' said Gardner. 'Xia will be back any minute.'

'Uncuff me, Joe.'

Gardner frowned at Bald. 'I'm tired of getting you out of scrapes all the time. I could just kill Xia and extract on my own. I get to keep the two million for myself, and you disappear from my life.'

Bald smiled on the inside at the thought of Land short-changing him to the tune of eight million. It only proved to him the legendary capacity Joe Gardner had for taking it up the shitter from the Firm.

'Just tell me what you want,' Bald said.

Gardner dangled the cuff key from his middle finger, as if trying to hypnotize him. 'You know what I really want?'

'Name it.'

'I want you to feel like I did back in London. The interview. Remember? How you humiliated me and said I wasn't up to the job? Because I sure as fuck remember. I felt like shit. I want you to feel the same way.'

Bald lowered his head.

'I want you to admit you're a useless cunt, John.'

Bald felt his head sink lower.

'Say it, John.'

Bald said, 'I'm a useless cunt.'

'And you've got a small dick.'

Bald said, 'I've got a small dick.'

'And Joe Gardner's a better man.'

Bald said, 'Joe Gardner is a better man than me.' He craned his neck at Gardner and evil-eyed him, then said, 'We're even now.'

'Not quite,' said Gardner. 'You're also going to renegotiate the split.'

'There is no fucking split.'

Gardner pulled back the key and said, 'Ninety-ten. In my favour.'

'You think you're such a clever bastard. But you need me,' said Bald. 'This whole area is swarming with jumped-up gooks in uniform. You slot Xia and they'll be serving you up a whole lot more than rice crackers. It's a two-man effort to get out of here.' He saw the undecided look on Gardner's face and continued, 'We'll fight back to back. Just like in the old days. You know there's no one better than me in a tight corner.'

'Ninety-ten. Take it or leave it.'

'Fine.'

Gardner unlocked the cuffs. Bald felt the blood pumping into his numbed hands. He tugged the nail out of his cheek and blood leaked from the hole. Gardner held back a metre from him, grasping the Five-Seven by his side. Bald quelled the urge inside him to beat him into next Tuesday. That training voice in his head was telling him: focus on the mission. Kill Xia.

Bald manoeuvred around the table and crouched by Hauser. The American was quietly alive. His breathing was now just one long, slow wheeze. There was more blood out of him than in. Should be dead. The warrior in Bald had to respect the fight Hauser's body was putting up.

He said, 'Tell me where I can find Xia.'

'Son of a bitch.'

Bald seized Hauser's jaw.

'I know it hurts. But I really need you to focus. Give me an RV and we'll put a round between your eyes. Get it over and done with. That's my best offer.'

Hauser tried to nod. His head wobbled, like he was shivering from the cold. He parted his lips a little. Gulped down air painfully. Blood bubbled and popped at the hole in his neck.

'She left already,' he barely whispered.

'Where's she going?'

'Back to the surface.' Each word sapped more of Hauser's strength. 'To meet the generals.'

Hauser gasped. His eyes whited out.

Gardner peered at the doorway and said, 'We need to leave, John. Right the fuck now. Before Xia gets away. She's the one with the ID.'

'Hold on a second,' said Bald, glaring at him. He looked back at Hauser. 'Before, when you said the deal with Xia went above the Agency, how far up the food chain was this shit going? All the way to the top?'

Hauser swallowed air and choked on it. 'Pentagon. Defence officials. Congress. Everyone.'

'And they were just going to let the Chinese nick your technology? For what?'

'John.' Gardner's voice was growing urgent.

'Debt,' said Hauser. 'We owed China two trillion. This . . .' His voice mutated into a gargle.

'What do you mean, "this"?' said Bald.

'Giving them the dust – this wipes the debt.'

Hauser pulled Bald closer and said into his ear, 'Finish it.'

Bald turned, faced Gardner and gestured to the Five-Seven dangling by his side. 'Give the piece to me.'

Gardner shifted on the balls of his feet. His arm locked in place. 'I'll do it myself.'

Bald shrugged as if to say, 'Fine by me.' He stood up and headed for the door, making way for Gardner to pony up to the American as he hacked his guts out. Hauser coughed and his mouth polka-dotted the floor with blood. Gardner didn't move.

'Jesus, my teeth. So cold . . .' Hauser groaned.

'Get it over with,' said Bald.

Gardner stooped low and pressed the muzzle tip at a spot roughly between the guy's eyes. He thumbed the safety control on the frame above the trigger guard. A red dot blinked. The Five-Seven was ready to fire.

'Hurry up, Joe,' said Bald.

Hauser closed his eyes.

'All that fucking *debt*.' Hauser forced the last word up like a shard of glass. Spat it out, like so much blood. 'Not just us. You too. All of us.' His jaw was shaking. His face was drained of colour. 'The Chinese will own everything. All of us. They've already won.'

'We need to go,' said Bald.

'All of us,' Hauser repeated.

'Now,' said Bald.

Gardner pulled the trigger.

The gun blazed blood red.

Bald and Gardner looked at each other. A shrill alarm rang out.

Bald was conscious of two silhouettes merging in the doorway.

fifty-two

2000 hours.

The two guards had a final shared second on earth, and they spent it looking curiously at Hauser, or rather at his brains freshly splattered over the wall. They had enough time to realize that something was badly fucking wrong. They also had just enough time to level their eyes at Gardner as he twisted around and directed the Five-Seven at their skulls. But they had no time to react. They were out of time, and luck. Two decisive double-taps in quick succession, four *ca-racks* amplified by the confined metal walls, two fluent sprays of blood from the guards' bellies. They dropped in tandem, and the pools of blood began forming separate rugs underneath their bodies.

Bald sprang to his feet and nabbed the Norinco one of the guards had unholstered. Its weight told him it was loaded. He pulled back the slider. There it was, nestled snugly in the chamber like a gold nugget buried in the guts of the earth: 9mm of bottleneck brass, quietly waiting to wreak serious damage on somebody. Bald released the slider: it shunted decisively forward. He and Gardner looked at each other. They were rocking. A team again.

'Where the fuck now?' said Bald, watching the bellies deflate on the pair of guards.

Gardner said, 'Xia's meeting is at ground level.'

'At 2130 hours, Land said.'

'No. We now know it's happening any minute.'

'Then we're gonna miss out.'

'We can take a short cut. Intercept Xia before she makes it to her meet.'

'How?'

'The same way I came in. The maintenance stairwell.'

'Who the fuck told you about this?'

'Land,' Gardner answered simply.

They hurried out of the interrogation room and back down the corridor, hanging a left in the direction of the freight lift. The route looked unfamiliar now it was bathed in violent red, the alarm cawing over their voices. Bald was in front. Setting the pace. Gardner at his back. Struggling to keep up. Both men had lost much of the fitness of their Regiment years. When he was younger Bald had been able to bust out a thirty-kilometre tab in his sleep and still have the energy to launch a frontal assault on an enemy position before breakfast. Now he was sweating out of his arsehole after a few measly minutes. After two hundred metres down the corridor Bald could make out the sequence of metal doors, a hundred metres away. He still couldn't see the maintenance stairwell Gardner had described.

Bald felt himself involuntarily slackening the pace. Partly that was down to his lack of fitness. But it was also because he hadn't had a drink since the Bowmore he'd necked in Mallory's office. That made it more than six hours since a drop of the jungle juice had passed his lips, and now he could feel the migraine scratching at the back of his brain again. Trying to break in and fuck his shit up.

You've come this far, he told himself. Get through it. Keep going and you'll be fucking rich.

Another big push, his lungs burning and his quad and calf muscles swelling, all the accumulated aches and pains of twenty years in the field coming back to haunt him now. Pains in his left knee, his right ankle, his ribcage and his neck, and the new addition to the family in his left shoulder blade. They formed a wall that Bald had to smash through with every step he took.

London. Mexico City. Clearwater. Tripoli. Jinchun. Bald had travelled tens of thousands of kilometres in search of Xia and the Intelligent Dust. Everything came down to this.

From somewhere deep in the fibres of his muscles, Bald found an extra five per cent. Gardner did too. They had both broken into a flat-out run, and now Gardner was drawing up alongside Bald, as if the two ex-Blades were locked in a race to the finish line. Bald's running gait became ragged, lurching, desperate. The air was filled with the pump action of harsh intakes and outflows of breath. They were willing their bodies to keep going.

They rushed past the dorms. Gardner halted. He yanked the handle on an unmarked metal door and slipped inside. Bald followed. They were in a cramped stairwell, with a spiral staircase twisting vertiginously upwards as far as Bald could see. There were fewer lights in the stairwell than in the corridor, and the red was a shade or two darker. Gardner began shuttling up the staircase, Bald in his wake, saying, 'You sure this is a short cut? Xia's taking the lift.'

The further up the stairs they ran, the more muffled the sound of the alarm became. Now it was a low, timid squeal. Gardner said between long in-breaths, 'She won't be able to use the freight lift. I set the alarm to go off in the maintenance stairwell. That automatically disabled the lift. She'll be using the steps in the old access shafts they built to help people get to different levels of the city.'

'And there's a lot of these shafts?'

'It's an underground city – there's a lot of everything. But we can get to her before she reaches the bunker.' He glanced back at Bald and grinned. 'As long as you can still hack the pace, John.'

'Never lost it, mate.'

Up and up, until they had gone through so many revolutions that Bald was beginning to feel disorientated. He didn't know how many steps he'd scaled, or how fast. He was only conscious of the sound of his own breathing, the thump of his heart, and the sweat washing down his chest and back.

And then they came to the top of the staircase, and Bald saw there was no door, but an overhead metal grille fixed a couple of metres above the landing. Gardner reached up to the grille, digging his fingers between the metal bars. Then he pushed upwards on the balls of his toes and the grille easily sprang up, which told Bald that Gardner had loosened it on his way down. Gardner gestured for a lift, and Bald boosted him up to the surface. Then Gardner hauled up Bald. He emerged into another drab corridor soaked in red light. This one looked like the engine room of the city. The area that kept everything else ticking. Drums of pungent chemicals lined the passageway, and beside them were fire extinguishers. Bald noticed exposed electrical cables and lead pipes, thick as tree trunks, with corroded valve wheels.

Then he saw her. Twenty-five metres away. She was carrying an orange Pelican box by her side.

His first thought was that Xia had clocked him and Gardner, because she was belting away from them.

His second thought was: the ID.

'*Stop, stop, stop right fucking there!*'

Xia ignored Bald and ran even faster. Bald lengthened his stride. He was breathing hard, like he'd just donated a fucking lung. He chased Xia along the corridor. He glanced over his shoulder: Gardner was five metres back now, and bringing the Five-Seven to bear. Ready to pop a round out of the snout.

'*I said, fucking stop and put the box down.*'

Xia kept on running.

A distinctive *ca-rack*. At Bald's six o'clock. He twisted and saw a tongue of flame licking out of the Five-Seven's muzzle: Gardner unloading a single round at Xia. He heard him shouting, '*Stay right where you are. Don't fucking move.*' He looked back at Xia. Two more *ca-racks* splintered the air. Rounds flashlit the corridor and ricocheted off the ceiling in a sharp one-two, dying somewhere in the distance.

Xia stopped in her tracks.

Bald was thirteen metres short of her.

'Give me the dust,' he shouted.

Xia said nothing.

'Hand it over, or I'll turn your face into a fucking pot noodle.'

'Let me go,' she said. 'You can keep the dust but not me.'

'Sorry, love,' said Bald. 'You and the dust come as a package.'

Suddenly an industrial clang sounded. The red lights were killed. Bald was plunged into a morbid, midnight darkness. He could hear the slow death of the distant generator.

'Can you see her?' he said.

'No. Can you?' said Gardner.

Neither of us has a bead on the bitch, Bald thought.

'Oh, shit,' said Gardner.

Light seared into Bald's face, instant and harsh. Like being hit with a snowball made of ice. It stunned him. He shut his eyes but he could still feel the light behind his eyelids, bleaching the lizard part of his brain. Then he sensed the far-off hum of power returning to the generator.

He opened his eyes a sliver.

Xia had vanished. The lights further along the corridor weren't working. Bald could see thirty metres ahead, and beyond that was the flat darkness that she had evaporated into.

'Where's she gone?' Bald shouted at Gardner.

'There's an emergency lift at the end of this corridor.'

Then Bald noticed the Pelican box. He raced over and knelt down beside it. It was a Storm model. The shell was injection-moulded and built from high-performance resin. There was a pressure relief valve on the front to let air in and keep water out. There was a press-and-pull latch fixed either side of the flexi-grip handle. Bald laid the box flat on the floor and flipped a button. The latches flipped.

Bald opened the box.

It was empty. He stared vacantly at the honeycomb-shaped interior for several long seconds and felt his head clouding with rage. Then he stepped away. Gardner was at his shoulder, saying, 'John? What is it?'

Bald didn't answer. He shot upright and broke into a run. Towards the emergency lift. He was running on adrenaline, and the stuff was effective fuel, powering his legs like turbo-diesel. Soon Gardner was flagging, falling further and further. Bald had always had the edge, fitness-wise, over him. Lights glimmered and winked forty metres down the corridor, at the lift. They yielded up Xia. She was twenty metres from the lift. The same distance from Bald. He tore along at full pelt. He felt the air corroding in his shrivelled lungs like battery acid. His adrenaline tank was almost empty. His body was begging him to *stop*; his mind was imploring him to *keep fucking going*. Xia was twelve metres ahead. Ten from the emergency lift. He looked back: Gardner was lagging far behind him now.

Fuck it, he thought. Gonna have to finish this on my own.

Eight metres to Xia.

Six to the lift.

Then Xia was stepping into the lift. It was no bigger than a phone booth. Bald forced a last desperate sprint, pushed through the open door and lunged at Xia before she could press the button. His outstretched right hand grabbed her by the shoulder and sent her into a spin. She went through a one-eighty arc, then suddenly Bald found his eyes drawn to her left hand. It was bunched up into a fist and twisting at Bald. He saw a ring on her middle finger. Connected to the ring was a dagger blade that ran the length of her hand and up into the sleeve of her Mao suit. The dagger's tip was a couple of inches from the joint on the ring and looked menacingly sharp. Bald had enough time to realize this. But not enough to dodge the sharp tip.

It perforated his right shoulder, grinding its way through sinew and muscle. Bald did what all fighters are trained to do, and absorbed the pain. Focused on his own game plan. He dug his fingers into Xia's shoulder and sent her crashing against the metal wall of the lift. In the next half-second he launched a palm strike at her left wrist and she dropped the dagger. Xia tried to jerk a knee up at his balls but Bald stamped on her toes. She screamed. Her screams echoed off the walls of the corridor. Now Bald snatched a clump of her satin hair and smacked the back of her head against the lift wall repeatedly, until Bald heard the hard crack of her skull splitting open. He threw her to the floor. He tugged her hair back and drove her face into the ground. She was kicking and fighting and flailing, but Bald was in control of the situation. Xia was in his world now. And she was about to find out just how dark a place that was.

Her face made a satisfying *thwack* as the bones in her nose fragmented like broken china. Bald made her kiss the floor a second time, grinding her face into it. Her legs stopped bucking. She was submitting.

Bald wasn't finished.

He rolled Xia onto her back. He wanted to choke the life out of this fucking evil bitch. He wanted to see the look on her face when she drew her last breath. A splinter of her nose bone had dislodged and was prodding out of flesh beneath her right eye. Her nostrils had deflated to a couple of pin-prick holes, like tyre punctures. Bald seized her neck with both hands. Pushed his thumbs in on the cartilage of her thorax. Xia couldn't breathe.

Then she did a funny thing.

She smiled a mutant smile.

Bald relinquished his grip a little.

'What's so fucking funny?' he said.

Her smile mocked Bald. Gnawed at his bones. At his dignity and self-respect.

All this way, all the bloodshed and the sweat, and all she gives me is a fucking smile.

Xia's mouth was a soup of bloodied gums, brutalized lips and shattered teeth. Her nose was obliterated. The whites of her eyes were blood-red. Her cheeks were swollen and cut. Bald shook her and lifted her head. Blood spewed out of the back of her skull and splashed onto the floor.

'The dust,' said Bald. 'Give it to me.'

'You're too late,' she said, her voice sounding like a gag reflex.

Bald grabbed a fistful of Xia's hair and tugged it until the roots were ripping out of her scalp. She responded with a fit of giggles, flashing her mangled mouth with its graveyard of broken teeth. Blood seeped from her gums and streamed down her chin. The giggles turned throaty and her nose was making a slurping sound, like milkshake sucked up through a straw.

Bald pounded her face. Over and over. Until his knuckles were red raw and her whole face collapsed and the giggles curdled and died.

Footsteps pounding at his six.

Bald gave Xia his back. Gardner was racing towards him, Five-Seven lowered by his side. His eyes settled briefly on Xia. Then he levelled his gaze at Bald. Kept the weapon at his waist.

'Shit, John. What have you done?'

Bald didn't answer.

'Where's the dust?'

'She didn't say.'

Gardner's face hardened. 'Christ, you killed her before she gave up the dust plans?'

Bald didn't answer.

'You stupid fucking idiot, John. You just screwed the mission.'

fifty-three

'We need to find the dust,' said Gardner.

'It's gone. We'll never find it. And if we can't, no one at the Firm can. We'll just tell Land we burnt the plans. By the time he realizes we sold him a lie, we'll have cashed our cheques and sodded off out of the country.'

But Gardner had tuned out of the conversation. He was quiet for a few moments and then he shot Bald a wide-eyed look and beat a rapid path back down the corridor. Away from the lift.

'Joe? What the fuck's going on?'

'Just follow me and do as I say.'

A hundred metres on, Gardner stopped by the door of a utility room. He gave the knob a twist and gestured for Bald to enter. But Bald gestured for Gardner to go first. Gardner gave him a dirty look, then stepped into the room. Bald followed close behind. He couldn't stop thinking about how Land had trusted Gardner with the underground city blueprints. There was only one reason no one had shared that int with him, he knew, and that was because he was a rogue. A renegade. Whereas Gardner was a corporate stooge. He had his head shoved firmly up Land's arse. This wasn't the first time, either, Bald told himself. In Rio, in Gibraltar, in Serbia, he'd done Land's bidding. Been his bitch. Gardner didn't have an independent bone in his body, and that enraged Bald.

The utility room was as small as a bachelor's wardrobe. It reeked of antiseptic. Attached to the wall were signs bearing hazard symbols. Metal shelves were stacked with industrial cleaning agents and tools. A larger shelf unit held a dozen canisters of propane gas.

Gardner grinned at Bald. 'Propane gas explosion,' he said.

'You're thinking . . .'

'Blow the whole city up. It's the only way of making sure the dust is destroyed for good. There's a generator powering this fucking place, so there has to be a fuel source somewhere.'

'We could use that as a liquid accelerant.'

'This much gas, we could bury this chunk of the city for ever. Xia said it was sealed off anyway.'

'The Chinese invented gunpowder, right?' Gardner said. 'So let's give them a proper display, Regiment-style.'

He began unloading a canister from the rack. The big, grey canisters were covered with dents and rusting from being knocked around. Gardner propped the first canister upright. Meanwhile Bald returned to the corridor and scouted both directions for guards. A minute later Gardner came out and headed for a firehose unit mounted on the wall. He smashed the glass front with his elbow, removed the hose and hauled it inside the utility room. No sign of any guards. Bald peered through the door. Gardner was checking that the valve of the canister was shut off by rotating the handwheel clockwise. He removed the valve's protective plug and, taking the end of the hose, fitted the female connector over the valve.

'Give me a hand, John.'

After a final check in both directions along the corridor, Bald removed the cover from the wall-mounted air duct, grabbed the nozzle end of the hose and jimmied it into the hole. Bald knew that a secure underground facility needed two things in constant supply. Oxygen and power. The air ducts would be powered by a fan system somewhere along the line. Now they would help flood the city with the propane. But the explosion of canisters by themselves wouldn't be sufficient to destroy the city and with it the Intelligent Dust. For that, they'd need to generate a much bigger explosion. The propane would be like a lighter striking a length of det cord. It would be the initial spark, leading to something much more noisy.

'Like the good old days, mate,' said Gardner.

'Mates,' said Bald. 'Yeah.'

Gardner twisted the valve on the canister anti-clockwise. There was a sputter and then a brief squirt, and finally a rapid hiss as highly pressurized gas flooded through the hose and gushed into the air duct. Bald could smell ethanol in the air as it filtered through the underground city. Silent, invisible death.

'Hurry it up,' said Bald, checking his Aquaracer. 'Eight minutes left.'

'That's hardly any time. Look, I'll pump this little lot out. Get your hands on that accelerant so we can get this thing nailed once and for all.'

'Roger that.'

Bald exited the utility room and carried one of the gas canisters two-handed down the corridor as he followed the trail of the overhead fuel pipes. They led him a hundred metres further down the corridor. All the way the generator's noise was building to a tremendous hammering din. Bald could hear distinct parts of the generator shaking and grating. He knew he was getting close. Then another fifty metres on the pipes swerved right, and Bald chased them around the corner, and found himself facing the generator.

Bald placed the gas canister next to the air duct nearest to the generator. Arranged in a snooker triangle next to the generator were four large fuel drums. With his hands free he wrenched the lids off each drum and knocked the drums onto their sides. Heavy, slick diesel fuel spilled out onto the floor. He rolled the drums around to make sure the fuel covered a wide area. Then he cranked the valve on the canister and let the propane seep into the air duct. His eyes began to sting. Powerful fumes filled his throat, like swallowing paint stripper.

2125 hours.

Five minutes to get their shit together. Get on that fucking emergency lift.

Bald powered back down the corridor. He found Gardner in a small kitchen two doors down from the utility room. Gardner had emptied the contents of half the cupboards onto the floor. Plates, cutlery, pans, kettles. From this carnage he had picked up a toaster. Bald saw a couple of thick dossiers lying on the table beside the toaster. Gardner plugged the toaster into the mains. He had stood the final propane canister next to the toaster. The valve was already open, hissing out lethal fumes. The kitchen seemed eerie. But there was no dust, as you'd

expect in a place that hadn't been used since the invention
of Internet porn. Everything seemed clean and polished.
Maintained.

'All set,' Bald said to Gardner's back. 'There's enough
fuel back there to make Hiroshima look like kids messing
around with a box of matches.'

2128 hours.

'Two minutes,' said Bald.

Gardner nodded. 'Let's do this.'

The dossiers were almost too thick for the slots in the
toaster, but Gardner managed to wedge them in. Bald had
to admit the paper was shrewd thinking on his old mucker's part. The dossiers would take time to heat up before
catching fire. Perhaps as much as a minute. They would
use that time to bug out via the emergency lift before the
fire ignited the propane.

The light on the toaster flared orange. The timer was
set.

Sixty seconds.

Gardner hurried out into the corridor, Bald alongside
him. They ran at breakneck speed towards the lift. The
migraine was brewing again in Bald's head, but this wasn't
the time to slow down.

Forty seconds.

As soon as the dossiers caught fire, the propane gas
would ignite. The explosion from the gas would channel
through the corridors and into the rooms, into every corner
of the underground city that had an air duct. All the way
to the generator unit. That initial explosion of propane
would trigger a second, much more violent explosion as

the diesel fuel caught ablaze and acted as an accelerant. Bald pictured it spreading ferocious, skin-meltingly hot flames through the city, incinerating everything in its wake.

Xia. The Intelligent Dust. The underground city.

Thirty seconds.

Bald and Gardner raced on, each forcing the other to demand more of himself. They saw the emergency lift twenty metres up ahead. One final push. Do or die. Bald ran at full pelt, he and Gardner hitting the lift with twenty seconds to go. Now Bald thumbed the button and the mechanism growled and the pulleys sighed and the lift shook itself from its stupor, and at last they were shuttling upwards. Away from the gigantic homemade bomb beneath their feet.

Fifteen seconds.

Then it was ten seconds till party time and they had risen just ten metres above the shit, and Bald willed the lift to rise faster.

Five seconds.

Twenty metres clear.

Three. Two. One.

Thirty metres above the underground city.

BOOM!

Bald first felt the explosion in his bones. It shuddered through his body, shockwaved through his jaw and echoed in the shoulder he'd busted in his fight with the road sweeper. The pain seemed to shake the loose parts of the bone a little fucking looser, like stones in a paper bag. Except each jangle felt like someone was twisting a kitchen knife into his shoulder. And then the first *boom* was superseded by a deep and thunderous *whoooshhh*. Successive *booms* sounded out in the background as the rest of the propane canisters exploded and ignited the diesel fuel. The lift growled. Bald lost his footing. Fell flat onto the floor and felt the metal beneath him heating up. The *whoooshhh* kept on coming, like a wind gusting across a churning sea. Bald's fingers blistered. His eyebrows singed.

Bald felt his brain thumping inside his skull. The beat of the booms channelled along his jawbone. He scraped himself off the floor. His skin was hot like warm dough. Noxious smoke and fumes belched out of corners of the metal box. Gardner had fallen over too. The two men didn't so much as look at each other. What if the explosion busted the lift?

They stood up and waited, letting the shudders play themselves out in their bones. There was a grinding noise, as if something had jammed and was trying to churn itself free. The lift had stalled. It shook for three long, stubborn seconds. Then it stopped shaking. The grinding lifted into an optimistic whirr. And now the lift made one last tremble and shook itself free, heading upwards once more. Heat was still rising from the floor. And now Bald and Gardner dared to look at each other.

The deed was done.

Xia was dead.

Intelligent Dust was history.

Bald was going to be cunting rich.

The lift reached the bunker level as the clock ticked to 2132 hours. Gardner wrapped his right hand inside the sleeve of his overalls and shunted the door back. Bald said, 'Good thinking, Joe. Don't want to lose your wanking hand too.'

Bald felt chilled air washing over his face as they debussed from the lift and emerged into a room so small you'd have to leave it just to change your mind. Gardner heaved open the door opposite them, which took them into the bunker. All the guys in white coats and black suits had fucking legged it. The test range was abandoned. Which gave Bald an idea. And Bald was never one to let an opportunity slip by. He raced over to the thirty-six-barrelled machine-gun and lifted it off the rack, surprised how light it was. This '36', he figured, was probably constructed from some kind of hi-tech carbon fibre, the same stuff they build F1 cars from.

Something else caught his eye. A projectile grenade launcher shaped like a bloated Tommy gun, jet-black, with a six-cylinder chamber. An M32 grenade launcher. Bald tried it for size. It was impossibly light: under 4kg. There was an optic target range-finder mounted onto the rear of the weapon. The grenades loaded into the chambers were 40mm High Explosive variants with a kill radius of ten metres and an effective range of more than three football pitches. Bald slung the M32 over his shoulder and quietly congratulated himself on finding this treasure trove. The M32 was already on the market but the 36 was still only an idea in the heads of most defence officials. When he was out of here he'd hawk the 36 on the black market, no questions asked. It should fetch him a tidy sum – perhaps a couple of hundred thousand. More, if he sold the technologies to the Russians so they could pick apart the designs. If he did that, he could be looking at millions.

Gardner frowned at the M32 over Bald's shoulder and the prototype 36 in his hands.

'What are they?' he said.

Bald grinned. 'Beer money.'

The door connecting the bunker to the staircase that led up to the memorial hall was open. Whoever had been last

to leave had forgotten to haul it shut. Now Bald followed
Gardner as he charged up the stairs and into the hall. A
small door on the left took them out into a lavishly decorated courtyard. There, concealed behind a morass of
ginkgo biloba trees and lilac shrubs and corroded statues
of dragons, stood an ornate metal gate. Gardner pulled it
open; the hinges creaked like old hip joints.

They emerged at the rear of the hall. Night had sucked
what little colour there was out of the land, turned everything a greyish brown, like decaying fruit. The sky was
pleated with purples and blues. A full moon. No stars.
Bald scanned the landscape left to right. A ribbon of
desert stretched out for a couple of hundred metres. At
the far end it sloped down to a river bank above water
that flowed bright yellow, like someone had coloured it
with a highlighter pen. Bald briefly wondered what kind
of fucking toxic shit had been dumped in there. The river
swerved through the land, slithering this way and that.
It was widest at a point to Bald's ten o'clock, a hundred
and fifty metres or so, and approximately half that width
at his two o'clock. Beyond the river lay five hundred
metres of lonely, knuckled terrain peppered with weeds
and rocks. That slab of land appeared to Bald the loneli-
est place in the world. It rose on a fifteen per cent incline
before plateauing out into a gentle green forest. In the far
distance Bald spotted molar-shaped mountains capped
with iridescent snow.

'Kazakhstan,' said Gardner.

'A shithole never looked so fucking good. How far to
the RV?'

'Two kilometres the other side of the border. Kargol is at
the base of the mountain range,' said Gardner, referencing

a handheld GPS navigator he'd stashed in his overalls pocket. 'I put us at exactly a kilometre east of the border.'

'Pissing distance,' said Bald. 'How's it feel to be rich, Joe?'

But Gardner didn't answer. Something had caught his attention at his six o'clock. Bald chased his line of sight. He was looking back towards the square, four hundred metres east of their position. The area was coated in a treacle-like blackness, and for a few seconds Bald failed to see what had spooked Gardner. Then the darkness resolved itself into murky outlines and dull shapes, like a poorly developed photograph.

And now Bald saw it too.

A neat line of lights glowed at the front of the square, near the spot where Bald had arrived in the police Jetta, some way from the memorial hall and from Bald's and Gardner's present position. Small and white, like pills. Twenty, thirty of them. The pill-lights were travelling at a hell of a speed because soon they had crossed the square and were heading towards the memorial hall. At three hundred metres from Bald and Gardner, the shapes around the lights came into focus. Camouflaged Beijing BJ-212 four-wheel-drives. They looked similar to the old-school Land Rover Defenders. The BJ-212s illuminated bulkier, much slower vehicles swarming the area to the south of the hall. The turbocharged diesel engines of these slower vehicles droned and sputtered as their dual-rubber road wheels and track rollers loped over the rugged terrain. Each had a periscope eye scouring the land ahead of it. Above the small hatch on the front of each hull there was a 12.7mm cannon and, either side of these, four 76mm smoke-grenade dischargers. Type 89 armoured personnel carriers. A double-dozen of them in a single row. Two hundred and fifty metres away now: they were closing in on the two operators. The APCs halted abruptly.

Ramps lowered. Soldiers disgorged.

'Oh, fuck,' said Bald. 'There's a shitload of them.'

fifty-four

More soldiers debussed from the APCs. Bald quickly gave up trying to assess the enemy strength. Each Type 89, Bald knew, had a two-man crew and was capable of carrying thirteen additional personnel. So twenty-four APCs equated to a maximum of 360 pairs of boots on the ground. Three hundred and sixty soldiers plus armoured support versus two ex-Blades, one of them with a migraine buzzing inside his head like an angry hornet and a shoulder joint turned to mush, and the other with only one good hand.

The People's Liberation Army soldiers were lit up by the headlights of the BJ-212s v. Bald could now see that they were decked out in four-colour woodland-camo uniforms with field caps and spit-polished boots, and they were wielding assault rifles. At two hundred metres it was impossible to make out design features, but Bald reckoned they were QBZ-95s. The PLA had one style of rifle for their soldiers and they either liked it or lumped it. The QBZ-95 was chambered for the 5.8x42mm Chinese-manufactured cartridge, and its box mag held thirty rounds. It was effective up to a maximum range of four hundred metres from shooter to target.

'Fuck me,' said Bald.

The soldiers didn't divide into groups or try to out-flank Bald and Gardner. They saw no need. When your force outnumbered the opposition by over 150-1, you didn't need to worry about complicated tactics or elaborate pincer movements. You could win the battle simply by steaming in directly and applying rapid, overwhelming force. A reasonable battle strategy, perhaps, based on the principles of sound logic and safety first. Just two men: it would be easy to overpower them.

But these weren't just two soldiers. They were ex-SAS, and the Regiment was unlike any other military unit in the world. Regiment operators specialized in overcoming vastly superior enemy forces and weaponry. They were trained in the way of the guerrilla, in the code of the spy and the philosophy of the survivalist. Bald and Gardner, and Blades like them, had been outnumbered and outgunned more times than either of them could remember.

Bald and Gardner broke west. They headed towards the river, and the Kazakh border. Away from the Chinese army, and the APCs and the BJ-212s. Away from the flare of the gunfire and the headlamps lighting up the desert floor. Bald willed his body on. His muscles no longer hurt; they were dead. The pain had jumped ship. Two hundred metres from the small army on their tail. A hundred to the river. He shut out the pain the only way he knew, by focusing on the positive. Told himself, get to the river. That's your first RV point. Forget about everything else. Look, you're just seventy metres from the river – fucking nothing. A few more strides and you'll be in the water.

Then the 12.7mm cannons on the APCs pissed all over Bald's optimism. Several of them opened fire simultaneously, their repetitive *tumm-tumm-tumm* banging at his six o'clock like a din of a ceremonial drum roll. Bald glanced back across his shoulder. Fist-sized clumps of earth were flung up into the air. Rocks the size of footballs were being flipped like coins. The world suddenly reeked of burnt gunpowder. The first wave of rounds had landed short and now Bald and Gardner were thirty metres from the river. Twenty metres and the second wave fired. This time the 12.7mm rounds landed wide. Bald caught sight of them in his peripheral vision. A couple thudded into the soil three uncomfortable metres from Bald. The APCs were finding their range and it would only take them a second more to get an accurate bearing on Bald and Gardner.

Fifteen metres from the river and Bald heard the ground erupt behind him, and heat pressing against his back and neck, and he heard the *ca-racks* of massed assault rifles. Bald instinctively dropped his head and tucked in his arms, presenting as small a target as possible. The night sky cracked and popped with the incessant rattle of gunfire. Bald knew he was in the shit, big time. Now he was ten metres from the river, 5.8x42mm brass breathing down both men's backs.

There was a sharp, two-metre drop where the land fell away to the water. The river bank gave Bald and Gardner precious cover against the rounds unloading at their six. But it would only keep them protected for as long as they were concealed below it and the PLA forces remained topside. Gardner edged backwards towards the river, until he could see the advancing soldiers and vehicles, while Bald canvassed the area on the other side of the water. Rounds were spattering into the soil just above their heads.

'What's the situation?' Bald shouted.

'Ninety metres,' Gardner shouted back. 'Moving this way – and fast.'

Bald examined the 36 prototype in his hands. 'Let's give them something to think about. I'll put down rounds on the fuckers.'

'Fire and move,' said Gardner.

Bald pointed out a scrape on bumpy land midway between their position and the border. It was a hundred metres up on the other side of the river, fully two hundred metres from them. 'See that scrape? That's our next RV point. Once I put rounds down, you break for the RV. Then you return the favour.'

'Then you're gonna have to sort me out with some kit,' Gardner said, pointing with his eyeballs to the M32. 'I can't cover you with the Five-Seven. Not against these pricks.'

Gardner had a point. The effective range on the FN Five-Seven was fifty metres. Anything over that, you might as well be throwing matchsticks at the bad guys. Bald grudgingly parted company with the M32. Gardner tucked the Five-Seven into his overalls and inspected the M32. There wasn't much to inspect. Firing the M32 was like operating a personal computer: all you had to do was point and click.

Rounds skipped and flitted above Bald, bolting like shards of light over the bank and striking the gradient on the opposite bank. That confirmed what he had already suspected. The elevated ground at the Kazakh border was exposed to the line of fire from the PLA soldiers. Before they could leg it to Kazakhstan, they'd need to put them down, and make them stay down. The RV scrape was just three hundred metres from the border on an incline. Bald reckoned he and Gardner, going at a fast stride, would need a solid minute and a half to reach Kazakh soil.

He rolled back onto his front. Lifted his head over the parapet just enough to establish a bearing on the soldiers coming at them from the east. A group of ten had powered ahead of their mates. Now they were seventy metres away, the stocks of their QBZ-95s tucked tight to their shoulders, their eyes lining up Bald and Gardner in the NV optics. Tracer rounds were barking out of the spouts and lighting up the desert in reds and yellows and greens. They spat furiously into the ground in front of Bald, flinging hot dirt into his face.

He hoisted the 36 so that the barrel ends were resting flat on the lip of the bank. The weapon had a hooded-post front sight and an aperture rear sight that looked as though they had been copied straight from the QBZ-95. They didn't feel properly lined up to Bald. Some engineer had probably welded the fucking things on. Bald used the sights anyway, figuring that bad sights were better than none at all, and lined up the ten nearest soldiers as best he could. Their shit training was betraying them. They were sticking close together. Safety in numbers, but a bad fucking mistake in a firefight. That close together, if a round missed one target it could just as easily strike the next guy.

Bald tensed his finger on the trigger mechanism.

The soldiers were fifty-five metres from Bald. Rounds split the ground an inch in front of his face. He depressed the trigger, but only for a moment.

The 36 made a sound like a buzz-saw firing up. It lasted for perhaps half a second, then it phased out. Bald spent the next half-second wondering if the weapon had jammed, or there had been some kind of misfire, as is common with prototype designs. The gun hadn't jumped in his hands. Nor had he felt even the slightest recoil from the discharge. But then he clocked smoke fluting out of the thirty-six barrels and he lifted his eyes and saw the group of soldiers crumpling, nine of them folding inwards, their arms and legs and heads splintered like they were made of cheap wood. All kinds of shit was oozing out of their bodies. Bowels and innards and organs splashed to the ground. The tenth guy staggered on. His left arm finished brutally at the elbow. Half of his skull had been blown away. He somehow managed to scream with no jaw.

A light pop came from Bald's nine o'clock: Gardner discharging a 40mm grenade from the M32. The round tunnelled through the air and detonated on impact with the ground, spitting out a backcharge of smoke and flames that engulfed a dozen soldiers, and following it up with a jet stream of molten metal and fragmentation that detached limb from pulverized limb. The soldiers weren't just slotted. They were chop fucking suey.

Twenty more guys were speeding past their decimated mates. Fifty metres. Forty-five.

'These bastards just don't give in,' Gardner growled. He unloaded a second 40mm grenade. *Pop–thud–scream*. Three sounds that were music to Bald's ears. The round vaporized half a dozen more soldiers.

'Fucking run, Joe!' he boomed.

Gardner pulled back from his firing position to Bald's nine and scooted down the river bank. He broke the water and began wading across as fast as he could go. But the water was sludgy and waist-deep and Gardner was clearing just a metre a second. He held the M32 and the Five-Seven above his head to keep water out of the chambers. A hundred metres to cross before he'd hit dry land. A hundred metres of exposure to incoming rounds, a hundred seconds in which he might take a round in the back. Bald needed Gardner alive if he was ever to get out of the shit. He spun round and faced the soldiers rushing at him from the river bank. He targeted the twenty guys pounding towards him. They were forty metres away, surging past the tangle of body parts and patches of burnt flesh scattered across the ground and spraying wild single-round bursts at Bald.

Another terse depression on the trigger of the 36. Another flash of noise. Another puff of smoke. The rounds whacked through the line of soldiers, wrenching limbs from torsos, punching fist-sized holes in chests and blasting kneecaps to white dust. All twenty dropped. Forty-two KIAs total, no survivors. Bald was amazed by the stopping power of the 36.

Seven more soldiers had manoeuvred into a thin line behind their mates in the hope that the guys ahead of them would take the brunt of the impact. But the 36's rounds lost none of their stopping power after punching holes through the first line of soldiers. They passed through flesh and muscle and carried on out the other side, penetrating the soldier immediately behind with as much force and violence. One guy dropped to his knees, squealing like a fucking pig. A neat circle of rounds had smashed into his groin and torn him a makeshift vagina. First his bowels hit the ground. Then the rest of him flushed out too. Another guy had a puncture in his neck wide and long, like a slashed tyre. He had his hands on his mucker's shoulders, silently begging for help and inadvertently spraying blood into his eyes.

Make that forty-nine enemy slotted. We might just make it, Bald allowed himself to think.

He spotted fifteen guys storming at him from his ten o'clock. Jesus, he thought, they just keep coming. Another frontal assault. The soldiers were so close he could make out the details on their faces. But to him they all looked the same. Then their rifle muzzles sparked. Flames licked out of the muzzles. Gunpowder corroded the air. The night had been cool ten minutes ago. Now the air was over-cooked. Rounds zipped and yawed past Bald. The soldiers were shooting on the hoof. A good fire tactic if your ambitions started and ended with putting rounds down on a general target. Pinning an enemy down. Not so good when you were trying to actually hit somebody.

Again Bald squeezed the trigger.

The 36 fumed. The rounds sliced and diced the fifteen soldiers. Body parts rained down. Faces and hands and feet were burnt crisp, like meat left too long in a George Foreman grill. Guts were incinerated and testicles blown to shit. Forty-nine dropped soldiers became sixty-four. A further group of eighteen soldiers hit the deck, reasoning that to be a coward was better than to be chopped up into a thousand tiny pieces. They were forty metres back. A line of fifty or more soldiers was behind them.

'John!' Gardner calling at Bald's six o'clock.

Bald rolled over onto his back. Gardner had trudged through the river and climbed up onto the far bank. He was climbing the incline towards the scrape. He hit the RV and gestured to Bald. *Fucking hurry up.*

First, Bald thought, he needed to give the eighteen closest soldiers the good news. There was a forty-metre gap between those guys and the next nearest grouping. Put them down and he'd have a window of opportunity to dash for the RV. Bald positioned himself so he was looking back at the desert floor. At the eighteen. One of them, a short, squat guy built like a tree stump, was on his feet. His uniform boasted a different insignia from the others. A single gold star against an olive-green background. A rupert, thought Bald. The guy barked orders at his men and now the eighteen rediscovered their manhood and picked themselves up off the floor. They were dangerously close, so Bald sprinted down into the river. Rounds slapped into the wet soil on the far bank. Bald quickly discovered that it made no difference how hard he tried to run: the river bed was porous and the water was like sludge. It was like wading through quicksand. Hot lead broke the surface, sending jets of putrid water into the air and drenching Bald.

'Give me some fucking covering fire!' Bald shouted at Gardner.

No answer.

What *is* he doing?

Bald glanced back. The eighteen guys were gunning down towards the river. Eighty metres, but they were eating up that gap with every passing second. Half the guys stopped at the edge of the water. Bald was sixty metres across the river, waist-deep in the gunge, struggling on. Nine soldiers were hurrying upstream to the narrowest point of the river in an attempt to flank him.

Storming through the last few metres of the river, Bald hit dry land. *Pop–thud–scream.* A third round unloading. As Bald ran he turned to face his three o'clock, to see where it had landed. It had smacked into the group of nine PLA goons heading due east along the river for the narrowest crossing point. One soldier was miraculously still standing. The explosion had ripped away the lower half of his head.

Bald was fifty metres up the bank now. Fifty to the scrape. Gardner discharged a fourth round at six guys moving tightly together down the bank. *Pop–thud–scream.* Bald closed the gap to forty metres. Then thirty. Rounds were slamming and scorching all around as the soldiers threw the kitchen sink at Bald and Gardner. Every last soldier was breaking towards the river bank. A hot circle of pain hit Bald. Blood leaked down his leg. He'd been struck in the back of his thigh. He automatically slowed to a crawl. Every time he had to extend his leg the muscles fired jolts of intense pain into his brain. He could hear, and feel, the squelch of muscle around the trapped bullet, the tip grinding against his slow-twitch muscle fibres. He was sick in his mouth. Gardner unleashed a fifth grenade at the river.

Pop–thud–scream.

But there were too many of them.

Last stand, thought Bald. Take as many of these pricks with me as I can. He eased his finger back on the trigger of the 36. They were in his face. He had to drop them in the very next second.

Click.

Out of ammo.

Now you really are fucked, Bald thought.

Then the ground trembled.

A pause.

It trembled again. Rocks shook; the soil shifted; a dislocated roar came from beneath the ground. Bald looked back across the river, at the square. The soldiers' heads had turned too, and they saw the memorial hall spew orange and black mushrooms into the air. The horizon lit up like a fireworks celebration, and all three buildings in the square were obliterated. The seismic force of the explosion was way above the power generated by the propane and diesel fuel.

Bald thought, the Chinese have been storing bombs in the underground city too. Suitcase nukes, warheads, experimental bombs – it didn't matter to him. All that mattered was that the explosions had just saved his life.

The soldiers were standing still. Some were retreating. The others didn't know what to do. Bald hit the scrape. Gardner hauled him up. Bald could feel the energy from the explosion in his feet. He could hear the screams and gunfire of the soldiers drowned out by something much more sinister and devastating. The soldiers had dropped to their bellies at the lip of the river bank, next to the spot where Bald had ditched the 36, and put down three-round bursts at Bald and Gardner. At a range of more than two hundred and fifty metres the chances of them scoring a hit were slimmer than a cunt hair.

Bald spotted the Five-Seven next to Gardner. He seized the semi-automatic and sprinted out of the scrape, eyes totally focused on the border. Three hundred metres to freedom. The rounds being fired at their backs were impacting further and further away from their position. Craters were punched into the soil. A yellow sign carried a warning in Cyrillic and below it one in Chinese. Bald didn't speak either language but the Kazakh flag at the top told him they had reached the border.

The gunfire from the soldiers dimmed to a distant patter, like raindrops lashing against a window pane. And now they reached the top of the incline and hurtled across the plateau. They left behind the smouldering earth and the river turned to yellow sludge. They left behind the carpet of dead soldiers and the underground city. They left behind Xia and the dust.

They left behind all of it.

They carried on for a single exhausting kilometre. Bald was half delirious with thirst. The migraines whispered to him in the back of his head, voices like crazed psychos in an asylum. The desert floor soon swirled with dust. Bald was close to collapsing. His fingers reeked of gunpowder. He felt the bullet lodged in his thigh. He was drenched in cold sweat from the waist up, and toxic river water from the waist down.

But he had the Five-Seven, and he had Gardner in his sights.

He raised the pistol level with Gardner's head.

Cocked the hammer.

Gardner froze. Turned slowly on his feet.

Bald said, 'Don't tell me you didn't see this coming.'

'But I saved your life, John. We're even!'

'You're a bigger mug than I thought.'

Gardner closed his eyes. Sweat dribbled down over his blood-stained eyelids. He took a deep breath, like a politician rehearsing a speech, and said, 'There's no fucking reason to do this, John. We've done the op. We can get our money from Land and go our separate ways.'

Bald said nothing. Gardner opened his eyes and stepped forwards. His mouth was flecked with spittle. His eyes were burning red.

'I was only following orders.'

'Yeah,' said Bald. 'That's the problem.'

'Fuck's sake, I saved your arse today. If it wasn't for me Hauser would have finished you. We're fucking even.'

Bald calmly shook his head.

'The only way you and me will get even is when you're six feet under.'

He pressed the Five-Seven's muzzle against Gardner's forehead.

'No,' said Gardner.

'Yes,' said Bald.

He tensed the trigger. Gardner went wild.

'*NO!* Jesus Christ. Don't do it, please, John . . . you fucking cunt . . . think about what you're fucking . . .'

fifty-five

China-Kazakhstan border. 2259 hours.

The bullet never came. Joe Gardner watched Bald crumple to the grass and the Five-Seven drop from his grip. Bald had clamped his hands at the sides of his head, like he was trying to plug gaps. He squinted and made a weird groaning noise. First he dropped to his knees. Then he sprawled onto his side and rolled back and forth. Gardner had heard rumours about Bald. About how he had never really recovered from that headshot in Kosovo. Gardner had dismissed all that shit. Anyone who met Bald for the first time was likely to conclude that he was unstable. But now Gardner was seeing first hand just how badly the head wound had afflicted Bald.

The Scot prised an eye open. His lips were cracked. His eyes were bloodshot and his skin bleached beneath a thumbnail of greasy sweat.

'Help me,' he said hoarsely.

Gardner said nothing. He bent down and gathered the Five-Seven.

'Joe . . .'

Gardner pointed the Five-Seven at Bald and pulled the trigger. Bald blinked. But nothing happened. Then Gardner checked the chamber and emptied the clip.

There were no rounds in either chamber or clip. Gardner chucked the empty clip, fished out the fully loaded one from his utility belt and inserted it into the underside of the Five-Seven's grip. He was about to stand up when he noticed Bald struggling to say something. His lips were barely parting. Stale, wordless air drifted out. Gardner leaned in, and listened.

'I just need . . .' said Bald, then his voice drifted. He swallowed hard and went on, 'I just need . . . a drink.'

Gardner said nothing. There was a small part of him that knew it would take great pleasure in slotting Bald. But the greater part of him knew that to kill him would be going against everything he'd ever stood for. Christ, if he pulled that trigger then he was no better a man than Bald himself.

He patted Bald gently on the shoulder. Then he stood up.

'Please . . .'

Gardner cast one final look over John Bald. At the man who had once been both a hero of the Regiment and his best friend. Now he had a bullet in his leg and demons in his head and he was dying in the arse-end of Kazakhstan. Gardner considered he was doing Bald a favour. He would never find peace in this life. Maybe the next life was where he belonged.

'A wee fucking drink . . .'

Gardner bid Bald a silent goodbye.

Then he turned away from his mate for the last time and carried on down the scabbed field, following the coordinates that had been plotted into his GPS navigator. These took him on a bearing towards the valley. Soon the ground became lush with grass and the air cooled and the sky sprouted diamond stars. But Gardner saw no signs of civilization. The valley appeared completely uninhabited. He made the next kilometre and a half in good time, and according to the navigator he was now just five hundred metres east of the RV. He looked west, at his twelve. A rutted mud path led down the valley. And parked by the path there was a black Mercedes E-Class with heavily tinted windows.

Gardner strode over to the Merc.

As he approached, a rear passenger door opened and the polished tip of an Oxford brogue swung out, followed by a dainty white-trousered leg. Leo Land planted his feet firmly down on Kazakh soil, stretched and took a long drag on his Montecristo. He walked towards Gardner with an exaggerated grin and a bounce in his step.

'Where's Bald?' he said.

'He's fucked,' said Gardner.

The grin on Land's face went supersize.

'Well done,' he said. 'Bloody well played. I knew you'd come through for us in the end, Joe. And the Firm will show you its gratitude. Count on it.'

Land reached into the inner pocket of his white jacket.

'Here's how we say thank you in Whitehall.'

He proudly handed Gardner a dog-eared cheque. Next to 'Payee' Land had scrawled 'JOE GARDNER' in rough capitals. On the second line he'd written 'TWO MILLION POUNDS ONLY', and he'd put a line through the third. 'Watts and Co.,' Gardner read. He'd never heard of them.

'Don't spend it all at once,' said Land.

Gardner looked at the cheque, folded it in half and tucked it inside the left breast pocket of his overalls.

Then Land said to Gardner, 'Before you toddle off, I've got one last gift for you.'

'What's that?' Gardner asked. He was thinking, John Bald is dead and I'm rich as sin. How much better is my evening going to get? Then he saw Land pointing at something fifty metres away.

'You see that clump of rocks?' Land said.

Gardner squinted. 'Yeah, I see it.'

'Now look a little closer.'

Gardner made out a figure kneeling beside the rocks. A woman. He recognized her immediately from the hotel in Libya. Rachel Kravets. Gardner stared uncomfortably at Rachel, and she looked indifferently back at him, and he wondered what the fuck was going on.

Land circled Gardner, gave him a comforting pat on the back.

'I'm sorry it has to end this way, Joe,' he said. Then he chuckled to himself. 'Actually, I'm not sorry at all. This works out just fine for me. Not you, though.'

Gardner felt Land withdraw his hand from his back. In his peripheral vision he saw him returning to the Merc. The engine was gunning. But Gardner was transfixed by Rachel. He watched her reach for an object resting on top of the clump of rocks. He clocked the distinctive outline of a rifle barrel glinting in the moonlight.

He watched her aim the sniper rifle at his head.